Pythagoras
the
Mathemagician

Pythagoras the Mathemagician

FIRST SUNBURY PRESS EDITION
Printed in the United States of America
October 2010

ISBN 978-1-934597-16-3

Published by:
Sunbury Press
Camp Hill, PA
www.sunburypress.com

Camp Hill, Pennsylvania   USA

Acknowledgments

Many have contributed their efforts to this historical novel. It is indeed my honor to acknowledge Mr. Jamil Ghaleb, an artist, painter and musician, for reading this novel and presenting me with his honest and truthful comments; Dr. Sami Makarem, Ph.D in Philosophy, and Professor of Arabic Literature at the American University of Beirut, for his valuable advice on the contents.

And last but not least, I should also express my appreciation to Editor Claudys Claude Kantara for her excellent comprehensive editing and literary input. Great thanks to Ms. Wasilia Yapur for revising the text in its English form and commenting on it.

A loving thanks to my friends: Elena Ramia, Fouad El-Hajj, Nouha Yammine, Corine Jabbour, Charles Frangie, and Vera Abu-Mehrez, for their individual support and care.

I am also grateful to Mr. Lawrence Von Knorr, the Publisher who had given me a great opportunity to publish my novel in the USA. Special thanks also go to the staff at Sunbury Press.

Karim El-Koussa
Ehden, August 1, 2010

"A thought is an idea in transit"

Pythagoras
c 570 BC – c 495 BC

Preface

Back in the old times, in the faraway distant past, from the shadows of days and nights, Humanity emerged by a strange deed of the scheme of life to evolve into tribal and restricted social structures. These small, incomplete societies developed later on into great civilizations; some of which prospered into nations that rose like the glorious Sun from the East.

Egypt, the mysterious *Land of Ham,* with all its magnificent pyramids and temples, formed a main part of this Ancient World, along with the remote Mesopotamia, also called the *Land of the Winged Gods,* and the mystical India or what was known as the *Land of the Yogi-Magus.* Not too far away, an equally great and ancient civilization, evolved to mark the history of mankind and change it forever – it was the Phoenician nation.

A nation of love, peace, and harmony, this great civilization harbored neighbors and foreigners besides the original inhabitants of the Land of Canaan. They all cohabited in an authentic spirit of fraternity.

Originally widespread, the Phoenician Land stretched out from the ancient city of Ugarit, in the North, to *El Arish* of Egypt, in the South. Whereas to the East stood majestic mountains and vast plains overlooking, to the West, the Great Mediterranean Sea.

One of the most attractive places in the ancient world, the Phoenician land welcomed people from different cultural, religious and social backgrounds. The land bloomed with this amalgam

1

of variety that cohabited peacefully, forming a cohesive human bouquet.

This ideal society did not last however, as ambition and greed forcefully led tribes and nations to the Land. In the 14th century BCE, Indo-European tribes, such as the Hittites, invaded the Phoenician nation, as did the *People of the Sea* around 1200 BCE. Semitic tribes, like the Assyrians, brought on their shares of violence as well around 700 and 600 BCE.

Cruel nations lurked like voracious vultures in wait of the death of their prey; a prey that bled profusely; a sacrifice offered to the gods for mankind... and the agonizing nation wondered in crucial pain: what kind of gods would allow such agony; such satanic killing and barbaric destruction.

Invasions and wars eroded the Land, reducing its size dramatically to extend then from the South to Mt. Carmel and from the East to the Mountains of Loubnan (Lebanon) and the plains of Galilee. Ugarit, in the North, remained an essential part of the Land, whereas the Mediterranean Sea, in the West, became just a Phoenician lake.

Yet, the Land would not die, nor would the soul of the Phoenicians. These fierce survivors prevailed, faithful to their God, the Most High Al-ELYON, and to the mission of love and peace He had inculcated in their minds from their earliest beginnings, and down through their social and religious development. In fact, on the walls of their temples, the doctrine shone in everlasting wordings, instructing them to plant *Love and Peace all over the face of the Earth*. That was the *bona fide* mission that kept their spirit alive.

As a matter of fact, the Phoenician Society was a social order whose members practiced what they preached. They lived lives of justice and freedom and conveyed knowledge and wisdom to others. The Society truly longed for *Immortality*.

And so, in order to keep the legacy of this outstanding nation well alive and immortal, a Phoenician genius appeared in the course of history to change it forever. His teachings in philosophy and his religious doctrine came about to shape western philosophical thought and all world religions.

Without him, where would the great Greek philosophers Socrates, Plato, and Aristotle be?

His name was Pythagoras and his ministry spotlighted mathematics and magic. He was Pythagoras the *Mathemagician*.

And the descendents of this exceptional Phoenician nation are the Lebanese of today.

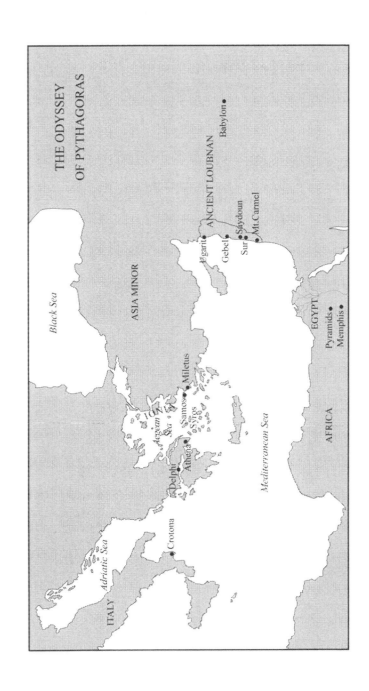

THE ODYSSEY
OF PYTHAGORAS

Black Sea

ASIA MINOR

Ugarit
Gebel
Sur
Saydoun
Mt.Carmel
ANCIENT LOUBNAN
Babylon

IONIA
Aegean Sea
Samos
Chios
Miletus

Delphi
Athens

Crotona

ITALY
Adriatic Sea

Mediterranean Sea

AFRICA

EGYPT
Pyramids
Memphis

4

.1.

The Mediterranean World

The chronology of Time marked the years around 575-570 BCE on the Mediterranean coast. Flat stones, perfectly aligned in a structural design, paved the long pier of one of the most important and earliest harbors in the world; Saydoun (Sidon). This Phoenician city reached its peak around the 12th and 10th century BCE, playing a spiritual, scientific and economic key role in the Mediterranean culture. Such major impact has prevailed through times until the present date.

Tradition conveyed that the name of that coastal city related to Saydoun, the elder son of Canaan; father of the Phoenician race. A powerful figure of his time and a charismatic leader with a magnificent vision, Saydoun had built the city in his name, nearly three thousand years BCE.

This port city carried its name that correlated to the act of fishing, as well; having been one of the most vital food sources for the inhabitants of that area. In fact, the majority of the Saydonians had acquired a solid reputation as successful fishermen, whereas the minority in the city was regarded as great *fishers of men.*

On the long dock, stood the lovely Parthenis, her eyes to the horizon reflecting on the past. The orange–red globe of the Sun, shrouded by thin layers of clouds, blended with the Phoenician waters. A flock of sea gulls flew by and their shadows drew swift forms on the beach. The palm trees swayed softly: silent witnesses to the confident departure of the majestic Phoenician vessels. Heading in all directions, they exported wisdom and knowledge, along with their national products of purple linen clothes, metalwork, wine, salt, perfume, cereal, and glazed faience. The traders exported to the world the most refined jugs of glass and clay, as well as engraved vases and exquisite jewelry that Saydoun manufactured on a grand scale. The world ahead would also be expecting their raw materials of pine and cedar wood considered by Europe, Africa and the Americas to be of great value.

On their way back, the traders would import gold, iron and lead from the western coast of the Black Sea; copper from Cyprus; precious stones from India and the Far East; ivory from Africa; papyrus from Egypt, silver from Spain; and lead and tin from the land of the Britons. They would also bring in, among other products, precious ebony, silk, horses, spices, amber and incense.

The Mediterranean Sea, once described as the Phoenician waters, was like a beehive where ships sailed in and out in an eventful yet systematic rhythm. Within all that apparent chaos, there was a certain hidden order that confused Lady Parthenis at the harbor. Her big brown eyes reflected admiration towards the harmonious maneuvering of the sailors taming the great crashing waves; the sound of which reached her like a musical hum. Sweet yet strong, the scent of the salty water filled her with a strange, stimulating sensation.

A soft breeze wafted her flax blue tunic and the pink veil around her head shaped the curves of her face whose softness mirrored her mid-twenties. Her elegant hand touched the sapphire necklace around her fine neck, nervously, as she sighed deeply for patience. Her husband was scheduled to arrive today from Greece, and his two-week long trip had felt like an eternity to her. A Surian (Tyrian) merchant, her husband Mnesarchus[1] constantly sailed the Mediterranean Sea aboard his ship; Astarte, the Lady of the Sea, represented by an impressive statue of a siren at the front.

And here it was, emerging proud and confident among the other boats. Parthenis smiled in relief, then with pride. Splendid, the *Lady of the Sea* revealed, gradually, its upper human figure. As the Astarte navigated closer and closer, the lower fish form of the statue came to sight. The vessel finally docked at the pier to release, and moments later, dozens of voyagers disembarked on the already busy port. Parthenis watched them with interest as they stepped out hastily. She could detect the artists among the merchants from their colorful attire. Their cheerful expressions denoted their relief at reaching their destination safely. These travelers belonged to different Mediterranean countries, and, as she always did when in the port, she examined them with pleasant curiosity.

Soon, she grew impatient at not seeing her husband. She stretched her neck, her eyes searching, and then she smiled widely at the man rushing to her. She admired his long, curly mane and his tanned, bearded face that gave him the look of a man in his early forties. His bluish-purple tunic, wrapped by a brown leather belt at the waist, shaped his stout shoulders. His patent force and

---

[1]   It is said that Mnesarchus, father of Pythagoras, was a merchant from the Samos Island in the Aegean Sea; center of Phoenician commerce. The name Samos probably derived from the Phoenician word 'Shamos' (Shamas or Sun). In the same line of discovery, the Aegean, a Phoenician civilization, was the base of the Grecian civilization, as claimed by many historians. Thus, Mnesarchus would be of Phoenician roots. Our ancestors conveyed to us that Mnesarchus was born in Sur (Tyre). Neanthes, one of the early sources, claimed that Mnesarchus was Tyrian by birth, thus, not a Tyrrhenian; as some have also suggested in an attempt to tarnish the truth.

enthusiastic appearance overwhelmed her with a feeling of expectation. Edging nearer, he went down on his knees and kissed the ground of his homeland. His eyes brightened warmly at her advanced pregnancy, lifted up to hers in love and then back to the round form of the new life her insides nurtured. His hand reached to it. He touched her, ever so softly, ever so tenderly, confusing her by such an unusual public display of emotion.

"I can feel him moving," he finally blurted out overwhelmed. "Our baby boy... moving in a harmonious rhythm inside you, my dear. How beautiful!"

She blushed and gave him a timid smile. Her hand joined his on her belly. With her other hand, she caressed his thick wavy hair.

"A boy? What makes you believe that, dear?" Her soft question teased him.

His smile broadened with a steady confidence that expressed his male satisfaction. He leaped to his feet, grabbed both her hands in his and said, "Beloved Parthenis, I carry with me great news! I will tell you it all on our way home."

He led her through the crowded port and, once on the quieter boulevard, he brought her, by the shoulders, closer to his side to continue walking at a calmer pace. Dusk was falling peacefully on them.

"I met a friend of mine, a Greek merchant, upon my arrival in Athens," Mnesarchus said, finally. "I told him about your pregnancy and he was truly delighted by the good news. He advised me to consult the oracle of the Temple of Apollo in Delphi; one of the most famous Temples in all of Greece. Well, dear, I did! And the priestess told me that *we will have a son!*" Mnesarchus announced with a cheerful tone of pride.

"Oh dear!" Parthenis exclaimed with a frown of disapproval.

A firm believer in the Phoenician God *AL*, she doubted that followers of gods, other than hers, could possibly predict the unknown. This information could very well be just a deception. Anxiety and curiosity left her mystified.

She probed for more, "Mnesarchus, my love, I want you to be honest with me. Your words left me wondering. Please tell me! Do you really believe in the prediction of that priestess? I mean... how is it possible, really, that she could discern the unknown? You are very well aware that her religious beliefs are different from ours!"

"Oh Parthenis, I'm telling you what she told me! I believe in what I heard. You should have seen that priestess. It seemed to me... hmmm, how should I put it? It really seemed to me as if she moved through a great mist far, far away beyond this world as if she was communicating with something invisible... an *invisible power!* You should accompany me on my next trip, and see for yourself. That, of course, if you wish." He looked at her inquiringly.

She stopped and gazed pensively at the sea sending its soft waves along the beach.

"Where about is Greece?" She asked, suddenly excited at the prospect of a trip with her husband to that exotic land she had heard so much about.

Delighted, Mnesarchus turned to point towards the northwest. Standing there for a while, the couple held hands. Parthenis rested her head on his shoulder, closed her eyes, and took a deep, long breath.

* * *

The couple reached the paved alley leading to the *souk*. Palm trees, on both sides, made their promenade more enchanting, as did the soft light of the oil lamps that hung on the road's pillars. The night had fallen by then; yet the shops, productive

9

still, conducted their business with the same dexterity. Some merchants engaged in stocking their newly imported merchandise under the curious eyes of eager buyers.

Most imported metals would reach the factories, directly at the outskirts of the *souk*, and even farther away to the legendary industrial unit of Sarepta (Sarafand). Located fifteen kilometers south of the city, the factory and its skillful artisans continuously produced fine chiseled works of art.

Saydoun had gained a vast reputation for its social and medical services, some well advanced, like dental treatments. Phoenician doctors in the city had come up with an ingenious concept of twisting pure gold wire around loose teeth to hold them firmly in place. Spirituality assumed a role in the medical field as well. The Saydonians took pride in their curative god *Eshmun;* known as *the god of medicine*. Originally an ordinary man, Eshmun had turned into a god because of his power to heal through the gifts of nature.

Both, natives and foreigners enjoyed the vivacious city. It seemed as if life pumped vigorously in the hearts of the people, in the fauna and flora, inside the houses and on the streets. Life vibrated energetically everywhere!

Music drifted from the right corner of the plaza. There, an aged musician sat on a flat stone, playing his lyre with a young flutist standing at his side. Charmed, people gathered around them. Some sat right there on the floor. Others stopped to listen. Enchanted smiles expressed the mood that the musicians contributed to create for the pleasure of the citizens and visitors. The breeze of the night wafted around the delicious smell of food, tempting many towards the nearby tavern. In fact, Phoenician cuisine was favorably reputed all over the Mediterranean.

"Don't even think about it! I have prepared a special dinner for you at home!" Parthenis teased her husband, whose eyes had widened at sight of the restaurant.

He laughed out loud then brought her hand to his mouth for a resounding kiss that made her blush with pleasure. "Let's go home then," he proposed with enthusiasm and turned her around towards the exit of the *souk*.

She giggled as she tried to match his fast steps. She then slowed down gradually, her eyes caught by the magnificent sight of a colorful array of flowers.

"Mnesarchus!" She called him back and stopped in total admiration at the display of the florist and the captivating aroma that drifted from that diverse arrangement. A particular flower took her breath away.

She heard her husband whispering tenderly in her ears, "The white rose of course."

She nodded with a grin and watched as Mnesarchus dropped a coin in the hand of the florist, drew out the rose and offered it to her. She gazed at it for a while, lifted her loving eyes to him in thanks then kissed him softly on the cheek.

His eyes warmed in hers then, speechless, he grabbed her arm to walk towards the residential area. They made their way, uneventfully, through the houses of limestone, all similarly shaped, in both rectangular and cubical forms, with open windows on the sides.

Upon spotting her home, quite different from the general lots, she smiled with tender pride at her husband's achievement. Different from that of his neighbors, he had constructed his house with stone and roofed it with Cedar wood. He had made it a point to expand his backyard with a bountiful garden. While most people could not afford to have their houses built in the same way, Mnesarchus had dedicated all his efforts and smart trading to afford his growing family a trouble-free life.

11

As soon as they were home, she marched decisively to the wooden pillar in the middle of the house and lit the oil lamp, there steadily suspended. She turned a discreet look at her husband dropping at once on the couch. She refrained from commenting on his weariness, cautious not to hurt his male pride. She instead rushed to set the dinner that she had previously prepared in anticipation of his homecoming. In fact, she had most of it primed and ready to serve the husband she loved so dearly. She warmed the stew of meat and vegetables and a delicious aroma rose at once. Freshly picked for the meal, the vegetables and fruits she set on the table appealed at once to her husband's senses who leaped to his feet the moment she turned to him an inviting smile. They settled at the wooden table, elegantly wrought by a Saydonian carpenter. From the window, draped with an elegant purple curtain, the moon appeared to smile at the peaceful reunion of the couple.

* * *

The Sun appeared on a new day from behind the mountains of Eastern Loubnan. Sunrays stretched over the land as the birds launched their musical rhapsody. The fauna awoke to another day of survival in the nearby forest and the surrounding fields. A brisk aroma drifted from the cypress and olive trees as the morning dew covered the land. The populace breathed, with satisfaction, the refreshing morning air before they moved on to their daily routine, as Parthenis did.

Yet she had awakened earlier than that to bake some bread and cakes for her husband. He had joined her later on and waited now, for her, in the garden. She stepped up with the baked meal and glanced at him while setting the breakfast table. Gazing pensively at the Murex Hill in the distance, he took a deep breath as if wanting to take in all the glorious aromas of the early day. He

12

turned to her a childish smile, and sighed with satisfaction. Their eyes met for a tender moment. This was their favorite time, when they both would sit in their garden for their first meal. At her gracious gesture of invitation, he joined her at the table.

On the narrow path alongside their garden, Saydonians sauntered towards the hill with baskets of murex shell on their arms. Some hummed a merry tune, while others chatted cheerily. In a friendly manner known to the inhabitants, they all waved in turn to the couple and their smiles broadened as Mnesarchus and Parthenis returned the greetings with the same enthusiasm.

As if suddenly remembering something, Mnesarchus leaped to his feet, surprising her, and rushed to the joyful procession. Amused, she watched him choosing with eagerness some of the precious purple linen. He then instructed them to prepare for him two sumptuous robes of the Royal Purple.

'A month, no later!'

She heard him and recalled him informing her, the eve before, that some wealthy Greek traders had shown high interest in that rare ethnic product. She did not need much to guess that he planned to sell these precious robes to them on his next trip to Greece. She tilted her head sideways with a grin of understanding as he joined her back.

"Yes dear, soon we will sail to Greece," he affirmed, smiling back at her.

"In a month?" she exclaimed.

"Of course, my love! I can assure you that we will enjoy it a great deal. I will introduce you to many of my friends. You will like them, you'll see!

"I guess I will, Mnesarchus. Who are they?"

"Some famous painters and poets," he said excitedly. "Others are successful merchants and there are even some prominent politicians!"

13

She chuckled at his unconcealed enthusiasm. "I'm really looking forward to visiting Greece and meeting all of your friends, dear, but..." she hesitated pensively then decided to state her mind. "About the priestess you mentioned... Well, I'm not sure..."

"Not sure of what, dear?" he seized her hand over the table and probed her eyes for her hidden concern.

"It's hard for me to believe her!"

"My love, I'm not trying to persuade you of her legitimacy. Just grant her the benefit of the doubt until you meet with her. Sounds fair?" His eyes were intent on hers.

She knew her opinion mattered to him, the way she cared a lot about him. This matter was important to him, so she would concede for his sake. She sighed.

"Fine, dear, since you insist. But I still prefer to consult our priests in Gebel. We both know for certain that the power of *AL,* our God the Most High, is with them."

"I don't mind at all, dear," he rushed to agree, apparently relieved. His hand started caressing hers warmly, his eyes tenderly in hers. "We shall definitely pay them a visit soon, and that's a promise!" He asserted all too happily.

Parthenis sipped at her milk with great relief. When, the day before, her husband had talked about Delphi with so much faith, she thought or rather believed that he had had a change of heart and fine-tuned his mind to the gods of Greece. She knew for sure now that her doubts were not founded. She looked at him.

His eyes were elsewhere...

* * *

The procession of the Murex Experts arrived at the hill that had built up by the accumulation of waste from the purple dye factories behind it. Their silhouettes faded away in that direction. It was by strategic choice that the Saydounians had opted for this particular location to the East of their town. As the wind would blow downward, so would the intense smell wave away from their city.

There inside, in total secrecy, the Experts cracked down the small shells of Murex[2] to extract the mollusks and then place them in large tanks over a low fire. Carefully and attentively, they conducted their undisclosed process of producing the purple dye. Later on, exposed to the Mediterranean sun, the mollusks would decompose and take on a yellowish pigment.

The Phoenician artisans would gently heat up the newly obtained liquid for almost two weeks. They would then add some unknown chemical formulas of their creation – probably made from Lemon extract. The skillful manipulation of the process would generate a selection of unique shades of colors that varied from soft pink to deep violet, also known as *Royal Purple*. These magnificent permanent colors would also be used to dye the finest textiles of linen and flax, imported from Egypt on a regular basis. The outcome introduced to people the pleasure of fashion at all times.

Undoubtedly, clothes made from *Royal Purple* stood out in beauty. They had gained favor with Phoenicians of wealth and high social standards. In fact, that unusual textile of rare quality had earned its royal surname because kings and rich elite of foreign nations sought it, regardless of its high price in gold that only their wealth could afford!

The Saydounians, like the Surians, both famous in the production of purple dye, had made it a point to conceal their artistic formula at all costs. As a matter of fact, workers of these factories had

---

[2]   The Murex is a sea snail found only on the Phoenician coasts.

related how each one of them would be inspected scrupulously at the end of the working day, and that, to ensure that the secret recipe would not be stolen. This meticulous, strict control had allowed the Phoenicians to implement a worldwide monopoly over that amazingly beautiful craft of their own invention.

* * *

The Sun rose above the peak of the Eastern Mountains. From behind the Murex hill, appeared two women in traditional clothes. They walked down the path to Mnesarchus' house, in their hands: two boxes and a papyrus. They opened the iron gate of the garden and halted at the reigning silence. They looked at each other for a moment then, without a word, they closed the distance to the backyard door. They knocked softly and waited. Getting no response, they placed the package and the papyrus on the doorsteps with great care, and, without looking back, made their way out.

Parthenis woke up, relaxed and refreshed from her good night's sleep. She drew the curtains to the sides, opened the window, and took a deep breath with a sense of contentment. Something under her window, right there at her doorstep drew her attention. She urged her steps to the backyard door, and opened it with caution. Her eyebrows lifted in surprise at the brown packages left at her doorstep. She glanced in wonder, left and right, and far beyond where her eyes could reach. No one could be seen. With a deep frown, she gazed down at the package: two wooden boxes and a roll of Papyrus. A breeze wafted softly and a strong smell of Cedar reached her senses. It was then while bending down slowly, that she distinguished the Phoenician characters on each of the boxes. *Royal Purple - 1 Piece.* On the other side, the words read *Made in Saydoun, Phoenicia.*

16

She smiled, then giggled. Those would be the outfits her husband had ordered a few weeks ago. She carried the package inside the house and restrained from opening it, or reading the papyrus. *Mnesarchus would do it later,* she thought to herself. As she turned to go back to her room, she recalled that the trip to Greece had been confirmed, and the fate of her future child would soon be revealed by the oracle of Delphi! Although she greatly doubted the revelation of the priestess, trepidation overwhelmed her. When she stepped back into her bedroom, she smiled at her husband waking up.

"Good morning," she greeted him cheerfully and went to lay a soft kiss on his forehead.

He returned the greeting as he tried to grab her back to him, but she eluded his hands gracefully.

"Time for breakfast, husband!"

He groaned in disagreement. Giggling, she turned to the window and gazed for a while at the colorful little bird, sprinting from one branch to another on the olive tree. *Strange,* she thought to herself, *it resembled the legendary Phoenix!*

* * *

It was a lovely morning in which the crowd at the busy Saydounian pier seemed driven by an energetic will; the *will of life.* Consorting under the Mediterranean Sun, traders, merchants, artists, and scholars intermingled in social conversation. They appeared longing for an adventure, an adventure filled with the spirit of belonging to the courageous, loving, and caring family of mankind.

Elegant in a blue-flax tunic, her head veiled with a white scarf, Parthenis, aided by her husband, made her way towards the "Astarte". Behind them, two young porters carried their luggage with a grin of expectation. The couple slowed down here and there on their way to the "Astarte" as friends and

17

acquaintances would greet them. Parthenis stretched her neck above the crowd to gaze at their ship. The *Lady of the Sea,* with the huge eyes lost in an eternal gaze, its posture in advance, appeared eager to initiate another trip through the infinite world of the ocean.

She felt her heart beating faster as Mnesarchus helped her climb the thick wooden steps tied together with strong ropes that brought them on board. Truth be said, she had rarely traveled overseas. For her, this date would stick in her memories forever as a brave new day. From on board, she gazed at the town she had dreaded to leave, even if for a short period of time. She loved her house and her chores as housewife. She liked her neighbors and the friendly people of her hometown. She sighed deeply, inhaling courage and determination for what awaited her. Their destination should be reached and their goal accomplished. There was no going back now!

"This way, dear," Mnesarchus invited her to follow him, and she did, with a dynamic return of grins.

Her steps, firm yet graceful, her head straight, she walked, unconcerned, past the men jamming the boat. Mnesarchus came to a halt at the entrance of the pilot's compartment. She stepped closer to him as the noise impeded them to communicate. He kindly gestured her to precede him a step down then to the left. She did and then halted, taking in the quietness of the confined interior and the strong smell of the narrow aisle. She frowned as her mind tried to assess what her senses detected. There was more to the smell than humidity. The cedar wood all around her spoke of long voyages on the seas through the powerful aroma it emanated.

"Parthenis?"

She glimpsed at Mnesarchus above her shoulder and gave him a reassuring smile before

18

moving on. Identical doors of natural wood lined up on both sides of the passageway. She did not need to turn around to check for their porters. She knew for a fact that they would not miss this opportunity for a tip from her husband, known for his generosity.

"Our cabin is number five, just ahead, dear..., the next one to the right," Mnesarchus guided her from behind her back.

She stopped in front of the door marked number 5, in Phoenician form, on a bronze plate and glanced back at her husband for confirmation. At his nod, she opened it and stepped in.

"So, dear, this is your personal lodge," Parthenis exclaimed cheerfully, her eyes browsing the modest surroundings in which her husband always traveled.

"So it is, my love!" he replied with the same enthusiasm and turned to signal to the porters to leave the luggage at the side of the only bed in the room. He then dropped a few coins in the extended hands of the porters whose eyes brightened at once. Parthenis refrained from laughing at seeing the boys bowing in gratitude several quick times before they dashed out, one after the other. Her heart went to her husband for his kindness to others.

Her attention reverted to the room they were to inhabit for the duration of their trip. Small, yet comfortable, the place appealed to her. The purple bed linen looked remarkably clean as did the two weaved, colorful carpets thrown on the wooden floor. In a corner, a terracotta jar of water stood by an iron strut carrying a large wash basin of flowery ceramic. The opposite corner presented some hooks on the wall for their clothes. Brand new candles and a small bouquet of white roses graced the small wooden table near the window.

"Oh dear, how thoughtful of you!" Parthenis exclaimed and rushed to smell the bouquet of her favorite flowers. She then looked curiously from the small window at the activity unfurling on the long pier outside. She laughed at the vibrant scene. At once, the strong arms of her husband wrapped around her waist. She rested back on his warm chest and closed her eyes with contentment.

"Departure in ten minutes!"

She snapped her eyes open at the call that reverberated to her from the outside.

"It's the Captain," her husband explained.

"Everybody on board!" the call reiterated with more authority this time.

She veered to face her husband. Her heart pounded fast. Her hands sweated on his chest. His eyes sparkled in hers, perceptive of her excitement.

The adventure was about to begin!

* * *

Parthenis and her husband hastened out to join the travelers who submitted to the routine checkup of the traveling documents. The couple did not need to undertake this routine since Mnesarchus owned the ship. However, she had insisted not to miss the gathering and meet their journey's companions. At detecting that she was not the only woman undertaking this voyage, she felt relieved, even if the male gender surpassed by far the female voyagers.

Mnesarchus led her by the waist to the banisters, away from the crowd and to a spot where she could watch leisurely without being pushed or harassed. Soon, the "Astarte" moved slowly away from the pier. Parthenis focused her attention on the manpower at work. On one side of the ship, forty muscular men occupied two ranks, one above the other. They rowed with all their power in a harmony that seemed to follow the rhythm played by a young flutist.

Mnesarchus explained to her the rowing technique invented by the Phoenician sailors through their expertise in the art of navigation.

They, as such, far bypassed the Egyptians who still used large canoes that required hard, thus less efficient, paddling.

Attentive, she watched how the captain and the pilot, along with the flutist, commanded the rowing. It amazed her that the flutist coordinated the exact tempo of the rowers. Like a Maestro who would direct a musical symphony, he brought the whole team, including the pilot and the captain, into perfect harmony. This unity favored the speedy maneuvering of their navigation in gaining considerable time. The captain, from his side, kept a watchful alert while guiding their vessel out of the harbor with an admirable precision.

When they made their way farther into the sea, they increased the speed. The statue of Astarte, steady in its position, appeared to part the waters, directing the ship into the very heart of the Mediterranean Sea. Three boats of smaller size, with wooden heads of horses at their front, escorted the "Astarte". The captain shouted his orders, and a sailor ran to the five-meter high mast in the center of the deck. In a matter of seconds, he untied the bulky knot and pulled down the thick ropes. A huge cylindrical canvas unfurled at once to catch the wind. The "Astarte" propelled forward, slicing the surface of the sea in a white foamy crease.

Thirty-two meters long and six meters wide, their vessel comprised plenty of space for people and merchandise. For the moment, most of the local merchants rested on the other side of the deck facing the rowers, whereas their trading goods were set neatly in the center.

By mid-day, they encountered several other boats, somewhat similar to each other. The "Astarte" made its way through, proudly different in beauty and shape. Trepidation faded gradually as most of the voyagers sought rest in their rooms.

"Our lunch will be served any time now, dear," Mnesarchus informed her, "Aren't you hungry?"

"Already?" She lifted her eyebrows in surprise. "I mean, is it lunch time?"

He laughed out loudly. "I'm glad you are enjoying the trip from the very start," he teased her.

She chuckled then, and, seized his hand to have him lead the way to their lodge.

The moment they regained the privacy of their room, she untied her veil and graciously shook her head to release her long mane.

"Mmm, it does smell delicious," she exclaimed with a look at their meal ready on their table.

Mnesarchus laughed, "So, you are hungry!"

"Of course! With all this excitement...!"

"Adding the fresh air of the sea that stimulates the appetite...," he insinuated jokingly.

"Oh dear, I am so happy I came along!" She threw herself in his arms in a spontaneous expression of gratitude and joy.

"Same here, beloved," his voice sounded hoarse with emotion. He cleared his throat and added, "Let's eat."

She complied and settled on the wooden chair weaved with thick rope. He joined her at the table facing her. He divided the warm bread and shared it with her while she served him some stew.

"I am really thrilled, Mnesarchus! I am, very much, looking forward to seeing Greece. When do you think we'll be there?"

"No more than seven days from now," Mnesarchus replied, amused at her eagerness. "I'm really glad you came along," he added seizing her hands tenderly. "You'll see. We will enjoy all of it. Greece is a wonderful place to visit! You'll love the Temple of Apollo in Delphi as well."

Parthenis listened to him expounding on all the amazing places planned for her visit. She could almost envision them all. His fervor grabbed her dreamily. The great city of Athens and its wise men! The Agora square and its many grand public buildings! Proud sculptors exhibiting their fine pieces! Poets and poetesses reciting the most beautiful prose! The Acropolis! The beautiful colossal statue of the goddess Athena! The shrine of Zeus!

His eyes were bright and wistful. Parthenis knew then that his love to this particular country surpassed by far all the others he had visited.

"Some wine, dear?" She proposed, grabbing the clay jar on the table. At his nod, she poured some of the *drink of the gods* into his cup and filled hers with some fresh water.

He raised his goblet, toasted to their life together, sipped on his red wine, and leaned forward, "Do you know what the most beautiful thing I have ever seen, is?"

"What is it, beloved?" She asked puzzled.

"Your eyes!"

Before she could react, his lips were on hers, kissing her passionately.

Caught in the magic of the moment, time seemed to cease.

* * *

Later in the afternoon, Parthenis stood on the banister admiring the sunset. The sky changed its colors gradually as the sun made its slow decline behind the horizon. She shivered with some strange emotion. Feeling so close to the sun, at the very moment of its merging with the sea, confronted her with a phenomenal mystery. The fiery planet appeared to inflame in protest at touching the water of the ocean that swallowed its glory all too slowly as if tasting a delicious victory over a different yet powerful element.

She welcomed the warmth of Mnesarchus' hand on her shoulder. It brought her back to reality and to a sense of security she had felt lacking in front of such a majestic occurrence. Comforted, she felt indeed, when his hands wrapped around her belly and pulled her softly back to his solid chest. She smiled at his words of love whispered so closely to her ears and shuddered with emotion at his breath on her neck. He rested his forehead on her left shoulder for a long moment, as if lost in the enchantment of her softness. The amber colors of the sky showered them as time reached dusk with all its secret beauty. There, connected in body, heart and soul as never before, they both shared a unique moment of peaceful love.

Time seemed to stand still for both of them. The activity on deck had subsided by now. Mnesarchus turned her tenderly to him seeking the love of her lips.

"Eh... Sir...," a hesitant voice interrupted the couple. "Excuse me, sir... It's the Captain... He, hmm...," the boy who uttered these words kept his eyes riveted on the sea, to avoid looking at them, as Parthenis noticed with amusement.

"Yes...?" Mnesarchus replied slowly yet his tone hinted his irritation. Then, as he glared at the boy, his wrinkle of annoyance vanished to leave place to a sparkle of amusement in his dark eyes. He certainly deemed the embarrassment of the boy as amusing as she did. "Come on boy! Spit it out!"

The order shook the boy who spun on his heels to face Mnesarchus. "Captain Hamelkon, Sir!" He rushed on his words. "He requests the honor of your presence at his table for dinner... Sir!"

"And so it will be!" Mnesarchus exclaimed in agreement and Parthenis burst out in laughter.

* * *

Edging his fifty, Captain Hamelkon had a lean physique, and a thick black beard smeared with the white color of age, same as his hair that reached his shoulders. The stiff look of his tanned face reflected his strong character. Parthenis imagined reading a long story of experience in his deep black eyes shadowed by thick peppered eyebrows. A crooked nose, denoting determination, traced a long length from the linked eyebrows down to his thick moustache. The deep wrinkles on his forehead and cheeks enhanced the impression of a charcoal drawing.

Hmmm... Interesting, she murmured inwardly, but there was a kind of perturbed feeling that inhabited her at first. Yet, she soon changed her mind about him. His impeccable courtesy, lit at all times by an effortless smile, made her feel at home. He, in fact, attended to all the guests with a cheerful mood yet with respectful manners, making of the dinner gathering a very enjoyable evening.

From the lavish clothes and heavy jewelry of the four other male guests, Parthenis knew of their wealth, the way she recognized their profession from their conversation in trades and merchandise. She delighted in a meal of well cooked and finely served meat. Servants constantly filled the cups with red wine of excellent quality, or so she assumed from the enchanted expression on her husband's face. She would not drink herself for the sake of her unborn baby.

From the very start of their meal, Captain Hamelkon captivated her, and all the guests, with his narration of strange stories about the seas and the lands he had explored in his many trips. Fascinated, she watched how he engaged in his tales as if reliving them. He related his adventure across the *Pillars of Melkart-Hercules* when he had commanded a large fleet towards Bar-Tanak[3], the

---

[3] It is said that the word *Britain* comes from the term *Prutani*, given to the Celts by the Romans. We, however, believe that the Phoenicians gave to Britain the name *Bar-Tanak*, meaning the Land of Tin. History and Archeology reveal that Britain was the Phoenician secret reservoir of tin they used to trade or bring home.

Land of Tin. Parthenis could not get her attention away from him.

At moments, she envisioned herself in that exploit. The tension seemed to take on everyone around the table. The merchants gawked at the Captain, their eyes bright in expectation and their wine untouched on the table, anticipating the end of the story.

Mnesarchus seemed more composed, sipping his wine quietly, yet his eyes focused on him with amused interest. Parthenis assumed that he had heard this tale once before, or maybe more than once, but he still felt absorbed, sharing with his captain the same attraction for the sea.

"Tell them about the land of the black-skinned people!" Mnesarchus exclaimed.

"How about the times I docked at *Marsa-El*[4] in Europa[5]?" He proposed in reply, his eyes mischievous.

"Later... later!" Mnesarchus waved his hand in the air in dismissal. "The land of the black skinned people first!" He incited flippantly.

"Yes, please!" The guests pleaded almost in one voice.

"So be it!" The Captain snapped with a resounding clap of his hands. He brought the cup of

---

[4]   The establishment of the port of Marseilles in France was for long credited to the Phocaeans, a people of Asia Minor, of the Ionic civilization and the port Massilia was called as such from the 6th century BCE. However, we believe that the Phoenicians founded it nearly at that time and called it *Marsa-El*, which means the *Docking of the Phoenician ships of El!*

[5]   The name of the European Continent, *Europe*, derives undoubtedly from *Europa*, the daughter of Agenor, King of Tyre. Legend says that her brother Kadmus went searching for her in Greece after she was kidnapped by Zeus, the most High God of the Grecian world. During the many years of his search, Kadmus introduced the Phoenician Alphabet to the Greeks and founded many cities; the most famous among them was Thebes.

26

wine to his mouth, drank all of it, placed it down on the table and went for his new story.

The Captain controlled their night and dreams, dragging the time far beyond the sleeping hour, and capturing them, one more time, in his world of exciting adventures…

* * *

The next day, the deck experienced its usual morning activity as soon as the sky tinted with the colors of dawn. The rowers positioned themselves to sail at a faster speed when the first sunrays highlighted the soft waves with a radiant touch.

Moments later, they ceased their rowing efforts to allow the navigation to direct its course. Parthenis enjoyed the scene along with a few passengers strolling around leisurely. She breathed deeply the fresh air of the awakening day. The sea conveyed to her senses its briskly salty scent. She felt at peace, somehow. The feeling escorted her all day, until a strange sensation seized her later at night.

She stood there at the banister, admiring the rise of the full moon that painted the dark water with timid rays. The sea looked infinite to her; a dark ocean at sleep through which the "Astarte" abdicated to the current and to the sudden wind.

An odd sensation of apprehension overwhelmed her when she pondered over the unknown mystery of that immense body of water. She heeded behind her the sound of footsteps approaching her steadfastedly. She tensed for a moment when it edged closer then she veered at once to face the intruder on her thoughts. Captain Hamelkon came at a respectful halt and distance from her, took off his cone hat and greeted her with a contrite smile.

"Pardon my intrusion, my Lady. I was conducting my tour of surveillance and saw you from my cabin. And so, I have come to check on you. My apologies, again. Is everything alright?"

"Yes, Captain, thank you," she replied with some reservation.

"Are you enjoying the night view?"

"Yes, indeed, I am." She granted him a graceful nod of her head before adding, "I would say, it is quite relaxing and calm." Then after a slight hesitation, she commented, "A little bit strange though..."

"Yes, quite understandable," Captain Hamelkon agreed, keeping to his distance out of respect for their cultural values. He gazed pensively at the ocean and said as if thinking out loud, "The ancient people of the Earth deemed the Sea a frightening mystery. They wrongly presumed it to be the habitat of gigantic monsters and outlandish creatures. They in fact imagined them appearing behind the horizon. For centuries, people believed in such tales, until, of course, our ancestors broke through that ancient illusion when they ventured into the vast ocean. Eventually, what they found beyond that imaginary borderline was nothing more than human life and habitats. However," he paused to turn his eyes at her and declared, "Sea monsters, legends tell, existed in immemorial times in the scheme of nature."

The brief sparkle in his eyes when he looked in her direction betrayed his anticipation for a reaction of dismay from her; dread or fear.

She smiled faintly at his attempt to assess her courage, and uttered calmly, "Yes, I'm well informed of such legends. People are usually prisoners of their own fear of the unknown. Only those who dare facing their demons prevail, and, of course," she added evenly, "to acknowledge the borderline between reality and illusion demands courage."

Stunned by her reply, he gawked at her for a moment then slightly bowed his head in respectful acknowledgment, not of her statement but of her level of reasoning, as if she had just passed a test of some sort. *Men!* Her mind snapped in frustration. In a proud move of her head, she directed her attention to the game of the moon rays on the dark waters.

"My lady, allow me," the Captain finally said with a hint of apology. "I know of the educated level of our Phoenician women, and of them being looked upon as exceptional. I am honored to join my voice to the general praises. Phoenician ladies stand out indeed from among their sisters in the world I have visited."

The praises did not move her. She knew of her value very well. "The honor is all mine in being a descendant of such awe inspiring people," she murmured, more to herself than to him.

"And you honor us, my lady," the Captain replied at once with sincere admiration.

She knew what he meant. He was, of course, referring to her courage and intelligence, yet he should know that Phoenician women were not of the weak and superficial type. They had proved it through the ages, and she was but one among all the others. At the thought of her roots, a new sensation of tranquility enveloped her.

"How did you become a sailor, Captain Hamelkon?" she asked, half turning to his direction.

"It is in the family, fair Lady. When I was a little boy, my grandfather used to narrate stories to me about the sea. He told me of the strong connection that bounded him to the immensity of the water world from the onset of his travels."

Parthenis understood then that she, in fact, shared this feeling towards the sea as well; a unique feeling that belongs to all those who sailed through it. *It is just another state of mind processed by Nature*, she reasoned.

"My grandfather told me that people were strongly convinced that the world ended behind the

Pillars of Melkart," the Captain resumed, then pointing to the West, "there, in that direction." He grinned with a hint of irony. "So, one day, he decided to go see for himself what the end-of-the-world looked like!"

"He must have been quite an intrepid man, your grandfather," Parthenis commented, sharing his amusement. "So, what happened?" She encouraged him to continue. Somehow she felt connected in soul with the old man.

"Well, when the boat crossed through the *Pillars,* he was astonished at the fact that the navigation continued without incident or drama. The world just extended farther and farther away!" He laughed and shook his head in glee. "He was a new sailor at that time, a neophyte in the Art," he felt like explaining his grandfather's candor. "The other experienced sailors cackled at his bewilderment of course, and kept teasing him during the entire journey. Eventually, the captain explained to him that the concept in itself was just a rumor fabricated by our Ancestors to scare away other nations from sailing through. The captain concluded, *'Son, this is not the end of the world, but the beginning of a new world!'* The stated revelation anchored in my grandfather's mind forever."

Parthenis stared at Captain Hamelkon pensively. Their eyes met in a moment of understanding, linking the souls of their Ancestors who had mastered the seas and far beyond that.

He sighed then released with confidence, "We know the wind and the current of the water!" Examining the sky above, he added, "But that's not all. We, Phoenician sailors, depend much on the stars to navigate. If you really want to reach your goal," he gave her that kind of intense look that usually preceded a major announcement, "then, fair Lady, you have to follow the stars!"

He excused himself and walked away.

But Parthenis would indeed follow the stars...

Her stars...

* * *

On the afternoon of the seventh day, the "Astarte" arrived safely at the port of Athens. The passengers rushed out, eager to stand on firm land; the land of Greece! Parthenis had waited for this moment with the same fervor. She had craved to experience the world from a new perspective. The moment she set foot on the shore and smelled the new exotic fragrance in the air, she knew that she would like it here.

"Welcome to Greece... Lady... Sir...!"

The greeting ensued from an old man with a bald head and a long white beard. He murmured the word *Phoenicians* with a look of appreciation at their ethnic outfits.

"Sir needs a ride to the city?" He proposed pointing a wrinkled hand at his two-horse stagecoach a few steps away.

From his spot, Mnesarchus assessed the status of the horses and the wagon with a critical look. He then negotiated the price for the service before agreeing.

And so, after some young porters set their luggage in, the carriage took off towards the great city of Athens. Despite the dust that the horses lifted in their path, Parthenis appreciated the efforts of the old driver in maneuvering smoothly. She overlooked the uncomfortable ride on the jagged road to concentrate on the new panorama that unfurled along their path. Plains rich with vine and olive trees outstretched from both sides of the road.

She discerned some farmers working the lands and detected the songs of dozens of women picking dark grapes, depositing them on large baskets. Children played in the field. Some ran around each other, while the older ones carried the filled baskets to a destination she could only guess.

31

She beamed at the scene that reminded her of the harvest season in her homeland.

Ahead of them, some mountains took shape little by little. The more they neared their destination, the larger the mountains appeared. Finally, they neared the impressive gate of the city wall. Parthenis lifted up her eyes, in awe, at the mountain on which stood the magnificent metropolis of Athens.

"Amazing, isn't it?" Mnesarchus remarked with a look at her.

"It is indeed," she breathed out in a murmur of awe.

"Originally, the city initiated on the rock of the Acropolis, two hundred and seventy meters above the sea level," he explained. "Upon flourishing and developing, it spread around the hill from all sides, and then all the way down the ancient fortress where the Athenians now live. Today, Athens has become one of the most important cities of Greece!"

Parthenis did not answer, for their carriage was, just now, slowly penetrating into the city, and a whole new world of sight and sound unwrapped around her, taking her breath away. She took in, at once, the remarkable dynamism of the city through its activities, colors, assortment and beauty. There were sculptors almost everywhere; busy shaping stones into fine-looking statues. In the plaza square, just there, below the northwestern road to the Acropolis, poets recited their prose and hymns to whoever would show interest; and many did!

"Sappho!" Their driver announced, indicating a woman of medium stature, violet hair and dark-purple tunic. "She is our pride, this poetess. She always presents us with the most sensational poems and elegies in town!"

With curious interest, Parthenis examined the young woman of ivory face and honey smile. She stood, barefooted, two steps above a small crowd. At her side, a beautiful girl played the lyre while the poetess recited some poem of sensual wordings and melodic tones.

"She writes for various personages and genders, mainly songs of passion, love, yearning, and reflection," the driver expounded with fervor as he drove the wagon all too leisurely.

"Where is she from?" Parthenis asked, eager to know more.

"Sappho? She was born into an aristocratic family on the isle of Lesbos in the Aegean Sea. She is the most famous poetess in, perhaps, all of Greece! We call her a *lyrist* because her poems are performed with the accompaniment of a lyre."

"And who is the young lyrist at her side?"

"She is Gongyla, a beautiful rose with a Lydian lyre." With these words, the old man expressed his affection and admiration. "They both came together two days ago from Sicily. They are here to perform a daily hymn to the goddess Aphrodite. I think she will start right now, please listen to her... Lady... Sir...!"

And the couple did, the rhymes reaching Parthenis, melodious and warm, with some pitch of supplication that touched her deeply and echoed almost in every corner around the city square.

> *On the throne of many hues, immortal*
> *Aphrodite, Child of Zeus, weaving wiles — I*
> *beg you not to subdue my spirit, Queen,*
> *with pain or sorrow.*
>
> *But come – If ever before having heard my*
> *voice from far away You listened, and leaving*
> *your father's golden home you came in your*
> *chariot yoked with swift, lovely sparrows*
> *bringing you over the dark earth*
> *thick-feathered wings swirling down*
> *from the sky through mid-air.*

*Arriving quickly — you, Blessed one, with a
smile on your unaging face asking again what
have I suffered and why am I calling again*

*And in my wild heart what did I most wish
to happen to me: "Again whom must I
persuade back into the harness of your love?
Sappho, who wrongs you?*

*For if she flees, soon she'll pursue, she
doesn't accept gifts, but she'll give, if not now
loving, soon she'll love even against her will."*

*Come to me now again, release me from
this pain, everything my spirit longs to have
fulfilled, fulfill, and you be my ally.*

The crowd went cheering in ovations to the poetess
and the goddess Aphrodite. With the tip of her fingers,
Parthenis swapped a tear from the corner of her eyes.
"Amazing!" she murmured.

Mnesarchus grabbed her hand and leaned
closer to her ear.

"You like it, don't you?"

"You mean I love it!"

"I knew you would"

"Oh dear, this is just a completely different
world," she asserted without taking her eyes off the
scenes around them.

Mnesarchus chuckled quietly. "It is indeed,
dear. This is exactly the same impression new
comers get during their first visit to this great city."

"You can feel all this energy pulling you…
amazing…" she blurted out in admiration.

*Art is what the Athenians lived for and
survived on,* she remembered her husband
informing her back home. *It is the source of their
happiness and their source of life.*

34

She could not agree more now that she had witnessed the Athenian art expanding across the city in a rhapsody of colors, shapes and sounds.

Their driver ordered the horses and they finally came to a halt. The cart stopped. Mnesarchus helped his wife down with much precaution. She waited for him to supervise the unloading of their luggage. As he retrieved from his pouch some Athenian coins to pay their driver, three young men of poor attire rushed to offer their services in carrying their bags. Mnesarchus looked them in the eye for a moment, assessing their honesty. The instant he nodded in agreement, they hastily grabbed the luggage and followed the couple on their way to the *Agora* city square.

"Here we are, dear! Fascinating, isn't it?" Mnesarchus announced with enthusiasm at reaching the famous plaza. "As you can see, this is the heart of the public life of Athens."

Parthenis held on tightly to his arm to avoid being dragged off by the large crowd in the market place. Packed with fervent customers from different ethnicities, the borough captivated her utmost interest.

"Who are all these people? They don't all seem to be locals," she remarked.

"No, dear, they aren't all locals. Traders and customers seek this place from all the corners of the world."

"Hmm... Impressive," she thought out loud.

"See that old man leading a discussion over there?" He discreetly directed her attention to a small group of men intensely absorbed in a debate.

The old man in question carried his long white hair and neat beard with dignity. His white tunic with blue belt and sleeves enhanced his noble appearance.

"Yes, who is he?"

"He is Solon, the wise man of Athens. I bet he is exchanging some of his astute views with these citizens."

"Views on what, dear?" she asked curiously, "Politics?"

"Yes, and also justice, religion and economy. He is eminent in these fields. The two advisors at his sides are our countrymen, dear. Two notorious Phoenicians, "Thales[6] and ..."

"That man looks like my brother... what... is that Pherecydes[7]!" She wondered and yelled in surprise, interrupting him. "My brother Pherecydes!"

Mnesarchus burst out laughing loudly. "Yes, dear, your brother Pherecydes is here!"

She was in dismay, ignoring that her brother stood as the close advisor of the most famous Solon.

My brother is a private advisor of the sage! The surprising revelation reiterated in her mind. Pride overwhelmed her and tears of joy filled her eyes that riveted on her brother. *Not only one but two top Phoenician consultants!* She thought with pride as she observed both Phoenicians who appeared as magnificent as the High Magistrate with their white tunics trimmed with blue.

"Both Thales and Pherecydes are also the closest friends of Solon," Mnesarchus explained to

---

[6]   According to Diogenes Laertius and many other historians, Thales was the son of Examios, a Phoenician, descending directly from the lineage of Agenor, king of Tyre and the Father of Kadmus. Thales later left Phoenicia, migrating to Miletus, where he became a citizen.

[7]   Pherecydes was born in the island of Syros, a Phoenician settlement in the Aegean Sea. Diogenes Laertius affirmed that he was not only the maternal uncle of Pythagoras but his Master as well. Iamblichus, however, mentioned him as *Pherecydes the Syrian*, but, at the time of Pherecydes, the name *Syria* was not used at all and not even known. Iamblichus surely meant *Pherecydes the Phoenician*.

her discreetly. "They help him run the politics of this great city, even if on a minor scale."

Parthenis realized that her husband had been right about the influence of her countrymen in this foreign land. Its socio-political foundation certainly revealed the fingerprints of Phoenician philosophies and the spirit of their Art. She turned a more attentive ear to his explanations.

"Initially, the aristocratic *Eupatridae* families governed Athens. Then Solon took charge twenty years ago. He is the son of Execestidas; a descendant of ancient Athenian kings."

"So, he issues from a family high up," Parthenis concluded.

"Right," Mnesarchus replied with a nod. "Let's have a walk around the city square," he proposed and led her gently by the waist.

"But my love, I want to talk to my brother. I haven't seen him in two years." She gave Mnesarchus an insistent look.

"I'm sorry. We can't do that right now dear. We have to wait until they finish with their discourse."

The magnificent shrines and public buildings of different structures caught her interest straight away. She stopped for a while in front of the *Royal Stoa,* known also as the *Basileios*, and then moved to admire the Council House, or what was called the *Old Bouleuterion.*

"This is the *Heliaia*, dear," Mnesarchus drew her attention to a major rectangular structure. "It is the Supreme Court; the most important civil law court in the country, one of the biggest in the whole known world!"

Erected on a high ground, right there to the southwest corner of the Agora, the Heliaia faced the Old Bouleuterion on the west side. It formed a large square fence with no internal divisions or rooms, nor roof.

She frowned slightly then her eyebrows lifted at him in wonder.

"The hearings take place outdoors, under the sun," he expounded with a grin. "The Heliaia drew its name from the word *congregation* or *ecclesia*, meaning the Assembly; the Principal Assembly for Democracy."

From their spot, the couple could heed the voice of Solon that resonated strongly throughout the Agora. His words entered every ear, "The aristocratic control on the government: the *eupatridae*, must end! No more owners controlling the best lands and manipulating the poor by driving them into debt! The mission of this very council aims at subsiding the agony of the poor."

Parthenis and Mnesarchus veered promptly at the source of such a strong statement. Stunned, Parthenis gawked at her husband whose eyes widened then shrunk in utmost attention.

"Am I wrong, or this is really a..."

"Shush dear," he interrupted her kindly. "Listen..." he intoned in a whisper.

She did. And how could she not!

"When our farmers are unable to settle their debts, they are forced to become hard laborers!" Solon charged fearlessly. "This means that they become slaves in their own lands. This is unacceptable! We will introduce a new body of law that will be just. Just and fair to all people without exception! Especially in consideration of the poor who are inhumanly abused."

From the large crowd, voices rose in cheering approval. Mnesarchus grabbed her by the forearm and drew her closer to the stage where history was unfurling. Judging by the diverse attires evidencing different social classes, Parthenis noted that Athenians of wealth mingled with the underprivileged and listened to the sage with the same deference.

"We will redeem all dispossessed lands and all the enslaved citizens shall regain their freedom! The decree will be issued at the end of this pronouncement. Yet, rejoice people of Athens, as I assure you that the decree is in effect as of this very moment!" Solon proclaimed with fervor.

The crowd roared, applauded and burst out in an amazing display of exaltation. People shook hands and slapped each other's shoulders in congratulations. Slogans proclaiming Solon as *liberator* were hailed. Mnesarchus and Parthenis witnessed, in awe, the extraordinary moments of a powerful reform in the Agora of Athens. Parthenis had indeed guessed rightly!

Solon raised his hands to impose silence; yet to quiet down the jubilation of a mass that had long lost hope of improving their situation, was not an easy deed.

Thales climbed higher on the steps and shouted for silence. "My friends, that is not all! Listen!"

A wise man himself, and as highly respected as Solon, people shushed and turned their attention to him to heed what he was about to announce.

"Alternative jobs, like trades and other professions, shall be provided to those unable to work the land and become farmers. The new coined money you've seen around lately, have been issued within a better quality and standard, and we have casted them especially for the Athenians."

"Soon, we will introduce new weights and measures to encourage and develop the trade of our Athenian products through the mercantile world. And we are talking about all our products, including our olive oil, grains, wines, and potteries!"

Applauses resounded and hails stirred the Agora. Awe and admiration brightened the eyes riveted on the wise men, as if this wise trio announcing the great news were life saviors. Parthenis felt the contagious excitement and she joined in clapping for the orators. Her husband laughed in amusement.

Apparently, Thales had more announcements to make for he did not wait for the crowd to shush again. But then he gave the podium to Pherecydes who stepped in and proclaimed loudly, "Fair citizens! The rich among you shall replace the *eupatridae*. We will organize a survey of yearly earnings that would be fundamentally calculated according to the commercial transactions of our principal products. To achieve that objective, we will divide you into four groups. Political privilege will therefore be approached accordingly. Hence, each one of you is entitled to attend the General Assembly, the *Ecclesia*, or the Sovereign Body, and to participate in the making of laws and decrees. You will also elect officials and listen to appeals of the most considerable decisions of the courts."

Impressed, Mnesarchus and Parthenis looked up at the wise men with great respect, as did the crowd. Mnesarchus edged closer to Parthenis to whisper in her ear with emotion, "This is history, my dear. What we are hearing now is the laying of the foundation of one of the most important codes of human life to date. It is indeed an evolution of social structure!"

Parthenis stood still, absorbing the revelation in its entire immensity. She turned then to read in his eyes the confirmation of such extraordinary news. She was speechless. The voice of Solon drew her attention back to his speech.

"The poorest among you may have to work, one year after another, on a new Council of Four Hundred, which will prepare business affairs for the General Assembly. However, the highest positions in the new government will be reserved for the citizens of the top two income groups."

Solon took a deep breath and closed his eyes for a moment in which every mind present there awaited in suspense. Nobody dared disturb the silence that reigned. Everybody held their breath in expectation. The seriousness of the moment kept them hostages to the unspoken meditation of the High Magistrate.

Parthenis could have sworn she heard the mass breathing out when Solon reopened his eyes. She sensed the vibrations of their forthcoming trepidation. Solon gazed down at them before his intense look got lost in the horizon.

As if staring into the future, he declared slowly, measuring his words one by one, "My people, today, we place in front of you the foundation of the future democracy."

The words of Solon, the Athenian statesman, legislator and poet, resounded like a strong pledge. He had spoken of a social structure with a proper place and function for each class within. He had just proposed a solution to some major problems that had been weighing on them for many years; a solution based, not on revolutionary forms, but rather on a global reform, both economic and political.

Mnesarchus whispered to her, "Even in his poems, Solon tackles the socio-economic differences."

Parthenis edged closer to him and asked in the same tone, "Tell me about it, please."

"See, he recently wrote these verses:

'Some wicked men are rich,
Some good are poor;
We will not change our virtue for their store:
Virtue is a thing that none can take away,
But money changes owners all the day.'"

The evening fell on the Agora by the time the wise men bid their farewell. The crowd dispersed with the Athenians rushing to their families. On this

41

third night of the full moon, the news of a major reform would be announced in every home.

Eager to speak to her brother, Parthenis struggled against the current of people in order to make her way through. She finally reached the spot where the wise men had reigned over the crowd a while ago only to face her own disappointment at noticing that Pherecydes had disappeared out of sight without knowing of her presence.

There, near the royal porticoes, some finely carved wooden tablets stood on an axis. Parthenis approached to read the inscription:

New Laws of Athens
On display for all the citizens to see.

- *Honor the Gods.*
- *Be convinced that virtue and integrity are more honorable than the oath.*
- *Respect your parents.*
- *Make yourself busy with the serious things in Life.*
- *Know to obey in order to succeed in leading.*
- *Do not consult the attractive, but the beautiful.*
- *Take reason for guidance.*
- *Do not lie.*
- *Do not walk with Evil...*

Before she managed to read through the remaining laws, the sound of running steps echoed behind her and she veered abruptly. She breathed in relief at seeing her husband. His frown and tightened lips reflected his worry.

"What it is, honey?" she asked in dread.

"Goodness, Parthenis! I've been looking for you all around!" he retorted in a suffocated tone.

"Oh, I'm sorry, dear. I was just trying to reach my brother." She smiled and edged closer to caress his chest in reassurance.

But he did not seem to let it go. "Please, Parthenis! What were you thinking of to meander here all alone? Can't you see the place is deserted and too dark for your own sake? And the baby... have you thought of our baby?"

Parthenis examined her surroundings for the first time. She blushed at her impulsivity, as she was not the kind of woman to take things lightly.

Apparently, Mnesarchus realized her discomfiture. He sighed deeply then took her tenderly by the shoulders and said in a soothing voice, "Come on. Let us call it a night. I admit the day was quite unusual. A good rest will do us both good. The porters have delivered our luggage to the inn already and the comfort of our lodge is waiting for us."

He walked with her through the narrow streets. The silence in the night took in the sound of their footsteps joined by the tuneful hum he intoned softly to her.

* * *

On the second day, Parthenis walked the city square with graceful confidence at her husband's side. She ignored the male admiration she drew on her way and kept to her queenly bearing. Despite the warmth of the city, she had thrown a light, purple cape on her shoulders. Her brown silk tunic fell loose on her body without the belt she had discarded due to her advanced pregnancy. A blue ribbon held her black tresses high at the back of her head while some untamed curls spread out on her forehead. A necklace of gold and amber decorated her bosom and matched the bracelet on her forearm nicely.

Mnesarchus, walking proudly by her side, carried one of the most beautiful artifacts his fellow countrymen had ever manufactured; the *Royal Purple*. The couple headed to their meeting with the wealthy buyer.

"Mnesarchus... oh... Parthenis!" A familiar voice shouted with a startling tone from behind them and they both stopped at once.

"Pherecydes!" Parthenis exclaimed gladly at seeing her brother at last, and rushed into his arms.

"What a surprise, Parthenis! I didn't know you were in Athens."

"We came yesterday. And I saw you, Pherecydes... with Solon... and...," Parthenis blurted out her words with excitement. "I had no idea! You have become a sage and a close friend to Solon, the wise man of Athens!"

Pherecydes responded to her excitement with a wide grin.

"Oh Pherecydes, that is indeed a great honor to our family!"

"Parthenis, fair sister, what a joy to see you! It has been a while now!" He hugged her again and snapped a resounding kiss on her forehead. Gazing at her face lifted to him, he asked "So, how is the future boy of our family?"

"Oh, you too?" Parthenis stepped back in surprise. "You also know about the baby boy?"

Pherecydes and Mnesarchus burst out laughing.

"I've really missed you, fair sister!"

The family reunion engulfed her with an amazing sense of belonging. Moreover, the fact that her own brother, a wise man himself, had just declared his belief in the prophecy of Delphi, added more validity to her search. She somehow felt confident about the outcome and anticipated her encounter with the famous priestess.

Later that day, Pherecydes accompanied the couple through the lively city. They headed towards the Acropolis where the old city had once stood. Out of love and consideration for the fifth month pregnancy of Parthenis, both men took their time up the long stairway to the huge temple. They constantly urged her to pause and she welcomed those short stops where she rested on the platform along the stairway. The heat would momentarily lessen on her skin, as the gentle fingers of the breeze would touch her hair and caress her cheeks, refreshing her stamina and inciting her to move on.

They finally reached the entrance and stepped inside the hall. Parthenis breathed in delight at the cooler temperature of the interior. A colossal statue of the goddess Athena (Promachos) stood impressively in the center. Built up through the years in beauty and majesty, the structural design met her eyes in fascination.

"The altar of Athena," Mnesarchus whispered to her, directing her attention to the left. "She's the goddess of Mind, Art and Sciences. Worshippers present her their sacrifices by burning cows and sheep."

"I see," Parthenis commented pensively then took a look over her shoulder at a large hallway where there reigned the shrine of...

"Zeus," he explained, attentive to her every move. "This is the shrine of Zeus, king of the Greek gods."

She turned to give it her full attention, and as she stepped forward, he took her hand to walk towards the shrine, with her brother at her other side. Their steps echoed in the colonnade, empty but for the presence of a lonely man in a white and blue tunic. His head slightly bowed on his thoughts, he paced the hall with his hands behind his back.

"Thales!" Pherecydes called out, recognizing his friend.

Thales halted, grinned and came forward to meet them. Introductions soon made, they all partook in a friendly conversation.

Parthenis listened to him with respectful attention. She restrained from asking a particular question that tantalized her mind. After a while, she grew restless and decided to put it forward.

"The Oracle of Delphi?" Thales repeated. "I did pay her a visit once and that in spite of my doubts. Call it curiosity," he added with a witty smile. "The truth is that I refused to believe her at first, putting it all on account of her imagination. Yet, what she had foretold to me back then did occur later on and in such a precise way that I had to admit that she was not the fraud I had assumed." He paused on a certain hidden thought of his, sighed then declared, "After that, I cannot but believe that all things are *full of gods.*"

"Do you mean to say that all things are full of divinity?"

His dark eyes brightened with a new respect at her sharp deduction and he advanced, "Yes, my Lady, this is exactly what I meant."

His assertion created enough reason in her mind to yield her closer to the authenticity of the Priestess. She had to convince herself that a man of such wisdom and soberness like Thales could never claim anything more than the truth. She read the sparkle of relief in her husband's eyes.

She nodded with a bright smile.

"I understand that you are finally okay with our visit to consult the Oracle." It was more of a question than an affirmation.

"Yes dear, I am okay with it."

Thales approved of her decision with a nod. "I advise you to visit on the seventh day of the Delphic month. It will be the birthday of the god Apollo thus the best timing for a consultation."

"Three days from now," Pherecydes noted.

"Oh!" She murmured, suddenly realizing how soon it would be.

"We should be on our way by tomorrow then," Mnesarchus decided in a serious tone. "It will take us two days to reach it."

Parthenis grabbed her brother's arm and asked, "Would you come along, Pherecydes?" A note of imploration betrayed her.

He stared at her with an encouraging smile. "I wouldn't miss it for the world, beloved sister!" He patted her hand then kept his on hers as if to infuse her with courage. He looked at Thales and said, "Would you join us, my friend?"

"I Sure will!" Thales accepted the invitation with patent enthusiasm.

Parthenis rejoiced at the thought of having the company of all three men in that important journey. Somehow, it made her feel more secure.

There existed only two options for those who marched to meet their destiny. To journey alone, or with those who might share the same fate.

And in this case, it concerned the revelation of the fate of a future Phoenician boy, and all of them were highly interested in heeding the prophecy.

Very early at dawn the next day, the carriage left the city still asleep in tranquility. The group reached the outskirts of the city of Thebes at the time the sun was edging the horizon.

"Our first stopover," Pherecydes announced in relief. "Thebes, my friends, is one of the many Grecian cities founded by Kadmus, our notorious Phoenician!"

"Is it so?" Parthenis straightened up on her seat.

"True," Thales confirmed with his deep, serene voice. "When the god Zeus kidnapped *Europa* from Phoenicia, Kadmus undertook, in secret, a long search for his sister. During those years he worked on colonizing several cities and civilizing the Greek nation to whom he introduced the phonetic Alphabet."

Parthenis knew that famous story of her great Ancestor, but to come to see one of his achievements was something overwhelming. They soon reached an inn, west of Thebes, and stopped for their breakfast. They decided to extend their stay to allow Parthenis to visit the city. During their lunch time, she engaged in conversation with Tales and her brother. With grace and sincerity, she expressed her pride at their improvement endeavors. She openly spoke of her emotion at witnessing the historical social and economic reform they had proclaimed a few days earlier.

By the evening, exhaustion took the best of her. Her silence betrayed her at the dinner table, so did her reluctance to stand up and continue the journey. She gratefully welcomed her companion's sudden decision, claiming, all at once, that the wooden cottage was too beautiful and much too appealing not to reside there for the night.

Early in the afternoon of the following day, the group reached some stately fields that stretched wide beneath Mt. Parnassus. On one of its many superposing slopes, stood the Temple overlooking, with all its beauty, the valley of the Plistus River. Considered as the most holy place in Greece, the temple of Mt. Parnassus was known as the navel of the world.

The group stepped out of the stagecoach at the outskirts of the Temple. Parthenis wished her physical status would allow her to stretch out her back like her companions did. She instead contented herself in bracing in deeply the fresh air that enlivened her. Her fatigue waned gradually. Her eyes relaxed at the amazing view below the mountain and she felt a delicious sense of peace. Only then, did she decide to proceed with her visit. From the carriage, she retrieved a package containing her offerings, brought from Lebanon, especially for this visit. This one contained a ritual cake and Cedar incense for the God Apollo, the Sun.

They entered the Temple from the East side in deferential silence and halted at the altar for Parthenis to present the Priests with her parcel. Thales came forward and offered to stand as the sole sponsor of the consultation. The Priests agreed and scheduled their session for the early morning of the next day. They invited the group to stay overnight in the dormitory of the pilgrims near the Temple.

At dinner time, Parthenis met Pythia, the Priestess-Medium. Now in her fifties, Pythia assumed, among other tasks, the role of attending to the female visitors. The presentation was done and the Priestess off to her duties elsewhere.

"Pythia was a young virgin chosen from among the poorest families in the region, as is the tradition here, to serve the Temple," Thales addressed Parthenis in a low voice. "Living a life of asceticism since then, she resides in an annexed secluded room. She is not much of a talkative person, Parthenis, so please don't take it personally when she attends to you tomorrow morning," he added with a hint of a smile.

And so it happened. Pythia woke her up at sunrise and attended to her ritual bathing in the Castalian spring. Afterwards, she escorted her to the Cassotis sacred spring to drink from the pure water of its source.

When the ritual ended, she escorted her to the main entrance of the Temple. On a golden plate above the entrance, words written in different ancient languages intrigued Parthenis who stopped to read "Man know thyself..."

Once inside, she followed Pythia a few strides to the right and down into a small, low ceilinged cell built in the rock. The cold engulfed her. With fascination and dread, she watched the Priestess-Medium performing some formal procedure. All too slowly, she mounted a brass tripod angled into certain mystical mathematical degrees. Parthenis deemed the tripod to hold some sacred meanings. Pythia had already placed it over a crevice in the ground through which emanated prophetic vapors. She then went on chewing some shrub leaves from the sacred Laurel tree of Apollo.

There in complete silence and dim light, an intense fog of fumes engulfed her to throw her at once into a trance. She appeared moving into another dimension that could be spiritual. Smoothly and easily, she appeared to grasp that other arcane world as if gifted for such a strange exploit. Thales appeared behind Parthenis and, as he had previously promised to be her sole sponsor, he stood there silent, watching...

A priest of the Temple came forward and interpreted to her ears the unfurling scene.

"Pythia is communicating with the god Apollo. She will now speak with the mouth of Python; the Serpent of Wisdom."

Parthenis felt spellbound by the incoherent words that spurred out of the odd woman. She felt grateful to that priest when he explained the strange verses to her.

"You will have a son, Parthenis.... A great man he shall be... He shall play a major role... in the evolution of the Human race...."

In a motherly instinct of protection, Parthenis covered her belly with trembling hands.

Her own son... a great man who will affect the entire Human race?!

That was a lot for her to absorb at once. She remained still though as the revelation continued from the mouth of Pythia and interpreted at once by the baldheaded yet bearded, tall priest.

"Your son, Parthenis, will be born in Saydoun. At the age of one, you must take him to Gebel... to be baptized by the Priests of AL... there in the Adonis River...."

Parthenis shivered with emotion. Such a prophecy could not have been uttered but by the foremost spirit of Al-Elyon; the God-Light, the Most High. Overwhelmed, she fought back her tears.

Pythia slouched to the floor and went silently subdued. Parthenis stared down at her motionless body with anxiety then assumed that the vision had ended at that. She turned to the priest. He remained silent. Confused, not knowing what to do, she then turned to Thales for reassurance, and at his nod, her concern faded away. He smiled with what seemed to her an expression of satisfaction and divine hope. Her heart beat faster. She drew her shivering hand to her mouth to abstain from screaming out her elation. Then, without further ado, she veered on her heels and rushed out.

As she crossed the threshold of the exit door from the West side, she came to a quick halt, went back on her steps, looked up at the inscription above the door and read the golden sign. *"...You will know the secrets of the Universe and the gods"*.

She frowned in concentration for a while. Her intuition told her of the importance of solving this puzzle. She recalled what she had read on her way in from the Eastern side. She grinned. Composing both sentences into one, she said out loud: *"Man know thyself... You will know the secrets of the Universe and the gods"*.

The moment she pronounced the mystical message, her baby-boy moved in a circular motion inside her womb.

.2.

Birth[8]: On the Path to Greatness.

Athens rejoiced in a festive mood. Locals and visitors alike anticipated with excitement the evening presentation of the theatre[9] show; so did Parthenis! From her window, she watched in fascination as the artists and their assistants bustled all day with their preparations. Setting up a stage was not as easy as she had assumed, and the dedication of these people to every single detail amazed her. She welcomed the distraction. A dreamy state of mind had subdued her into an atypical quietness since her visit to the Oracle of Delphi two days ago. Back in Athens now, and with all these vibes of exhilaration in the air, she finally woke up to her usual self.

At the fall of evening, the square ignited with hundreds of colorful lights that took her breath away. A vibrant music drifted all around the square, and people started to fill the area, not only with their presence, but with their laughter and chats. Parthenis grew restless. She paced the room back and forth. She halted to look from the window for a while, then back to her pacing.

---

[8]   It is traditionally known that Pythagoras was born on the isle of Samos. Neanthes, from his side, claimed that Pythagoras was in fact born in Tyre (Sur), a coastal city of Phoenicia. Iamblichus, in his book Life of Pythagoras (p.3), stated that Pythagoras was born in Sidon (Saydoun), also a coastal city of Phoenicia.

[9]   Theatres developed colossally later during the Hellenistic period.

"Take it easy, dear," Mnesarchus admonished her kindly then engrossed again in the reading of some documents.

"Come on, Mnesarchus! Pherecydes and Thales should have been here already! What is keeping them?"

"We still have some time before the show starts, Parthenis. Don't work yourself up now. It is neither good for you nor healthy for the baby."

She sighed in loud complaint and went to the window. She noticed that the theater team had already disappeared behind the installation. "Oh! They are about to start! We are going to miss it, Mnesarchus!"

"We won't dear, I promise."

It was then that she heard the knock on their door. She pivoted on herself and dashed to open it revealing Thales and Pherecydes. Her husband chuckled in amusement.

"Let's go, let's go!" She rushed them out excitedly.

Thales and Pherecydes stared at her for a moment then, as they seemed to understand her impatience, they laughed and followed her quick steps out of the inn and past the road to the square.

The moment they reached their table, Captain Hamelkon stood up to greet them with his distinctive cordiality and they all sat to enjoy their evening. The play absorbed them all at once. Three talented actors presented a series of dramatic and tragic scenes which themes tackled the social life of the Athenians as well as the political and military ones.

Their richly colored costumes of extravagant patterns brightened the stage. Their cloaks opened up on their adorned robes that topped some festooned boots. They used genuine human hair for a more realistic impression. Their masks portrayed different facial expressions at each scene. Accordingly, they succeeded in representing several characters of gods, legendary figures, famous people, women, and animals.

Captivated, as was the large audience, Parthenis forgot all about her dinner on the table. She would dry a tear or two at a dramatic act, and clap her hands in appreciation at the end of each scene. Mnesarchus drew her attention to her meal at every entr'acte. It was then that she noticed that some affable waiters constantly passed by their table to pour more wine in the goblets of the men.

During one of these entr'actes, she made it a point to converse with Thales and Pherecydes. "I couldn't help noticing your major influence on the Wise Man of Greece. I am sure he relies much on your advice and contribution of thoughts and wisdom."

Thales blushed and abstained from answering; probably out of modesty, she thought.

Of a more extroverted personality, her brother prompted, "Thanks for the praises, fair sister. Truth be told, we are both honored to be his advisors!"

"Sure, sure, my dear brother," she teased him. "We are all honored indeed, but still, modesty on the side, you are doing really great!"

Pherecydes abstained to answer. Something in the conversation of Thales and Captain Hamelkon had grabbed his attention. He leaned forward on the table to listen to them. Parthenis imitated him, guessing from his focused features that this might be quite an interesting discussion. They debated over Astronomy. Both Thales and the Captain proved to benefit from a wide knowledge of the sky and its heavenly bodies.

"Thales is a notorious scientist himself," Mnesarchus murmured close to her ear. "Fifteen years ago, or so, he predicted, rightly, a solar eclipse."

Impressed, she examined the wise man as if seeing him for the first time.

His voice drifted deep and even. "I strongly advise you, dear Captain, to take into serious consideration the Stars of the Chariot in your navigation. Follow the Ursa Minor, or the so called Little Bear, rather than the Ursa Major, or what we call the Great Bear."

At these words, Parthenis felt a sudden kick inside her. She instinctively placed the palm of her hand on her tummy.

"Are you okay?" Mnesarchus hurriedly asked; his eyes dark with concern. His arm wrapped around her shoulders.

"Yes dear!" She smiled broadly. "It's just the baby kicking."

Pherecydes chuckled then, his eyes bright with emotion. "Tell me, sister. How is it going with your preparations for the birth of our new family member?"

The question redirected the general conversation to the main subject of her presence in Athens. The men offered her suggestions of all kinds, based on what they knew from their families or what they had heard. They all acted as concerned as the father of her unborn child. She ended laughing with hilarity.

Their happy chitchat continued all the way back to the inn where the group halted under a pine tree to admire the stars in silence.

Captain Hamelkon coughed discreetly to break the silence. "We should sail back home in a couple of days Sir," he addressed Mnesarchus. "I thought to remind you in case you still have any unfinished business in town."

"Thank you, Captain," Mnesarchus replied calmly. "We are done with what we came here to do, and we are very much looking forward to our return home."

The Captain lifted his eyebrows in surprise. "No regret whatsoever to leave the Great City? I had the impression that you were enjoying your stay."

"Oh but we are!" Parthenis exclaimed. "It is that... well," she hesitated.

"A great event awaits them in Saydoun," her brother came at her rescue with a merry mood.

"They have a lot to prepare," Thales dashed out.

"You mean the baby," the Captain uttered.

"Not just the baby!" Mnesarchus insinuated jovially. "Is it darling?"

Parthenis grabbed his forearm with both hands and lifted a bright smile at him. She then leaned her head on his shoulder. She met the happy faces of Thales and Pherecydes, yet they all abstained to discuss the prophecy in front of the Captain.

Confused, Hamelkon looked at them in turn yet desisted from asking for clarification. He bid them goodnight with a slight, yet respectful nod and walked away without a question. Parthenis watched him as he scratched his head, glanced at them above his shoulder then continued on his way, scratching his head again. She chuckled, amused by his puzzlement.

Pherecydes bent to smack a brotherly kiss on her forehead, and, as he did, he whispered in her ear, "I will be praying for the prophecy to become a reality, and for you to have an easy and safe delivery."

"Thank you, brother dear," she replied with sudden emotion.

* * *

The tranquility of the Grecian waters surrounded the Phoenician ship. The couple leaned on the banister, waving farewell to Thales and Pherecydes at the shore. The "Astarte" stirred slowly away from the Athenian port. In a mist of time, Athens faded like a land of ghosts. Images from Delphi could still be seen, but not for long, Parthenis thought, as, in a while, it would be as invisible to them as the world beyond to the mortals. Only the memory of places would remain alive in her mind; Delphi in particular because of the prophecy. At this very moment, she fathomed the enormous responsibility that befell on her at carrying in her womb a kind of savior; a future great man. With every internal motion of her unborn son, she braced more and more the magnitude of such an event.

Why me? She wondered for the hundredth time since she had heeded the prophecy. *Will I be up to it?*

She shivered with angst at the idea of failing the mission that had befallen her.

At night, the Polar Star - the *Phoenician Star* as called by the Phoenicians themselves, and later by the Greeks - shone brightly in the vast firmament. From her spot on deck, Parthenis gazed at the reflection of the star on the surface of the water. She recalled the statement of the Captain, at the start of their trip, on the extent of their dependency on the stars for navigation. She pondered on that fact while her mind mulled over a name for a child of such great destiny. She knew somehow that the star of the sea held the answer to her query. However, no matter how hard she tried to read the message, the letters remained concealed inside the Light of the Star.

She waited...

With a sudden sense of urgency, she felt she needed Mnesarchus at her side at that very moment, so together, hand in hand, as one thought and spirit, they could decipher the name of the fruit of their love.

She had to wait though until the next morning to tell her husband about her nightly inquiry with the stars.

He grabbed her hand to urge her patience and replied in a tender tone, "Parthenis, my love. I fully understand your concern, but there is no need to rush. Come on, dear! We still have almost four more months ahead of us! By then, we will have decided on the name," He promised and she appreciated his attempts to reassure her.

Yet his kiss met but her lips twisted in disappointment.

The "Astarte" edged closer to the harbor of Saydoun on the seventh day, while the sun slipped in the horizon with all its golden warmth. A serene tranquility ruled the port ignited with hundreds of soft lights. From afar, the temples of the city materialized in an aura of enigmatic holiness. The city appeared lurking in religious silence.

However, when the ship docked at the port, the city revealed its real aspect. For Parthenis, it was like a sudden sprint of life. Citizens bustled on their daily tasks. Curious foreigners halted to watch the ship. Porters scuttled in competition to catch some wealthy travelers and gain a few coins. Anxious merchants paced the pier in wait of their new goods. Families waved with cheerful hails at their beloved ones reaching home.

Dusk had passed away, when the travelers disembarked eagerly. Mnesarchus and Parthenis waited for the first moments of rush to lessen in order to go ashore. Having bid farewell to the Captain, they stepped on firm land with a sense of relief. Mnesarchus gave his instructions to have their luggage delivered home. Relieved from that burden, the couple, hand in hand, took the dimly lit alley towards the city. The road conveyed them to the Souk on their way home. Parthenis sighed in content.

"Oh goodness, I really missed my hometown!"

Mnesarchus smiled at her. "I wish I could say the same, my love, but the truth is that I seldom miss any place in particular. I got used to different countries and long trips."

"Of course, I see." she sighed with a hint of sadness then groaned gently, "You are always on the move, always traveling and trading."

"Did I hear a complaint here?" he taunted her and prompted to take her in his arms.

She sighed again, feeling tired by then. "It's just that I can't help missing you when you leave."

"I know, my love, but rest assured, this will change in time."

She leaned on his chest, wanting to surrender to the comfort of his warmth. He kissed her forehead, lifted her face to him by the chin, and murmured, "We're almost home, sweetie. You are exhausted. Hold on there! A few more minutes and we will be home."

"Home...,' she intoned after him.

"Yes dear, home."

A sweet fragrance of Cedar welcomed them in their abode, along with a balmy sense of security. She knew that even Mnesarchus yielded to that invisible, yet substantial, power of belonging. He had admitted that to her once. She remembered his words whose deep connotation she now fully understood for having been away for a while.

Wherever we go, we will always return to our homeland; there, where for the first time ever, we came to see the light of life.

* * *

As early as the following afternoon, the expecting parents initiated their preparations for the birth of their first baby. They roamed the souk in look for some baby clothes, bed linens, and other related items. As they moved from shop to shop, the news of her pregnancy spread through the market. The villagers stopped them to convey their best wishes. Some took their time to converse with them, some gathered around them with advices and suggestions. Their genuine care and happiness touched Parthenis deeply, especially when some cheered at her passage: "A firstborn is always a blessing to celebrate!"

Over and over again, she would heed the same wholehearted murmur: "A child is to be born to Mnesarchus, a successful trader and to Parthenis, a fine lady!"

Could it be the enthusiasm of the Saydounians that made the announcement spread fast and far? Or was it the premonition of some great news? The fact was that it crossed the borders to reach *Sur*, the birthplace of Mnesarchus.

* * *

The expecting parents kept the secret of the prophecy concealed to most, unwilling to share it with people around the Phoenician coast, and not even with their closest neighbors. Only a few relatives were informed in secret. Some of them believed it and rejoiced. Others, however, remained skeptical, giving to time the benefit of the doubt.

And time passed...

The pregnancy of Parthenis advanced into her eighth month smoothly, allowing her to enjoy every moment of it. Every preparation related to the coming birth was a feast in itself. She felt overwhelmed with love; a new love she experienced as the days elapsed quickly.

Eventually, house chores became restricted to the minimum as her pregnancy reached its end. As a result, she dedicated more time to weaving and sewing for her baby; an activity that helped her control her trepidation. One particular morning in which she woke up heavier than usual, she sat on her comfortable couch to knit a baby blanket of purple and blue wool. Joining the twitter of the birds at her window, she hummed softly her own version of motherly glee.

She heeded the sound of graceful footsteps on her front yard and she stilled in wonder for she did not expect anyone at this hour. The three knocks on her door brought her slowly to her feet. Cautious, she glanced from her window. Two strangers in white long robes stood on her porch. She noted the blue belts around their waist and the blue cone hoods on their heads. Their bearing bespoke of calm confidence.

"Priests?" she murmured to herself with a frown of surprise.

With the palm of her hands, she prompted to wipe off some wool threads from her dress, tucked her hair back to give herself a proper appearance and took a quick, inquisitive look at the neatness of her living room. Only then, reassured that her house was impeccable to receive, she opened the front door.

A blue pair of eyes, limpid as diamonds and warm like a summer sky, met hers for a moment. She felt seized, then lifted in space and time; a strange feeling than infused her with peace.

"Yes?" she managed to blurt out.

Both priests pulled their hoods backward and greeted her in a serene voice, "Peace be upon you, fair lady."

With a reserved hint of smile, she nodded slightly and uttered with courtesy, "And upon both of you as well. What brings you, holy men, to my dwellings?"

Although clean and their beards neat, their sandals denoted the dusty deed of a long trip.

"We have come in peace, my lady, from the Holy Land of our God El," the eldest declared with a gentle voice then added in confirmation, "From Gebel."

The name echoed in her soul like a melody.

"We have received a specific *message* concerning the singular baby your womb nurtures," the youngest priest declared. Despite his composed voice, the sparkle of his black eyes betrayed his enthusiasm.

She shivered then exclaimed with fervor, "Go ahead, tell me!"

"My Lady," the older priest addressed her. "A brilliant spirit has exceptionally evolved in your unborn child who is to become a great man of wisdom and authority."

First, the prophecy of the oracle, and now, the message of Gebel! She was inwardly astonished.

As if sensing her state of mind, he paused for the time she took to absorb his revelation. Although she remained composed with dignity, her stillness must have betrayed her internal turmoil. Or was it the fact that she gawked at him for a long moment? Finally, he gave in to his fervor and his serene voice broke in greeting, "Blessed are you among all ladies of Canaan-Phoenicia!"

The unusual salutation confused her, yet she maintained her apparent self-control. She bowed her head slightly in respect to the spiritual message brought to her by the Priests. She closed her eyes, envisioning the oracle of the priestess at the Temple of Apollo in Delphi.

Silence prevailed...

A woman of sense, more down to earth than any, she dwelt in doubts for a moment at the possibility of such a mysterious matter.

She decided to face the transparent blue of those eyes. It was then that she deciphered the answer of his soul. *Destiny.*

The priests of the God Al-Elyon, the Most High, had just revealed to her the destiny of her family. She smiled in acquiescence and felt peace at once.

Only then did the Priests bid her farewell. At a standstill on her porch, she gazed at them, departing without a single look back, as if another mission awaited them elsewhere. Their silhouette, bathed in mysticism by the sunrays, soon disappeared behind a house at the end of the road. She sighed deeply, wishing all of a sudden that she could call them back; these Priests of the Temple of Adonis.

Adonis... the young and beautiful god of Gebel!

Adonis... the god who incarnated the cycle of nature to emphasize the spring and assert the resurrection of every atom in the kingdom of life!

Parthenis welcomed her husband home that same evening with a serene smile. When told about the holy visit, he frowned pensively for a while before he raised his face and both hands up in prayer. With no comment whatsoever, he remained lost in his thoughts until dinner time.

"What is it, dear?" Parthenis finally expressed her concern. "You have been silent since you came home!"

He stared at her for a moment in which she titled her head to the side and flaunted at him a flirty grin meant to make him smile.

"Parthenis, we have to talk about that whole thing," he answered in a serious tone. "We better keep this to ourselves."

"You mean the visit of the Priests of Gebel and their great message?"

"Right! Admit that it is a bizarre announcement and even more impressive than the prophecy of the oracle back in Delphi."

She absorbed the whole significance of his request. Pensive, she conceded in a murmur, "Sure dear. It is a wise decision."

"No one should know, Parthenis, not even any of your relatives or mine!"

"Don't worry my love," she prompted in a higher pitch meant to express her total agreement and reassure him. "I shall conceal it all until you say otherwise."

She granted him, then, a bright smile. The fervor in his eyes soothed down. His frown faded.

His features loosened up. He sighed loudly and relaxed back on his chair.

"How about deciding for the name of our son?" She proposed in a jovial tone, wanting to redirect his thoughts to something less worrying. "Don't you think it is time?"

He smiled widely. "Sure! Tonight, before you fall asleep, my fair lady, we will have the name of our son!"

And so they did. After a couple of hours of deliberation, Parthenis beamed with satisfaction as her eyelids closed. The last thing she murmured, all too tenderly, was the name of her son.

Pythagoras[10]...

* * *

Pythagoras, the prodigy child, opened his tiny eyes to life on the month of April; the fourth of the year, and the beginning of a new season, Spring. Proud and delighted, his parents, along with their relatives and neighbors, surrounded his cradle in a cheerful mood. The aroma of incense and Cedar wood wafted through the house in celebration. Joy and tears of happiness marked the event.

From the city square to the neighboring houses, and all through the city, the public announcement reiterated, "A child is born to

---

[10]   There are many different explanations for the derivation of the name. It is suggested that the name 'Pythagoras' came from 'Beth-agor' which means in Phoenician, the 'house of the mountain god' or 'house of the red soil' (clay). It could be true since Pythagoras was considered as the son of the God Al-Apollo. Some have strangely suggested that the name is derived from the Sanskrit word 'Pita-guru' which means the 'house of the spiritual Master' or 'the spiritual Master of the assembly' (school). To others, as it is known traditionally, Pythagoras is a derivation from 'Pythia-goras' which means the 'Speaker of (like) Pythia' or the 'Pythian Announcer'.

Mnesarchus, the successful trader and Parthenis, the fine Lady!"

Saydoun and Sur received the news, yet only the priests of Al-Elyon in Gebel comprehended the real magnitude of this event. So did the new parents who acknowledged the fact that their tasks extended beyond the typical parental duties of raising a common child. Thus, they committed totally to the rearing of their son. Mnesarchus decided to desist from travelling as much as before in order to contribute quality time to his new family and help his wife with the responsibilities of realizing the prophecy.

> *Prophecy; that mental revelation of the unknown divine; an aspiration that evolved into faith in the advent of a great man who will contribute to a better humanity; greatness of those which humanity calls saviors!*

Henceforth, the parents would have to see to the materialization of that prophecy. As such, they beheld the revelation in the heart of their inner realm as it became the very essence of their existence.

In accordance, their life took another course. It shifted from rearing an ordinary child to one destined to be a divine and revered man.

> *Divinity, that hidden course of the evolution of Nature and the Manifestations of God...*
> *Divinity, that essential part of every being living a spiritual life across the universe...*

* * *

Unease with the new environment of air and light, the infant whimpered. Voices drifted to him. Indistinct objects floated in his range of vision. As most of the time, he craved for the comfort of his previous abode. He groaned, wishing for that unique

65

embrace of late to enfold him in its warmth. *The soft voice* and familiar scent constituted his harbor of peace and fulfillment. His insides ached again so acutely that he screamed for the *soft voice* to come closer, lift him and feed him.

A spasm of nostalgia gripped him. He missed the aquatic dim state of his earlier comfy existence. His body shivered and yelled.

The *soft voice* did not delay to come. "Hush baby, hush, don't you cry, my love."

The soft hands lifted him and he felt lighter, then warmer when embraced to his source of food. The anguish of this array of discomforting emotions waned. Happy again, soon to be content, he delighted in the melody the *soft voice* hummed; a melody he had come to cherish and expect. A deeper voice, now familiar to him, drifted closer. The infant opened an eyelid and, as he breastfed from the spring of his contentment, he examined the smiley strong face that took shape gradually. His instinct impelled his hand to that direction. A new sense of security wrapped up around his fist and spread through his being.

* * *

A year later...

The light of the day gave way to the dusk of the evening as the sun faded away. The mystery of the night spread over the Phoenician coastal cities to be soon brightened by a full moon that took over its ruling throne among the stars.

Mountains and hills consorted in lifting their splendid heads towards the celestial realm. They stood majestically, resisting the course of time. A peak of one particular mountain emerged different from the others that night, glorious with religious chants of the priests and priestess. In the valleys, the harmonious rhythms echoed, so did the proclamation of the special event by these guardians of sacred sanctuaries.

66

The nation, akin the priests, anticipated in prayers and praises the dawn of the coming day...

* * *

A majestic natural bridge led to the entry of the Afka Grotto in Gebel; the *Holy Land of El*. Sunrays broke through the apertures of the mountain and into its heart, diffusing in a visible spectrum of light. From there, the *Kaddosh River of Adonis* exploded in a chain of waterfalls. Cold and powerful, the river flowed through chunks of rocks towards the bosom of the valley.

Many forms of vegetation inhabited the riverbanks and filled the fissures of the rocks all the way down to the valley floor. Spring bloomed with all its beauty. Soft and pure air stirred through the evergreen flora and forest. Nature, what a phenomenon!

On either side of the valley, and in the heart of the adjoining mountains, Nature, as well as human hands, had carved in numerous caves to protect living beings from both the fierce winter and the fear of the unknown. Men and women had also dwelled in these caverns, much too often, in hope of spiritual enlightenment.

On the top of this Great Mountain of Gebel, stood in magnificence two major temples; one in dedication to Astarte, the goddess of fertility; and the other to her lover Adonis, the god of resurrection.

Tradition in Canaan-Phoenicia, and especially in Gebel, required from the families to bring their children to be blessed in these temples. The priestess of El, in the Temple of Astarte, would bless the female children, whereas the priests of Al would consecrate the male children in the Temple of Adonis. Later on, if wished so, those anointed boys and girls might choose to serve the sanctuary at an older age.

On that particular morning of spring, in celebration of the sacred, the burning incense blended its scent and fumes with the candle lights inside the Temple of Adonis. Elated, Mnesarchus and Parthenis stepped in with deference and walked to the altar. Pythagoras, now one year young, cuddled in the arms of his father. On both sides of the aisle, twenty priests, clothed in white robes with hoods, sleeves and belts of blue color, bowed their heads in respect. Their hoods covered most of their faces. Their grave voices chanted to the god Adonis some hymns that resounded all over the sacred place.

The ritual was about to start.

Reaching the altar, Mnesarchus handed over his son to Parthenis, and they both turned to face the High Priest in expectation. Splendid in a white robe, he wore a golden cone hat on his head. He raised in a long moment of reverence the golden cup of wine in one hand and the piece of bread in the other.

"Elim Shalam Likum," he greeted them, paused for a moment of profound meditation to invoke the spirit of El upon him, then, addressed baby Pythagoras solemnly, "In the name of El, the Most High God, and in the power bestowed in me, I, *Man-Ka-El*, declare you blessed, my son, now and forever."

At that, he placed the wine and bread down on the altar and bowed in prayers for the manifestation of the mysterious moment of unification. He brought together the wine and the bread inside the sacred cup[11] then drank and gave to the parents and the child of prophecy to drink.

Only then did Parthenis lower her son on his feet slowly and with caution. Under the proud looks of the father, and the tearful eyes of the mother, Pythagoras took his initial steps and made his foremost walk into his destiny.

* * *

Pythagoras grew up into a handsome and gentle child. Before he reached his seventh year of age, he started to accompany his father to the small isle of Samos where they owned a residence. Facing the city of Miletus on the Aegean Sea, Samos comprised the heartbeat of the Ionian culture and luxury, and stood out for its excellent wine and fine red pottery. With its strategic navigation location, Samos ensued as one of the most important commercial centers of all Greece. It imported textiles from inner Asia Minor and developed an extensive oversea trade.

However, such wealth and prosperity did not withstand when a great famine ravaged the island. Eager to assist, Mnesarchus strove to bring in major corn supplies that eased down the predicament on the islanders. In appreciation of his humanitarian support, the authorities granted him citizenship when the isle recuperated some semblance of a normal life. Eventually, Pythagoras became a citizen of Samos. The majority in the isle called him *the long-haired Samian* but most people knew him as the son of Mnesarchus, the Phoenician trader.

---

[11] The ritual of *Wine and Bread* was first mentioned in recorded and biblical history with Melkisedek (Melchisedeck) who was the Phoenician priest of Al, the God the Most High. It was considered as the most sacred Phoenician religious and spiritual rite of all times. Melkisedek was recognized as the outstanding teacher of righteousness and the King-priest of the city of Ur-Shalim, later known as Jerusalem.

Even as a child, Pythagoras, with his alerted demeanor and brilliant eyes, reflected an acute intellectual curiosity. During a sea voyage to Greece, Pythagoras, only seven years young back then, stood with his father on board. His curious eyes wondered at the vast ocean. Mnesarchus held his small hand tightly and observed him discreetly.

Like his mother before him, the strangeness of the sea seemed to fascinate him in a paradoxical sensation of dread and calmness. When the shadows of the night gloomed over, he drew closer to his father. Ignoring the lit torches around, his instinct impelled his attention to the source of light in the sky. Riveted on the stars, his eyes expressed puzzlement.

He lifted his hand as if to touch them, frowned, then pointed his index at the sky and asked candidly, "Father? What are these shiny little things?"

"We call them stars, son. Phoenician sailors rely very much on them to navigate ships like this one. A group of stars are called a constellation. Can you see this group of shiny points?" He pointed at that direction.

"Yes," he dragged his answer in wait for more.

"These are the Stars of the Chariot..."

"Stars!" Pythagoras snapped, impeding his father to continue his explanation. "Stars look very nice, father," he commented with a grin. "But, I want to know what they really are. What they are made of. You understand, Father? I want to know their nature, and why they shine so beautifully at night. Do you know why, father?"

Mnesarchus gawked at his son in awe and went speechless for a while. He then scrutinized the stars in a new perspective, wondering about their nature for the first time in his life.

"Well, father?" Pythagoras insisted, pulling him by the sleeve to draw his attention back to him. Mnesarchus stared back at him, his eyebrows lifted with a mixed feeling of amusement and embarrassment. The fact was that his well-known education did not include Astronomy. Then, his work and travels had never granted him much time to tackle such studies. To his knowledge, only two people could answer such a question; Thales and Pherecydes! Maybe, if his son prevailed in such direction, he might find him good tutors to help him delve into that mysterious world.

"Honestly, son, I don't really know what to tell you," he finally answered. "But don't you worry. Your uncle Pherecydes and our friend Thales could educate you in this matter in due course."

His curious child gave him a hopeful grin and his eyes brightened in expectation. Luckily, he did not insist further that night.

Yet, Mnesarchus guessed that this incident might ensue as the start of many quests to come. His son had just given him a flicker of the ingenious mind that would probably develop and expand with age. Mnesarchus witnessed the dim glimmer of an aura evolving out of the inner realm of his child.

Such sagacity needed nurturing, thus the loving parents never objected to any of his educational endeavors. On the contrary, they highly encouraged their son by cultivating this spirit in him in all the ways and by all the means they could afford. His father initiated him on ships, trades, and the geography of the Mediterranean Sea. Pythagoras proved enthusiastic interest in all these matters, except for trading.

At fourteen, he convened a few times with Pherecydes who strove to protect the sacred prophecy. At a later stage, his uncle afforded him several encounters with some of his erudite friends. Pythagoras impressed them all with his modest attitude, his serene voice and his words full of wisdom. In time, he succeeded in surpassing all the other young disciples in the comprehension of the divine wisdom.

* * *

Pythagoras lived through the blessing of brotherhood when his parents brought to life two more sons. When he turned eighteen, he experienced the acute grief of losing his father. Peaceful and painless, death snatched Mnesarchus in his sleep while far from his homeland.

The sad news hit Saydoun with deep sorrow. Heartbroken, Parthenis wailed and sobbed in excruciating pain over the loss of her husband. Her two other sons[12] wept loudly. Pythagoras, however, shed but silent tears.

Abiding to the will of Mnesarchus, the family undertook to bury his body in Sur, his homeland, there where his Ancestors rested. Thus, his last navigation ever, took him on a journey, for a week, towards his last dwelling.

A profound sadness reigned over the funeral ceremony. Pythagoras froze in coldness when the inert body of his beloved father was placed inside a white marble sarcophagus. The priests covered the leaden face with a golden mask. Several villagers approached the coffin then to lower it inside a deep crypt in the earth. A moment of deferential farewell impelled them into stillness before they pulled over the white marble stele. The final habitat of Mnesarchus embraced him forever.

Pythagoras closed his eyes tightly then opened them to read on the marble above the burial the name of his departed father. The Phoenician inscription marked also some words of tribute,

---

[12] It is widely believed that Pythagoras had two brothers by the names of Eunostus or Eunomus, and Tyrrhenus or Tyrenus. No sisters of Pythagoras were ever mentioned by historians.

"Mnesarchus, the notorious wealthy trader". On top of the marble, a fine sculpture of Mnesarchus stood to remain there for the posterity.

The authorities of Sur presented their final tributes to Mnesarchus. As in a horrible nightmare, Parthenis heeded their speeches. Such tragic moments brought her crashing down to her knees in lamentation. Her head between her hands and her moans unrelenting, she deplored the loss of her beloved. Her sons surrounded her to bestow on her some comfort. Yet, at that dark time of great grief, nothing could console her.

How would she?!

How would she ever cope without Mnesarchus at her side? She missed him already! Memories of their moments together flashed in her mind; scenes of love, scenes of laughter and scenes of support and care. Her body trembled, the cold of despair numbed her hands, the air seemed to lack in her lungs, and something hard and heavy caught her by the throat. In an instinct of survival, her head snapped up as she strove to breathe.

As if sensing her internal misery, Pythagoras grabbed her by the forearms, lifted her to him and enfolded her tightly in his arms. He caressed her hair and murmured soothing words of comfort. A kind of peace invaded her. Calmness subdued her into a state of total numbness despite the loud weeping of the friends and family around her.

Mnesarchus, the loving father and husband would be certainly missed, but so would the caring friend and the supportive neighbor that he had always been to everyone.

On Parthenis befell now the heavy burden of raising her three sons all by herself. Yet, she knew that, for being the eldest son, Pythagoras would have to assume the major part of the family responsibilities, notwithstanding the vacancy left by his father.

73

The gentle voice of the Priest of Baal-Melkart broke through her apathy, "This stele represents Beth-El, the House of God. It stands in watch over the dead body of our beloved Mnesarchus while leading his spirit through its final journey. In truth, my fair lady and dear people, take comfort in the fact that death is only a passage into another stage of existence."

At that sentence of conclusion, Pythagoras stiffened as in alert. Parthenis felt it and a particular thought brought her tears back. Mnesarchus would have commented that such a strong statement would dwell in the acute intellect of their son for as long as it would take him to find his own answer.

Mnesarchus! Her heart screamed in ache. Her vision blurred and she felt uncannily feathery as she drooped into vacuity.

* * *

Grief would not wane with the months that followed. Yet, her pledge to her husband concerning Pythagoras kept her moving on with more determination than ever. She visited Ionia and Phoenicia for the appropriate experts who could lead her son all through his primary formation. Her efforts ensued successful as they agreed to grant Pythagoras access to the writings of the most significant issues of life.

Hermodamas, the nephew of Creophylos of Samos, taught him music, poetry and the Homeric epics; both the Iliad and the Odyssey. These various subjects of interest constituted important and preliminary studies into the sacred knowledge.

That was but the beginning of the cultivation of his educational zest.

Parthenis never ceased to provide him with all the requirements for him to quench his thirst in the pursuit of wisdom.

* * *

The early sunrays spread smoothly over the land of Ancient Loubnan. Dusk faded and silence waned at the melody of the birds praising the glory of sunrise. They, among themselves, could only understand the hidden expressions of their musical communication.

Pythagoras heeded them in his sleep. He woke up to their call and rushed out in response. Somehow, he fathomed the code of the secret chants of these creatures of the air. He observed their quick fly from a tree to another and then up towards the realm of the sky. With his extraordinary sensitivity, he deciphered their songs as a message of freedom.

He beamed with joy then began to whistle, driven by an instinct, an unconscious behavior, not to imitate them, but to reach such state of unfeasible freedom. Wings he had none, he sneered at himself and headed to the fields that stretched out in front of him. Sauntering north now, he entered Bustan el-Sheikh, the *Garden of the Sheikh*. Fragrance of orange fruits flooded the atmosphere. The drone of the cascading river resounded from nearby the majestic Temple of Eshmun[13].

He halted in a moment of hesitation then decided to enter the sanctuary. He stepped inside in time to witness the scene of a curative ceremony that a minister performed on a sick child. On the wall, behind the Priest, a golden plate illustrated the engraved image of Eshmun; the god of healing. He appeared standing with all his glory, holding in his hand a scepter entwined by a red serpent.

Pythagoras observed the parents of the child with some emotion. They seemed to believe that the god would soon cure their son. The father carried his offering of gratitude; a statue of marble

---

[13]   Eshmun was the Phoenician god of medicine. His Greek counterpart was Askelepius.

75

representing their sick child. The priest grabbed the infant gently by his tiny feet and immersed him in a pool of holy water, drawn from the sacred spring close by. He repeated the ritual immersion seven times then handed over the kid to his parents. The mother prompted a large towel around him to dry him up. The ritual ended there. To a grateful father and a hopeful mother, the priest announced that the divine medical art would take effect in the coming few days.

On their way out, the parents beamed with hope. Their expressions reflected appreciation and faith in their god Eshmun, the divine healer. The Saydounians had declared him as such after his many healing miracles.

Pythagoras smiled, sharing their optimism that their child would be freed from his disease. Yet this particular concept dwelled in his mind as he left the Temple. He halted in the shadow of an orange tree to meditate. He embraced the reality that what humans basically sought was total freedom from what weakened them. And so, some prayed to the one God, others prayed to the many gods. Yet, all prayed for their salvation.

How many yet would find salvation, remained a major question in his head. Would the sick baby make it? Pythagoras wished he could be of help. A sense of distress and discomfort engulfed him at realizing his incapacity. The feeling followed him all the way back home.

He entered the kitchen where his brothers had already started their mid day lunch.

His mother, her face in angst, exclaimed, "Goodness, Pythagoras, where have you been? You can't possibly run out of the house so early in the morning without leaving a notice!"

"Good morning to you too, mother!" He greeted her teasingly, to calm her down.

"Pythagoras!" She admonished with a look meant to shame him, yet he knew that her anger was only based on her anxiety.

"I'm sorry, Mother." He edged closer and kissed her cheek. "You're right." He grabbed her to him by the shoulders in a pleasant way and winked at his brothers.

But she would not let it go. "Where have you been all this time?"

"I went for a morning walk, Mother, and visited the temple of the healing god," he said with an even tone and took his seat at the head of the table.

When he glanced again at her, he met the surprise in her eyes that hooked his for a while. A current of understanding passed between them, and she sighed. She of course knew him well enough now to comprehend his true nature. His spiritual curiosity and aspirations were nothing new to her.

They ate in silence for a while. Pensively, Pythagoras savored the warm stew of lamb meat and vegetables. His mother placed in front of him some steamed rice and green salad.

"In my childhood, mother... I was sick sometimes, wasn't I?" He broke the silence, then paused, unsure on how to phrase his question.

"Well, yes, son, like all children do, here and there. Why do you ask?"

He fiddled with his napkin for a moment. "Did you ever take me to the temple and pledge to the god Eshmun to cure me?"

"Oh... No my dear! Your father never accepted such a thing. It's not that he was not a believer, on the contrary. But, he always stated that these rituals were not certain. See, he would not jeopardize the health of any in our family. We once called in the best doctor in the country. That, I recall well." Parthenis extended her hand to grab his, over the table, and smiled to him before declaring, "You were rarely sick anyway, son, and it was never dangerous."

He smiled back in relief and his respect for her increased. In the silence of his heart, he thanked his late father for making the right decision on that particular matter.

While his mother cleared the table to set the dessert, he pondered over the sick baby in the temple. "Too bad, really...," he murmured in a sad tone. "Those parents I saw at the temple today... I'm sure they didn't have much of a choice."

Parthenis halted with the plate of fruits in her hands. She looked at him with puzzled eyes. His brothers gawked in confusion and waited.

He sighed inwardly then explained, "I mean... they looked poor... don't seem to have the financial capabilities to have their child treated by a doctor. Oh the irony of fate!" He added with fatality, his tone broken with emotion. Before he bent his head to hide his tearful eyes, he noted the seriousness in which his family stared at him. He kept silent...

* * *

Sunset colored the beach of Saydoun. Under a palm tree, Pythagoras delighted in the game of the sea waves and the music of his lyre. Having studied the science of music for some time now, Pythagoras became well versed in its use.

As per the legend, Hermes-Enoch had invented this musical instrument with four strings upon the four elements of Nature. It remained unknown who exactly added the fifth and the sixth strings. Terpandres of Lesbos, a Greek musician, introduced the seventh string at a later stage.

In the horizon, the orange solar disk grew bigger before fading bit by bit in the heart of the Mediterranean Sea. The musical rhythm of his lyre, soft and nostalgic, echoed in the silence of the falling night to bestow on him a tranquil sense of peace. He had acquired this habit of seeking shelter in his music when sadness troubled his heart. In Saydoun, he was known as the *long-haired musician*.

With the spread of darkness and the increase of the stars in the sky above, Pythagoras rested on his back to admire the beauty of the galaxy. He continued playing his music. Millions of tiny spots illuminated the Heavenly Matrix. They appeared boundless to him. Again, like always, he wondered about their nature, their age, and their movements; the answers still unknown to him; a dilemma in the world of forms.

Dreams invaded his imagination, passion filled his heart and peace seized his mind.

* * *

The first sunrays of the day caressed the surface of the sea at the Saydounian harbor. On the pier, Pythagoras hugged his tearful mother. He caressed her shoulders to sooth down in her the pain of their farewell. His heart ached in silence at her holding on to him one more time as if finding hard to let him go. They both knew that his trip would drag longer this time. They had discussed this all week, and she had assured him, sharing in his joy at sailing towards his inevitable fate. Yet, at facing the cruel reality of his departure, she revealed her distress. Pythagoras understood her very well.

"Don't worry mother, I will be all right!" he reassured her in a cheerful tone. He could not say more. His eighteen years of youth still lacked the strength of the consoling words adults excelled in.

As if the words failed her also in her pain, she nodded. At this moment, he could swear hearing her heart murmuring, "I know that, my son..."

His brothers hugged him with affection. The youngest grabbed him tight, his small head on his chest. Touched, Pythagoras swallowed hard. He patted his back in a paternal way and brought to him his second brother by the shoulders. He would miss them also. His last words to them, before they broke apart, came out deep from inside his soul.

"Take good care of mother."

He then gestured them to run behind her as she staggered back towards town, forcing her head up.

The moment they disappeared from his sight, Pythagoras boarded the ship, ready to sail towards the Aegean Sea. His destination was the isle of Syros, originally a Phoenician colony. Pythagoras had sent his uncle Pherecydes a message the previous month, informing him of his arrival. By now, his uncle would be expecting him with eagerness as he had urged him many times to come dwell in his abode and learn from his long years of experience and wisdom. Profoundly influenced by the Phoenician and Egyptian priests, Pherecydes became the aim of Pythagoras.

Reaching the beautiful domain of his uncle, a week later, he felt home right away at the warm welcome he received.

Pherecydes did not dawdle in initiating his role of tutor. Early the next day, as the sun rose, he invited Pythagoras for a walk amidst the exotic plants of the isle.

"Let me tell you, son, about the gods of Creation. Zan, or Zeus, is the Ether. Kronos is the Time, and Chthonie is the Earth-goddess. They are all immortal," Pherecydes advanced his own theory on the creation of the universe and its evolution; a Cosmogony that Pythagoras was about to discover.

His eyes closed, Pherecydes continued, "Zan, the Creator, ornamented Chthonie, the Matter, with shapes, forms, proportions and images of the universe. Kronos, the Time, stood still and waited patiently until the creation occurred in him."

"And how did the creation happen?"

"Ah! Good question. The creation of the universe ensued when Zan, the universal Eros, joined together all the opposites in the old matter. He formed as such a harmonious whole of existence."

"Oh!" Pythagoras murmured his surprise, too subtle for his uncle to hear.

He suddenly sensed that this day, and actually his entire stay, would be a marvelous journey in the *magnum opus* of his uncle's mind whose thoughts were in a way complex, yet remarkably simple; two different paths to the mysterious inquiry of the unknown.

Pherecydes, a believer in the immortality of the psyche, introduced him also to the ideology of reincarnation. Pythagoras, was astonished when his uncle informed him that he had recognized *Aithalides*, the son of Hermes, to be one of the former lives of his nephew: him Pythagoras! Accordingly, Pherecydes awakened in him the memory of his past life, and stimulated his own *anamnesis*. He, as such, granted him the power to recollect the cognition and consciousness of his previous lives.

The wise man strongly advised him to benefit from the caves around the domain to dwell sometime like a hermit. Caves, his uncle explained, constituted receptacles for those who sought illumination and aspired to awaken the divine within themselves.

Weeks passed from his initiation and Pythagoras walked the path of knowledge more at ease. Day after day, he connected deeper and deeper with his inner thoughts. Bit by bit, he discovered the essential steps that would enable him to control their revolving process within his active mind. Maybe, after all, that was the preliminary phase of every student wishing to penetrate the world of Sophia.

On a young clear night, he sagged on a wooden bank at the terrace to enjoy his lyre. He closed his eyes for a moment to absorb the profound notes that echoed in the stillness of space. Yet, nothing was ever still; Pythagoras recognized. Everything moved harmoniously to transform all forms and images in the wide space around him.

In his transcendental state of mind, Pythagoras remembered his father and the game of his fingers on the Lyre, refined to gentleness. He improvised tones that expressed his nostalgia for his late father. The velvety softness turned melancholic. He truly missed him.

He ignored when and how Pherecydes came to be seated at his side. His uncle did not interrupt him. He just sat and absorbed the improvisation of the notes that talked of longing and love.

"What do you think happens when people die?" Pythagoras finally asked him through the sound of his music.

Pherecydes seemed to understand, his eyes sympathetic in his for a while, before turning his attention to the Mediterranean Sea ahead.

"The moment of Death in this world is the moment of Birth in another existence that we cannot perceive by our senses. Yet it does exist in its own way, and in its own reality. The soul is immortal, son."

Pythagoras breathed, deeply in, the statement that succeeded in appeasing his angst at the fate of his father. Yet, the concept of immortality sprouted in his mind; key-words that unleashed his imagination once again into a world of unknown probabilities.

A world that exists in its own way and in its own reality, Pythagoras murmured in the stillness of time.

In fact, the concept of death and rebirth set his mind free from the barriers of the flesh and into a profound state of reflection.

* * *

Early in the morning, after almost seventeen months, Pythagoras sailed to Miletus; a coastal city of Asia Minor to meet with Thales in his residence. A wise among the wise men of Athens, Thales stood out as a renowned figure all around the Mediterranean world. His teaching method has influenced many people, including Pherecydes.

A poised and composed character by nature, Thales welcomed Pythagoras with a warmness that was rare to him. He willingly accepted him as a student and introduced him to his selective circle.

The rumor spread fast that Thales had adopted a new student possessing a great light in his being. That young man dressed in purple, the Phoenician of uncommon acuteness, was therefore well received by all.

In the few days that followed, Pythagoras never stopped shuffling ideas and thoughts on the creation of the universe as per the theory of Pherecydes. Moreover, the concept of death and its hidden secret puzzled him to a large extent. Life and death became his major concern.

Alone with his thoughts at sunset, he found shelter in the coolness of the shadow of a big Cypress tree. His Lyre subjected to the skilful game of his dexterous fingers. He relaxed with the intention of dismissing, for a while, the absorbing analytical world of late. At this moment, he needed to reach a serene frame of mind, and access the more complaisant and blithering place that was for him the world of music. That stance represented his method of meditation; a kind of soul therapy.

Dusk descended on him then the evening reigned, yet he remained in his calm state of meditation. When the moon grew bigger in its ascent, he slackened down on his back to admire the galaxy. Without stopping his play, he turned his face sideway to the view of the Aegean Sea. The crystalline water of the sea reflected in beauty the mysterious lights of the heavenly bodies above.

It was then that he heard the slow footsteps of Thales. He glanced back without stopping his music. Apparently respectful of the magical melody, Thales remained silent as he slouched under a cypress tree behind him.

Pythagoras pivoted his attention back to the sea and to the game of glitters the stars reflected on the surface. He observed their beauty in the sky. "What could be the essence behind all of what my eyes see?" He wondered out loud.

"Eternal Water[14]," Thales, with his clear, yet irregular, voice answered. "Eternal water is the essence of what we see of matter all around us."

"Water!?" Astonished, Pythagoras lifted his weight on his elbow to look backward at his tutor.

"Yes, Pythagoras. The whole universe is a living being nourished by the exhalations of water."

"Oh! And what has made you reach such a bizarre concept?" he probed curiously.

"To be truthful to you, dear Pythagoras, I have never invoked the gods, or even sought supernatural answers for my queries. My long observation of nature made me discern the importance of water and its great role in the existence of all matters and life. Hence my realization that everything is ultimately made of water."

Pythagoras frowned in deep thoughts. He engrossed in analyzing the probability of such a mind-blowing theory. *If this is true, then there is something not quite proper...* He pondered.

His lips tightened on a particular contemplation. He shook his head in forethought, and deepened in his assessment for a while before revealing his comment to his teacher.

---

[14]   In the myths of many ancient civilizations, water was considered as the primeval substance of creation.

"I must say that I agree with you on the prime necessity of water in nature and, eventually, in life. However, I find it hard to believe that water could be at the essence of everything living all around me," Pythagoras argued, challenging the wise man. "There must be something more energetic, more sublime than water!"

Apparently incited by the sharp argument of his student, Thales stood up as quickly as his old body would allow him and hastened his heavy steps to edge closer to him. Their eyes met as swords would do; Thales squared him down while Pythagoras defied his master for a more convincing answer.

"To the ignorant, water is just water!" Thales snapped between his teeth. "But, to you Pythagoras, because you have dared probing for more, water is an allegory of the primeval spirit!"

Pythagoras widened his eyes.

Thales diverted his to the darkness of the sea to continue his explanation with an amazing calmness, "Everything that exists and pulsates around you is in fact of psychic nature. There is a soul to the world; a Universal Soul!"

Pythagoras leaped to his feet speechless, yet he faced but the back of his Master disappearing in the shadows of the trees.
He turned slowly towards the sea then closed his eyes to allow his spirit to immerse in the sound of the waves. He smiled as he finally realized the mode of thinking of Thales.

In fact, the wise man was probably one of the very few who had dared to declare a one-essence for the whole existence; a unity of the phenomenal world!

During the few months that passed, Thales continued creating great impressions in the mind of his student. He taught him how to be moderate and in control of his thoughts and feelings, the way he helped him in replacing superstition with reason and logic. Thales, in fact, held the merits of bringing into the Greek world both Mathematics and Astronomy; sciences he had acquired in Egypt and the East.

He, Pythagoras, became very interested in both sciences; Astronomy being the evolved derivation of the most ancient science of Astrology.

In Miletus, he frequented classes which lectures could be of interest to his quest of knowledge. At the invitation of his Master, he attended once a discourse on Geometry, Astrology, and Cosmology given by Anaximander, one of the pupils of Thales. As per Anaximander, Earth was situated in the middle of the world. Very few of his ideas held much of significance to Pythagoras. Yet, he remained there for some time out of social respect, and maybe from some bit of curiosity on his side._

"In truth, there is no God who created the Universe," Anaximander stated boldly that day. "I believe in the Infinite, the Unlimited and the Undetermined as the only real God. The whole Universe was never created and will never be destroyed. It is dead and blind!"

And that was the end of it for Pythagoras! He never attended a lecture again. He opted instead to focus on the teachings of Thales, whose depth and intelligence rooted in the True Science and thus, were of more interest to him. Thales deemed the Universe to be animated. In parallel, Pythagoras considered that the concept of a Universe being dynamic was more realistic and rational.

* * *

Five years went by with Pythagoras pursuing his assiduous initiation under the dedication of Pherecydes and Thales. However, his thirst for more knowledge would not find its satisfaction. He felt that many of his questions remained imminent.

86

Time had come for him to leave.

A couple of days before his departure, on a sunny midday, he convened with Thales in the open yard of their residence. There, seated on a wooden bench, the birds twittering around, they held their last private meeting. Flowers of all kinds and scents enhanced the beauty of the Cypress and olive trees that surrounded the domain.

Pythagoras sighed deeply at realizing that he would miss this favorite spot of his. He glanced at his Master and asked, "What is, in your opinion, the most difficult thing in life?"

Thales answered without hesitation, "To know thyself!"

Pythagoras nodded, pensive for a while, then put forward, "What is the wisest thing then?"

"Time, son," came the calm reply of the Master.

"Time…" Pythagoras murmured.

"Right!" Thales confirmed along with a nod of his head. "See, Time in truth, discovers everything, and the wisest feats a man could do in his life is to control it."

"I see," Pythagoras muttered, admiring the depth of his wisdom. "It makes sense, really. And, in your opinion, what could be the fastest thing in life?"

"It is the Spirit, for it runs in all directions. It is everywhere!"

There was silence for few seconds.

A time to meditate…

And the most pertinent question ensued a moment later, "What is God? Who is God?"

"God, my son, is what has no beginning and no end; the Most Ancient," the voice of his Master, as his answer, came composed and confident.

Silence prevailed again. Pythagoras waited for one of the new students at the house of Thales to serve their tea and leave before resuming his questions.

"I was wondering Master, what could be the most beautiful thing in your point of view."

"The world, for sure!"

"The world? Why is that?" Pythagoras stared at him in puzzlement. He did not expect such an answer at all!

"The world, my son, the world! For it is the work of God!"

"I see...," Pythagoras muttered as he pondered over the statement for a while then asked, "How about the biggest thing?"

"Certainly the Space for it contains the whole."

Impressed, he stared at the wise man who glimpsed at him with a witty look. They both shared a smile of complicity as if Thales understood what the eyes of his student conveyed of high regard.

"Go ahead, continue!"

"They are a few more," he warned him with a grin.

"I can handle them," Thales snapped in good humor.

"I bet you can!" Pythagoras replied and burst out laughing, joined instantly by his Master.

"Okay, then. Here goes the next: What is the most powerful thing in this world?"

"It is the will of necessity, because it comes always at the beginning of everything desired."

"Everything desired! What do you mean by that?" Pythagoras frowned, totally confused.

"There is nothing in the world that is not for man to look at, to enjoy, to feel, to grasp... everything you see is desired, whether consciously or unconsciously, because everything in the world is beautiful for it is the work of God." Thales explained with joy in his mind, his eyes brightened. "Only by the power of will, of necessity to have what your heart and spirit desire, that you achieve what you want."

Silence reigned once more, and once again, Pythagoras plunged in deep thoughts. He could not just stop now, his curiosity grew bigger and bigger at the outstanding words of his Master.

"What is death?"

"Death is not any different from life, Pythagoras. They are the same."

Thales waited apparently for the next question but Pythagoras needed to mull over such concept of similarity.

"Any more questions?" The Master tempted him.

"Yes, actually, just a couple more. How can people reach a point in which they can live a life of justice and respect?"

"Hmmm..., well... Let's say this utopia could only be attained when we all stop doing what we blame others for!"

Pythagoras waited for him to sip his tea and advanced his next question. "What is the easiest thing?"

Thales chuckled then and stood up. He gazed at him with a witty sparkle in his eyes. "The easiest thing, young man, is to give advice to others! And I advise you to return to Phoenicia and then head to Egypt. There, you will certainly learn more about the deepest meanings of life."

At that, Thales walked away without a look back.

Pythagoras deemed that somehow his pace became slothful, the curve of his back more accentuated and his hand trembled more than usual on his wand.

So long, Master... Pythagoras murmured, his heart aching. *I shall miss you too...*

* * *

And so, on a night lit by a full moon, Pythagoras left Miletus, sailing to Samos, his second country. At the time, the Lydian king

Croesus ruled all the towns of Asia Minor, including Samos. The Great Persian King, Cyrus II, defeated and killed Croesus and seized all the towns under his Achaemenid Empire. History marked the time around 547 BCE when his Persian general Harpagus imposed his control on almost all the Greek-Ionian towns. Consequently, the political situation in the rest of the Greek world changed in a significant way.

When Pythagoras reached Samos, turmoil still prevailed. He worried that the inherent tension caused by the Persian rapid control would be an impediment to his studies. Without hesitation, he decided to follow the advice of Thales at once and pursue his quest for knowledge in Phoenica and Egypt.

On the third day, he embarked on a Phoenician ship in destination to Phoenicia. The sun lowered in the horizon when the ship moved away from the isle. Standing on the deck, his hand on the rail, Pythagoras reflected on the education acquired in the past five years. He acknowledged that all these intellectual acquisitions constituted only a simple introduction into a world of a different nature; a world that only a few people would dare to approach.

Through the previous ages, many had tried to venture into the deep secrets of knowledge and failed to persevere on that mysterious path. The reason could only be the *fear* that confined humans in the realm of illusion of a world created only by their weak minds. Such limitation could only yield to them the familiar and the complacent of what their aptitude could be; simply dormant minds.

On board, Pythagoras continued his meditation. The breeze wafted to him the freshness of the ocean air and its distinctive smell. Droplets of water sparkled on his face. He leant his elbows on the banister to gaze at the mysterious depth of the ocean.

To know thyself... was the most difficult thing in life. He remembered that answer by Thales. *"Man, know thyself... You will know the secrets of the Universe and the gods".* He recalled the words of his mother; wisdom inscribed at the temple of Apollo in Delphi. *"Man, know thyself... You will know the secrets of the Universe and the gods",* he repeated out loud.

Through his diverse readings of late, Pythagoras had discovered that such wisdom, first taught by Enoch-Hermes-Tautus, the father of wisdom, was basic to the mysteries of Egypt, Canaan-Phoenicia, India, and Babylon. Pythagoras craved to know himself as the rare *Initiates* had done before him.

However, the path towards such achievement would ensue difficult to undertake as it required from the seeker both the will and the faith. Pythagoras harbored no doubt in his mind that to reach such a marvelous goal, he should fully commit himself.

He admitted to himself that his previous studies in Poetry, Music, and Cosmogony, as well as in Geometry, Astronomy, Astrology and Theology had revealed to him nothing more than an alluring glimpse of the Reality he sought.

Many questions hustled and bustled in his hungry mind while his eyes browsed the vast sea and the ship moved forward.

How does the phenomenal world function? What is the essence of the realms of consciousness and unconsciousness? How could we direct our vital energy? How could one indulge in the dimension of the spirit and the psyche?

The answers to such queries, he deemed, lurked simply between the lines of his completed

91

studies. They were riddles that could be solved. He grasped the certainty that he would have to walk the path of *Hokmah*, Wisdom, and remained totally awakened and aware of its sagacity.

He lifted his eyes to the sky and breathed in deeply with a sense of relief. *Right! Once I gain that infinite knowledge, once I know myself, I shall know the secrets of the gods and the universe!*

He smiled in defiance...

.3.

Temples of Canaan-Phoenicia

The trip from the city of Miletus towards the Phoenician land was uneventful, yet filled with hopes and aspirations for Pythagoras. All the way along the Mediterranean Sea, he recalled with fondness the past five years he had spent in the Ionian Isles, seeking education with great teachers.

When the ship approached the port of Saydoun, a few days later, he inhaled deeply the smell of his Ancestors in the blend of aromas drifting to him from the shore. Only then did he realize the real extent of his ache towards his country of origin. He has missed it indeed! His longing turned to trepidation when a few minutes later, the ship slowed down at the proximity of the shore, and made a smooth maneuvering towards the ancient long pier. The active mood, sound and smell of the busiest harbor of all time in the Mediterranean world blasted him. His heartbeat precipitated and grabbed him by the throat.

The ship finally docked.

At this breathtaking moment, Pythagoras disembarked with quick steps. The instant he touched the firm land of his Ancestors, he went down on his knees, laid his trembling hands on the soft sand to sense its ancient power, and, with loving deference, bent to kiss the ground. *Home!* His heart rejoiced. He grabbed sands in his hands, and stood back on his feet, gazing far towards the city with eyes blurred with tears.

Shouts on the pier brought him back to his senses. He grinned at the scenes that animated the port around him. Families received their beloved. Porters rushed to potential clients. Sailors bustled on their final tasks. Buyers dashed to merchants who showed off their newly imported products with grand smiles.

The July afternoon sun blasted in full, and Pythagoras decided to hit the road home without further ado. His luggage could wait for tomorrow. The ship would not sail soon and the captain had agreed to keep them on board until the next day.

Reaching the Souk, Pythagoras meandered through its narrow roads. Memories of his father gushed at him. He could almost see him again around the market selling his products, discussing prices, laughing with his peers. Pythagoras remembered watching him with the pride of a child, as he traded between Loubnan and Greece. Suddenly, a tear blistered in the corner of his eye...

"We have fine pieces of glass! We have pottery, too!" A merchant called out in a rhythmic tone that resembled the tempo of a kind of song he seemed to recall enjoying.

Pythagoras snatched his thoughts away from his memories and forced himself back into the present.

"We have *Royal Purple*! The Robe of Life!" A call propounded in a dexterous rhythm, similar to the previous. The voices of the sellers on all sides formed together a spontaneous musical concert.

Pythagoras chuckled in glee and, in the silence of his heart, wished prosperity and success for all of his countrymen.

In a light spirit, he left the souk, heading North through a paved alley of flowery shrubs and cypress trees. He hastened his steps towards the residential area twenty miles farther ahead. Emotion slowed him down upon nearing his parent's house. His heart beat faster. He felt like laughing out loud. His eyes blurred. *Home again!*

The door flew opened before he even knocked. In the blink of an eye, the form of a woman, who might have seen him from the window, dashed for him, grabbed him tightly, wept words of love, hailed words of greeting and praised God El for his safety. The *soft voice* of his childhood, to which he had first awakened to this life, engulfed him in its motherly love. He, the grown up man, the scholar of wise men, the learner of self-control, regressed to the state of infancy as both mother and son lived the compelling emotion of their reunion.

"Mother...," he finally managed to murmur and, grabbing her by the forearms, he gently pushed her away to look at her face. Her mid-fifties did not alter her beauty whatsoever, on the contrary!

"Son! My beloved son!" She repeated again and again, as if the intensity of the moment impeded her to utter any more than these words. Her eyes, bright with tears and joy studied his. Her trembling hands seized his face, shaped his features and caressed his cheeks.

Pythagoras feared the emotion would be too strong for her to handle. He cleared his throat twice to urge her softly, "Let's go inside, mother."

His arm enfolded her shoulders and he led her inside and straight to the couch. He sat at her side, holding her hands, and smiling at her with affection.

"No luggage?" She suddenly blurted out fearfully. "You are not coming to stay?"

"Of course I am, mother!" he rushed to ease down her rising anxiety. "I was in a rush to see you so I left them in the ship for tomorrow." He brought her hands to his lips and kissed them with loving respect.

She smiled brightly, yet her tears would not dry on her face. "My beloved son... almost five years...," she murmured with some trouble. "You know? Time has been slow, too slow... waiting for you. I counted the days, the weeks, the months. The years slipped away one after the other...," Parthenis related, in those few words, all the anxiety she had lived in his absence.

"I'm sorry, mother, to have put you through this," he apologized with sincerity. "I missed you too, but time is wise, I tell you. No matter how or for how long it runs, it always carries along new and great discoveries."

Parthenis froze in awe and scrutinized him with curiosity. He inwardly smiled at her patent realization that her son belonged now to a circle of a different nature.

The circle of a new life that propels, in neither slow nor fast rhythms, but in that of a single beat; articulates words of tranquility, peace, and wisdom.

"May the God *El* bless you always my son," she said after a while. "I have prayed every day that *He* may protect you and guide you in your expedition. Now, I know that your journey was really blessed," she ascertained with finality.

Pythagoras smiled at the hint of pride in her statement, yet restrained from any comment.

Silence prevailed for some time, each in their deep thoughts.

"Mother, where are my brothers?" he finally asked in a murmur, trying to keep his eyes opened.

"They are still at the Souk...," she answered, turning to him.

And before sleep enfolded him in its restful realm, he perceived the *soft voice* whispering tenderly, "Welcome home, son."

* * *

Early the next day, Pythagoras woke up with renewed energy. The delicious aroma of local cakes and fresh milk wafted to his room from the backyard. He sprinted to the window and glanced at his brothers settled at the breakfast table. He had truly missed those delicious cakes of his mother. He hurried to put on his tunic with a beam of anticipation. *Home again!*

He rushed out of his room and to the garden, eager to meet his brothers again. Less emotional than his reunion with his mother the previous day, this reencounter with his brothers was nevertheless impelled by cheers and warm greetings. They had indeed grown up, these beloved brothers of his, to be able to control their tears of joy and endorse a merry attitude!

Reunited again, the family sat around their meal. Before they took their breakfast, they saluted the soul of their father, who rested in peace in the abode of the Eternal.

They soon became engrossed in catching up on the years they had missed in each other's lives. Thus, Pythagoras came to know, with pleasure, that both his siblings excelled at their careers, one as a trader and the other as an artisan. Parthenis, meanwhile, seemed to delight in every moment of her family get-together.

"How is your uncle, Pythagoras?" she finally managed to inquire.

"The wise Pherecydes, dear mother, is getting wiser, day by day!" He replied in good humor. "He is truly close, so close, yet…." His words remained suspended in the air. He wondered how to explain to her his deep perception on a matter that was beyond her understanding. He then smiled at her and said, "He is fine, mother."

His brothers stood up then, to start their working day. By turns, they tapped him on the back in a friendly manner, leaned to kiss their mother on the cheek and left with their good wishes for a good day to all.

Alone now with his mother, Pythagoras conveyed to her his intentions to pursue his quest for knowledge and wisdom in the educational centers and the temples of his homeland. She demonstrated enthusiasm in encouraging him and her blatant faith in him touched him deeply, so did the adoring smile she granted him in return.

No more than a few days afterwards, Pythagoras undertook a dedicatory journey to Sur to visit the grave of his father; his first instructor. Facing the marble headstone with the memorial sculpture of his father, that afternoon, he read in a whisper: "Mnesarchus, the notorious wealthy trader."

Tears betrayed his self-control. He swallowed hard, inhaled deeply and lifted his face to the sky, striving to master his emotions as Thales had taught him. Recalling his Master did him well. The memory of their discussion on the concept of death flashed in his mind, and so did those words of wisdom.

He glanced around the graveyard of his Ancestors and murmured, "Such is life, after all. Every instant some people die, and some are born. It is a never-ending cycle that would definitely reach - if there is truly an end - a state of transformation!"

He deposited some flowers on the tomb and remained bent, in his prayers. Before he stood up to leave, he murmured softly into the sweeping breeze, "Father... may the God *El*, the Most High, bless your soul. Rest in peace."

Heading out, he stopped for a moment at the gate and turned a last look at the cemetery. Deep in thoughts and prayers, his mind spoke to his aching heart.

Life and Death...

*What a strange
phenomenon indeed!
It utterly controls our
mundane existence.
Although life and death
are one against the
other, both are
inseparable and
inevitable.*

With a lighter heart and a new wisdom, he climbed into the horse-carriage after ordering the rider to head back to Saydoun. His plans awaited him in his hometown and he was keen to proceed.

* * *

Saydoun stood out as one of the most famous Phoenician cities at the time. Aside from the fishermen who lived and prospered in that coastal city, *fishers of men* emerged from the region, taught the nation and spread around. Henceforth, the coastal city became an educational center sought by many of those in quest of a deeper knowledge of life. From Saydoun, also surged exceptional men, like Mochus, born not long before Pythagoras; a *Kabir*[15] of Canaan-Phoenicia; the land of civilized humanity.

A physicist and a teacher of the science of Anatomy, Mochus had shone for his scientific skills and profound insight on Sophia, or wisdom. His reputation extended throughout the Mediterranean world. While most people indulged in believing superstitions, Mochus had adopted reason and calculation. He had discovered the particle of matter

---

[15]   Kabirim is a Phoenician word that means the Elder Ones, thus the Wisest. The Seven Kabirim often mentioned in the Phoenician history were: Enoch, Melki-Sedek, Melkart, Sanchoniaton, Kadmus, Mochus, and Eshmun.

that could be decomposed and called it the *Tom*[16]. In consequence, he came to be the first person ever to theorize on the existence of the particle.

The Tom is decomposable, Mochus had taught in his theory.

Highly impressed, Pythagoras pondered over the cerebral ability of Mochus that had brought him to discover such a decomposition.

He must have been a genius!

Apart from his close circle of students, Mochus had kept the method concealed. However, such a great discovery could not remain padlocked for long and it had started to spread recently.

Pythagoras first learned about Mochus and his school from Pherecydes and Thales. Unfortunately, Mochus[17] was long since dead when Pythagoras started his earliest quests for knowledge. Thus, upon his return to Saydoun, he joined the descendents of Mochus who initiated him for months in the sacred teachings. As such, Pythagoras came to learn the theory of the *Tom*, known also as the *First Essence,* and defined as the primary principal of the total existence of the whole universe. These teachings also included studies in Cosmogony, Physics and the Science of Anatomy. He, in reality, opened his mind to the internal and external body organs. He learned how they functioned, and how the whole body acted as a cosmic element. In short, he came to meet with the Microcosm that he was.

---

[16] The Tom, as called by Mochus, was later copied by the Greek scientist Democritus who called it Atom, referring to the particle of matter that cannot be decomposed. With the advance of science, Mochus was proved right that the Atom is in fact decomposable.

[17] Some historians claim that Pythagoras received knowledge directly from Mochus. We, however, strongly doubt that.

During a lecture that Pythagoras attended at a major educational center of Saydoun, he heeded the wise masters with their long beard and capes. That day, they narrated the story of a great Priest-King. A descendant of Saydoun, the founder of the city, his name was Melchisedeck.

"Melki-Sedek was a Kabir in the Land of Canaan," one of the wise men declared. "The fact that he was such an extraordinary and righteous man created a legend around him stating that he had no father and no mother."

"He was a High Priest, probably the first High Priest of our God the Most High, Al-Elyon," another wise man stepped in. "Being a Kabir, he is said to have also initiated Abra-om[18] the Aramean into our Phoenician religion of Love and Peace."

The eldest sage declared then, "In the name of the God *AL*, Melki-Sedek performed the most sacred ritual of all times, that of the Bread and Wine. He reigned powerfully over Ur-Shalim as a King-Priest of Peace!"

Fascinated, Pythagoras pledged inwardly not to miss any of these lectures. Thus, with every conference attended and newer information acquired, he delighted more and more on the topics tackled.

That particular day, the sages related how, some few hundred years ago the Saydonian priests had developed the primitive musical forms into what would come to be called the *Sacred Music*. Eventually, it became one of the most essential ingredients in holy ceremonies and religious rituals.

"Music! Why music? We often ask ourselves. How does it affect us?" One of the masters proposed. "Does anyone in this group know?"

---

[18]   Was it Abra-om the Aramean wanderer, or Abraham, mentioned in the Old Testament, a minor Initiate from Ur, a Chaldean village near Babylon? Are they the same and one person? Only time will tell!

At the silent response of the group of students, Pythagoras decided to advance his personal concept. Confident and poised, he stated his thoughts.

"Music enters the heart to awaken our deepest and noblest emotions. It refines our mind and calms down our restless and fierce desires. Consequently it releases the spirit into a world of a higher nature."

Silence grabbed the audience in awe.

The sages gawked at his direction for a while before they reacted at once.

"Impressive!

"Beautifully said indeed!"

"Absolutely true!"

Murmurs ensued from the audience of students.

In fact, the sacred teachings in Temples and educational centers had integrated music in their curriculum long before Pythagoras was born. However, no one in that classroom had seemed to comprehend or know the exact essence of music better than him.

The eldest wise man stepped forward and asked him, "What is your name, young man?"

"I am Pythagoras, a pilgrim and seeker of Truth."

The eyes of the sage warmed and brightened. A hint of a smile appeared under his white thick moustache. His peers nodded in approval. Students, however, glared at him with mixed feelings apparent in their eyes riveted at him; puzzlement, awe, and envy. They seemed confused.

"Well, Pythagoras," the eldest priest addressed him with his creaky voice. "In your case, I strongly recommend that you continue your pilgrimage in the Temple of Eshmun. Let the God *Al* be with you, my son!"

At the mention of that temple, Pythagoras visualized at once the healing ceremony he had witnessed before his departure to the Ionian Isles. With that image, surged the sadness he had experienced at his incapability to help; a feeling whose impact continued to affect him to date; thus, his reluctance to seek the sanctuary. However, the wisdom he had acquired with Thales and Pherecydes impelled him to grab another opportunity to fathom the secret of the healing god of his Ancestors.

Therefore, *Sofia* took him, a few days later, to the Temple of Eshmun. There, he met with the newly elected High Priest. Had he been a commoner, he never could have benefited from such a privilege. However, Pythagoras, a true seeker of Truth, treaded the path towards enlightenment. Thus, in the privacy of his chamber, the High Priest convened with him. They tackled, in an insightful way, the science of Therapeutic healing.

"The water in the pool where children are placed is naught but an accelerator of the healing process," the High Priest revealed. "Water, my son, is a very pure element of Nature. It does not only wash out all the dirt from the body, but it also allows a certain feeling of elation."

Surprised, Pythagoras muttered, "Hmm... interesting." He needed more explanation, "So, it is not the water that heals."

"Not exactly, yet, it does work as a purifier," the High Priest admitted and leaned closer to confide in a low voice. "Truth be told, my son, it is the will within me, Abdu-Eshmun, combined with the power of Theurgy that processes the healing."

"If so, then, I could enjoy the same will!" Pythagoras thought out loud. Then, incited by excitement, he inquired, "How can I have the power of Theurgy?"

"With all due respect to the capability of your mind, Pythagoras, and to the great energy that radiates from you, I must say that it is not yet the time for you to have these powers. You are only a beginner, and, the road is way too long. Be patient!" His forthright words, stated so firmly, echoed mightily in the ears of Pythagoras.

His mind went on alert.

So it happened that Pythagoras made his primary steps into his Initiation, there in Saydoun, where he had come out of the darkness and into the light of life. Soon, he came to acknowledge that the more he tackled the sacred teachings, the more the road appeared endless.

How deep could he really fare into the secrets of religion, divinity and the universe was yet to be known. Still ahead, the great mysteries hidden beyond the phenomenal world, lingered, awaiting him.

* * *

A week later, Pythagoras sought the calm mood of the golden sandy shore of the city of Sur. There, under a palm tree, he found a haven where he retreated with his Lyre. Unconcerned by the sand that spattered on his comely purple robe, he delighted in the breeze that wafted through his long mane and caressed his face. A sense of peace engulfed him. He meditated on the mystical musical tones his lyre generated in the air and past the sea waves.

Sur, the *rock*, the birth place of his father, related somehow to the city of Gebel, *the Sacred Land of El*. They both constituted, from times immemorial, the cradles of the Society of Sacred Builders. Temples, castles and even houses, built all over the Phoenician coastal cities, carried the fingerprints of that secret society. And that included many of these constructions in the villages of the mountains.

Pythagoras had only recently come to know about them and wondered. The Secret Builders did not limit their exploits to the land in which their

104

society blossomed, but had successfully extended all over the reachable and unreachable world.

While in Greece, some Phoenician sages had revealed to him that the Sacred Builders endorsed a very strict selection in their acceptance of builders and workers among them. They, like the Murex Experts, endorsed a stern vigilance in the management and secrecy of their work.

Scrutinizing the shore from his spot, Pythagoras imagined those Sacred Builders departing from there and spreading all over the world, with their skills as wealth to contribute to other nations.

At the thought, a sense of nostalgia drove the cadence of his fingers on the lyre, producing harmonious tunes that conveyed his emotion. In his mind, he gave tribute to all the great men and women who had sailed from that same shoreline to venture to worlds unknown to them; worlds they had ended up civilizing!

And many they had been!

Kadmus...

One of the Kabirim, he had sailed to Greece to import to its nation the tablets of a sacred system of writing, the *Phonetic Alphabet* invented by Thor the Geblite. In consequence, Kadmus had changed the life of the Greeks forever. With the Alphabet, he had taught them to manifest their thoughts on Egyptian papyrus imported by Phoenician traders. Kadmus, this great Phoenician, had also built many Greek cities, like Thebes.

Elissa...

The name flashed in the mind of Pythagoras, along with the great deeds of that Tyrian princess. Known as Dido by the Romans, Elissa had sailed towards the black continent, built the city of Carthage on the coast of Tunisia, and became its queen, sometime around the year 814 BCE. Carthage, or *Kart-Hadasht,* was known in Phoenicia as the *new city* in order to distinguish it from an older Phoenician outpost, namely, Utica.

Of course, Carthage was not the first Phoenician colony ever established by the Phoenicians.

King Hiram of Tyre...

That Phoenician king had dispatched artisans to build the Temple[19] of Jerusalem. Pythagoras recalled the Phoenician sages of Greece and Saydoun narrating that story to him: "Jerusalem, my son, was founded by the Jebusites, a Phoenician tribe. They named it *Jebus* initially. Throughout history, the city changed its name several times. It was called Ari-El, meaning the *Hill of the God El.* Later on, Melki-Sedek wished to dedicate it to Shalim, the son of El, so he called it Ur-Shalim. However, when he ruled the city, people designated it as the City of Peace because he was known as the King-Priest of righteousness. The Romans, later on, named it *El-ya.*"

"And so, by historical necessity and logic," the sages had continued, "the Temple of Jerusalem was, in fact, the Temple of Shalim. King Melki-Sedek specially requested its construction for King Hiram, known also as Ahiram of Sur. Henceforth; the Temple of Jerusalem is simply a small copy of the Temple of Melkart, previously built in the great city of Sur."

---

[19]   The Hebrews narrated a strange story in their Old Testament about the existence of a Temple built by Solomon the son of David. They alleged that Solomon had received assistance from King Ahiram of Sur, and his expert Mason, Hiram Abiff. What might be true though is that the Hebrew people were only nomads and used to worship their national god YHWH inside a movable tent. Long before that time, the Phoenicians and their brothers, the Egyptians, were both great nations of Sacred Builders.

Pythagoras pondered over those facts. He thought of the major contributions his Ancestors, the Phoenicians, offered to the people of the world.

The name of Thales flashed in his mind.

How can I forget Thales, my great teacher!

"Thales, oh Thales!" he whispered. Emotion grabbed him by the throat, his eyes blurred and his fingers stopped their musical game. Just yesterday, the news of his death had reached him. He had refused to believe that his beloved teacher had passed away to another life. However, at this very moment in which Pythagoras recalled that great Phoenician who had made such a difference in his world, he was impelled to mourn him.

He murmured the words that the messenger had ascertained reading the epitaph of Thales:

> *"This tomb is so small, but the fame of the man had reached the sky, it is that of Thales, the Wise."*

He repeated them in the silence of his grieving heart as a tribute to the great man that Thales had been. Gathering his courage, he shook off his state of grief and leaped to his feet.

He meandered in the city with no particular aim, until he found himself facing the Great Temple of Baal-Melkart[20], the Lord of Eden.

One of a kind in all of ancient Loubnan, the Temple stood majestically impressive. At each side of its entrance, two winsome pillars stood as guards to the main door of Cedar wood. One of them was made of *Hajjar al Urjouwan*, the Purple Stone, or Ruby, and the other shone as Crystal or Pure Gold.

---

[20]   Herodotus, one of the great Historians who lived between 485 – 425 BCE, asserted seeing the whole Temple of Baal-Melkart at Sur, and that was surely after Pythagoras' time.

He stood in awe, once again, in front of its greatness. Today, however, he decided to enter its abode and convene with the priests.

With confident, yet reverential steps, Pythagoras entered with the intention to listen and learn from the High Priest Ieto-Baal, whom he had already befriended.

Ieto-Baal, the Hierophant of Baal-Melkart, received him for the first time into the secret domain of the society. They soon engaged in their meeting.

"One night, a long time ago, a great rain and wind storm struck hard on our city," Ieto-Baal related in an even voice as if he had narrated this story hundreds of times. "All the bamboo houses crashed down, so did all the trees of the city. A powerful thunderclap hit the adjacent forest and set it on fire. The fiery flames devoured almost every tree there in less than an hour, leaving in its wake an incredible devastation. The disastrous fire spread to the city, burning it down to ashes and killing a large number of its residents."

"Very few survived. Among them was a man called *Ieosos*. To his luck, he found only one tree on the ground that had not been touched by fire. He trimmed off all its branches, put it in the water and sailed the sea. Upon reaching the island of Sur, not far away from the city of Sur, he erected two pillars, one for the *fire* and the second for the *wind*."

"Once done, he faced them abashed, wondering what they really meant to him. He realized then that they represented the two powerful elements of nature that he could not control; fire and wind. Thus, he decided to worship them, although..." Ieto-Baal paused on a particular hidden thought of his.

Pythagoras took the advantage to comment, "Do you mean to tell me that the pillars were the first symbols of worship ever and that it happened here in Sur? That's enormous!" He exclaimed.

108

"Yes son... kind of," the High-Priest Ieto-Baal answered with pride. "Yet, bear in mind that *Ieosos* did not worship them because they were mere pillars he strove to erect. They, in fact, became the symbols of both fire and wind; two fearsome elements hidden within the power of nature. He just feared them as such and believed them to be deadly measures which gods used in their fury against people."

He paused for a moment to wipe the sweat off his forehead and drink from his goblet of water.

Pythagoras remained silent and waited...

"These two pillars that you now see on both sides of our Great Temple do not, however, represent fire and wind at all, not anymore," he revealed with his eyes widened on Pythagoras as if to emphasize his statement. "They actually symbolize Justice and Mercy; the two great functions of the Universal God Al-Elyon!"

"The Temples that the Sacred Builders built, and continue to build to date, are divided into three parts. Let me put it this way: to enter the Temple, you initially walk between *The Pillars*, that is the first part. You then reach the second part that we call the place of *The Saint*. It is there that incense is burned in the altar. From there, you continue straight to the last section, *The Saint of Saints;* where the statue of the God *Al,* or *Baal,* stands."

Ieto-Baal stretched his back to look above Pythagoras' head towards the closed door of his chamber. Reassured of their privacy, he relaxed to pursue his explanation, yet the tone of his voice remained low in conveying what was concealed to the commoners.

"In the eye of the common believer, the Temple is a sacred place where people practice, be it in the outside hall or around it, a ritual of faith that a priest celebrates to a certain god. However, what people do not really know is that some special geometrical calculations were taken into

109

consideration, and effectively used, in the sacred building of most of our great Temples. In fact, these special geometrical calculations generate a kind of divine receptor. They help the Temple absorb the energy of God the Most High *El*. This is part of the hidden reality, or shall I say, its esoteric side," the Hierophant concluded with finality and looked straight into the eyes of his student.

"But... uh...," Pythagoras blurted out in confusion. "What does that lead us to understand?"

The Surian Hierophant stood up, glanced down at his student for a moment, and without further explanation, walked out of the chamber. Pythagoras was stunned as the door closed behind his tutor and intrigued by the secret message that was left for him to decipher; a mysterious riddle whose great meanings Pythagoras intended to discover.

* * *

To Pythagoras, the days seemed to end swiftly, the nights, by contrast, appeared to lengthen, abiding by a slothful rhythm. Yet, he cherished those long nights he spent under the Lebanese sky. Wearing his purple robe, he ambled barefooted on the sand of the Surian beach. Like a monk would, Pythagoras reflected on the arcane character of the Temple.

In a mechanical motion, acquired in childhood, he bent to grab a murex shell and brought it to his ear. The sound of the ocean whooshed deep and mysterious. For the first time, Pythagoras discerned the physical reality of the sound, and halted in suspense, as he tried in body, mind, and soul, to fathom its message. From the abyss of its many years of existence, past memories of the sea echoed the voice of silence in his inner realm, whispered into his mind, merged with his spirit, and vibrated within his body.

Upon heeding this revelation, Pythagoras realized the power of his own three dimensions; his tri-une nature of being. He felt the excitement of edging closer to the answer of his query. He sank to his knees at once and his finger scribbled fast on the sand the strange puzzle the Surian High Priest had left behind.

He read the words, once then twice, a smile lifting his spirits, his heart beat accelerated and... *eureka!* A tremendous relief triggered a compelling laughter from the bottom of his being and lifted his face to the stars in delight at the wonderful discovery.

The three divisions of the Temple... They are simply an allegory of my tri-une microcosmic being! It is who I am! Who everyone is!

As a neophyte, a true seeker of Truth, he had ultimately found the real Temple of God. But what should be done now, Pythagoras thought, was to complete the work started by God. *It would be up to us to finish it, so that we may become what we are, temples of the Divine Light,* he concluded then deepened on the concept of who he really was and who he would become.

Then, quiet was his mind.

Silent was the night.

* * *

Days passed with Pythagoras advancing in his journey of edification. The nights would find him at the shore in meditation. In that particular evening, few days after his significant discovery, Pythagoras meandered on the beach. He cherished the gentle breeze and the sound of the waves that flirted with the shore of the Surian Island. The stars spread their splendor all through the vast clear sky where the moon ruled in grandeur.

According to an ancient legend, Astarte, the goddess of fertility, had once made a star fall to the ground on that Surian Island. In consequence, it became a sacred place.

Pythagoras continued his way to the Great Temple. There, he paused for a moment to admire the game of the moon rays on the finely carved stones of its façade. With quiet steps, he entered the gate by the two pillars.

He came to an abrupt stop and turned around. Was it the sound of the wind, or had he really heard a strange voice addressing him in a mysterious language? Cautiously, yet fearlessly, he retraced his steps and stood for a moment between the pillars. The voice, *their voices probably*, whispered to his heart, songs of resistance; resistance through the ages by challenging the evil and the injustice of this world.

Their message was clear, his mind, heart and spirit bowed in homage and respect. With pride and a renewed confidence, he entered the Great Temple and crossed the Saints into the Saint of Saints. There he halted a second in front of the statue of the god Baal-Melkart then continued down to the underground chamber where Initiations often took place.

Inside the secret domain of the Society, the High Priest Ieto-Baal welcomed him formally and offered him a seat at his side. On the wall behind the altar, an engraved image of a serpent with a Phoenix head, stretched from the center of a burning circle.

Confused by the possible meaning of the engraved scene, Pythagoras, dressed in a purple robe, addressed the High-Priest, "I have seen the serpent before. It was in the Temple of Eshmun. They informed me there that it symbolizes the art of medicine that remains incomplete without the scepter of the healing god."

Ieto-Baal nodded and his bottomless eyes encouraged him to pursue. So he did, "It looks different here, kind of bizarre, I must say. What do these images symbolize?"

The reverend nodded again, slowly and went on with his explanation. "The serpent was considered divine to Hermes-Enoch-Tautus, the first Kabir in our Land and in Egypt as well. It is, in fact, a very special creature; the wisest of all animals. It breathes stronger than any because of the fire element that runs at a very high speed through its entire body. This same fire grants the serpent a great power for maneuvering and the capability of an extraordinary bodily modulation."

Astonished, Pythagoras remained speechless in spite of the many questions that unfurled in his mind concerning that creature. Ieto-Baal seemed to have more words to add and more secrets to reveal. Pythagoras listened.

"There is another essential feature concerning the serpent. It has the power to live for a long time. You may certainly wonder about that and ask how it is possible. You are actually asking yourself this question right now." The High Priest glanced at him with a witty look, grinned and continued, "Right! Well, hear me out! The serpent in fact goes on fasting to escape the aging process!"

"What?" Pythagoras exclaimed, incredulous. "How strange! And how...? How does this eccentric feat occur?"

"As a matter of fact, the serpent remains still and stays stagnant during the whole winter until it ultimately shrinks. And when this happens, it immediately gets rid of its old skin. A new, bright one then forms to reveal a younger and more vivid serpent. Life never stops growing in this amazing creature, that's a fact!"

Totally wordless, Pythagoras slouched back on his seat. No questions whatsoever came to his mind. He sat still, assessing the information of such a strange natural phenomenon.

Silence prevailed as Ieto-Baal seemed to give him time to absorb the revelation. The moment Pythagoras turned his face to him; the High Priest proceeded with finality. _

"To the Initiate, the serpent is the symbol of immortality and wisdom. It defeats time. Our priests named it *Agatho-daemon*, the Good Spirit. The circle you see on the wall, my brother, represents the world in its latent form." He indicated the image on the wall before pursuing his tutoring. "When the Serpent appears in the center with a Phoenix head, it means that the good spirit is moving and turning the world with the power of the fire element. The fire element is the energy; life energy!"

This imperative exposé continued till dawn and throughout the following nights for three consecutive months. Eager to learn more and more, his thirst for knowledge never quenched, Pythagoras participated in all the rituals of Initiation; the same initiation that the Phoenician Hierophants have always performed by the cult of Baal-Melkart, in the city of Sur.

* * *

A soft wind of the divine breath gushed over the face of Pythagoras, as did the mysterious heave that impelled him down the sacred valley below. The full moon shed timid light over the flora and the rocks; its silvery rays caressed the smooth surface of the water of the Kaddosh River, the Sacred River, also known as the Adonis River.

To some, the River sprang out with all its power from the grotto of Afqa that the hand of nature had formed in the heart of the Holy Mountain of Gebel; the Sacred Land of El. The river continued its way down, in earnest, to merge with the Mediterranean Sea.

However, to others, the River abounded with no beginning and no end, the image of its water unscathed and forever clear, while in a soft, continuous movement, the river stretched out towards the beyond; *the unknown.*

Alone, Pythagoras strolled that night in search of peace of mind, energy for his spirit and shelter for his body. Past the enchanted valley, he climbed the Great Mountain up to the majestic Temple of Adonis reigning as a crown on the impressive green eminence.

An hour later, having reached the Temple, he directed his steps to the annexed monastery, and without hesitation, knocked at the heavy door. He introduced himself to the young priest who opened for him, and stepped inside. The Priests of Adonis, gathered in prayer, turned to look at him while the young priest announced his name. Silent surprise met the nightly intrusion into their sacred sanctuary.

A voice rose in a murmur of awe, "Pythagoras... Pythagoras, the true seeker!" The High Priest, the Hierophant of the resurrected god, moved forward and grabbed him by the shoulders, studying his face with a glint of affection in his eyes.

"Oh... you have grown well, my son. I am Man-Ka-El. You don't know me, uh, and how can you, but I remember you very well! I had the joy to bless you by the power of El in the Temple of Adonis when you were one year old... one year old."

"Oh... I see...," Pythagoras finally understood the warmth with which the High-Priest had just welcomed him. "It is an honor for me to meet you, your Holiness," he added genuinely. "I did not know that time would offer us an opportunity to meet again! What are the odds?"

Man-Ka-El chuckled. He was newly elected to the High Priesthood when he baptized Pythagoras almost twenty three, twenty four years ago. "Time... hmmm... I always knew that I would see you here one day, son," he declared briefly in explanation and turned him towards the other priests who stood up to welcome him as warmly.

Pythagoras was invited to spend the night, and so he did.

* * *

Between the holy walls of the Temple, the second day, Pythagoras received the exceptional gift of knowing the *Secret of the Alphabet*. The Phonetic Alphabet, invented by Thor long ago, carried in its foundation the fundamental keys to a mystical music that had produced, at a later stage, the scale of seven notes.

Imbued with the new education of the day, a bit tired, Pythagoras stepped out and found an isolated spot in the garden to play his music. There, at the peak of the Mountain, his gentle fingers stroke the four strings, his mouth emitted tunes based on the seven notes, and his heart intoned the amalgam of tones and notes that echoed in the valley below. Pythagoras sang his love for that spiritual place, so peaceful, so inspirational always... all the time.

Inside the walls of the sanctuary, time drifted and Pythagoras progressed further in his initiation at the hand of the High Priest that became for him a fountain of knowledge from which he drank eagerly. In the secrecy of the private chamber, they sat that day, face to face, on the cedar wooden table.

"The very first stone building that used special geometrical calculations and the science of numbers occurred here in Gebel," the High Priest asserted; his voice low in spite of their seclusion. "I suppose you have formed, along the path you have treaded, quite a good idea of geometry? Haven't you, my son?"

"Yes, I have," Pythagoras answered evenly.

"Good...! What about numbers then?"

"Numbers? Hmmm... well, I guess they are but mathematical tools," Pythagoras replied with a

116

shrug of his shoulder, then, with sudden doubt, he asked, "Aren't they?"

The Hierophant of Adonis stood up, not too pleased. All too slowly, he turned around on his student, scrutinizing him all over. Uneasy and confused, Pythagoras swallowed, once then twice. He watched as his tutor walked back to his seat, veered to him, leaned forward with his palms on the table, and stared deeply into his eyes.

"Pythagoras!" he uttered without anger. "Heed me! There is a part of numbers which is indeed of a mathematical nature. That is quite correct! However..." He left his sentence in suspense to edge closer to him, an inch or two from his ear and whispered, "There is another side of a more sublime nature, and that's what I am trying to tell you..."

Before Pythagoras could conquer his astonishment, Man-Ka-El marched out, leaving him puzzled to the very last of his brain waves.

* * *

In the months that followed, Pythagoras dwelt peacefully in his little room inside the monastery. His assiduous mind, however, would not rest as he spent most of his time in perfecting his music and unveiling the secret of numbers.

One night, while perched on a rock above the bottomless valley, playing his lyre, the tunes suddenly performed a swift descent and ascent, between the valley and the sky. That astonished Pythagoras but, nevertheless, he delighted in the outcome. The melody he had composed, accidentally or not, had just created an invisible bridge between Heaven and Earth, and by such, mystified his whole existence.

De facto, Pythagoras discerned the existence of a harmony between these two distantly opposed places. That harmony, currently generated or always existent yet hidden, unveiled its secrecy to

Pythagoras. With the powerful perception of his inner ear, developed through the years, he heeded the music that the Earth emitted, synchronizing and harmonizing with the aria that the Heavenly bodies diffused.

Harmony... he murmured in awe. *Harmony of the Spheres... What a phenomenon!*

By necessity and from that very instant, he decided to call this very natural phenomenon, the *Harmony of the Spheres.*

Resting by the Adonis River the next day, Pythagoras reflected for a while on the Harmony of the Spheres he had detected the night before. Satisfied by his discovery, he turned his complete attention now to another important issue; the secret of the numbers!

What could numbers be other than mathematical?

What could be their esoteric side?

Up until now, he reasoned, everything around me moved in a perpetual motion of music, shapes and colors. This could be the mathematical side of their existence. However... what could the other side be, the sublime side; that complementary, yet unseen, mover of life?

Moments passed...

MAGIC! Pythagoras deducted in a flash. *Of course! It cannot be anything other than magic!*

"Yes!" he shouted.

Numbers are the essence; the measure of all things. The whole existence is naught but of a Mathemagical dimension; a real state of concatenation and an infinite frame of becoming!

He smiled at his smart deduction, and then resumed his meditation, deeper and wider.

And yet different sensations of different places were recorded in the hall of time and space: Above and Below, Intellect and Instinct, Unconsciousness and Consciousness, Logic and

Illusion, Freedom and Slavery, Good and Evil, Love and Hate... Heaven and Earth!

With the fervor of a novice, eager to communicate his discovery to his tutor, Pythagoras leaped to his feet and rushed to the Temple. Without halting to take a breath, he scuttled in and through the halls, and past the priests that snapped their heads up from their tasks in surprise. Without decelerating, he threw an apologetic grin in their direction, reached the door of the private chamber and came to an abrupt stop in front of his tutor. Impassioned by that wonderful feeling of accomplishment, he conveyed to him what he had come to discover.

Man-Ka-El did not react nor comment.

This man, the man in purple standing in front of me now, is a true seeker of truth; he is really on the right path towards wisdom. The High Priest mumbled in his heart.

He simply gawked at him directly in the eyes, nodded silently with a little grin then took his usual seat. Without further ado, he uttered evenly, "There is only one God, Al-Elyon, the Most High and the One," his calm voice issued a totally new topic, moving the conversation up to a higher level.

Chilled by the lack of interest of his tutor, Pythagoras gawked at him in a moment of disbelief. Yet, the introductory words captivated his interest at once. Trained by Thales to master his self-control, he quickly swallowed his disappointment.

Man-Ka-El rubbed his long white beard as he waited for Pythagoras to resume his seat. In his eyes, a glint of approval, *maybe of admiration*, lifted the spirit of Pythagoras up again.

"Along with Al-Elyon there was Anat-Astarte, described as his wife and also his sister," the High Priest continued as if he had never stopped. "From their union, came Baal-Adonis, the synthesis of that ancient perception of Reality. Adonis is then regarded as the manifestation, or the incarnation, of the God. This is the Holy Trinity, the Great Mystery of all times."

"And what is El?" Pythagoras inquired leaning forward to heed the answer. At noticing the lifted eyebrow of his tutor, he hastened to clarify his question, "I mean... How do you define Him in a more... let's say, exact theological word?"

"*Al* is the *One*; the first Light. Period! The Sun is his physical reflection, for it is the most precious and the most powerful element of light and fire. The Sun gives heat to our globe, the Earth, and life to its creatures. The Sun reigns over time and organizes it perfectly. It also controls and best coordinates the movements of all other Heavenly bodies around it. Occasionally, Time - or what we also call Kronos - manages to escape from the Sun, and in consequence, nations lose their tracks! They undeniably stagger through a path of illusion, darkness and diversion."

Thoughtfully, Pythagoras contended in a murmur, "I see what you mean... I see that." Then, looking back at him, he posed a pertinent question, "Who is Anat?"

"Anat, my son, is the female principle, the *virgin lady*. She comes second in the Trinity. *El* requested from her to plant the soil with love, pour peace in the bosom of Earth, and multiply love in the heart of the fields. She abided with absolute devotion and delivered their son Baal-Adonis to be the Savior of the world."

Man-Ka-El paused for a second. He stood up, joined his hands behind his back and quietly paced the chamber in front of Pythagoras. "The child came as the supernatural synthesis of their Divine Union, so to speak. He happened as the manifestation of Good Will to all nations. He transpired as the incarnation of Love and Peace; a way for the salvation of mankind. He came, died, and resurrected. He saved the faithful, defeated Kronos, and touched immortality. And so, the son of the first Sun became a second sun to reign over life," Man-Ka-El ended with eloquence the exposé that revealed the basis of their theology.

Pythagoras felt overwhelmed by that astonishing, and yet clear, description of the three main divine principles that composed the core of his Ancestral religion.

What a resolute way of seeing things, he thought, *changing and moving them from a limited perception to an infinite visualization.*

It should have happened. It could happen. It happened and it will happen. It will happen only by the good *will* of the mind and the *faith* in love and peace; as soon as they inhabit the life of a person, they can be stretched out all over the face of the Earth.

Individual consciousness certainly leads to collective consciousness, he concluded. *Yet, Kronos stands still...*

Deeply convinced, he absorbed this theology. He deemed it an evolved religious system; a valuable allegorical look over mankind in general, and individuals in particular, and that included their salvation, their spiritual evolution and, hence, their resurrection.

* * *

Clothed in purple as always, contemplating nature from his favorite spot on the rock above the valley, Pythagoras pondered over the issues of religion. A breeze wafted from the valley and, in its course, the trees swayed, the leaves rustled, and the birds fluttered their wings away from the branches hovering over them. Pythagoras closed his eyes for a moment, relishing in the musical combination. He inhaled deeply the peace and joy that the song of nature granted him.

From his spot, Pythagoras watched the great Phoenician Temple of Astarte, lingering in his view, right on the summit of the Mountain of Gebel.

Women, like their goddess in a previous undetermined time, came to mourn the death of Adonis. They wept, lamented and pounded their chests. Somewhere, a flute gushed out melancholic notes. The echo on the adjacent mountains, and deep down the valley below, conveyed the sounds of memorial mourning to Pythagoras.

He looked down the valley and to the Adonis River whose water appeared tinted in a blood-red hue. Most probably from the red soil of the Mountain, Pythagoras reasoned. He knew too well that the devoted believers deemed it to be the blood of their god Adonis wounded to death by a boar, some say, by a lion. The mourning ritual continued until the rebirth of life on the third day. The resurrected sun then shone intensely upon the Holy Mountain and its Sacred Valley. On that special day, the believers gathered from all around the area, their heads completely shaved. As per the religious ritual, the god Adonis would come to life once again and ascend straight to Heaven.

In their faith, they believed that the Naaman flowers in and around the river that day sprang from the blood of Adonis. These scarlet anemones bloomed beautifully on the surface of the water and on the river banks. They would console the goddess Astarte in her grief for these flowers have resurrected from the blood of her divine lover as living proof of his immortality.

On that sacred day of resurrection, and in the secrecy of the grotto of Afqa, Pythagoras stood reverentially in front of the High Priest of Gebel. Ready to receive his baptism directly from the source the Kaddosh River, he knelt in veneration, his eyes riveted on the pure original water.

Man-Ka-El proceeded. "In the name of Adonis, the son, the resurrected god, and by the power bestowed upon me, I, Man-Ka-El, baptize you, my son, with the Kaddosh water," he proclaimed, firm with faith, as he dipped

Pythagoras' head three times in the water. He then uttered the mystical words of blessing; "The spirit of the rising god is resurrected in you, Pythagoras, now and through the eternal cycles."

* * *

The great Hierophant of Gebel advised Pythagoras to seek the meaning of the mystical words of baptism somewhere else. In order for him to understand the deep secret of the self, Man-Ka-El suggested that he experienced an absolute meditative solitude in one particular sanctuary – the Grand Temple of Mt. Carmel. Pythagoras was informed by Phoenician Initiates that Mt. Carmel happened to be the ultimate abode, at the time, for such an exploit that might bring about some kind of illumination. Mt. Carmel, being the most sacred of all mountains and the most inaccessible to the populace could definitely be the best of choices.

Also called in Phoenician *Karm-El* - the *Generous Vine of El* - Mt. Carmel harbored a Phoenician Temple dedicated to *El* and his son Baal or Adonis, united as one, in the form of *El-Baal*. The Temple, long erected on the top of the Mountain, always received, in the sanctuary of its walls, those thirsty for the drink of the gods.

All around that Holy Mountain, from the bottom base and all the way up, small temples stood here and there. Many natural grottos dwelt in the area, carved in splendor by nature into the rocks and improved, later on, by human hands.

Beside the Great Temple of El-Baal, there existed another important one dedicated to *Ashirai* (Asherah); the Mother-Goddess of the Phoenicians. Ashirai was the virgin lady Anat herself; the Queen of Heaven who had planted the soil with love, poured peace in the bosom of Earth, and multiplied love in the heart of the fields.

Phoenicians, Egyptians, and other adepts from neighboring countries, all around the

Mediterranean world, often sought to find enlightenment inside these monasteries and grottos where they would dwell in total seclusion. Hence, Mt. Carmel, cradle of the monastic and contemplative life, stood as a shrine to the Virgin Lady Anat, the God El, and their ever young and beautiful son Adonis. For the believers, Adonis incarnated the cycle of nature and emphasized the spring; the resurrection of every atom in the kingdom of life.

Highly recommended by Man-Ka-El, Pythagoras was at once recognized and admitted into the Great Temple after a few days walk in the wilderness. As a matter of fact, the Temple of Mt. Carmel had long decreed very strict entry rules, and never received common visitors. The outcasts, the ill-mannered and the non-qualified students, included, among others.

Inside the Temple, the teachings of the *Great White Fraternity* anchored in the minds of all the adepts. The adopted system of teachings went far back in time to Enoch-Hermes-Tautus, the founder of the First Religion. Since then, it became the spiritual endeavor of the Canaano-Egyptian Monotheistic Fraternity. *De facto*, the members of this fraternity sought and believed in the resurrection of the self up into its higher level, and in the immortality of the spirit.

On the walls of the Grand Temple, some unique, delicately engraved symbols sided along a number of particular inscriptions for the neophytes to contemplate about in silence. No questions whatsoever were allowed to be asked, not even a word was to be heard. The only sound that resonated between the walls of that Temple remained that of the thoughts echoing in the mind of every seeker.

Separated from all the troubles and worries that burdened the profane world outside, Pythagoras spent most of his days and nights, and

124

for almost three months meditating as a hermit on one single symbol. One symbol among many! From the very first moment in which he had stepped inside that Temple and that particular symbol had been all the focus of his attention.

The symbol reflected a horizontal line connected to another vertical line; a cross. Called the *Sacred Tau*, that cross, discovered by his Ancestors, rooted in time to the faraway days of Enoch-Hermes-Tautus. This exceptional charming symbol became the subject and the object unified in the mind of Pythagoras.

As usual, in silence, the doors of perception in his mind opened widely to the cognizance of the secret he sought. His transliteration revealed simultaneously the Horizontal Line as the Stagnant Matter, and the Vertical Line as the Moving Energy, or the Living Spirit. Accordingly, Pythagoras became more conscious than ever that the point of intersection between these two worlds was undeniably the Universal Mind; their point of balance, the First and Final Equilibrium.

It all makes sense to me now, he muttered in his heart to restrain breaking the rule of silence. *And hence, on a relative human scale, the intellectual thinking mind of the human being could only be the primal, and yet final, mover of his or her two other dimensions; the spirit and the body.*

The ultimate fusion of all, to Pythagoras, could only happen when the rational human mind would connect with the Universal Mind.

Now, how does this Rising occur? Pythagoras mulled over the concept for a long, long while. Yet he ended smiling, his heart rejoicing at his new discovery.

Deep down inside himself, in his most secret and sacred realm, a great light shone bright. A revelation arose. There existed *a man, a mortal god,* on the lengthy path to become, *an immortal man, a god.*

On the Phoenician coast, almost when the sun was setting in the horizon, a small boat landed. From his spot at the peak of Mt. Carmel, Pythagoras watched for a moment. Long tutored in ships by his father during their long trips together, Pythagoras recognized this one to be of Egyptian origin. Without any further delay, he leaped to his feet and scuttled down the steep mountain and straight for the ship at the shore.

For the first time in, perhaps, a year, panting and gasping to regain his breath, he heard the sound of his own voice addressing the sailors, "Are you heading to Egypt?"

They nodded and stared at him in puzzlement. Pythagoras felt their eyes examining him all over with curiosity.

"When?" Pythagoras yelled to be heard above the sound of the great wind that wafted through the coast.

An old man, apparently the captain, loomed from behind the sailors and screamed and gestured for him to listen to his reply, "Not before early tomorrow morning, my friend. The wind is crazy, so is the water. We are staying overnight."

Pythagoras nodded and grinned widely. The hope of a new venture into the world of discovery streamed through his blood like the rush of a water current. He waited for the Captain to step on shore and approached him eagerly.

"That suits me perfectly well. Would you count me in?"

The captain chuckled and shook his hand. "Sure will, Phoenician! Just don't be late tomorrow or we'll leave you behind."

And as decided the day before, Pythagoras, dressed in purple, his lyre in one hand and a small bag of personal belongings in the other, embarked at dawn the following day. Wordless, he paced the boat, looking for an isolated retreat where he sat in silence. And silent he remained for a couple of nights and days.

The sailors would throw speculative looks in his direction, yet none dared to disturb him. Devoid of food and water, motionless as if in a trance, Pythagoras undertook his trip to Egypt.

Then, all of a sudden, on the fifth day, he woke up to the life around him and instantly into social exchange with the crew. With gentleness and tranquility, he began conversing about the sea and its mysteries. He asked them where they planned to disembark in Egypt. The old captain pointed his finger towards their imminent destination, *the Delta of the Nile.*

"Is Memphis that way?" Pythagoras asked.

The old man, wrinkled by age and weighed down by life, might have known from his purple robe and his question that he was a seeker of wisdom.

"Yes, it is not far from there," he answered with a reassuring smile.

On the eleventh day, the boat reached the shore of the great city of Memphis, at the early break of dawn. Physically tired from the trip and weakened by his long fasting, he welcomed the help of the sailors in stepping down ashore. His legs failed him and he slumped on the sandy ground.

Before bidding him farewell, the captain set on his lap a basket of fruits, urging him to eat. A sailor brought to his side a jug of fresh water. Sagging on the sandy floor, his eyes foggy, his ears alien to the noise around him, Pythagoras perceived their silhouettes fading away in the midst of what appeared to him like trees strewn over the Sahara.

Slowly and cautiously, he drank from the jug, and then grabbed a peach. In fact, he took his time in eating the various delicious fruits laid in the basket in front of him. Gradually, he regained his power and senses while his consciousness flooded back to him.

Moments later, he opened his eyes fully, and beheld himself reposing under a palm tree, on the soft sand of Egypt; the land of mysteries *par excellence.*

4.

Egyptian Mysteries

Memphis!

Like the virtual reality of a long fancied dream, Memphis appeared impressive. Although its greatness, long related by both his teachers: Pherecydes and Thales, had remained vivid in his mind; to come and see the metropolis, for the first time, beheld quite an impact on Pythagoras.

He assessed his six years of Initiation in the holy sanctuaries of his homeland. His last conversation with Thales in the backyard resurfaced in his mind.

The easiest thing is to give advice to others... And I advise you to return to Phoenicia and then head to Egypt. There you will certainly learn about the deepest meanings of Life.

Thus, here he was, elated with a new hope at the turn of his twenty-ninth year of age, in these times: 541 BCE. Warmed up by the Egyptian early sunrays, he headed towards the city, ready for his new journey into the meanings of life no matter how profound.

He followed the sandy road through a massive forest of palm trees. The remarkable obelisks along his way seemed to foretell the gateway of a mystical world he intended to explore. Various statues of different shapes and sizes stood along the lane he traipsed. They appeared welcoming him into the realm of mysteries.

Pythagoras knew that inside the Egyptian sacred sanctuaries lived true magicians who possessed the profound erudition of the occult sciences, or what the sages called *the divine knowledge*. His insides quivered in anticipation of what awaited him ahead; the secrets of the gods!

From afar, a temple appeared encircled by palm trees. A silhouette in white, probably a Priest, stood on the steps of the entrance. The man turned in his direction as if he had sensed the advent of some foreign energy. Pythagoras felt the eyes studying his every step as he moved forward. He fathomed those eyes of wisdom, which only great teachers could command, in order to discern those walking the circle of wisdom and mastership. He shivered before warmth braced him as the vibrations of the priest reached him from that distance. He wondered about that subtle, yet real, phenomenon: the sage probing the aura of a real seeker of Truth.

All of a sudden, the man in white vanished and a couple of servants appeared waiting for him at the entrance of the domain. He refrained from showing his surprise and followed them through the vast front yard and up the few steps to the temple. There, another silent servant led him to an interior court.

Pythagoras halted in awe.

Ten Colossal Lotus Pillars beset the patio. They held, with all their might and purity, nothing less than the sacred Solar Arch!

"Behold the Great Temple of Osiris!" The servant heralded in a strong voice. The vibes resonated like drums proclaiming the sanctity of the place. With silent steps that contradicted the verve of his recent herald, the servant walked out.

Amidst the Lotus Pillars, Pythagoras remained alone with his amazement. *The Great Temple of Osiris!* He mumbled in admiration and reverence.

The Pillars exhibited some hieroglyphic writing and images of Pharaohs, divinities and stars. Topping them, the Lotus shone in a harmony of red, blue and green colors. The pillars reached the ceiling of an amazingly painted sky. Figures of the winged golden disk spread amid a myriad of stars. The celestial Nile, there depicted, showed the navigation of some sacred barges that transported the deceased to the other world.

Frissons of awe cooled his skin while he tried to absorb the wondrous sight. Suddenly, he discerned some imminent vibes in the air. He stood on alert. A faint sound of steps ensued from behind him and impelled him to glance over his shoulder.

There, a few inches away from him, stood a bald, white man with a scepter. Taller than the average man, dressed in a white linen tunic and papyrus sandals, he carried his trimmed beard almost to his chest. Under the refined eyebrows, his black eyes, outlined with golden tint, hooked him; the same deep eyes that had previously probed him while nearing the temple. Pythagoras turned completely in order to face him. Wordless, they both remained for a while, as if, in this arcane land of Egypt, souls should meet before the human minds communicated.

The Priest, with all his physical being, reflected utmost serenity. His fervent inner light sparked out and glowed in an enigmatic manner. Pythagoras yielded to the beam that penetrated through the windows of his soul to meet his spirit, and the sacred incarnated impulses within him. He felt total peace in unveiling, to the soul of that

Egyptian priest, the real identity of his being on the path to spiritual enlightenment.

It was only then that Pythagoras took note of the extravagant attire of the holy man. A large blue and gold necklace dangled from his neck. A thin blue linen belt wrapped the waist of his white robe. Heavy bracelets of gold adorned his wrists and upper arms.

"Phoenician, aren't you?" The Priest brought him to focus his attention in a leveled voice. "I can tell that from your purple tunic." He pointed his scepter at Pythagoras' outfit, and granted him a hint of a grin.

Pythagoras nodded in tranquil silence.

"Ah! I knew it!" the Priest exclaimed, clapping his jeweled fingers in self-acclaim. He edged closer in small, yet quick, steps. "What is your name? In which city were you born? Who are your parents?"

Pythagoras grinned inwardly at the sudden interest that sprinted out from that odd personage. In a composed voice, he introduced himself. "I am Pythagoras, native of Saydoun. My father Mnesarchus was a merchant, trading all around the Mediterranean. My mother Parthenis is a widow now. She takes care of my two younger brothers."

"Ah, I see!" The Priest muttered then probed for more, "In which Temple have you been instructed?"

"Actually, I undertook several apprenticeships in all the temples of Canaan-Phoenicia; Saydoun, Sur, Gebel...," Pythagoras answered quietly. "I became a brother of the Great White Fraternity in the Temple of Mt. Carmel."

Calmly, he dug his hand inside the leather satchel and retrieved a roll of papyrus handing it to him. "Here is a letter of recommendation[21] from the High Priest of the Great Temple of El-Baal."

The Egyptian Priest shook his head in gentle dismissal. "No need. Keep it with you, Pythagoras, I believe you. My name is Sonchis. From here onward, I will personally assume your tutoring. Follow me, please."

Pythagoras abided with a hidden sense of relief.

They walked, side by side, the long path of a wide hallway. Pythagoras tried not to appear overwhelmed by the magnificent architecture and sublime decoration. The countless drawings in different hues and themes on the walls, as well as the huge pillars, denoted, indeed, the great artistic skills of the Egyptians.

The magical reality of the fused colors astounded him. Golden yellow, red, turquoise and white tones blended to interpret their divinities in human and animal forms, along with other strange shapes. The sandy hues of the background emphasized that mysterious impression. Pythagoras marveled at the extraordinary skills, yet restrained from halting in order to keep up with the resolute steps of Sonchis.

They crossed the threshold; large doors leading to the outside, then strode through a long and narrow alley deep inside a lofty rock. Upright slabs and grand sphinxes were aligned on both sides of the passage. Pythagoras sensed a strange

---

[21]   Some early biographers and historians claimed that Pythagoras received a letter of recommendation from Polycrates, the tyrant of Samos, to Amasis the Egyptian Pharoah, who then introduced him to the Egyptian priests. This letter, they maintained, was not effective, for Pythagoras was not accepted at Memphis or Heliopolis, but at Diospolis (Thebes)! We however do not believe in this historic analysis. First of all, Pythagoras left Samos to Phoenicia and then to Egypt before Polycrates came to power in Samos. Secondly, he was surely admitted at Memphis.

presence watching him. He looked around him without stopping, then over his shoulder and up towards the ceiling. From this confined alley, all that he could see was the light blue ribbon of the sky.

They reached a high wooden gate, belonging most probably to a temple inside the rock. Towering pillars, delicately decorated, framed, from each side of the door, the majestic sculpture of a goddess.

In a queenly posture, her face veiled, she sat on a magnificent throne. A solar-disk with two horns crowned her head. Her hand, positioned on her lap, held the *Ankh*; the Egyptian cross of life, both physical and eternal; the key of the Nile. The other hand carried the book of Mysteries to her heart.

The effigy and its mysterious posture puzzled Pythagoras, so did the strange Hamitic characters inscribed at its footstool. That mixture of both Phoenician and Egyptian tongues read "No mortal has ever lifted my veil."

"This is Isis, the holder of magical secrets," Sonchis whispered to his ear, soft enough to sound like a reverence, yet not sufficiently low to impede the words from echoing before they waned in the mystery of the place.

"Behind this door resides the domain of the occult mysteries. Look at these two pillars, Pythagoras. The red one symbolizes the ascension of the spirit, up towards the Light of Osiris. The black one stands for the captivity of the spirit in the world of matter."

Pythagoras took his time to scrutinize the statue. He wondered about the similarities between these pillars and the two others at the entrance of the Great Temple of Baal-Melkart, back in the city of Sur.

The even voice of Sonchis broke into his thoughts. "Anyone who would venture inside our secret sciences and doctrines would be risking his life," he warned Pythagoras who turned his head to gawk at him. "The weak and the evil would fail, but the strong and the good would reach wisdom and immortality. Through the years, many qualified fellows have dared stepping through this door. Very few, however, have succeeded in achieving their journey and becoming authentic Initiates."

Sonchis paused for a moment in which his eyes seemed to scrutinize the soul of Pythagoras.

"Think carefully! Think well, Pythagoras," the Egyptian priest insisted in warning. "Consider the danger you might encounter beyond that door. You can still reconsider and back off now before it is too late. For when this door opens for you its covert trials, you can never pull back!"

The admonition, though substantial, crashed against the wall of determination Pythagoras had endorsed since the very first moment of his journey. Well aware of his mission and fate, he still deemed his Initiation to be the only essence of his life.

If I recoil now, I would lose it all, he asserted in the secret of his mind. The strength he embodied had always characterized him from others anyway. Doubt dwelled not in his brainpower. Only will and faith prevailed, and now, they impinged on him stronger than ever!

"I shall carry on. It is but my free will to proceed based only on my personal choice," he rendered with total confidence.

Sonchis smirked then nodded pensively several times. A spark of admiration brightened his black eyes. Thrilled to venture into that unknown perilous world, and confront all the challenges that lurked ahead, Pythagoras smiled.

"I'm ready," his voice surged out cold with tenacity.

"There are some things to undertake first. Let's go back!"

"What?" Pythagoras astonished with growing disappointment.

"In time, Pythagoras... in time," Sonchis advised for patience and marched away.

Pythagoras had no other choice but to follow him back to the interior court. There, Sonchis halted right under the Solar Arch.

"The servants will take you from here. A group of priests should be waiting to meet you by now. You will join them for ten full days and nights in which you should refrain completely from meat and wine. During this period, you should endorse total silence, listen to sacred hymns, and practice the rites of purification."

At seeing him walking out, Pythagoras asked in surprise, "How about you?"

Sonchis halted for few seconds as if astounded by the question then turned to him slowly. "What about me?"

"Aren't you joining us?"

The Priest hooked him with his intense look as he marched back to him with his small, quick steps. "Pythagoras, the Phoenician. My Initiation has been achieved long ago. I'm the High Priest of the Great Temple of Osiris."

Pythagoras gasped and gawked at the holy man.

"The servants should be here the moment I leave for they are not allowed to see my face." At that, Sonchis bowed his head slightly, turned on his heels and disappeared behind the doors of the big hall.

Pythagoras ignored how much time elapsed before he felt the presence of the servants behind him. He shook off his dismay and turned towards the servants. Wordless, they gestured him to follow them. He abided without further ado. Resolute, he marched behind them and towards the first phase of his Egyptian Initiation. As Sonchis has just informed him, the meditation and purification chambers awaited him.

* * *

Ten nights later, Pythagoras paced back and forth the great hall of the Solar Arch. He halted, glanced at the door then resumed his pacing again. He had been anticipating that moment since the very first day of his abstention period. His fretfulness finally ended at the appearance of two men of particular attire. Of similar mid stature, they looked oddly alike with their tanned skin, impassive faces, trimmed eyebrows and large black eyes outlined with blue tint. Long turbans, of green and yellow stripes, covered their heads all the way down to their shoulders. At their waist, a thick leather belt held their only piece of clothing; a colorful skirt that reached their ankles. Other than that, heavy jewelry adorned their bared chests and arms.

Dispassionate and silent, they bowed their heads at Pythagoras. Guessing that they had come for him, he hastened in their direction, and continued his way past them. They caught up with him halfway through the narrow alley leading to an ancient gate. Could it be that of mysteries? There, he cut his vehemence short and waited for them to open his way in. They did, looking astounded by his eagerness.

A semi-dark vestibule, partially lit by some torches on the walls received them in its cold smell of confinement. They continued through a rocky path. Pythagoras glanced curiously on both sides at the weird statues of human bodies with animal heads. He discerned among them some lions, bulls and serpents. Reaching the end of the path, he halted when the peculiar assistants did. There in front of him rested a skeleton on a bier; an uncanny mummy standing at its side. *They must symbolize death and immortality respectively*, he levied inwardly.

Always wordless, his escorts pointed at a dark aperture in the wall. It was large enough to constitute the entry of a tunnel, yet not sufficiently so to permit an easy access through it without crawling. Confused, Pythagoras hesitated for a moment in which he tried to assess the path ahead.

A dry voice broke the stillness, "You can still forget all about it," the assistant on his left suggested with a hint of caution. "The door behind you is still opened. You can walk back."

A moment of quiet coldness ensued. A moment of weighty reflection elapsed.

Pythagoras inhaled deeply, lifted his chin up, shrunk his eyes on the hole and, with all the willpower he felt within, he enjoined, "No! I'm in!"

"Very well then," the other guide replied evenly, yet Pythagoras perceived a pitch of admiration in his icy voice. "You are on your own now," he warned him as he handed him his torch. "Go ahead!" He snapped, veered on his heels and strolled away with his friend without another word.

The sinister sound of the door closing behind them resonated through the rocky hall. A feeling of dread and excitement overtook Pythagoras at this moment in which he faced the inevitable unknown. He walked back to scrutinize once again the walls around him, the statues, the skeleton and the mummy, then stood still in front of the locked entry door.

That is it then! So, let's do it! He cracked out with finality.

He marched decisively to the entry of the tunnel and bent on his knees to peer in.

Excitement flooded through his veins. The corner of his mouth lifted into a smile known only to those readying for a battle whose victory they have secured.

The *Temple of Mysteries* waited for him.

Head first, he crouched his body, elevated a knee then the other and pulled himself inside the tunnel. He crept through with caution. An acute odor of cavernous moist and ancient soil wafted to him. Cold accentuated as he progressed on his hands and knees. He heeded the sound of his robe tearing at his shoulders and knees before he felt the scouring ache on his skin.

He continued.

The narrow tunnel lengthened to a point where he almost doubted the reality of what might, or might not, lay ahead!

He sweated profusely.

Air flattened around him. Oxygen exhausted from his lungs. By necessity, he stretched down on the ground and heaved his body forward with the aid of his arms; an inch at a time... He crept through with much trouble. Unexpectedly, the tunnel widened, just enough to reinstate his hope. He lifted himself on his knees and dragged his torch to look ahead. It seemed an endless way, but that did not sorely try his inmost dedication, so he clambered farther and farther, continuing his way through.

The humidity he sensed after a while intensified. He came in contact with the squashy texture of mud that turned thicker and thicker as he advanced. He halted and squeezed himself in a sitting position. He needed to rest, to stretch his legs and to ease his constricted muscles.

He breathed with difficulty.

He deemed wiser to carry on, instead of lingering there, where the air lacked in a precarious way. The thought of being buried alive made him quiver in panic, yet he prompted to control his weakness.

More determined than ever, he went back to his endless crawling. And crawl he did, faster and faster, striving to conquer that underground adversity. His mind calculated the time at which he had first entered through that hole.

Almost an hour! I think it has been almost an hour!

At that particular moment of fretful awareness, he reached the periphery of a large aperture. *Finally!* His soul screamed in victory. He pushed himself to break out of that calvary. His hope was short lived. He lost ground, flew in the air, and crashed painfully on a hard marble floor.

He strove to catch his breath, sweating heavily from terror. He looked around him then burst into a nervous laughter. Evaluating quickly the terrible experience, he deducted that he had just overcome the difficult trial of *the Earth element!*

He stared up at the aperture of the tunnel he had just conquered and, shaking off the upshot of his dreadful crash, he took control of himself, leaping to his feet.

He knew that more tests awaited him. With renewed stamina, minutes later, he followed the only long alley that stretched in front of him to the right until he reached a barricade of progressive burning fire.

He froze.

Am I really supposed to cross this huge door of fire? How?!

His wits labored for a plausible solution. He frowned, searching his mind, thinking, deliberating... He shook his head. *Impossible!* His heart yelled in revolt. He leaned on the rocky wall; his eyes furious on the fire. After a while, he slouched to the cold floor, closed his eyes and tilted his head back. He breathed slowly and deeply to control his emotions and master his fears.

Do not feel the fear of the fire! Try! Try...! Try to overcome it! His inner voice wafted then insisted on the words that echoed deep into his central realm.

Do not feel the fear of the fire... Try to overcome it!

He snapped his eyes open, probed for a hidden message on the rocky ceiling, shrank his eyes in concentration, then slowly stood up on his feet and approached the fire, closer and closer.

He froze.

Impossible! He muttered and his laughter resonated in the narrow path. *An illusion! It is but an illusion!*

Relief embraced him in its gentle strength. His mind appraised the fire for a while. He realized the visual hoax fabricated by the Egyptian Hierophants as part of this unusual system of trials.

Not wishing to loiter any longer, he gathered all his energy and, in one swift movement, launched his body through. He attained the safety of a chamber and veered to glare at *the element of Fire* he had just conquered.

He grinned.

Yet, he had no time to relish in his victory. The earth cracked under his feet and he glided into the darkness.

An abyss... *Death!*

Terror burst out from his mouth in the form of a baleful scream that echoed behind him. He held tight to his torch as if his life depended on it.

Quick! Quick! His mind urged him for a solution.

What solution? His heart rebelled in despair and accelerated its beats that pounded horribly to his ears. This could not be another trick of the Egyptians! That was real! The blast vacuumed him further and further down to a point of no return.

Pythagoras tightened his eyes close. He breathed deeply. Forcefully, he strove to disregard the potent sensations around and inside him. He focused his mind on his body.

He controlled.

He mastered.

He exerted all his physical power and snapped his eyes open. His hands and feet hurled out in blind search for any solid contact that might come as a plank of salvation. *Nothing!* He heaved himself to swerve in the air, changing his point of vision. He saw it then; an aperture to his left! In a supernatural effort, new to him, he summoned all the energy left in his being and leaped.

His feet touched ground. Tears of triumph streamed down his face. His muscles released at once their previous spasm. He slumped to the ground. At this very moment, he just wanted to forget all about the tension he had just endured.

He stretched down right there on the cold ground, and closed his eyes. He sought for self-control, breathing deeply and slowly. He fixed his thoughts on one particular point in the back of his mind, the vision of a flame, that of the torch in his hand. It was still lit despite it all.

Tranquility started to engulf his body. His clarity of thoughts came back to him. Only then did he allow himself to return to the reality around him. He murmured, "*The element of Air!* Of course, I just overcame the trial of the Air element!"

His joy lasted only for a few seconds for as he stood up and took a few steps to the left, a powerful heave jerked him into a new chasm to dart him, in shock, in a body of water. Depth sucked him down. Total haziness encircled him. But he could feel the water. He was drowning!

He fought.

The element of Water launched a war against his life. He held his breath to propel his body upward. He lifted his eyes in quest of the light of hope. Darkness above weakened his courage, yet his determination to survive dispatched him further up and to the surface. He emerged, inhaled the air that lacked in his lungs, coughed forcefully, then breathed again and almost yelled. He swerved on himself quickly, sensing the potent presence of a danger. Then he heard a powerful movement in the water, he could not discern what it was. However, a soft blaze in the surroundings revealed parts of them. He saw them then, on the water of what appeared to be a lake, those horrible reptiles that could devour him mercilessly; *Crocodiles!*

The fierce reptiles surely saw him first for they spurted in his direction. Horror paralyzed him. *No!* His mind urged him to master his fear. He darted his body forward and, without releasing his now extinct torch, he swam for his life. A sudden current yanked him down. He sank for few seconds then hauled his body upwards. He launched himself toward the surface. He swam with the strength of despair to a ridge that he could barely see.

His limbs started to give in to exhaustion. His movements lost their speed. His breathing rhythm decreased. His face went under water. He was about to surrender when his hand touched the solidity of ground. He lifted his head above the surface of the water and roared in relief. *Safety!*

He dragged himself up the muddy ridge and sprawled onto the ground.

Water element, I got you! His heart shouted in triumph. He ducked the wooden base of his torch in the mud as a sign of victory, and snapped out loud, "I got you indeed!"

Pythagoras, his favorite purple tunic all dirty and torn, lay on his back with an amazing feeling of relief. He worked on catching his breath; panting in delight at having succeeded the ordeal of the water element. His tears mingled with the water on his face. Gradually, exhaustion took hold of him but he did not allow nature to take over and drift him into the comfort of greatly needed rest.

On the contrary, in the midst of confusion that swallowed his mind for a while, his eyes browsed around, in angst, then riveted on the lake in front of him. The muddle in his mind cleared off steadily. All the hardships of his recent tests seemed to have completely vanished. He straightened up into a sitting position and undertook a calm assessment of what he had undergone. A sense of triumph, new to him, invigorated him when he realized that he had

142

succeeded the tests. He had certainly controlled the four elements; the passive and the active ones!

Pythagoras fathomed the extent of his success. He acknowledged the four qualities and importance of these four elements; dryness integrated in the Earth, heat in the Fire, humidity in the Air and coldness in the Water. By means of their characters, the elements would either act upon each other, or would be acted on; thus their active or passive values.

Pythagoras recalled the lecture of his teacher, Thales, on the subject.

> "According to the strength and degree of their motion, active elements impress a definite and precise character upon the passive elements. Thus, the active elements are the Fire that is basically connected with intuition and energy, and the Air that is associated to the mental realm and to the communication ability. Eventually, the passive elements, by their inactive qualities, receive the impressions of the active ones. Thus the passive elements are the Water that relates mainly to feelings, and the Earth that is linked to caution, patience and practicality."

Pythagoras envisioned his Master, Thales, conveying this knowledge to him. The thought infused him with a renewed determination to overcome the imminent challenge ahead. His eyes explored the darkness. There was a soft glow nearby. A small sphere of light shaped a narrow stairway in the shadows. His hands searched the sand around him for his torch. He went on his knees, his hands frantic in quest. *Yes!* He murmured the moment he touched the wooden handgrip and then leaped to his feet. His steps leaden still by the exertions of the recent trials, he forced himself towards the stairs.

The spiral steps, cut into the rocks, led him to a round gallery. There, beautiful effigies stood magnificently lit with torches on their sides. He lifted his own, edged it to the flames of the first statue, and waited for the fire to dry the moist out. Prudently, his eyes roamed around then halted with curiosity at some symbolic frescos brilliantly painted on the walls.

His torch finally ignited. He stepped back and elevated his light to examine the fresco.

"Welcome to the Gallery," the voice of a tenor bashed the silence.

Pythagoras startled and veered swiftly.

There in front of him stood a tall man in weird attires. His yellowish beard reached his chest as did his hair. His large robe of burgundy velvet matched the peculiar turban around his head. What attracted Pythagoras the most was the contrast of those small amber eyes with the dark skin of the man. *A Magician!* He amazed secretly.

"Welcome to the Gallery, and Congratulations!" The Magician finally said; his eyes witty. "You have succeeded the tests of the four elements. You have just earned your access into my world!"

Pythagoras nodded in thanks, unable still to find his words.

The Magician smirked, knowingly, as if mocking him. "I'm the Guardian of the Sacred Symbols," he declared with his arms widely opened in a theatrical manner. His amber eyes shone.

"I... I am Pythagoras from-"

"Yes, yes I know," he interrupted him with a dismissal gesture of his heavily jeweled hand. "Come on, let's move on!"

In spite of his blunt ways, the tone of his voice was amiable. Pythagoras guessed that he would have to get used to the frank manners of his new teacher. He dashed behind him.

The Guardian walked with him by the frescos. He showed him the numbers, and the letters of the Alphabet, written under each one of the twenty-two paintings.

"These twenty-two letters represent the *Alphabet of the Occult Doctrine*; the absolute principles," he explained in a serious tone. "They are the secret keys of the universe. Should you comprehend their esoteric meanings, and learn to use them by will, you shall be able to obtain wisdom and power."

The Magician waited for a reaction from Pythagoras. It came in the form of a simple nod of understanding.

He answered the silent reply with certain humor, "Very well, then. Let's proceed! These secret keys, the 22 letters of the Sacred Alphabet, are divided as follows: Three letters stand for the three elements of Fire, Water and Earth. The fourth, the Air element, is so unique. The Ancients consider it as the link and the primary mover of the other three elements, thus it is not included herein."

He stopped at that to inquire with inquisitive eyes, "Are you following me, son?"

"Not quite..." Pythagoras answered with bewilderment showing on his face. "Why Air is considered to be so particularly above all other elements that it should not be represented in a letter of the Sacred Alphabet, while it should, I think." He continued in good humor tinted with defiance. The subject had grabbed all his attention.

"A good observation, son, but heed me. Air is like the spirit, a mover of things. When it moves, it moves from all directions. None of the other elements can do that. My fellow Egyptian priests have long learned from our god Thoth that in the beginning there was a Primal Wind, Air, in the form of a breath of mist and darkness. There was also *Môt*, the formless Primal Mud, the primordial form of Earth. The Primal Wind fertilized itself and

145

became *Rûah*, Spirit, while Môt became the Cosmic Egg. The cosmos was born when *Rûah* opened the Cosmic Egg, and this eventually led to a separation of the Elements."

Motionless as never before, Pythagoras listened attentively to the Magician, almost hypnotized by the words he thoughtfully uttered. Nothing really came up to his mind for a discussion. He just murmured under his breath, *Air is not an element, but a resemblance of the spirit!*

"Fine then, let's proceed! There exist seven planets that influence the Earth and its inhabitants to a great extent. They are the Sun, the Moon, Saturn, Jupiter, Venus, Mercury and Mars. They are manifested in seven letters. With that in mind, there are now ten letters and there remain twelve out of twenty-two. Correct!?" The Magician inquired with a witty smile as if he was playing with numbers and shapes; Pythagoras nodded. "Well, the remaining twelve letters are the images of the twelve signs of the Zodiac."

Pythagoras remembered at once the teachings of the Sacred Alphabet back with the Hierophants of Gebel. Indeed, the system of teaching of the Egyptian Guardian differed in many ways. His transmission of the knowledge of the Sacred Alphabet seemed to take a more practical way. *Hmmm... How interesting!* He thought in anticipation.

"Are you following me, Son?" The Magician snapped with a frown.

Pythagoras wanted to chuckle at the question that appeared to be a pattern of his new teacher. Yet he did not. He simply answered, "Always!"

"You should. I count on it!" the Magician said bluntly and reverted to his lecture. "When each letter of the sacred language combines with its associated number, it affects, to a significant extent, the tri-une dimensional worlds of the spirit, the intellect and the matter," he stressed each word as if the neophyte needed that emphasis to understand.

Pythagoras grasped the full meaning when he recalled his experience with the deep sound of the murex shell back on the Surian beach.

> *...The sound of water with past memories of the sea echoed, inside his inner realm, the voice of silence that whispered to his mind, merged with his spirit and vibrated with his body.*

Such a mystical experience had made him fathom, back then, the power of his three dimensions; his tri-une nature of being.

His discovery of the Harmony of the Spheres, afterwards, in the Mountain of Gebel had ensued as a confirmation of that existing bridge between Heaven and Earth.

"Are you following me, son?!" The voice of the Guardian of the Sacred Symbols propelled him back to the purpose of his presence there.

This time, the Magician caught him indeed distracted by his flashback. He felt some heat on his face under the accusing amber eyes. Because lying was not part of his nature, Pythagoras opened his mouth to apologize.

Impeding him to do so, the Guardian cracked at once, "Shall we proceed?"

Pythagoras nodded and diverted his eyes. Yet, at the loud chuckle that cropped up, he turned to look at the Magician. Surprised, he followed the glimpse of his master on his own attire. Pythagoras gazed down and blushed at the sight of his torn out robe that appeared more black than purple. He shrugged off his shoulders with fatality. What unsettled him more at this moment was the blunt character of the Guardian rather than his own physical appearance! When he looked up, he noticed that his master had already moved on. He rushed to join him.

Side by side, the teacher and the neophyte walked through the gallery. They stopped in front of a painting picturing a royal person in a white robe, a scepter in his hand and a golden crown on his head.

"Well, let's see Pythagoras!" the Guardian taunted him. "Can you explain the significance of this painting?"

"Sure!" Pythagoras took up the challenge with confidence. "The white robe signifies Purity. The scepter stands for Mastership, while the golden crown means the Kingship."

"Not bad, not bad at all," the Guardian replied wittily. "What else could the golden crown mean though?"

"What do you mean?"

"There is more to this illustration than the physical appearance of... hmmm... a clean wise king," he tempted him again.

Pythagoras stood alert. His new teacher might consider himself funny, but his brusqueness submitted Pythagoras to a new challenge by the minute.

At his discomfiture, the Magician sighed loudly and explained, "It is not wrong if you don't know what the answer is, son. The golden crown means the Universal Light. Every will that unites with God, for the manifestation of Truth and Justice, will dwell inside this Light. Accordingly, the will participates directly in the Divine Power over the existential life. It is an eternal gift to the free spirits."

Pythagoras pondered over the revelation. *A Magician!* He mumbled in the silence of his mind. To his surprise, the Guardian respected his silent meditation. Not long enough though!

"Any questions?"

"Well, yes," Pythagoras replied. "What are the letter A and the number 1?"

"They symbolize, in the spiritual world, the Absolute Being from whom life sprang. In the mental world, however, they mean the Unity and the Equilibrium of life. On the physical plane, they personify the Microcosmic man who, by expanding his occult faculties, elevates himself up into the spheres of infinite Macrocosm."

"Very interesting!" Pythagoras exclaimed, impressed by this new system of Initiation.

The Magician smiled and continued his interpretations on the meanings of each painting. Pythagoras began to perceive the inside significance of the sublime ideas and images they embodied.

The lesson ended as they reached a small door on the rock. The Magician levied the heavy bolt and opened up to a dusky grotto.

"Go ahead! The servants will help you clean up. I'll meet you later in the Chamber above," the Guardian informed him, pushed him gently forward and closed the door at once.

In the grotto, the same assistants greeted him with the same impassive faces. They led him to a lavatory where they subjected him to a cleansing process that included washing with hot water and soap, shaving his head and beard, and changing into a dry white linen tunic. Pythagoras welcomed the refreshing feeling, and of course, the food they lay down for him in a low table of carved brass in a private luxurious room.

He relaxed on a comfortable couch, content that the tests had finally ended. Feeling victorious, he began to enjoy the calmness that enveloped him. The sound of music drifted, tender and soothing, from somewhere in the background. The melodious tones engulfed him gently to convey him into a journey of dreams. So tired, his eyelids gave in as the tension of his muscles waned.

149

Pythagoras woke up from his sleep to the sound of exotic music. He smelled a powerful aroma of jasmine and roses in the room. Something felt strange to him. He opened his eyes to astonish at a feminine silhouette swaying to the musical rhythm behind a white translucent curtain. Her body moved languorously and enticed his basic male instincts.

The woman appeared from behind the curtain, a wholesome embodiment of female beauty. He swallowed hard. Her long black mane waved down on her golden skin. A sheer blue tunic barely covered her beauty. All too slowly, the curves of her body undulated as she closed the distance to him. With every one of her steps forward, her hips stirred in an erotic manner that warmed his insides. Her powerful sensuality blazed the blood in his veins.

In her hands, a silver cup of red blooming roses fused out an arousing fragrance that caressed his skin, warmed his senses, and fueled his desires. He lifted his weight on his elbow to ogle at the exotic woman. Her big black eyes and full lips tempted him. Dazzled and totally mesmerized, he leaped to his feet, hesitated a bit, thought for a moment, but then with uncontainable strange impulses he dashed to grab her by the waist. He brought her body tightly to his and his other hand fondled her breasts. Her dark eyes hypnotized him.

"Are you afraid of me, handsome man?" she murmured in a guttural voice.

His insides quivered with reeling want. His hands shaped her feminine curves and further down to caress her hips.

"Go ahead, love," she incited him, encouraged him, and stimulated his male desire to a point of no return.

His mouth neared hers as she whispered, "With my body, I shall give you the prize of the winners... the oblivion of pain... and... the cup of happiness."

He halted, just an inch from her parted lips. Somehow, her words had slashed his mind like a sword and blasted him awake from the lecherous tension in which he had basked.

Temptation...

He became conscious, all of a sudden, of the fact that he was about to jeopardize all that he stood for. She must have sensed his hesitation for her attempt at seduction intensified. She stroked his chest, grabbed his hand, kissed his fingers, and her eyes hooking his, dragged him to the couch.

Pythagoras beseeched all the powers left in him to fight the fervor that burned his flesh. He snapped her hands away. He stood up with an immense exertion of willpower. She seized his hand. She tried to pull him back to her. He refused to yield, however hard it felt. He snatched himself away from her enticement. He marched to the middle of the room. He veered angrily and glared her straight in the eyes.

"Touch me not woman, for I have not yet come to my higher-self! You know this, don't you?" He raved and ranted. "You aim at slowing my progress by engaging my sexual desires, don't you? You, woman, are stepping on my way. Get out!" Pythagoras fulminated, but more at himself for having risked falling into temptation.

The Nubian woman lowered her eyes in surrender. Her attempts to seduce him failed. She stepped back and back, all too slowly...

Suddenly, priests in white robes stormed in with bright torches. They chanted hymns to the goddess Isis. The woman sneaked shamefully behind the curtain, never to be seen again. The priests surrounded Pythagoras and led him to the Sanctuary of Isis with all the due honor of a winner.

A semi-circular formation of some dozen Magicians received him in that hall. The priests joined them to seal the Assembly circle. The statue of Isis stood majestically at the heart of the Temple.

151

A golden rose ornamented her breast and a seven-ray crown covered her head. Her son Horus rested in her arms.

The High Priest of Osiris, the Hierophant Sonchis, appeared in splendor in the middle of the Assembly. Wearing his white linen tunic topped by a purple robe, he opened his hands to greet him. In a ceremonious tone and strong voice, he announced, "Pythagoras, Son of Phoenicia, Seeker of Truth and Wisdom, here and forever, pledge silence and submission to the Occult Doctrine!"

Pythagoras straightened up. He inhaled deeply then, his eyes straight in those of the High-Priest, he proclaimed his oath.

Only then, did Sonchis welcom him officially in the secret circle of Isis, accepting him, in the name of the Assembly, as their brother and future Initiate.

Elation overwhelmed Pythagoras.

I am now a disciple of Isis, a son of Isis, like Horus! His heart exclaimed, his spirit heightened, his eyes moistened and he shivered with emotion.

In the company of all the Magicians and Priests around, he felt the manifestation of a strong divine presence. The sphere of Truth seemed to draw a path for him to walk, and open a door for him to enter.

But... how? He wondered with sudden anxiety. _

* * *

A few days later, Pythagoras traipsed the Sahara; Memphis to his back and the Pyramids as destination. Under the blaze of the Egyptian sun, he moved on. His steps immersed in the softness of the golden sand. The small dunes merged all around him. His step unhurried, his heart in marvel and his mind pondering over the world of mystical meanings.

Like all those prophets, holy men and sages who had preceded him in this path, the Sahara welcomed his probing for wisdom and for the purification of thoughts. In fact, traveling through the Egyptian desert created in his mind a sort of inexplicable state of existence. It just puzzled him to a degree of madness. This emptiness, the very void all around him, made him wonder about how minuscule he really was. Like a drop in the ocean, he was just a white mark in the infinite golden sand.

At night fall, he tackled more than the strong darkness and the sharp cold. A world of illusions parted its doors wide open to snare his mind in its chimera and deception. Pythagoras feared losing his direction. Within the chaos that framed his senses, strange voices emerged from and through the wilderness.

Voices of Elves, *Jinnis*, Angels or Demons! He wavered.

No, wait a second! His wits urged him to listen carefully. His inner ear tuned in to the voices. Thus, the musician with a perception powerfully developed through years of playing music, him who had decoded the Harmony of the Spheres, rebutted as false the voices emitted from the Sahara. He marched farther, fearlessly. He acknowledged the weird voices as nothing more than the sound of the silent night; the echoes of his loneliness distorted by the most natural phenomenon of all, nature itself!

After all, that is what makes of the Sahara an enchanted habitat, he muttered with a smile.

From afar, the Sphinx and the Pyramids finally materialized in his sight. Moon light shaped the gigantic mystical forms with a magical blend of beams and shadows. There they stood, in all their glory, amidst the Egyptian desert, resisting the course of time. He trembled deep inside as he felt their energy vibrating all around. He halted for a moment of awe then pressed his steps forward, quickly. His mind pondered on their mystery, speculated on their existence and strove for answers that would not come into light.

What do they stand for? What is there inside the Sphinx? How was the Great Pyramid built? Why? What does it hold inside its walls? Is it Numbers, Immortality, Reality? What is it? What are they?

The questions scuttled inside his head, unruly like the blowing dust of the Sahara that began to gust on him.

Two spots of light materialized in front of him. They moved, swayed and edged closer and closer. Two men appeared with torches in their hands. They greeted him cordially as if they were expecting him. Pythagoras examined them in a swift gaze. Both dark and bald, the men looked strangely similar. Their muscular and hairless bodies were bare but from a long skirt, of colorful stripes, belted at the waist. Their darkly outlined eyes emphasized their tattooed eyebrows and thick lips. Without further delay, they rushed him towards the monuments. They guided him to an entrance located between the Sphinx and the Great Pyramid. Two other similar men stood in guard with long spears in their hands.

"This takes you to the underground of the small Temple of the third Pyramid," one of the sentinels informed him then added in clarification, "the Pyramid of Men-Kau-Ra."

The guards browsed cautious looks around before rushing him inside.

This tiny structure is surely a place inaccessible to the common people, Pythagoras deducted.

"This is the *Hat-Khet*, the House of Body where studies are conducted," the guard notified him and added respectfully, "I am instructed to escort you to your room at once." His striking white teeth sparkled when he grinned widely. "I understand you shall be spending the night."

And the months and years to come... Pythagoras formulated in the silence of his heart. *It will be a long journey, indeed!*

To his escort, he answered with a simple nod.

Soon, he entered a small austere room. The moment the door shut behind him, he dropped in exhaustion on the narrow bed.

He closed his eyes.

Silence filled the place.

Inside the *Hat-Khet*, Pythagoras initiated his journey of studies with the Egyptian Priests and Magicians. The **1ˢᵗ degree** of his education took him numerous years. He studied the organic constitution of human beings and animals, as well as vegetables and minerals. He poured over the circulation of blood, the muscular system, the respiratory system and the functions of all the four kingdoms of nature.

The program, more advanced than any previously acquired, boosted him forward to the level of physician. He came to peruse the natural constitution of the four Kingdoms of earthly life. That was a direct indulgence into the **Natural Magic**, so to say.

Meanwhile, he put his solitude to good use in his Spartan room plunging into the scholastic ocean of Cosmogony and elementary Geometry. In the Hall of the Temples, he acquired his instruction on the Hieroglyphs. That Egyptian system of writing allowed him access to the odyssey of man, and the story of human civilization.

Years later, dressed in a white linen tunic and fully equipped with his new erudition, Pythagoras penetrated into the House of Soul, known as the *Hat-Ba*. The second in size and importance, it was situated inside the exterior Temple of the Khaf-Ra Pyramid. The House of Soul received the more mature seeker of Truth that he had become.

Gladly surprised, he met Sonchis there. He entrusted his mind willingly to the High Priest of Osiris who instructed him on the science of Esoteric Physiology[22].

His **2nd degree** Initiation started!

In the years that followed, Pythagoras acquired the knowledge of the Astral Plane. He mastered the skills of developing and directing the mysterious fluid that manifested into vital force. That force allowed him substantial mastership over both the physical and ethereal dimensions. In fact, these occult studies of the so-called **Astral Magic** granted him the power of magnetism and therapeutic healing.

During an afternoon break from his intensive studies, Pythagoras relaxed on his chair. While meditating on the science of Therapeutic healing, he recalled his talk with Abdu-Eshmun, the High Priest of the Temple of Eshmun...

> *Water is just an accelerator of the healing process, a highly pure element of Nature that works as a purifier...*
>
> *The healing operation actually happens through both, the combination of my will, I, Abdu-Eshmun, and the power of Theurgy...*
>
> *It is not yet the time for you to have these powers. You are only a beginner, and, the road is way too long. Be patient, my brother...*

---

[22] Esoteric Physiology is an old system that shows the centers of force in the body of the human being. It is a system similar to the Hindu Yoga. These centers are called Chakras, and they are seven, distributed along the spinal cord. Two currents of energy, a positive and a negative, surround them.

The words from his past echoed in his head. He grinned with a sense of thrill and triumph. Now he could affirm that his time had certainly come to possess those healing powers!

His smile froze all of a sudden. He frowned. In a blast, he realized that there existed, undoubtedly, a major relation between Phoenicia and Egypt, be it religious, theological or spiritual. *Amazing!* He whooshed in astonishment.

The voice of Sonchis whispered in his ears, "These powers that you are gaining now, Pythagoras, are very dangerous."

The sound and the warning propelled him back to the present. His body tensed in order to heed what his teacher intended to tell him. He abstained from turning to look at him. He just sat straight and waited.

Sonchis pursued his arcane message, "You have to be extremely careful, Pythagoras, when using them. They could hurt as much as they could save. Behold nobility and high spirit always when enacting the splendid feats of such supremacy."

Pythagoras gave his teacher a courtly nod, somehow offended that Sonchis might assume that he would ever misuse such powers. He need not be told that if these acquired secrets were to be used in contradiction to their good principles, the negative ramifications would certainly rebound many times, and cause him major suffering.

The Temple of Osiris received Pythagoras two years later for his Initiation into the **3ʳᵈ degree level**. The exterior of the Temple related to the Great Pyramid Khufu. The Greeks called it Cheops.

There, in the secrecy of the Osiris shrine, Pythagoras submerged in the mysterious world of the science of Astrology. Known also as the **Cosmic Magic**, that discipline engrossed him in both its exoteric and esoteric perspectives.

The exoteric side showed him the position of the planets and their harmonious movements in our solar system. The esoteric aspect unveiled the different vital forces that the planets emanate to ensure the perfect balance of their spatial existence. The science of Astrology, in fact, came to confirm his past revelation, in the mountain of Gebel, on the *Harmony of the Spheres*; the phenomenal balance between the Earth and the Heavenly Bodies. Thus, music and numbers appeared of sound value as well in the sacred sciences of Egypt.

And furthermore, during the long years of intensive studies in the *Hall of the Great Mysteries,* as called by the Egyptian priests, Pythagoras reveled in being the disciple of Isis. He actually stood in front of the great triad of Horus, Osiris and Isis. Osiris, so regal, wore the most majestic of the Pharaoh's crowns, the *Atef* white crown, and carried the royal crook and flail. To his left, the Patron of the Temple, the goddess Isis who was the holder of magical secrets, wore a disk on her head edged by two horns, those of a cow, and from the fingers on her left-hand dangled the *Ankh*. For these sacred moments in which he stood in the presence of these effigies, Pythagoras really felt like Horus the Elder, their only son, with a falcon head, standing to the right of his father.

Three years later, Pythagoras entered the realm of the **4ᵗʰ degree** through the science of the **Celestial Magic**. Consequently, he acquired the power that allowed him to perform magic on the living. This paranormal ability granted him authority over the spirits of the dead, as well, to help them in their final journey towards their spiritual resurrection into the sphere of consciousness.

Inside the *Place of Purification*, the most mysterious and ritualistic chamber of the Temple, Pythagoras joined the priests for a cleansing sacrament. They surrounded a long wooden bier where the corpse of a recently deceased brother rested. Two statues of lions, with hefty tawny manes, stood on each side of the corpse; their heads bent, yet their huge eyes watchful in protection. Two other statues of lions, apparently alerted, crouched on their tufted tails. A flambeau on a lotus pillar provided enough light for the three priests, known as the embalmers, to operate. The Mystery Superior directed them.

Profuse sacred incense burned from the four corners of the hall and wafted an intense fog and scent. The portrayed image of the Jackal-Headed god, Anubis, the divine embalmer, took one side of the wall. Priests, all in white, made their reverential way in, one after the other. They carried, with deference, precious funerary articles in both hands. They aligned behind the bald embalmers and waited. On a table, at the side of the corpse, surgical instruments and several Canopic Jars waited to be used.

Specially built for such a funerary purpose, an underground duct, connected to the Nile, streamed water in through a canal, at the ground level of the Chamber. A basin received the water to be used by the embalmers, and so they did, washing the body with meticulous and measured gestures. Once the ceremony of sanitization was done, they used extreme caution in creating a sideway incision to remove the intestines and then the liver and the lungs. Through the nostrils of the corpse, they sneaked a sharp heated iron and cut the brains into segments which they extracted slowly through the same conduit. They then washed the organs in palm wine, covered them with perfumed gum and placed them, with reverence, in four different Canopic jars[23]. They kept the heart

---

[23]   Canopic Jars were four and used by ancient Egyptians during the rituals of mummification of usually a priest or

intact within the body, for they deemed it the *Seat of Intelligence.*

In turn, the priests behind the embalmers stepped forward to pass on the precious funerary articles in their hands. At that, the embalmers filled the body cavity with myrrh, cassia, and other pungent zests. They anointed the corpse with sacred oil and resins. They then stitched up the notch and wrapped it tightly with fine white linen bandages.

A mummy... the corpse laid dormant before them.

A still moment of respect ensued.

The embalmers ended the silent contemplation when they proceeded to place some sacred strange amulets, of their own preparation, on the body. A priest stepped forward and rested the *Ankh,* the Egyptian cross of immortality, on the forehead of the mummy. The older embalmer received from his assistant the *Scarab.* In the belief of the Egyptian mysteries, that talisman, which symbolized the soul, would stimulate birth into eternity from that very moment. Thus, the embalmer placed it, all too slowly, there where the heart is. Finally, the priest carrying the golden mask edged closer. The embalmer used it to cover the head of the dead.

Forty days and nights later...

Dressed all in white, Pythagoras accompanied the embalmers into the Mystery Chamber. He waited in reverence for them to lift the mummy, with utmost respect, on their shoulders,

---

a pharaoh. These funerary vases of elongated form were made from various materials, including calcite (Egyptian alabaster), limestone, pottery, wood, and bronze. Each extracted organ would be placed in its own specified jar and never all organs in one. The covers of the jars would sometimes be modeled, or painted, to look like the head of Anubis, the divine embalmer, and, some other times, like the face of the deceased.

160

and then he continued the walk with them through a long corridor. They finally entered the *Funeral Chamber* situated by the side of the Nile.

The Solar Disk, *Ra*, reigned in the centre of the painted ceiling; there, among the Heavenly bodies depicted in a quasi-rotational movement. The dark-blue hue gave a breathtaking impression of the real sky at night. The Solar Disk radiated its divine rays upon the mummy, as if meant to provide it with the heat of life.

With the priests of Osiris around him, Pythagoras stood ready to perform his Celestial Magic ceremony on the mummy. He had religiously committed to guide the dead priest in his last journey through the after world. Incense burned heavily from all the corners of the Chamber and pervaded the air with holy fragrance.

"In the name of the great *Ra,* and by the power bestowed upon me, I shall guide you, brother Uah-hotep, in your final journey!" Pythagoras started with the sacred ritual for the resurrection of the deceased into the netherworld.

"The Ka, this spiritual vital force in you, represented by your two upraised arms, and your soul *Ba*, embodied by your human-headed bird, are about to separate now. Anubis, the guardian of death, expects you at the gate. You will meet him there and he will guide you with love. This is his name and, by the knowledge of the magical words, you will call upon him to unlock the entry for you and be your guide thereafter. Know that you will be the protégé of the goddess Isis from the very beginning, and all along your journey."

There was a long silence in which all there present envisioned the start of the journey of Uah-hotep.

"On the western mountains," Pythagoras intoned with a deep voice. "There, where the sun disappears from the sky, stands the gate to the world beyond. You are about to reach it, Uah-hotep," he guided the soul with gentle authority, his voice confident and his faith strong. "Anubis lingers in wait for you, my brother. Do you see him? Call out his name! Fear him not!" He commanded in encouragement. "Go ahead, Uah-hotep, cross the threshold to the Dark River in the *Gallery of the Night*. Sail with him, brother, sail on his boat!"

Pythagoras paused with a frown of wariness. He suddenly sensed a danger. The priests around him waited in prayers.

"Beware Uah-hotep!" He warned loudly. "You are crossing the gloomy Kingdom of Seth; the greatest enemy of Osiris! Move on! Move through! Fear not the evil ones; these gigantic baboons who will try to sink your boat to impede you from sailing farther!"

He took a deep breath. Prayers intensified around him in the hall.

"Uah-hotep!" He called out. "You must arm yourself with the will and the power to overcome these enemies of Osiris. Beware the Serpent Apophis who will attempt to block your way towards the free realm!" He warned the soul; his vision clear on the journey of the after-death.

And then...

"Yes, you made it!" He exclaimed in glee. "You have survived! But it's not over... March now towards the Stairs of Justice."

Long minutes elapsed and, in the Funeral Chamber, only the hum of prayers reigned.

Pythagoras raised his voice in sudden thrill, "You are there now! Go! Climb the Stairs of Justice ahead of you and behold the *gods of creation*. They are all present there, welcoming your arrival in the *Hall of Justice*.

"Brace yourself, against the imminent trials of the seven gates of the House of Osiris, Uah-hotep, there in the Field of Reeds. Should you succeed to cross them, behold the trials of the ten pillars that should lead you to the *Final Hall of Judgment*! Good luck brother..."

> *Uah-hotep knelt to kiss the threshold at the Hall of Justice. He stepped in with great reverence. The first part of his trial began with him reciting the 'negative confessions'[24]. Three beings, or three gods, guarded each of the seven gates. Uah-hotep confided on each one of them in turn. He called them by their names to confirm his knowledge of each one, and prove that he had nothing to fear.*
>
> *Every guard assumed the responsibility of a particular sin. There, judged and assessed by each of these beings, Uah-hotep denied having committed any evil action or sin._Only then, did the gates open their access for him, one after the other. He proceeded his way inside until he halted in front of the ten pillars, each of which was in the care of a god and a doorkeeper. Again, he addressed them in turn with confidence, and called them by name. He proclaimed his innocence of any evil deed, affirmed his purity of any violation and dirt, and confirmed his accomplishment of all the rites of purification.*
>
> *"Uah-hotep!" he heard the voice of Pythagoras, his sacred guide, calling him from Earth.*

Pythagoras called the soul of the priest again, "Uah-hotep, hear me out! Anubis takes you

---

[24] The Ten Commandments of Moses recorded in the Hebrew Old Testament do actually exist in the Negative Confessions mentioned in the Egyptian Book of the Dead and found in the Papyrus of Ani, 19th Dynasty sometimes around 1250 BCE. In addition, the Ten Commandments could be traced way back to Hammourabi and his Code, sometimes around the 18th century BCE.

now by the hand. Go with him, and proceed inside the *Final Hall of Judgment*. Osiris sits on his throne. Behold him anxious for your final judgment. Be ready to break through the second part of your trial. Be ready now, brother, to face your fate!

"Your heart will be, at any moment now, weighed against the Feather of Truth of the goddess Maat. Behold her, Uah-hotep, as she stands for justice, harmony and balance. Thoth, the Ibis-Headed god, will record the result while Anubis will carry out the process with careful consideration. Beware the monster Ammut as he keeps also close watch. If your heart shows wrongness, the devil Ammut will devour it. So be careful Uah-hotep! I wish for your good deeds in life to save you now, and help your way out of the *Circle of Necessity*."

This time, the silence that downed on the Funeral Chamber bore the heavy tension and anxiety of the priests for the soul of their brother, and the result of the judgment.

"Rightly! He was judged rightly!" Pythagoras proclaimed in glee. "He made it!"

The sound of general relief gushed out softly along with the vibrations of the happy hearts of all the fraternity there present.

Pythagoras closed his physical senses and opened the eyes of his soul to witness what dwelt above.

> *Uah-hotep pursued his journey to the Lotus Lake for his eternal purification. In the Fields of Yalu, the blessed, the sanctified soul, gained its everlasting life in paradise. From now onward, the soul of Uah-hotep would continue its life working along the Celestial Nile.*

"Very well done, Uah-hotep, Congratulations!" Pythagoras praised him on behalf of all the priests there present. "This is indeed a great achievement!"

In the Chamber, a general smile brightened all faces, but Pythagoras had still a major recommendation to convey. "Now, *Uah-hotep,* you must unite your spirit and vital force, the Ka, with your soul, the Ba, in order to form the Akh. This will be your fully resurrected and glorified form; your Spirit of Resurrection; the Akh symbolized by the crested god Ibis!"

Time on earth seemed to freeze for a while...

Then, in a high tone that resonated in the Chamber, Pythagoras commended, "Finish your journey now, Uah-hotep. Unify your mortal yet resurrected being with the Immortal Spirit, and by such, identify it with Ra, the Supreme Being!"

The stillness that followed was soon broken by a soft voice whispering, in a breeze, a spiritual melody.

> *"I was yesterday. I am today. And I know tomorrow. I am the beginning and I am the end... I am the master of my soul. I am Ra and the Supreme Being is in me. He embraces me deep inside his bosom. He is myself!"*

The beautified soul proclaimed as its final realization into the abode of Absolute Truth.

As above, so below...

Down on Earth, well equipped with the four degrees of Initiation, Pythagoras had certainly mastered his assignment. To succeed, he had allocated his long practice of all the four forms of Magic; the Natural, the Astral, the Cosmic and the Celestial. One more thing remained to end the sacred ritual of this spiritual resurrection of Uah-hotep's soul. With great eloquence, he spelled out the final incantation as instructed by the Great Magicians of the Temple:

"It is true, Osiris lives,
It is also true, the dead live,
Resurrect yourself,
You have your soul,
You, the reanimated one...
Come, oh god,
Isis is talking to you."

At this stage, the Ceremonial Magic ended. The priests placed the mummy inside a sarcophagus of stone. They added the four Canopic jars, and all the other belongings of the deceased to be used in his life beyond. They then carried the coffin out and buried it in the Grave Chamber.

There, Pythagoras lingered alone with his thoughts for a while.

His vital force had allowed him to see and commune with the gods. However, he recognized that he had succeeded because of the power of his consciousness, and his acting from the mental sphere. A *Magician*, yes indeed, he admitted, yet his journey to a higher degree did not end here. In the Egyptian system of Initiation, there remained in fact one more degree; the last one that would reveal the Sublime Truth.

Pythagoras intended to achieve it!

* * *

Pythagoras spent most of his time meditating and reflecting alone. Silence escorted most of his next years through this **4th level** of Initiation. Yet, he knew he was not totally alone since the Magicians and the Priests of the Temple surveyed him closely. He felt their vibrations around him at all times. In his many moments of qualm, pain and wonder, they would come closer to whisper words of encouragement in his ears, "Prevail... Be patient... Persevere!"

However, in his quest for inner truth, Pythagoras began to doubt his powers ever more, almost to the point of mislaying them. Nightmares tortured his sleep. In fact, to dig into his depth resulted in hardship. Truth seemed to be a reality higher than he had expected, and its essence much more important than all his previous long years of studies.

"What is Truth?" He would often shout in despair and his anguish would resonate in the cell where he resided like a hermit.

The sages believed that man could not know and obtain *Truth* unless it became an essential part of his being. Pythagoras acknowledged that his connection to the Truth did not lay on what he had learned, but rather on what he would become.

In his quest, he persisted on that concept to lead him. His adamant will and strong faith contributed to his finding of the right way. He steadily experienced the reality of his inner realm, and endorsed a complete detachment from the world of senses. In consequence, Truth itself, like the early sunrays surfacing the face of the Earth, initiated a long journey into his own being.

One day, walking with Sonchis in the Great hall of the Temple of Osiris, Pythagoras expressed his frustration, "When will Truth be entirely revealed to me? Will I ever come to know it?"

In response, Sonchis stopped and pointed at a Lotus drawn on the side wall. With his usual poise, he said, "Look well at the lotus, Pythagoras, and meditate." He gave him some time of silence then uttered, "Truth can not be given just to anyone. We usually find it in ourselves, or we simply don't find it at all! We cannot make *you* see it. No one can! Actually, you cannot be taught how to perceive its sublime power, for it is, in fact, inside you. Therefore, my brother, you alone shall find it when you are able to recognize its radiance within yourself."

Pythagoras stared at him pensively then turned to scrutinize the Lotus again.

167

What connects the Lotus to my goal at the moment? Where is the lead to my ultimate aim?

As if reading his thoughts, Sonchis explained, "The Lotus grows inside water for a long time before it blooms out on the surface. This is the reality, I must say, of the great hidden matters. Don't rush the blossoming of Truth, Pythagoras. It will certainly happen when the proper time comes."

"The Lotus is like you, Pythagoras. It contains the four elements. Remember! The four tests you undertook to enter the occult world have no other meaning than that of your desires, your passions, your doubts and your fears. Those four barriers are still holding you back from becoming what you are in reality," Sonchis ended with finality.

Pythagoras remained silent. He understood.

And yet!

Another long year went by. With valor and determination, Pythagoras persisted against the extensive tensions that weighed on him. He managed to conquer the illusions that invaded his inner realm. Ultimately, the time came in which the Hierophant decided that Pythagoras radiated an energy powerful enough. It ascertained his readiness. He was indeed all set to penetrate the last degree of Initiation and, as such, receive the ultimate reality.

The Hierophant summoned him to the Great Hall. "You have earned the right to adhere to the group of Initiates, my son, because you have felt Truth inside a pure heart; a heart loving of the Truth more than any. Congratulations!"

Pythagoras smiled widely, his heart elated.

"However," Sonchis prompted. "Bear in mind that no one has ever crossed the threshold of Osiris without passing by Death and Resurrection," his even tone alleviated the extent of the warning.

The words lingered in his mind that night as he stretched out to sleep under the stars.

The next day at sunset, Pythagoras and Sonchis stood admiring the Sphinx. They commented on how such a gigantic monument appeared to direct its looks up towards the *Constellation of the Lion.*

"The Sphinx is the entrance to the final Initiation," Sonchis explained. "It is *Horus in the Horizon.* Know this, Pythagoras: It represents the initial state of man. It informs us about the principal of evolution, and about the incarnated secrets of the complete theology."

"The Sphinx is the fundamental figure - the symbol - that describes justly the four elements. The hoofs of the Ox are the Earth element; it is the Beginning thus, the *Silence.* The upper body of the Lion is the Water element which is the Vital force thus, the *Daring.* The wings of the Eagle are the Air element; it is the Key to the mind, so eventually, the *Knowledge.* And, finally, the face of Man is the Fire element which is the Unity, therefore the *Will,* the will to become what humans are in reality."

At these words, the access to the final Initiation of Pythagoras heralded as if by a deed of magic. Under the head of the Sphinx, and in between its arms, the door unlocked to welcome him and his Mentor inside.

Torches on one side of the wall illuminated their way along the lengthy corridor. They reached the end halting in front of an enigmatic sculpture. Its right hand pointed upwards, and the left downwards.

"What do you think is the conundrum of that statue, Pythagoras?" the Hierophant asked in a serious tone.

Difficult as it came to be, Pythagoras focused on that enigma for a long moment. Deepened in his reflection, the *Magician* within Pythagoras grabbed a certain thread to an answer. Pythagoras dwelled on it for a moment. He hesitated.

He turned to probe the eyes of Sonchis for a clue then examined the statue again. He followed the direction of the right hand and spelled out, "Above..." He paused, shrunk his eyes on a thought, looked at the left hand and uttered, "Below..."

"As above... so is below...," he murmured what he deemed to be the answer.

A fearsome silence loitered.

As above so is below... Pythagoras repeated inwardly then veered to face his Master.

Sonchis nodded with a smile and a glint of satisfaction. Without further explanation, he turned on his heels, span to the left and disappeared through an opening in the wall. Pythagoras followed behind him.

A serpentine lane took them under the Sphinx and all the way under the Great Pyramid of Khufu. They continued through some passageways that led them to an enormous hall walled by huge granite blocks.

"The Chamber of the King," Sonchis explained to him in a whisper.

There, inside the heart of the Pyramid, three priests, with bright torches in their hands, stood in wait at the three sides of a sarcophagus. Their ceremonial white robes and purple tunics distinguished them to be second in roles after Sonchis. Distinctive coronets crowned their heads; each one different than the other. One represented the Moon, with a globe of two horns. The other embodied the Rising Sun, with the eye of *Ra*. The third, with a serpent, symbolized the Vital Energy.

Sonchis and Pythagoras joined them at the head-side of the sarcophagus. The mystical fragrance of incense permeated all over.

"No one can ever escape death!" Sonchis intoned and the fatalistic words resonated with the same dramatic sound as their full meaning. "Yet, every spirit is destined for resurrection!" He affirmed in faith then turned to address Pythagoras with

170

solemnity. "Here is the *Hat-Ka*, the *House of Spirit*. You will sleep inside this sarcophagus, Pythagoras, for three days and three nights until the light of the resurrected god Osiris wakes you up."

Without hesitation, Pythagoras stretched down inside the coffin and crossed his arms over his chest. In turn, the priests approached him to chant some holy lyrics and bless him with a sacred gesture of the hands. At that, they walked out.

Sonchis muttered some indistinct words of prayers over Pythagoras. Their eyes hooked for an undetermined moment then, with a last look of affection and admiration, Sonchis disappeared from his sight.

In complete darkness, the cold breeze of the Chamber initiated its pitiless sting on his body. His heartbeat pounded harder by the second. He perceived the sound of his heart intensifying before it slowed down dramatically. Numbness sneaked through his skin to reach his muscles and beyond.

Cold waned...

Sounds faded...

The aroma of the incense disappeared...

Darkness prevailed...

His last mindful apprehension of the physical world was that he was losing touch with reality. A powerful sense of lightness lifted him. He knew then that the ethereal part of his being had initiated his ascension through the gateways of eternity.

His Ka so to speak, his spirit, flew like a Phoenix throughout the spiritual spheres of space and time. He recognized the pulsations of life all around him, and acknowledged the eternal law of evolution. Shapes and numbers materialized, and his past lives unveiled their stories.

Pythagoras continued his ethereal journey through the deep mystical space without any awareness of earthly time.

171

Something unfathomable shone brightly from afar. He decided to approach it. He realized that, in fact, the bright form headed in his direction as if to meet with him half-way. 'The light of Osiris!' he anticipated in elation.

Edging closer, the light revealed its form –a star; a five-pointed star! Amazed, Pythagoras slowed down for an instant, yet the star pursued its fast approach. In a phenomenal spark, Pythagoras and the star collided and merged at once in one being. A great magnetic light diffused in the realm of darkness.

In ecstasy, Pythagoras understood that he had finally become what he was in reality: the Microcosm of the Macrocosm; the god in the heart of God.

The vision waned...

A heavy weight pressed on his body. Pythagoras felt his limbs once again; back in his earthly body. He opened his eyes with reluctance. The anxious faces of the Sonchis and the Priests gradually appeared staring down at him.

Dazed, he heeded their murmurs welcoming him back from his spiritual journey. Someone approached a goblet to his mouth for him to drink. The liquid reanimated his membranes and cleared the fog off his mind.

He rose up from his tomb.

"Here you are now resurrected!" Sonchis greeted him with patent joy. "You have experienced the Great Mystery of all time, Pythagoras. Three days and three nights! You have defeated death, and achieved actual immortality!"

Serene and silent, Pythagoras looked resolutely at him with the eyes of the wise.

"Come now! Let us celebrate the glory of the Initiates." Sonchis exclaimed. "You have become one of us; A reborn!"

172

His steps still unsteady, Pythagoras accompanied them to the south entrance of the Grand Gallery. They entered that hall which Egyptian Astrologers and Magicians have used at all times to observe the starry sky.

They waited for the very first sunray.

At that precise moment in which the beam of the Rising Sun, the Supreme Being Ra, struck the face of Pythagoras, the Hierophant turned to him.

"Believe now, Pythagoras, that *He* is in *You* and *You* are in *Him*. Believe that you are everything that is, everything that was, and everything that will be," Sonchis initiated him. "Pythagoras, you have become what you are!"

.5.

The Vision of the Master

Pythagoras succeeded his Initiation in Egypt as very few seekers of Truth could have done; the higher degree in the Great Pyramid of Khufu being the pinnacle. Such a major exploit changed his life for it led him to experience death and then resurrection within the Rising Sun; the Supreme Being *Ra*. After his accomplishment, he returned to the sanctuary of Memphis to assume his new position and responsibilities as the High Priest of Osiris.

Adamant to protect its great mysteries, Egypt has always strived to conceal their occult doctrine of Truth. Eventually, the great mysteries incited the curiosity and jealousy of other nations. These feelings spanned into hatred and greed. As history recorded, Cambyses II, the son and successor of Cyrus II, the Great king of Persia, attacked Egypt in the year 525 BCE.

His large and powerful army of ferocious Persian soldiers invaded the land of Ham. They burned down the religious cities. They destroyed the temples of Amon-Ra in Memphis and the shrines of Thebes. In an unbelievable phenomenon, the pyramids withstood all attempts of destruction. They survived steadfast and intact, as if protected by an unseen supremacy of occult power! Conversely, Pharaoh Psammetichus III and his

174

court did not escape their horrible fate, nor did the important Egyptian families. Forced out of their castles and temples, they underwent shame and humiliation. The Persians chained them and hauled them between the ruins, then beheaded them in public. History marked, in time, the political and religious execution of the powers of Egypt!

Pythagoras, aged forty-five by then, saw the end of his fifteen peaceful and fruitful years in Egypt. His continuous learning of the great enigmas of life came to an abrupt and painful halt. Imprisoned by the Persians, along with the other priests of Osiris, he was forced to leave the Temple of Memphis and the Egyptian land behind.

A life of exile into Babylon became his doom.

* * *

At midday, two weeks after setting out to sea, the Persian ship of prisoners reached the city of Babylon that Cyrus II ruled, approximately, since 539 BCE. A province of the great Persian Empire at the time, Babylon expanded inside massive walls. They exhibited colorful mosaic illustrations of animals, heroes and gods. Attractive, yet peculiar, various statues of winged gods loomed over the vastly populated city. The Ishtar Gate constituted the main entrance to the city. It guarded the Ziggurat that comprised a tower of steps crowned by the Temple of the god Marduk.

The Persian guards dragged Pythagoras and the other prisoners through the city and past beautiful castles, impressive palaces and grand platforms. In spite of his precarious situation, he could not avoid gawking in awe at the beauty around him, in particular at its suspended gardens. They soon reached their confinement in the Temples of the goddess Ishtar and the god Bel. These sanctuaries represented the Babylonian versions of the notorious Phoenician female and male divinities, Arstate and Baal (Adonis).

175

In the ancient tongues, Babylon[25], or Babel, *Bab-El*, meant *the Door of El*. Many races of different languages, cults and religions considered it a holy capital and sought it for their dwellings. They co-existed peacefully together, and created forcefully a lively culture of controversial human thoughts.

At the time, two major religions had survived the Persian Religious influence in Babylon brought by the Zoroastrian Magi, whose Persian adepts worshiped their alleged savior Zoroaster. In consequence, a large number of residents prevailed in their practices. The older form of religion that endured was that of the Chaldean Kabalists, followed by the religious doctrine of the Hindu Gymnosophists, better known as the naked wise men.

To Pythagoras, a seeker of Truth by birth, nature and fate, new horizons for more knowledge broadened widely. Although a religious prisoner in exile, he favored some liberty of movement due to his honorable stature as a High Priest of Osiris. He grabbed this opportunity with both hands, and proceeded in studying the various doctrines there present, and their secrets. As always, he strove to acquire more and more comprehension and enlightenment. He started his new journey of

---

[25] The Persians proclaimed the founding of Babylon to Semiramis, the legendary beautiful Queen warrior. Some historians accredited it to the Akkadians (2350-2150 BCE). Others claimed it to the Kushites. However, many believe that Hammourabi (Ammour-abi), the *Father of the Amorites,* founded Babylon or Babel around the 18th century BCE. The Amorites were Canaanite nomads from the northern-western mountainous regions of the Land of Canaan. Some claimed them to be of European origin. Yet, there is no truth in that. Ancient Egyptians had described them as people of great stature like the Enochians (the sons of Anak the Canaanite) with fair skins, light hair, blue eyes, curved or hooked noses, and pointed beards. It is most likely that the Amorites, of Canaanite origin, had interlinked socially and physically, with the neighboring Indo-European or Caucasian tribes.

knowledge with the Chaldeans from whom he would learn the Kabbalah for many consecutive months.

Savants and magi, the Chaldeans dressed up in particular attire. A black cloak covered a three-layered white and blue linen robe that displayed quadrangle patches of odd patterns. Known by their long curly manes and beards, they wore flat linen turbans. That particular headwear carried always a golden sign with the name of their Kabalistic Mystery God *Iao,* or *Yaho.*

Truth be told, the Babylonian Chaldeans had adopted their own concept of the Kabbalah, originally introduced by the Phoenician spiritual Enochian tribe, some time ago. From his education in Gebel and Memphis, Pythagoras knew that Enoch-Hermes-Tautus had initially acquired and accepted that occult spirituality from Angels on Mount Hermon in Phoenicia. Although Pythagoras deemed these Angels to be Higher Selves, he recognized that the authentic and more spiritual form of Kabbalah had originated from Enoch-Hermes-Tautus. The latter had based the dogma of that extremely clandestine system of Initiation on the esoteric meanings of letters and numbers, thus, the Ancient Scriptures. In fact, the Kabbalah meant *to accept* in the Phoenician language.

Previously Initiated by its original source, Pythagoras had already mastered this occult art. Therefore, he was perfectly able to discern many substantial differences between the original Kabbalah and the deviated one of the Chaldeans. As a matter of fact, by adopting the Kabbalah[26], the

---

[26]   With the Chaldeans, there occurred a strong deviation of the Kabbalah from its original Phoenician source. Later on, a cast of Chaldean priests from Babylon might have carried the tradition to the Land of Canaan when they occupied it with the help of the Persians and their propaganda. They became later known as the Hebrews, the Ebraniyine, or the *Abarou el-naher,* meaning *those who crossed the river.* They changed it once again and

Chaldeans had incorporated one of the most ancient languages on Earth. They then used it for the invocation of spirits, either in the written form of the talismans, or in the spoken form of incantations.

With nothing more to learn from the Chaldeans, a year later, Pythagoras moved on into the next phase of his personal agenda; the Zoroastrians.

Zaratas, the great Magus of that sect, and probably the most notorious at the time[27], welcomed Pythagoras in his realm. The Magus, with long hair and bearded face, was dressed entirely in white linen. His robe cloaked him by the shoulders. An amber belt bundled up his double girded tunic at the waist. Even the turban, which extended all the way down his back, was of white linen. Pythagoras came to know that Zaratas always kept the fire of his god Ahuramazda ablaze in a clay container.

For more than a year, the Magus Initiated him into an enigmatic science that would enable him infinite manipulation of the occult powers of nature. As explained to him, such operation would transpire through the *incorporeal fire,* or the Astral Light, that is diffused everywhere.

One day, Pythagoras joined him inside one of the most secluded areas of Babylon. There, in the covert bosom of Nature, away from the eyes and ears of the common people, Zaratas imparted his philosophy.

"There are two causes behind the existence of the Universe, the Father and the Mother. The Father is Light. He is the god of Fire; the good god Ahuramazda. The Mother, on the other hand, is darkness and cold. She is Ahriman, the god of evil."

---

deformed it even more to fit their new culture in a new land. It then became the esoteric and symbolic interpretation of their Old Testament having the Zohar, a classical form of it, at its core.

[27] The term *Magi* is the plural form of magus. Magi were priests of ancient Persia.

Shocked by such a statement, Pythagoras enjoined swiftly. "Why is that, Zaratas? Why is the Mother evil?"

"She is not evil in the literal sense of the word. No! She should not be considered as such, Pythagoras. What I meant is the following...." He rubbed his palms together, sighed loudly, and explained, "Ahuramazda, the Father, is the Heavenly god that formed the psyche, or the soul, to implement it in humans. The Mother is the infernal goddess that produced the physical life on Earth."

Pythagoras leaped to his feet in outrage and snapped, "So what! What's wrong with the physical life on Earth?! Come now, Zaratas! I still don't get this!"

He went pacing back and forth in front of the Magus, then, came to an abrupt halt and veered to face him. "Unless...," he uttered pensively.

"Yes, Pythagoras? Go on!" The Magus incited him with a witty look.

"Well, unless you mean to imply that the psyche - the fire, or the life principle generated in the Kosmos and humanity - is standing against, or let's just simply say, rising above, the physical mortal bodies of the living."

"Correct! This is the essence of all things. The metaphysical principles in the whole universe consist of both Heaven and Hell, or Earth... male and female, and so forth."

Pythagoras engrossed in his private deliberation on what he had just heard.

Zaratas, also an Astrologer, instructed him that day on the science of the sky and its rotating planets. He elaborated on their secret numbers, and the vast influence of their magnetism and electric effects on the lives of human beings.

At that stage, Pythagoras dwelt in some doubts. He had acquired the knowledge of an identical system back in Egypt. He fathomed inwardly the clear disparities between both systems.

The following days he spent with the Magus, in the bosom of Nature, impelled him to conduct a deep assessment on the Zoroastrian Initiation. Despite his conclusion on the peculiarity of these teachings, he listened intently to what Zaratas imparted.

"No evil matter shall ever destroy, or defile, the wisdom you acquired during the many years of your Initiation, nor shall they affect the purity of your inborn psyche," his commanding voice claimed high and loud, his eyes intense with a bizarre luminosity. "However, you should purify yourself from the pollution of your previous life. I shall teach you how!"

"When?"

Unconcerned by the fretfulness of Pythagoras, he stood up slowly. He took his time to arrange his turban, and fixed up his tunic. Only then, he edged closer to square him sharply in the eyes.

"Tonight!" he announced then chuckled.

Pythagoras released his breath.

That same night, Zaratas subjected Pythagoras to the service of Initiation of his dogma.

A dozen drummers performed their deistic soft rhythms while the Magus smashed a variety of magical herbs and plants. He mixed them together and blended them. He then placed the green mixture in a terracotta pot on low fire. Soon, a powerful aroma wafted around to stimulate the senses. Pythagoras deemed the herbal occult powers to be of foremost furtherance. Thus, he was not surprised when the mixture was used on him throughout the rite of purification.

The ceremony ended with Zaratas baptizing him in the Euphrates River.

A few months later, still a prisoner in Babylon, Pythagoras met with a Saddhu of India, a meeting he was looking forward to. His only attire consisted of a strange leather necklace, and a long white beard that contrasted with his brown face. In fact, the Saddhu, who strongly believed that the sky was enough to clothe him, appeared completely naked.

Pythagoras spent two years with the odd Saddhu learning the great discipline of Yoga. This sacred science never included spirits or planets, but only Man; the Microcosm of the Macrocosm.

"Your body, Pythagoras, is composed of seven Chakras. The sacred science of Yoga considers them the seven centers of Energy," the Saddhu explained. "Your mission is to awaken within you the Astral Light that the Ancients described as the Serpent of Fire; Kundalini! It is the Akasa of immortality and wisdom. You must lift it up along the Soushoumnâ, your spinal cord, till you reach the blossom of your Brahmarandra, your God-Head Lotus. Only at that stage, will you come to merge with the Total Consciousness," the Gymnosophist instructed him.

Yoga meant also Union. In some ways, it closely connected to the Esoteric Physiology; that sacred and highest form of Initiation Pythagoras had previously acquired in Egypt. Very few people had ever been accepted inside the Egyptian sacred shrines; Pythagoras being one of them.

Union, after all, remained what every Initiate of the ancient world longed to accomplish during his spiritual life. In essence, what all Initiates sought and strove for was a Union of their three dimensions, a Union with the world around them, and ultimately, a Union with the Essence of life.

Pythagoras had indeed reached such a state back in the Great Pyramid of Khufu, when, with the use of his will, he had entered eternity and gone into the bosom of the Source. That endeavor had allowed him to fly out of his material body and return at any desired time, attaining immortality by such!

He recalled the powerful words of the Priests of Memphis.

The science of numbers and the control of the will are the keys to the Real Magic that opens the gates of the universe.

Time elapsed...

Five years into his captivity, Pythagoras reached a profound insight. He ultimately concluded that all religions he had come to know by then sprang out of one single truth; the Enochian-Hermetist Truth, that which was immemorial in time! The Truth had been certainly transformed into many religions and transported to many nations around the world. Such a phenomenon occurred according to the degree of intelligence of those groups of people, and their social structures.

Obviously, very few nations had preserved its original form. Most of them had tolerated some minor or major deviations to occur along the process. In addition, Truth splintered in two sections.

The first was the exoteric, or the outside form of religion. It served the common people that conveyed it from a generation to another.

The second section was the esoteric, or the inside form of religion, ministered to the Initiates who then relayed it only to elite after elite.

There existed no doubt whatsoever on where Pythagoras stood from these two sections. Certainly a true Initiate, he, among the very few, had received the Truth from its original Phoenician-Egyptian source. He had acquired the Key to the Occult Science which was, without question, the synthesis of all doctrines. He had studied the past, understood the present and envisioned the future.

He had also witnessed the boundless human manipulation of the *divine right doctrine* by some rulers of nations; the alleged King-Priests. And along with the genesis of man, he had also

182

pondered over the history of many adjacent nations. Therefore, eager to convey the Truth in its genuine form, he longed for substantial changes, not only for the sake of those subdued by socio-religious tyranny, but for the sake of all men as well. In fact, he strongly aspired to freeing mankind from all the chains that impeded its evolution.

Time to decide!

Time to devise!

Yet, his incarceration hindered any possible initiative by him. He needed his freedom back at all cost. The time had come for him to go back to Greece. The personal mission he had just engaged himself in, by his own free will and choice, should be carried to accomplishment, whatever the cost!

His lovely mother Parthenis had told him once about the Prophecy of the Oracle of Delphi, and the similar prediction revealed by the Priests of Adonis. The certainty of his fate dawned on him clearly; a fate written beyond the memory of the manifested world, there where time had no limitation, and there where the past, the present, and the future strongly intermingled within one omnipresent frame of existence!

The Akashic memory had revealed to Pythia, the Medium-Priestess of the Temple, that he would be *a great man for mankind, a kind of a Savior.* Pythagoras started to believe it, now that he had finally come to realize the real significance of his life. *Nothing happens by coincidence!* He concluded with certainty.

The time has come for me to dash ahead with my mission! He decided more determined than ever.

In order for him to leave Babylon, and thus regain his freedom, Pythagoras needed to submit to the ruler of Babylon a written order from the King of Persia. He strove in vain for any means of achieving this, when, suddenly one day, be it by chance, or perhaps by divine will, he met a man from Samos; an old friend of his deceased father Mnesarchus.

That Samian, by the name of Democedes, dwelt closely to the King – being his personal physician. He felt compelled to help the son of his friend in all the ways he could, and requesting his liberation from the King was one of them.

And so it came to be, a few days later, that the King of Persia signed a royal decree fast dispatched to the ruler of Babylon for the immediate discharge of Pythagoras. Believing that the winds had finally changed their courses to ally with his mission at hand, Pythagoras rejoiced greatly in the news.

* * *

Never has Pythagoras felt as cheerful as on the day he sailed to his freedom on the ship that took him to Samos. Freedom, during those days, beheld simple meanings to him. It carried the smell of the sea, and the taste of salty breeze. He could see it in the unruly waves that hit the ship, and in the sunset of the infinite horizon. He sensed it in the fresh air he breathed, and in the meager meals he shared with the sailors on board. After he had come to endure the boundaries of captivity, he beheld minor details as significant blessings.

The ship finally edged closer to Samos. Anticipation made him restless. Only then, did he realize the depth of his nostalgia for his second home. Almost thirty years had passed since he had departed from Samos. That was definitely a long time!

He was turning fifty-one by then, and it was around the year 520 BCE.

The moment he disembarked in the island, Pythagoras faced a horrible disaster that killed his joy. Samos lay under the ashes of war. Downhearted, he walked the deplorable streets of his childhood. His recent years of confinement had isolated him from all occurrences beyond the walls of Babylon. On board, a sailor had informed him, vaguely though, that Oroetus, the Persian lieutenant and governor of Lydia, had launched since 547 BCE a war to expand the Achaemenid Empire. To face the reality of that aftermath dawned on Pythagoras painfully.

Pythagoras halted at the white marble fountain of the plaza to drink and refresh himself. He splashed water on his face several times in an attempt to cool his angst down. He then turned to observe the desolation around him. Deeply saddened, he slouched on the perimeter of the fountain.

"Shocked my son?" the quaky voice impelled him to turn around. A man, wrinkled by age, his back hunched, watched him with doleful eyes.

"What happened?" Pythagoras murmured.

"The war."

"Tell me about it," he implored him in a tearful tone. "Please!"

The old man shrunk his small eyes in wonder. "You are not from here," he concluded with insight.

"I am... was..." Pythagoras blurted out. "I was away." The simple words ensued heavy with his feeling of guilt.

The old man seemed to understand. He slowly closed the distance and sat at his side, yet did not speak for a while. Pythagoras waited patiently.

"It's a long story," the old man warned him.

"I'm listening."

The ancient man nodded then, his eyes to the horizon, he related, "Around 540-535, three brothers executed a rebellion against our oligarchy. Their names were Polycrates, Pantagnostus and Syloson. Many of our citizens supported them enormously. They captured the citadel of the city. Not so long after, Polycrates alienated his own brothers. He ordered the execution of his eldest,

Pantagnostus, and sent Syloson, his youngest into exile in Persia."

He went motionless in his thoughts... or was it his breath that he tried to catch? Pythagoras wondered about his age, and name.

"Polycrates was a popular man," the old man pursued the story. "He controlled Samos without changing the constitution. He created a new government and imposed his autocracy on its members, and on society. Of course, the old aristocracy opposed them. Some of them fled the island. The others were expelled."

"An oppressive ruler...," Pythagoras commented in a murmur.

"Yes, but Samos reached the height of its prosperity under his reign. He generated many remarkable public works that enhanced our city. Our school of sculptors attained a grand reputation, so did our institutions of metal-workers and engineers. Our people opened up trade with the Black Sea and Egypt. We were probably the first Greeks to reach the Straits of Gibraltar!"

A smile drew on his face. His eyes sparkled with pride. He stared then at Pythagoras expecting a reaction of some kind.

"It must have been days of glory for Samos," Pythagoras remarked with a smile.

"Oh yes! Polycrates even created a huge and powerful navy that, not only protected our city from all attacks, but also reigned superior in the Aegean waters!"

Impressed, Pythagoras advanced, more as a question than a statement, "It must have been quite costly on the city though."

"Not really. Polycrates secured the financial contribution of the Egyptian Pharaoh Amasis. This one deemed him a potentially useful ally against Persia."

"What happened next?"

"Well, Polycrates soon changed sides," the old man declared with a frown. "He joined the Persian King Cambyses II who invaded Egypt in 525 BCE. Three years later, a civil war broke out in the Persian Empire. Gaumâta, a Persian usurper, revolted against his King Cambyses in 522 BCE. Cambyses died before the open war began."

"Thus, Polycrates lost a strong ally with the death of Cambyses," Pythagoras deducted out loud.

The old man nodded. "He did in fact! During the summer of that same year, he was invited to Sardes by Oroetus, the Persian governor of Lydia. Oroetus was long appointed by Cyrus II, the Great king of Persia and father of Cambyses II. What Polycrates failed to see was that Oroetus coveted the Samian navy for himself. He wanted to strengthen his position during the chaos that had ensued at the death of Cambyses II. Oroetus tempted Polycrates with a lot of money that Polycrates deemed useful for him to control all of Greece. All that Oroetus requested in exchange was for Polycrates to save him from the Persian King who plotted his death."

"I assume that Polycrates fell in the trap of his own ambition," Pythagoras issued more to himself.

The old man gazed at him in a moment of silent surprise. "You can say so, yes," he admitted. "It was certainly a great offer of money and power," he added as if excusing the mistake of his past ruler.

"Too much ambition could be dangerous," Pythagoras commented firmly to reject the argument of the old man.

The ancient man rendered a deep sigh of fatality. "You're right, son. Your wisdom is praiseworthy."

"What happened next?"

"His ambition, as you rightly stated, cost him his life. Oroetus had him killed and crucified in

Sardes," he announced in a sad tone, and bowed his head for a while, engrossed in his own grief.

"Samos…," Pythagoras muttered at realizing the cost that the city must have paid because of the ambition and unawareness of its ruler.

"Yes… Samos paid a heavy price," the old man confirmed with tears in his eyes. "With Polycrates dead[28], Oroetus took control of Samos. The blow ensued very harsh on us. The Persian Achaemenid Empire had already expanded west towards Greece and the Aegean Sea. Their army stormed in on our beautiful island, destroyed it, conquered it and partially depopulated it."

By now, tears streamed down the face of the ancient man who had apparently undergone a lot of disappointment and pain. Pythagoras respected his grieving moments. He looked around the desolated plaza that he remembered full of life and activities. He recalled his years of schooling here.

"What happened to our temples and schools?"

"Most of them were destroyed or had their doors sealed, my son. A major damage, it is, since all our priests, scientists and poets ran away!"

"Oh, they escaped the tyranny of the Persian Empire, of course! A true cultural disaster!" Pythagoras exclaimed with frustration and discontentment. He worried then that the inherent tension caused by the Persian invasion would be an impediment to his mission. However, his determination to prevail overcame his concern.

---

[28] Historians believe that Pythagoras left Samos to Egypt and later to southern Italy because he refused the tyranny of Polycrates and his government. This is not historically correct. First of all, when Pythagoras left Samos the first time to go to Phoenicia and Egypt, Polycrates was not yet in power in Samos. Second, when he returned in 520 BCE, after almost thirty years, Polycrates had been killed two years earlier.

"You are aware, aren't you, that Darius I seized power in Persia?" The ancient man broke the silence. Without waiting for an answer, he continued, "He did, yes! He fought a civil war against Gaumâta and killed him. As such, he ended the chaos in the Persian Empire. He restored order, not only in Persia, but also everywhere the Empire extended. He succeeded in reorganizing the Achaemenid Empire. Oroetus was executed in Samos, and another Persian governor ruled us... for a while though, because Darius the Great needed a loyal Greek to preside over Samos."

"It happened that Syloson, the youngest brother of Polycrates, had met Darius in Egypt while he was a member of the guard of Cambyses. When Polycrates perished at the hand of Oroetus, Syloson asked Darius to help him recover Samos, his native land. Thus, when Darius became the King of Persia, Syloson hurried to the royal palace of Susa and got appointed ruler of Samos."

The old man turned to drink water from the fountain. Pythagoras watched his slow movements for a while then looked afar, his mind analyzing the war tales.

"You have changed, Pythagoras," the quivery voice of the old man rendered with emotion.

Pythagoras veered to him in bewilderment.

The old man smiled. "We thought you were dead."

"You know me..." the statement was more of a question.

"Your father was a good man, Pythagoras. A very good man indeed," the old man intoned with tears in his eyes. "I miss him. Samos misses him!"

Pythagoras swallowed the sudden tension that grabbed his throat at the mention of his father.

The ancient man sighed loudly. "I, among few, have survived times and illness, Pythagoras. I have recognized you for having known you in your youth."

The astonishment rendered Pythagoras speechless, so did the patent affection of the old man...

During the days that followed, Pythagoras made it a point to socialize with the citizens. Polite and courteous in manners and words, like the elderly remembered him, he gained the interest of most. His radiant serenity and wisdom impressed them. In fact, his inner glow and calm authority seemed to distinguish him as a man of divine inspiration; a holy man, almost an angel! That impression of him kept Samos forever bewildered.

As for Pythagoras, his stay resulted interesting, both to him and to the citizens. The elders decided to summon him to speak in public about his vastly acquired knowledge. Feeling honored by the noble request, he agreed, eager to guide and instruct the Samians. He deemed the event to be a divine sign to launch his mission.

And so, he did. He adopted the Egyptian symbolic and parabolic method of teaching to address them. Unfortunately, he faced an unexpected impediment. The Samians did not understand the profundity of his words. Mostly prosperous merchants from the aristocratic classes that had previously governed the city, they rejected his way and refused to acknowledge him as a sage. If truth be told, their incapability to understand lay on their unwillingness to comply with the commitments he proposed, and especially after the devastating war that stroke their island. After their recent predicament, their mood sought what was effortless and less demanding. In consequence, his teachings encountered total disapproval!

In fact, the spiritual and mathematical disciplines Pythagoras strove to introduce to the Greek Samians did not convene with their motives. His audience decreased by the day.

Yet, he prevailed!

Despair never dwelled in his heart or mind. Determined and assertive, the son of the prophecy stood up; he who became a Master with a vision! And his vision required from him to change the world around him, and make it a better place, with no room for ignorance and war, but knowledge and wisdom instead; a place nourished by the culture of peace.

Long days ensued with him immersed in meditation. He remained as such until he came up with a plan. If talking to the mass with its diversity did not serve his purpose, then he should try to focus all his energy on one single individual, someone with enough desire to learn the great teachings he was willing to offer.

The following day, he lingered in the city square, there by the fountain. With the quiet sharpness of an eagle, he patiently observed the people at their tasks, or simply passing by.

Until finally...

He detected the particular aura of a young man of robust body. Pythagoras did not waver in approaching him. The youngster looked at him in puzzlement. His eyes conveyed recognition for he had probably seen him during one of his sermons. Pythagoras engaged him in a social conversation. Eventually, their dialogue led them to sit at the marble steps of the fountain monument.

"What do you do in life, Eratocles?"

"I am an athlete!" the young man replied with a handsome prideful smile.

"How Interesting... Are you a professional?"

"In a way, yes, I am. I am seriously engaged in all the trainings for the coming Olympiad," he informed him with patent enthusiasm typical of the youth.

"In the Olympus, isn't it? Near the great city of Athena?" With the question, Pythagoras asserted his awareness of this important event.

191

Eratocles smiled his confirmation with a spark of anticipation in his eyes.

"That's remarkable, Eratocles! I wish you all the good luck in your endeavor."

"Thanks!" the young athlete exclaimed in thrill.

"Have you ever won a game before?"

"Yes, of course, but, honestly, only a few in my home village."

Pythagoras smiled at him with affection. He felt the hope and disappointment of the young man. He envisioned his trials and frustrations.

"You are opting for the ultimate prize then."

Eratocles looked at him in surprise. "You know about the Olympiad?"

"I guess I do. The first Olympiad started in the year 776 BCE. The greatest warriors, charioteers and athletes of the world traveled from all over Greece to Olympus to participate. The massive festival featured challenges of strength and speed."

Eratocles smiled widely. His eyes shone with expectation. He proclaimed out loud, "In the name of Zeus and glory, a contest of blood and honor, the Olympiad explores the raw competitiveness and passion the contestants bring into the arena!"

Pythagoras added with eloquence, "And it leads some to their ultimate glory, and others to their ultimate downfall."

Eratocles froze in thought.

Pythagoras rushed to comment, "I believe that the most important thing in the Olympiad is not to win but to partake. It is not the triumph but the struggle..."

"Sure! This is enough to bring honor to each athlete and to Niké, the goddess of victory!" Eratocles agreed; the sparkle back in his eyes. "Do you know that the winners of the ultimate prize are bathed in olive oil, crowned with an olive wreath, or laurel leaves, and celebrated?"

Pythagoras chuckled at his enthusiasm and nodded.

Eratocles followed his dream in words. "The fame of the champions follows them all their lives. They will never have to labor another day, or pay for food again, because of the grandeur their triumph brings to their home village! Did you know that?"

"I know indeed, the way I know that losing breaks the body, mind and spirit of these men."

Eratocles went quiet, his features lost their brightness. His stout shoulders sagged slightly and his eyes glared at the distance with a mixture of gloom and frustration.

"Come on, cheer up, my son!" Pythagoras exclaimed in an encouraging tone and a friendly tap on his back. "It is always good to exercise the body."

"Yes, but... you know...," the young man seemed aching to confide in him. "I have been practicing for so long... every day...! It has been my dream... my life aim... since I was a kid!"

"I understand this, but that is not enough."

"What do you mean?"

"Let me ask you something, son. What is your aim behind all your training?" His gentle, yet firm, tone commanded the full attention of the youngster. "Isn't it because of your wish to become a perfect athlete? An all time winner?"

Eratocles nodded hopeful.

Pythagoras pursued, "And of course for the ultimate Prize... the crown of laurel!"

The young man gave him a complying nod.

"Eratocles, exercising only your body will not get you close to perfection. You should also train your mind and your spirit."

"I don't understand..." Eratocles appeared confused, but eager to know more.

"See, man is a tri-une being. If the mind and spirit are not in good shape, then, I tell you, the body could never be. The perfect man is the one who succeeds a perfect equilibrium. And in order to reach such perfection, he should first unite his mind, spirit and body in one."

"I see..." Eratocles muttered pensively, as if trying to absorb its whole meaning. "But...," he hesitated to formulate his thought.

"Yes, son?" Pythagoras encouraged him with a gentle pressure of his tone.

"How to?" he finally exclaimed loudly. "How to undertake such a path to perfection? How to reach this unity you mentioned? It seems impossible!"

"No, my friend, it is not," Pythagoras kept to his firmly gentle tone. He deemed the moment appropriate to move into the next step. "In fact, this can be done. I can tell you how."

"You mean that you know how?" Eratocles exclaimed with expectation. "How then? Tell me! I know you are different from any one I have ever met in my entire life. I have attended a couple of your sermons. You have that... wisdom and... aura. Tell me, please! Do you know the way to train my mind and my spirit?"

Although Pythagoras had waited for this opening, he abstained from answering. He just smiled and hooked his eyes on the boy's. Time stood still for a moment. Light glowed from his soul to grab the young man in his charm, and impart him with his tranquility.

"Would you teach me, please?"

Pythagoras grinned, so did his heart in victory. He had just found his first disciple and, with him, the door to reach out to others in the long run. His insight did not betray him. The mass had not listened to him, nor had he managed to bring them into the circle of enlightenment, simply because their full attention had lacked.

His mission took off!

* * *

194

The Master started teaching Eratocles on the sciences of arithmetic and geometry. He conducted his demonstrations using an abacus[29]. Eratocles proved to be a neophyte of great interest. The sophisticated studies did not rebuke him. On the contrary, they absorbed him completely. Pythagoras trained his mind in the art of numbers and Initiated him on the marvelous discipline of mental refinement. Eventually, the bonds between the Master and his first disciple tightened.

They decided to undertake a tour visit to the major cities of Greece. They therefore left Samos and sailed together. They halted at the beautiful shore of Athena where they rested for the night in a small hut by the sea.

In the morning, they meandered in the streets of the city before pursuing in their journey. Their expedition took them through most of the cities of Greece where they visited almost all of the most important temples. Some welcomed Pythagoras as a true Master. Others invited him to sit with the Hierophants, give sermons and hold meetings.

Naturally, Eratocles became the first Pythagorean. Master and scholar continued across the high and wild mountains. They traversed the evergreen forests in destination to Delphi. Albeit strenuous, their long expedition granted them many experiences to enjoy, countless moments to learn, and lots of occasions to teach others. Amazing as it was, the natural environment filled them with awe and peaceful joy; the kind that only untouched nature could grant.

They finally approached Delphi. The city was situated beneath the cliff of Mount Parnassus, and above the valley of the Plistus River. Topped by a

---

[29]   The abacus is an ancient instrument, most probably Chinese. It has a frame with wires along which beads are slid for calculation.

splendid theatre in the heart of the mountain, the Temple of Apollo appeared upon a rocky platform. Like a glorious god on his throne, the most holy place in all of Greece, and surely the most impressive of all, received the morning light of Apollo; the God-Light of the Grecian world.

Legend related that, in his youth, the god Apollo had confronted and killed Python with an arrow. Consequently, the lair of the huge serpent of Mount Parnassus became the base on which rose his Temple.

Apollo, in fact, represented an esoteric reality, where the mysteries of life - past, present and future - anchored in the hearts and minds of the true seekers. Harmony between Earth and Heaven, and between body and spirit, would reach its achievement in the lives of people, especially the Initiates among them.

Pythagoras had intended to visit that particular Temple to revitalize the energy in the hearts and minds of its priests and priestesses. He, in fact, wanted to create a substantial effect in the soul of Greece.

Inside the hall, he encountered Theoclea, also known as Themistoclea. The priestess, famous for her inborn clairvoyance who was in her late forties. He perceived the glow of her spirit. However, he soon noted that her extrasensory perception lacked the full development much needed for her admission in the profession of Priestess-Medium, or the Pythoness.

As per the legend, the god Apollo himself had bestowed the gift of prophecy on the Pythia, the priestess of the Temple. In reverence, the Grecian rules of sanctity restricted the admission into the profession of priestess to very few young virgins, chosen from the poorest Grecian families. Theoclea formed one of that rare elite. She led a life of asceticism in the abode of the sanctuary, and resided in the seclusion of an annexed room.

During her first meeting with him, Theoclea addressed him with significant respect and veneration. She referred to him as the *Great Master*. Pythagoras knew that she had probably sensed his extra-sensory energy. Her receptive attitude eventually facilitated his aim in contributing a considerable influence, not only on her life, but also on the many around her. In fact, her conscientious stance and unruffled attention encouraged his words of wisdom, as did her sensible attitude.

Pythagoras and Eratocles spent the night there. They welcomed the much needed rest. Their expedition had ensued long and strenuous.

The Sun-Apollo rose on them, the next morning, from behind Mount Parnassus. The stones of the Temple warmed and tinted with gradual golden hues. The early Sun wrapped them in beauty as it smoothly penetrated into the heart of the sanctuary.

In a white tunic, bundled up at the waist by a blue belt, Pythagoras followed, with quiet steps, the entry of the sunrays into the main hallway. He joined the priests there gathered for their morning prayer. When the ceremony ended, they exchanged greetings and assembled to converse. They discussed the improvement of their priesthood, and the rejuvenation of the divine energy in their hearts and minds. From his side, Pythagoras participated in their conversation with great interest. Before the meeting ended, he requested their permission to Initiate Theoclea into his secret teachings. He imparted them with his strong belief in her capability to assume the role of their Priestess-Medium. Impressed, the priests granted him that unique permission.

And impressed the high representatives were indeed, as the Master would take his seat at the heart of the shrine every day to teach them on the occult doctrine. He would deepen his discourses on the future of the world, and the destiny of humanity. A man of vision, and a Master of thoughts, he contributed his influence in the process. He captivated their utmost attention with his narration on his long years of Initiation into the Phoenician mysteries. With the fervor of passion, and the deference of devotion, he faithfully imparted them with his lengthy edification from Egypt. The high representatives astounded at the mysteries of Isis, and the light of Osiris. They wondered at the fact that the Egyptian Initiation could expose the spiritual potentials of man. The concept turned to a major topic of debate. They tackled the immense possibility of man to become the Microcosm of the Macrocosm. The Master ended revealing to them the Great Mysteries of the gods descending to men, and men ascending to the gods.

Powerful and meaningful, his words penetrated their minds. He, the Master of Wisdom, the holder of the charisma of a god, enveloped them in his brightness, and fueled them with the incandescent flame of his acumen.

With the daily teachings of the Master, Theoclea received the same fire whose essence imprinted deep into her heart and mind. In her transparency, she communicated her changes to him. With prudence, Pythagoras escorted her imagination to worlds beyond the restricted human walls. She, his new disciple, lifted up her own mind beyond those margins in order to soar high into the infinite sphere of spirits and gods.

From her avowals, Pythagoras knew that the vague visions of her past trances had finally unveiled their blindfolds to allow her into the sphere of the spiritual virtual reality. Despite its similarity with her visible space, she fathomed the greatest difference between these two worlds. They both existed primarily in the level of vibration; faster in the spiritual space than in the material world. The balance between them existed in her mind, both conscious and unconscious.

Perched on his throne of truth, at the heart of the Temple, Pythagoras continued on his discourses of enlightenment. With a fierce passion, he spoke against wars and destructions that humanity instigated.

"War and destruction! Those ailments and tragedies we inflict upon ourselves through time, whether recorded or not in the history of our humanity! Those deeds, my friends, are always evil chapters in our human memory, in the reminiscence of our Mother Earth, and in the eye of our beholder, our Father who art in Heaven!" Pythagoras proclaimed out loud. "But know thee! The light of salvation is at hand! It is in the will of those who perceive the Divine Inspiration." He paused and closed his eyes for the time his mind took to orbit around the Truth.

Silence and utmost attention reigned in the hall as the Assembly waited with respect and anticipation. Pythagoras opened his eyes then to roam around the hall before he rendered his next tirade.

"It is to you, honest priests, and to all the prophets and sages, that the gods reveal themselves. The Sophia of the gods shines upon those who seek wisdom, whether they are priests, civilians or common devotees. However, those who abide to materialistic interests are rendered blind to the truth! They shall always remain prisoners to the darkness of their ignorance!"

Priests and priestesses, there present, absorbed those words in quietness. They appeared reflecting on their meanings and on the enormous responsibility that lay heavily upon their shoulders. Silent with their meditation they remained all day and throughout the night that ensued.

Among all, Theoclea was the most affected, thus the most advanced in his knowledge as she received a special teaching from the Master. Her life changed upon her new perceptions. She underwent a significant transformation, patent to all. Consequently, the priests did not need to deliberate further in assigning her to the vital role of Medium-Priestess. Her prophetic voice became indeed crystal clear, as did her visions. Theoclea became the Pythia of the Temple!

The night in which they celebrated the birthday of Apollo, Pythagoras and Eratocles witnessed, inside a small room of the Temple, the preparations of Theoclea for the ceremony of the Oracle. Dressed all in white, as a symbol of her virginity, she brought the receptacle of the laurel of Apollo with reverent gestures. These sacred leaves would permit her a deep, yet conscious, sleep. She chewed them slowly, her eyes closed as if savoring a delicious meal. On the ground crevice stood a sacred brass tripod, angled into numinous mathematical degrees. Prophetic vapors emanated from that rift to engulf the chair where Theoclea settled.

Obscurity reigned in the cell. Theoclea fell into a trance that should convey her into another spiritual dimension. She started crossing the borders of the visible world. She soon mumbled her first incoherent words. Pythagoras deemed them to be addressed to the god Apollo.

...By the mouth of Python, the Serpent of Wisdom...

Eager to decode her enigmatic words, he edged closer. With a low voice, he pitched into her trance, "Where are you, Theoclea?"

The words surged from the fog, husky and uncertain, "On my way up....I managed to leave Earth...."

"Very good, Theoclea!" He encouraged her, yet his voice remained deep and stumpy. "Have you reached the invisible kingdom yet?"

He waited patiently for her reply that took endless moments.

"Very close... very close now...."

The silence of patience inhabited the cell.

"Wow!" She finally uttered in awe. Her voice became clear, more confident, heightened by excitement. "I can sense it! The spiritual energy.... It is all around me!"

"Theoclea, focus with me," he commanded coolly. "Can you see the future? Something? Anything?"

"No, Master, not yet!"

"It is fine, Theoclea," he implied in reassurance. "You are still looping the spheres above."

"Yes, Master. I am," she confirmed his statement.

"I can feel the high level of your vibrations here. They are swift like the speed of light. You are edging closer, Theoclea!"

"I think so, Master Pythagoras. I think so!"

He waited for a couple of minutes before asking her again, "Where are you now?"

"I'm up.... Way up.... I'm floating inside the celestial realm!"

"Great! Go on! What do you see up there?"

"I see the gods! I see the bright light of Apollo!"

Her enthusiasm was contagious. Pythagoras smiled.

"What else, Theoclea? What else can you see?"

"Ah! Humanity, Master.... Humanity dawdling more inside darkness than light! War, Master! A lot of wars and human suffering.... Moments of peace are sparse... here and then in Times," she foresaw the future with patent pain in her voice. She seemed to suffocate in her words. "This dual correlation of war and peace appears unavoidable with humanity. It shall continue as such forever. There is no escape really," she grieved on her announcement, her voice husky and tearful.

"You, Master, you are a true messenger of the god Apollo. You will work in setting right the course of things. Sadly, your noble attempts will not last. At least, from what I foresee, you will have tried!" Her voice broke into a sorrowful tone.

Albeit bleak for him, the news did not perturb him. He remained poised and settled in his faith and belief. What mattered for him ultimately was the achievement of his mission on Earth. In truth, at this very moment, he felt particularly concerned about Theoclea and her tearful distress. He stared down at her with compassion. Her trance waned. Her consciousness restored, she opened her eyes. With the tips of his fingers, he touched her tears then tasted lightly their tepid bitterness.

The eyes she lifted at him carried an intense sadness that broke his heart. In an impulsive act of sympathy, he bent to hug her. He sought to absorb her cold in the warmth of his embrace. Desperate for reassurance, she ensnared him tightly. He patted her on the back in fatherly solace. He kept comforting her until her quivers and tears ceased, and her tension eased down.

Her questioning eyes then pierced his in search for an answer that could contradict the angst of her vision. Swiftly, Pythagoras turned his head away and squared Eratocles in the eyes; eyes as distressed as those of Theoclea. To confirm, to both his disciples, the veracity of her prophecy would mean to proclaim the inevitability of Human Fate; a revelation he had already foreseen, in successive frames, through his previous profound meditations.

Wordless, he walked out of the cell, followed closely by Eratocles mute in grief. The steps of the Master resumed firmly. Confident in the success of his present mission at Delphi, he looked ahead with anticipation. Nothing retained him there anymore. Like Theoclea, yet through a particular guidance prepared for them, the priests and priestesses had duly undertaken their Initiation into the Sacred Doctrine.

Time for Pythagoras to move on!

At dinner time, Pythagoras revealed to his hosts his decision to continue with his journey. Although expected, the announcement saddened the Assembly of the priests. They gathered around him to express their gratitude at the teachings he had so lovingly contributed. They affirmed having enjoyed every moment spent with him inside their sacred sanctuary.

Pythagoras urged them again to accomplish their new mission. Now, aware of their real duty, they pledged to abide at all cost. As they bid him and his faithful disciple farewell, he, from the depth of his heart, wished for them the light of the God El-Apollo to shine upon them, and all over the land of Greece, once again.

At dawn, Pythagoras and Eratocles left the Temple, almost a month after their arrival. With hopeful expectation, they undertook the road to their new destination.

* * *

Pythagoras and Eratocles stopped over in Athena for the night. They left the next morning on the first ship sailing to Samos. Upon disembarking in the island, Pythagoras decided to look for a place to reside outside the city. He opted for a spectacular cave at the foot of a mountain and made it his home[30].

He spent the next days and nights formulating his ideas, and expressing his inner love to Sophia. Eventually, his Divine Energy engulfed Eratocles with peace and remarkable inspiration.

At the emergence of spring, meditation carried Pythagoras to a new dimension of

---

[30]   It was probably Mount Kerkis.

deliberation. In accordance, he worked in devising an effective scheme to establish the school of his discipline. By one of these evenings, his silent concentration went so profound in his being that he switched into a different state of mind. It soon expanded beyond the world of senses.

The celestial dimension received his spirit among the radiant stars in the darkness of the sky... or maybe even further, into the first light of the Universe. The Universal Mind revealed, glimpse by glimpse, the intricate configurations of the infinite scheme of the cosmic life. The *Rising* transpired stronger, and more uplifting than ever.

And he, like never before, felt a significant spiritual inter-correlation with the Divine Will. He, and everything around him, in all directions and in all dimensions, became one single truth. A *Unity Point* of the manifested and the obscure, and of the created and the uncreated, shone brightly and radiated with energy inside and outside, linking the only one reality, and the many virtual realities, in one state of eternal balance.

Several similar cerebrations followed the sublimation of that night. Pythagoras managed to solve many other crucial issues in his other mental reflections. He also relied on mathematical demonstrations to develop and complete his science of the planets. As a result, he crossed far beyond the classical science and achieved thereafter a melodic formula of the cosmos. Such musical scale differed, in tonality, from one planet to another, through their calculated distances.

In consequence, Pythagoras became ready at that time to implement his grand vision of a cosmic harmony. From his home-cave at the foot of that mountain, just at the outskirts of Samos, he finally instigated his messianic mission to save the world, so to speak.

* * *

Long and deeply rooted in the heart of the great cities of Canaan-Phoenicia and Egypt, the knowledge of Sophia had lacked a complete acceptance from Greece. When, at a later stage, a cultural turmoil spread through and beyond the Mediterranean basin, the philosophical erudition of Sofia emerged to undergo a rapid ascension. The reputation of Pythagoras crossed the borders of Samos and broadened through the Isles of the Aegean Sea. It ultimately reached the heart of the Grecian world where his wisdom gained gradual admiration.

Eventually, the first tangible response surged from Samos. Young Samians sought his teachings on a daily basis to learn the basic principles of the perfect life. Soon, hundreds of youth from all around Greece joined him. They all craved to adhere to his Circle of Sophia.

Many remained and lived with him in his cave, becoming as such his life companions. That natural place of abode held a special meaning to him and Eratocles. As in all occult societies of all times, the cave represented the matter from which the world was made. From there, the souls would move out of their human prison in search of the light - the freedom - either by death, or by Initiation.

Among the hundreds of youth who attended his teachings on a daily basis, his live-in followers counted the thirty by then. They would all heed and learn his newly formulated discipline. Encouraged by the successful outcome, Pythagoras carried on with his mission, aiming at making of his audacious vision a reality.

With that perspective in mind, he decided to expand his quarters. He deemed the cave inconvenient for certain lessons. Therefore, he looked for another haven for the transmission of other parts of his sacred teachings. A place in the open air would be ideal, he decided.

His disciples reacted with cheers at the idea. They joined hands in renovating a natural rocky amphitheater with a view over the city. It formed a semi-circle, known as a *Hemikyklion*.

The surroundings bestowed on them serenity and peace. The nearby mountain would shield them from the wind, and grant them cool shades from the sunrays. There, surrounded by the abundant greenery and the musical twitters of the free birds, they would gather around the Master. In a friendly mood, they would meet to acquire the basic formation for their spiritual life. Among the thirty disciples, Pythagoras spotted some outstanding minds. Other than Eratocles, of course, names like Archippus, Melissus, Lacon, Glorippus, Heloris, Eurymenes and Hippon shone in the secrecy of his vision.

Some prominent citizens surprised him one day with their unexpected visit and urgent request. They needed him to represent them before the Greek Governor Syloson, the youngest brother of their previous Persian-allied ruler, Polycrates. They asserted trusting his wisdom. They urged him to handle the administration of the affairs of the city and heed their issues. In short, they wished for him to stand as their political leader.

Albeit surprised, Pythagoras did not turn them down. On the contrary, he considered their demand with thoughtfulness. The task would certainly require his active involvement, and consequently a major responsibility from his side. Yet, keen for justice to be served, he, the loyal citizen, conceded to their request. Since they granted him a great deal of trust, he pledged his best to succeed with that new mission.

His goodwill and determination did not waver in front of the many difficulties he soon encountered in his public and political assignment. Mundane laws were alien to him. He found himself unable to compromise or, even abide, by the metropolitan laws so wanted by the populace. In unison to that burdening task, his attention prevailed on his primary goal in life; Sophia, there in his abode and with his semi-circle of Initiation!

Soon, pressure weighed heavily on him. The fact that the Samians proved inflexible and even showed aversion towards his divine wisdom took him aback. They refused to even consider applying Sofia to their social lives. He realized with growing frustration that their first and last focus lay uniquely on the Laws of Man. They would not even accept the Divine Laws he, a messenger of El-Apollo, had brought them; although, all that he had required was for them to create a balance between the Divine Laws and the Laws of Man. Pythagoras faced his first major disappointment!

He withdrew into his own deliberation to ponder seriously on his fate. Inside the cave, partially illuminated with a candle, he thought things over.

What is the purpose of my mission?

What is the use of it if I am unable to help those in need?

How should I proceed if those who really need me are unwilling to heed my perception and accept it?

Should I abandon them?

Lost and confused, he recoiled into heavy deliberations that night. The silver rays of the moon sneaked inside the cave where he had retreated. Some of his disciples slept around him. The others took to the green pastures for their nightly rest under the stars; a respite which escaped the Master in his worries. He decided that sleep would not capture him until he could find a tangible answer to his dilemma.

Worries revolved to thoughts, and thoughts to meditations, and meditations to a deep trance...

The fog on his vision cleared up. The light of wisdom shone wholly above his God-Head. The essence of his mission materialized in a mysterious way in front of him, and so did the right steps to undertake. The idea of establishing a school of life became imperative in his mind. He foresaw a discipline that would reveal wisdom to men, and teach them the sciences of life. For that, he would have to create a perfect place of balance that could awaken, once and for all, the god latent in every human sanctuary.

For certain, no politician or businessman could ever pull through such an institution meant for the real Initiates, true Men and Women; those inspired Fathers and blessed Mothers.

Pythagoras still had to consider the right location. He would not consider Samos an option. As a matter of fact, in order to make his vision a reality, he needed to aim for a liberal country that would be more tolerant to new ideas, more lenient towards new understanding, and unrestrained from demagogic environments.

His idea of reform did not comprise any organized revolution against any state whatsoever. It rather aimed for a life of utopia that would provide, among other things, a complete free system of education for the youth. The initial and final implementation of his vision, however, would disallow at all cost all kind of rebellious and chaotic movements that could generate uncivilized confrontations.

From that perspective, the organization of his secular Initiation should be nourished by his wise concept of transforming, step by step, the rigid political constitution of a state into a sound adaptation of the knowledgeable Sophia. In other words, he envisioned the establishment of the *perfect city*, there where the Divine Laws and the Mundane Laws could be harmoniously united in the heart and mind of society.

However, such an ideal place for the induction of his unique project ensued harder to find than he had first expected. Most of the Grecian cities dwelled under tyrants imposed by the Persians. People could not elect their own governors. The remaining cities that had escaped Persian authority had fallen in the hands of fanatics who claimed to embody a *divine right doctrine.* Obviously, the false notion had given them freewill to govern the souls of people, and bury their relics in the matrix of time and space.

Pythagoras visualized the liberation of Human Beings. His sacred spiritual teachings would unchain them from the *circles of necessity* that bound them to Earth much too often and caged them inside the abode of matter. He would have to liberate them in order for them to fly up into the spheres of eternity. Only then, would they be able to become gods and goddesses with free wings; impulses of the *Universal Mind.*

Dawn cracked the darkness of the night when he stretched down to sleep; in his heart a broad smile, and in his mind a clear destination to his imminent journey.

A couple of hours later, he leaped to his feet with renewed vigor. He rushed to the river to wash. He marched decisively back into the cave where his disciples shared their first greetings of the day.

"We are leaving!" He announced high and loud.

"What?!"

Ignoring the general stupor, and the stunned faces of his disciples, he marched straight to his corner to pack his personal belongings.

"Prepare yourselves, brothers. We are leaving right now!"

"Leaving? You mean... leaving... for good?" Melissus stuttered, his eyes wide in disbelief.

With a smile meant to comfort his followers, he confirmed, "Yes, for good!" Pythagoras did not stop his task at hand.

Archippus scratched his head in puzzlement. He asked in an anxious pitch, "But... uh! What about Samos?"

"Come on, Master! What is in your mind?" Eratocles urged him in exasperation. "Tell us your thoughts, please!"

Pythagoras veered to address them, "Well my friends... the truth is that it is time for us to leave. We have a mission to accomplish, and it cannot be done here."

"And Samos?" Lacon exclaimed in wonder, mirroring the anxiety of Archippus.

"My heart is with the Samians, of course! Rest assured that I shall never forget about them, neither shall you. But, for now, we are leaving. My mind is set!"

"And where are we going?" Glorippus retorted in frustration. "Who need us more than the Samians?"

"In fact, there are some who do need us more. They are the young people of Magna Graecia. There, men and women are totally abandoned to themselves. They are in dire necessity of knowledge. And us, my friends, we are going to give them just that!"

Smiles drew instantly on their faces. Some cheered and others laughed in excitement. The Master had managed to infuse them with his enthusiasm, with just a simple tirade.

As a result, less than a couple of hours later, they left behind the cave that had sheltered them for several months. If some looked back with a sigh of regret, Pythagoras marched with determination, his eyes ahead on his mission. All of them, nonetheless, took the road down to the shore in a jovial mood. They reached the harbor at the time when a Phoenician ship finished disembarking its load of people and merchandise.

Half an hour later, the same ship transported them in destination to Italy.

PART II

.6.

Birth of the Pythagorean Society

Around the year 518 BCE, after almost twelve days and twelve nights into their journey, Pythagoras and his thirty disciples reached the city of Crotona, in the Gulf of Tarentum. Renowned for both its scientific and religious cultures, Crotona harbored mostly Mathematicians and Doctors, and stood as the noblest city in all of Italy. At this particular time in history, it faced a major crisis. Its ethical, political, and economical situations edged disaster!

Luxury products had overflowed for quite some time, causing an unstable economy. In addition, there existed an unbalanced political system corrupted by social and ethical vices such as injustice and inequality. Unity lacked among the citizens. These problems piled up to impair the city.

Pythagoras knew of these conflicts. Yet walking the streets of Crotona, with Lacon and Eratocles at his sides, and his neophytes behind them, he encompassed the true enormity of these socio-economic difficulties. He sensed the new challenge; a demur, indeed, but of a different nature than the one in Samos. In spite of the fact that the citizens worshipped the god Apollo, his determination to realize his vision prevailed against all odds.

"What are you thinking about, Master?" Eratocles asked him with a pitch of anxiety in his voice.

Without taking his eyes off the activities unfurling around them, Pythagoras muttered pensively, "My principles of reform, Eratocles... I

211

wish for the favorable reception of the citizens and the senate of Crotona."

Eratocles nodded without comment.

Lacon whispered to him with a witty grin, "The wish of the Master might come true!" And he chuckled.

Pythagoras glanced at him with an eyebrow lifted in question. "What do you know, Lacon, which I don't? A vision of some sort?"

Patently amused, Lacon chuckled again. Pythagoras gazed at Eratocles for an answer. He met but the broad smile of his first disciple.

"Okay! Let's hear it!" Pythagoras halted, demanding an explanation.

Eratocles volunteered to end his confusion, "Master, your reputation has preceded you here. You have already raised a lot of curiosity among the Phoenician sailors during the trip. So, obviously, they overheard many of our conversations on board and..."

"And," Lacon interfered. "They couldn't wait to spread the news the moment they stepped on firm land!" He commented in a jovial tone. "I heard them announcing the news of your arrival in the harbor!"

Pythagoras rubbed his beard with a simple comment, "I see... but it still does not make my wish come true."

"Maybe not," Eratocles replied evenly. "But wait until you hear about the eagerness of the Crotoniates to meet you."

"The holy and mysterious man," Lacon quoted respectfully.

Unaffected by the glorious praise and the patent admiration in the eyes of his neophytes, Pythagoras murmured musingly, "I see...."

All that he could focus on, for the moment, was his mission ahead. By this time, his other disciples had caught up with them.

"Master," Heloris approached him in a confidential manner. "The news is spreading fast all around. We overheard some citizens speculating about you, and your wisdom!"

"Yes, Master," Archippus asserted in turn. "Rumor has it that an official delegation is looking for you right now!"

Gathered around him, his disciples seemed excited.

"Not now!" Pythagoras decided out loud. "The trip was long and we are all exhausted. We rest for a couple of days. Then we will start our mission with a clear head."

"But...," Glorippus exclaimed in disappointment.

"No buts! They have waited all their lives for a change. Two more days will not make a difference at this stage. We need to be prepared."

And so they did...

Two days later, a beautiful sunny morning saw the Master all dressed in white, meandering the streets of the city with his group of young neophytes. Puzzled looks followed them, heads turned in their direction, and murmured questions drifted from here and there. Pythagoras greeted all these citizens with courtesy. Conscious of the crowd increasing behind him, he continued towards a small hill. Only then did he halt to sit down on the green grass. His disciples, the early Pythagorean neophytes, followed suit and settled into their habitual semi-circle position.

The crowd, mostly youth, assembled around them with curiosity. Muttered comments and speculations emerged from among them.

Despite the vibrations of excitement that filled the air, Pythagoras remained mutely engrossed in his meditation for some time. He collected his thoughts. He breathed in and out his sense of profound serenity. He knew such energy

213

would surge from him to reach the mass and grab their spirits. He harbored no doubt that his own aura acted as magnetism. He could feel it attracting their attention, which hooked on him.

When he felt the multitude ready for him, he stood up with the calmness of his sound confidence. His move brought about total stillness from the people. Talks ceased at once. He fathomed the hunger for knowledge in their eyes that pleaded for him to speak. It did not surprise him. After all, that was the reason which brought him here in the first place.

"My friends," he greeted them in a gentle yet strong voice. "Let me tell a story. There was once a man, young in age as most of you here. He lived in Saydoun; the city where I was born, in my homeland – Phoenicia," he added in explanation. "His father was a well-known fisherman who wished that his son assumed the same profession. And so, he trained him in the art of fishing. However, the young man was not happy at all. And do you know why?" He paused for his question to sink in their minds and draw their speculations. "Simple, my friends! It is because he failed in the business and its practices! Of course, we can all fathom his unhappiness at that failure."

Nods in the audience confirmed his statement.

He continued, "Despite it all, the young man abided faithfully to the insistence of his father. Every single morning at sunrise, he would sail in his small boat towards the far sea, and every single sunset, he would return empty handed. Things remained as unproductive for a long, long time. Until one day...," he waited for the moment of suspense to ensure their eagerness for more.

"Until one day, he felt deeply fed up!" He intoned with fervor. "Yes, my friends, he was so wretched by such a fruitless life that he decided to take his destiny into his own hands. He, therefore, sought to find something more successful to do."

He went for a silent break, in order for them to absorb the first part of the story. He sensed the tension of their anticipation. He let it be. He intended to give them enough time to identify themselves with the young character of his story. Only then would their mind formulate an outcome or a solution.

"What happened next?" A voice rose from the mass.

"Yeah, what happened? What did he do then?" Another question surged, eager for the remainder of the story.

Encouraged, many others enjoined with their questions.

Satisfied at the reaction of his audience, Pythagoras proceeded, "On his last day of fishing there, in the far-distanced sea, he faced in awe a sudden thick mist. A boat broke through the fog slowly and edged closer to him. The sailor, an old fisherman, greeted him. The young man noticed at once the baskets full of fish in the other boat while his were completely empty. He felt miserable. His shoulders sagged in defeat.

'What's wrong with you, young man?' The old man asked him gently.

Extremely frustrated, the youngster decided to confide in him. 'I've been sailing the seas for months now hoping to fish, and I have never been successful! Look at your baskets! They are full! Tell me, I beg you. Is it luck? How do you do it?'

With the calm patience known only to old fishermen, the fellow replied, 'Listen to me, young man. I went through the same thing when I first started fishing. I was actually as young as you are now! I spent many days and months trying in vain, until one day I found the answer. No, my son, it is not luck! It is a matter of love!'

'Love!' The youngster prompted in dismay. 'How is that? What has love to do with it anyway?'

'A lot, actually!' The old fisherman replied with passion. 'It has a lot to do with it! The answer to all the queries in life is always *love*. You have to love the sea to a great extent in order for it to reward you with the same sentiment!'

Before the young man managed to add another word, the boat disappeared in the mist, and the mist in the atmosphere.

Gasps ensued from the audience. People shared their thoughts and conclusions. Pythagoras waited for a while then concluded with a final statement, "And so it happened, young fellows, that the young man put his heart into his work with the sea. He therefore loved the sea, and the sea loved him in return."

He met fascination on their faces.

The tale was so simple and yet so profound. His sagacity informed him that some people among the audience might have understood the message literally. On the other hand, some others might be speculating on a connection that related them to the story.

He spoke then and a soft breeze in the air carried his voice. It touched their faces ever so gently to refresh them. It dispersed all around them and through the green grass. The leaves of the trees swayed to the musical sound.

"Fair brothers and sisters, there is an allegory behind this legend. The Truth I tell you! The sea is Sophia; Wisdom. Nobody can ever reach its Essence, or even get close to it, no matter how much one tries. Truly, one must love Sophia in order to come to know it. We could only realize such wisdom when we create a balance of the *tri-une* nature of our beings. Know thyself for the kingdom of Sophia is inside each one of you. And so, on your path, you must shed the light that leads you to it; for Sophia is the *Science of the Truth!*" the Master proclaimed with passionate faith. A divine grace brightened his sermon – his words of wisdom – that radiated energy; the way his smile and dignified god-like figure did.

"Are you the Wise One?" A young man asked him, his eyes widened with curiosity.

"No…, no! I'm not the Wise One, son. I'm the Philo-Sophia[31], the Lover of Wisdom…," Pythagoras proclaimed with modesty. "And I invite you all to share with me this beautiful love." He smiled divinely.

From that very first sermon, Pythagoras managed to capture the attention of the youth of Crotona. He lifted their minds towards the realm of Truth, and relieved them from the chains of fear that had impeded their search for the unknown.

After that first encounter with the Master, life in Crotona changed drastically for the local youth. They would follow him by the hundreds to the hill, perhaps even by the thousands. Young men and women would join him from every corner of the city to heed a new constructive speech every day.

Their minds attentive and their hearts willing to receive new edification, they listened to the *Lover of Sophia* addressing them with affectionate care. The Master knew very well that only his own language of love could reach their hearts, minds, and spirits. In his approach, he simply practiced what he preached.

---

[31]   Pythagoras was the first man in Greece, and around the Mediterranean basin, to use the term Philo-Sophia which means *Philosopher*, the *lover of wisdom,* or intimate friend of wisdom. Thus, he was the first true Philosopher.

Yet, to his surprise, some of the young Crotoniates there present at his daily speech insisted in comparing him to the god Jupiter. Others called him the Son of Apollo. To his big displeasure, some claimed him to be the manifestation of the God Apollo himself. He ached to explain that he was a simple man who had reached divinity through many years of preparation and purification of his innermost self. Yet, he judged the time inappropriate for such an honest announcement, whose profound meanings extended far beyond their understanding. He dreaded to be accused of blasphemies against the gods of Greece through ignorance. Hence, he decided to proceed slowly and wisely in relaying his teachings. Once done, he could connect the missing links behind the structure of the hidden Truth.

With his popularity increasing, and the meetings extending way up the hill, worry and anxiety unsettled the political body of Crotona. The Senate deliberated on some drastic actions to impede his sermons. Yet, they ended opting for more astuteness when someone suggested that this could simply be a momentary socio-cultural phenomenon.

Pythagoras disregarded this information that reached him. He prevailed with devotion in his role as Initiate. He had never intended to conspire against the State Council at all. His primary objective, in fact, was to urge the youth to cultivate their knowledge through constant search of the occult meanings behind the phenomenal world. The young Crotoniates in question proved a persistent commitment to his teachings.

The early mornings would witness his enthusiasm on his way up the hill, followed closely by his faithful disciples. As the sun resumed its kingly throne in the celestial realm, it would illuminate Pythagoras' path towards his own throne of mastership.

On that particular day though, Pythagoras felt driven by a new energy. Upon reaching the usual spot, he halted in astonishment, so did his disciples who expressed their awe out loud. The widespread field appeared jammed with a crowd larger than ever. Pythagoras sensed their passion in the vibrations drifting to him. As he moved forward, murmurs rose like a wave then settled into stillness. The circle of humans opened up to allow his way through, as he greeted them with a sincere smile of approval. It then closed instantly behind his disciples.

Upon reaching the center of their circle, he closed his eyes to absorb in his being the strange feeling that engulfed him. He felt so close to each one of them. His energy spread in all directions then fused with theirs. By the deed of a miraculous phenomenon, both dynamic streams fused and embraced to become one in the presence of the Divine Will.

"I wish you all a good and healthy life, fellow brothers and sisters," he addressed them with his typical tranquil strength. "You might wonder about me. You might wish to know the intentions behind my previous lectures and my future ones. You might harbor some doubts as well. Yes, you might! Yet, know this, my friends; I speak in the name of Sophia. I speak the Truth!"

Hails of encouragement responded him.

"Today, my message to you is of major significance. I ask you my friends that in your daily life, now and forever, you honor first the Supreme God El-Apollo in complete silence. Then, honor the Immortal gods and the Divine Law that has dispensed them. Always remember your oath in the act of worship. Next, honor the demi-gods[32], and lastly, the men of great deeds!"

"You surely dwell with lots of questions on life itself. Let me tell you: life is a continuity of events, shapes, and numbers that manifest in the course of time and space. The Truth I tell you! Evolution is the law of life! You must know, brothers and sisters, that in some way, you owe evolution to your parents. Thus, you are urged to take care of your elders!"

Pythagoras extended his hands out; one to the East and one to the West. "Respect your parents, and think highly of them. Love them and never give them grief, for they have loved you and cared about you, even before your birth. Listen to this, and listen carefully! You owe them gratitude akin a dead man to the savior who has resurrected him back to the light; to life!"

"Every morning, the sun rises from the East to eventually set in the west in the evening. This happens every single day. In truth, after the act of creation occurred and the process of evolution followed, this cycle of manifestation, which is taken for granted, is one of the greatest laws of nature. I tell you this: the East is much more honorable than the West, and so is the morning if compared to the evening. The beginning, which is the half of the whole, is more valuable than the end, the same way that life is more precious than death – its second half."

At that, he ended his speech with a vision for them to adopt.

---

[32] Demigods were very important in Greek mythology. The term Demigod is used to identify people for whom one parent was a god and the other was human. They were half mortals and half gods. Some were heroes, but not all of them. Among the most famous demigods were Achilles, Hercules (Heracles), Orpheus, Phaeton, Alexander the Great, Harmonia, and Niobe.

Once again, the large audience expressed their delight on his lecture and moral code. Certainly, his lectures initiated a difference in their thinking method. Their duties towards their parents, as well as the burdens of life and its many complications, appeared less complex! The youth started to absorb his philosophical introduction to matters. They, in fact, comprehended the truth his messages conveyed. His disciples relished in the success of their Master.

* * *

Pythagoras traveled with his disciples to the adjacent regions; from the closest city of Sybaris to the farthest one of Rhegium. He knew from the elders of each city he visited that, at some point in the past, these cities had endured unjust practices and slavery, and that the residents had turned against each other with brutality. At the time of his visit, corrupt manners still inhabited Rhegium, the last station in his journey before returning to Crotona. Acting at once, he sent his disciples to call on the citizens to assemble in the city square.

"Citizens of Rhegium, heed me! Our instinctive desires coerce us often into harmful deeds that destroy our families and societies," the Master introduced the issue at once. Standing firm in front of the multitude, he spoke with his distinctive poise. "My friends, the need to control and possess, cripples and dishonors our souls. Once we yield to these destructive impulses, disaster becomes the doom of our societies!"

"I tell you this: human beings tend to seek protection from the unknown, and all that they deem dangerous. To ensure their safety, they react in whatever way they consider valuable to their own security. That includes force at times! And force, my friends, always gives rise to aggression. Such perversity of the human mind triggers prejudice, and eventually enslaves the powerless."

"Listen and listen carefully! You should unite at once and adopt peaceful and loving manners. Reconcile with your enemies. Discard hostility, injustice, and slavery. This requires courage, so be courageous! But do it with humility and restraint. Commit yourselves to the love of liberty, to the practice of justice, and to a life of equality, for these are the true basis of Sophia!"

At that, he ended his message regarding a pertinent solution to their social issues, and ultimately for a better life.

Motionless, the citizens stood abashed by the strength of his wisdom that seemed to have struck their minds. Truthful and clear, his lexis of reform went straight to the point. It shook them to the last bone, to the last neuron, and to the last thought. He had just inspired them to seek a new horizon, and open up to a new adherence; an allegiance to a nonviolent and devoted humanity within the scheme of an evolving existence.

Pythagoras waited patiently for their reactions. Their eyes reflected a fiery ache to improve their life for the better. He read a new kind of desire in their pensive and moist looks. The dreamy nostalgia switched to a glow of hope, and then veered to fierce determination. Their faces brightened and their chins lifted. Women wept with emotion. Men turned to each other with a friendly smile. Some slapped each others' backs. Some shook hands. The elderly nodded several times with a sense of relief. The youngsters among them drew nearer to gawk at him in adoration.

Sensitive to their joyful vibrations, Pythagoras smiled with affection. Eratocles whispered in his ear, "Master, you have just succeeded in creating a new feeling in them; a new life!"

"Yes indeed!" he murmured in a husky tone. He turned to discern the same emotion in his disciples.

Lacon cleared his throat and asked, "Now what, Master?"

"We move on!"

"Where to?

"To the next city!" He commanded with a grin of triumph that all his disciples returned at once.

And so they fared back from one city to another with the same faith and determination. Delighted, they experienced equal emotional reactions in every city they visited. From Catanes to Himaera, Agrigentum, and Tauromenium – ending in Sybaris – Pythagoras made sure to leave the people with the profound mark of his philosophy. Satisfaction and contentment escorted them back to Crotona.

On their trail, all doubts about his nature and capabilities waned away; a path of light, strongly and surely, diffused far beyond the physical boundaries of the cities. He and his disciples preached a better life.

Wide and far, the news spread that the Master, with his profound wisdom, had surpassed the Greek sages and all the Mediterranean Hierophants known to humankind at that time. From then on, Pythagoras stood forth as the synthesis of the human *Hokmah par excellence.*

* * *

One day in early spring, the Master undertook a lonely journey through the fields that linked Sybaris to Crotona. He reveled in the mild weather and the fresh air. The rising sun essayed timid tints on his white robe, and radiant hues on the soft waves of the sea.

While treading on the shore, he caught sight of some small boats nearing the beach. He stopped to observe the local fishermen. Upon reaching dry land, they jumped out in a good mood and hauled their boats further in. They then proceeded in downloading their laden nets. Smiling at their happiness, he lingered around for a while. He halted near a group of three fishermen at their tasks of the early morning.

"Good morning, brave people," he greeted cordially. "A good catch today, it seems! Your net is loaded."

The elder one among them lifted bright eyes at him then replied, "Yes indeed. We fared the sea all night. Hard work pays back."

Pythagoras approved, "No doubt, you must wonder how many fish you caught today."

"Hundreds!" exclaimed the youngster, probably the son from his physical resemblance. The third man chuckled in delight.

"Hundreds? Are you sure?" Pythagoras uttered in amusement. "How about if I tell you the exact number of fish in your net?"

It might have sounded like a joke of some sort, but he knew for certain that these hard-bitten men would accept his challenge, no matter how gentle.

They went still for a while, perplexity showing in their eyes. Suddenly, they cracked open in disbelief.

"Come on! You don't believe yourself to be some kind of god, do you?" the son enjoined.

The father shook his head in annoyance, pointed his finger at Pythagoras in accusation, and admonished, "You know? We often hear of people alleging to know the unknown. And guess what... they always turn out to be nothing more than crazy fellows!"

A general guffaw mocked the Master who responded with a smile. Unscathed by the scorn, he browsed the sea with his eyes. The waves seemed to whisper to him, *Maybe it is time....*

Probably, why not? He thought, weighing the conditions appropriate for the manifestation of his divinity.

"Try me!" He commanded evenly and ceased smiling. With a serious confidence of his inner power, he stared at them in turn.

They came to a standstill, so did the silent moment that elapsed like a cloud of mist.

"I shall predict the exact number of fish," Pythagoras affirmed. "However, you must promise me something when my prediction comes true."

The son smirked and asked, "And what would that be?"

"You shall return the fish, alive, back to the sea."

The reaction came at once from the three fishermen.

"What?"

"It's our food in there, our weekly income!"

"Alive?"

"That's what we do for a living!"

Pythagoras raised the palm of his hands to command silence. "Leave your problems and worries to me. Have faith. I shall solve them all."

They hesitated. The son poked his father on the hip while he threw glimpses of dread at Pythagoras. They looked at each other with concern then the eldest scratched his head.

"Tell me, why should we do that?" The father flaunted in feeble flout.

"Because if you don't, you will never know if I can, or not, deliver what I promise," Pythagoras sounded calm but a hint of defiance lingered over their exchange.

"Okay then, say it!"

Pythagoras turned slowly to the net and stood still. His eyelids half-closed, he examined the fish, alive still but not for long.   Mist blurred his vision and the inner eye of his mind read clearly a three digit number.

He veered back to the fishermen and intoned with confidence, "153 fish[33]!"

"Is it so?" The eldest sneered and his companions grinned in derision. "Let's see then!"

They dashed to spread the contents of their net on the golden sand. Pythagoras observed the process with quiet vigilance. It took them a considerable amount of time to count them all, yet the fish remained alive in the presence of the Lover of Sophia.

With the last fish, they sagged back on the sand with livid faces then gawked at him, astounded. The number he had predicted was indeed exact!

Pythagoras felt a surge of fatherly affection towards them at their, suddenly patent, vulnerability. Smiling at them, his tone kind, he rendered, "You may now return the fish back to the sea."

They leaped to their feet, gathered the fish with fearful glances in his direction, and threw them all back into the sea. Having done that, they walked back to stand, in wait, in front of him. To their surprise, Pythagoras drew a few coins out of his pouch and handed them over.

The three men gaped down at the money then shook their heads in refusal.

"You have families to feed," Pythagoras insisted in a tone of authority.

---

[33] It is most likely that the number of fish that Pythagoras predicted was exactly 153. Pythagoras was known for his knowledge of mathematics and regarded 153 as a sacred number. It is used in a mathematical ratio called *the measure of the fish*. It produces a mystical symbol of the *Sign of the Fish* — the junction of two circles which generates a fish-like shape. This was an ancient Pythagorean symbol and used by early Christians to represent their faith. Could that miracle be true, or just a representation of a sacred geometrical formula? No one really knows!

The eldest, the father, took the coins with humility, "Thank you, uh... Master," he added, not knowing for sure how to address him.

Pythagoras smiled then requested their silence on what had just happened. At that, he moved on.

A few meters ahead, he sensed their presence at a respectful distance behind him. His intuition told him that they had followed him at once. He shook his head when he heard them asking people on the shore about him.

Naturally, the incredible story spread around, racing throughout Sybaris to Crotona, and even farther away to the city of Rhegium. His disciples informed him, later on, that much fervor and faith kindled the narration of his deed. Many called him *Pythagoras, the miracle-worker.*

Consequently, a large number of people showed eagerness to meet him, listen to him, or simply glimpse at the extraordinary Master. Citizens and visitors, from all around the Italian cities, flooded Crotona.

* * *

By that time, Pythagoras' fame had spread out and crossed borders. The Senate could no longer consider him a mere temporary socio-cultural phenomenon, but more of a tide in expansion that risked swapping them over. In addition, to deem him a charlatan would be a terrible mistake. The followers and devotees of this real, human enigma numbered in the hundreds. Capable of almost anything, they would stand up to keep and protect him if needed!

Pythagoras knew that these facts worried the State Council of the Thousand. The news reached him that the House of Senate had issued an urgent call to its members to discuss the matter in a closed summit. Thus, when a day later, they summoned him to their presence, he nodded with a simple smile and went to meet them.

In spite of their nervous stances and anxious looks, they welcomed him with honorable manners. The due greetings done with, the head of the Senate took his presidential seat to start. A blue shoulder-band covered the right side of his white tunic and blue trims enhanced the sleeves.

He pierced Pythagoras with sharp eyes and intoned, "Pythagoras, son of Phoenicia! We have heard what you have been teaching to our youth. It is all good... very good, in fact, all these social and moral codes," he emphasized with a waving gesture of his hand, "they are indeed commendable! Actually, we very much approve!"

The senators all nodded in confirmation.

"And yet!" he snapped. "We wonder, why? What is your intention in assuming such a burden all by yourself?"

The question carried more suspicion than caring concern. Pythagoras would not fall into this political trap.

"With all due respect, gentlemen, since you approve of my teachings, then, asking the reason – why – is of no relevance," he answered with the calm confidence known only to those who have deepened in the sagacity of life and beyond. "Behold, I do not carry the burdens of life on my own, we all do; we humans walking the troublesome path of this existence."

Silence reigned for a moment.

Time for them to think...

"What about that power of yours?" One of the high senators broke the silence in a challenging tone. He dashed towards him and looked him squarely in the eyes. "Yes! We heard about it! Some of us have even witnessed it. Come now, tell us! What is your mystery?"

Pythagoras held the accusing attitude in the power of his coolness. The senator hesitated for a second then charged on, "Allow me to ask you another question. What is that unseen power that allows you to guide the spirits of the people, especially those of our young men and women?"

"There is no mystery at all," Pythagoras replied in a serene voice. "That unseen power that makes you wonder is nothing more than the power of Hokmah; Sophia. It is there in each one of us, in each one of you, fellow men. It is just lying dormant, waiting to be awakened. The Truth I tell you; it is not a matter of me guiding the youth, but a matter of a fusion between my Essence and theirs. They are drawn to me in the same way that I am drawn to them."

Bewilderment walloped the administrators in total stillness for a while. They then gazed at each other in confusion. Soon, murmurs emerged as they shared their deductions.

Pythagoras waited. His powerful hearing skill grasped most of their exchange. He perceived their reassurance concerning their previous assumption that he might be a threat to them. They seemed to have accepted his words as honest and clear, and considered them of divine meaning. He sensed their vibrations of insecurity. They still needed an answer to one question; a dilemma that harassed their minds and hearts. He knew for certain what bothered them still, yet he waited.

At last, someone dared to put it forward. "We heard... hmmm... how should I put it? Well... We heard that you have performed a miracle. Some people see in you a god. Some regard you as the only manifestation, or one of the manifestations, of the God Apollo. Are you?" he snapped in accusation.

Pythagoras shook his head in amused disbelief. "Me... incarnating the god Apollo... or being his manifestation?" He exclaimed in their direction. "Aha... how could that possibly be? I was born to a woman. Don't you know?" He smirked, and they smiled back in relief. "Honestly, what

229

could have made you think that? Listen, I have informed the young Crotoniates of who I am, and I, here, reconfirm it to you, fellow brothers. "I am the Lover of Sophia. That's who I am!" The Master declared loud and firm. "I strongly recommend you bear in mind, at all times, that the act of procreation is sacred simply for being a natural phenomenon. You must always consider it with high respect. In truth, it is the only way by which myriad souls are incarnated into the world."

Even had they fathomed the depth of his statement, the senators could not have responded to it. Their concern appeared to focus on the nature and aim of Pythagoras. They, in fact, shared looks of reprieve and chuckled, amused at having believed the rumors and wrongfully accusing him.

Pythagoras sighed, inwardly disappointed by their narrow minds. He decided to advance the statement more clearly and proclaimed out loud. "Of course, reproduction is the way for the soul to reincarnate, but only in the manifested life."

Everybody went silent. The reaction he had wished for failed to ensue. Again, his last declaration went unfathomed. However, he regained some level of hope when they prompted to ask him to convene with them more often in the near future. They appeared eager to heed more of his wisdom. They – the actual leaders of the people – intended to communicate, in turn, his knowledge to their citizens.

Obviously, such a request from the Senate stood as a direct invitation for him to carry on with his vision and mission. He appreciated such a significant opportunity for expansion, to develop his concepts, and educate the general public. In return, Pythagoras reassured them that his teachings would not endanger the Dorian[34] constitution of

---

[34]   Dorians were an Indo-European population of the North. They migrated to Greece in the 13th Century BCE. They

Crotona in any way, but would instead confirm and enhance it.

The smiles they wore brightened the mood in the House of Senate. All their doubts, regarding him as a possible threat, vanished never to return again. Truth be told, Pythagoras embodied the characteristics of a Spiritual Reformer.

"Remember, honorable Senators. The city has been entrusted to your care by your ancestors. Your political positions in the government are a grant from your compatriots to you. What you have obtained is a common heritage to all. Hence, my recommendation is that you govern your country accordingly, and legate it, in due time, to the next generation with similar wisdom and value."

He moved around the circular hall of the House then halted at the center where he stood firmly and stared at each in turn.

"Please, pay attention to what I am about to convey to you now. These are major suggestions for the administrative running of your beloved city, Crotona. They are only five but of major impact. Listen!

- Be equal in everything you do to and for your citizens. Represent them honestly and serve them wisely as only true leaders do. If you ever need to make an exception, let it be through Justice. Only Justice should occupy a position of Authority. And so, be just, for every man and woman loves fairness.
- Be worthy of your words. Do not use the gods as objects of oath, for they must be dissociated from the laws of the city. Instead, make sensible choices in managing the government, and manage it rightly! This

founded Dorid and colonized Rhodes and some of the Isles of the Aegean Sea. For instance, Crete and Sparta were Dorian centers. In Crotona, Italy, their artistic and civil influence took up an important role.

231

should earn you a good reputation and trustworthiness, and allow you to resolve issues without the need of oaths.

- Be faithful in everything you do and undertake. Be truthful with everyone around you, especially with your friends, and in particular with your wives; these companions of your life! Abstain from having affairs outside the institution of earthly marriage. This is important for you to avoid the destruction of your family and of society, and to ultimately circumvent the bastardization of the nation.

- Be caring individuals so that you may prevent people from acting wrongly. Do not let them fear the punishment of law. Instead, instill them with a deep respect for good manners. Give them that opportunity, for it is the only *way* and the only *good thing* that makes them see the path of truth.

- Be cooperative with those who contradict you. Do not feel offended at all by their differing opinions. Instead, you should approach their ideas with an open mind. Try to benefit from their concepts before reaching a conclusion. I tell you: live democratically!"

The State Council of the Thousand remained seated for a long moment after Pythagoras had concluded his speech. Then, as if moved by the same spirit, they stood up together at once, and gathered around him in awe and admiration. They shook his hand, one by one, expressing their gratitude; praising his wonderful speech of reform and his remarkable suggestions.

In fact, Pythagoras, who really disliked politics, never meant to create a new form of government. That was never part of his actual mission. But necessity called upon him to act because of the many injustices taking place in the cities. His main focus bounded him to cultivate the youth's knowledge, the opportunity to extend his impetus to the governing class merged in as a must. He, in fact, wished for them to realize that their leadership should utterly harmonize with a philosophical way of life. Ultimately, the socio-political set of reforms and the moral-religious set of laws he communicated, to both the politicians and the people, contained none other than the authentic elements of wisdom; Sophia!

* * *

Months elapsed and Pythagoras succeeded in attracting a large number of rich citizens, including the majority of the Senate, and the young men and women of Crotona. Truth be told, the Master throve in restoring their independence and liberty. The Senate, who had come to trust him to a high degree, acclaimed his input as foremost. All the Italian cities – from the far-away Rhegium, to the closest, Sybaris – followed suit in accepting the same providence. Such an enormous accomplishment earned him more esteem than ever before. His ambition and willpower to improve human life created a breakthrough at that time. The rigid and long adopted systems in their social, cultural, and political context changed drastically.

Pythagoras persevered. With his popularity increasing, he came up with a plan to build an exclusive Institution for his disciples. Wealthy Crotoniates expressed enthusiasm and committed to support the noble project. Encouraged, Pythagoras proposed his idea to the House of Senate during one of their weekly meetings.

"An Institute? How interesting!" The head of the Senate exclaimed. "Let's hear it!"

Eager to advance his initiative, Pythagoras did not hesitate. "The project would form a fraternity of secular Initiates who would live in a community inside a school of life, without being secluded from society. Those among them who are found worthy of holding a tutorship (*Mastership*) would be immediately appointed to teach the sciences of: Mathematics, Physics, Psychology, and Religion. Based on the rules of the Community, the young men would be submitted to essential examinations before being admitted for further instruction. Under the guidance of the Grand Teacher (*High Master*) of that future prestigious scholarly Order, these young men would progress through different and successive degrees of Education (*Initiation*). And that would be intended, if I may say, according to their levels of intellect and their good will."

"Furthermore, those who wished to formally adhere to the Circle of Teaching (*Circle of Initiation*), and I mean those best qualified to become Teachers (*Members of the Inner Circle*), would be asked to relinquish their wealth to a curator. In case they wished to leave at a later stage, they would simply recuperate their money. Undoubtedly, there should also be a section for young women to favor from an adequate Education (*Initiation*) that better suits their roles in life."

Thrilled to have such an innovative institution in their city, the Senators promised to discuss it meticulously in private. And so they did during the several days that ensued. Their decision taken at last, they summoned him straight away.

An honoring welcome received him in the House of Senate upon his arrival.

"Congratulations, Pythagoras! The votes were unanimous in favor of the execution of your project," the head of the Senate informed him, at once, his tone official. "It is there, noted down on the calendar of our affairs for now and the years to come."

Amidst the sound of applauses, and overwhelmed by the apparent affection their smiles expressed towards him, Pythagoras delighted in the positive decision.

My vision will soon see the light! His heart cheered out. The Philosopher in him declared out loud, "I tell you this: the most excellent men of all times are the ones who can discern the benefits for their society. They are the ones who heed and learn from the useful events experienced by others before them!"

Flattered, they rejoiced openly in his statement.

* * *

Some three years elapsed in the memory of the people of Crotona before they, the disciples and followers of Pythagoras, smashed down a brothel at the outskirts of the city, on the order of the House of Senate. And so it happened that on the same spot, there on the hill, they began building a Temple meant for the Muses[35] in the year 515 BCE.

Evergreen trees fenced in the construction of that edifice. In spite of its unfinished status, one could already see the greatness and beauty of its structure. The gates already looked fabulous, and so did the well-designed gardens of beckoning fragrances. There in the middle, a very modest residence was planned for the Master. In his belief that he should always remain in the center, he had opted to build his house in the axis of the gardens. He considered this essential for his energy to radiate throughout the circumference. Moreover, such a position would make a strong statement that he would always remain close to everyone and everything without, nonetheless, taking sides.

---

[35] In Greek Mythology, the Muses are nine sister-goddesses presiding over harmony, arts, and sciences.

Months later, the construction successfully achieved; the Temple of the Muses rose in all its glory and majesty. It stood on the green hill akin a queen on her throne. Next, they commenced two novel constructions: a house for Pythagoras and two dormitories – for male and female disciples, and students within the starting community.

After settling down in his new house up the hill, a month later, Pythagoras considered that the time had come for him to speak again to the youth. He left his cozy dwellings and went to the city to commune with the young men gathered at the Temple of Apollo.

"Dear brothers! I came to check on you and see how you are faring."

Thrilled by his approach, they all shared the events of their week.

"Talk to us, Master!" they invited him to speak. "Tell us some of your thoughts!"

Pythagoras smiled at their eagerness. "Well, I will gladly offer you some important advice; useful stances that you should seriously consider as you walk the path of life. Heed me, for the Truth I tell you!

- Do not condemn anyone, and do not take retribution against those who condemn you.
- It is easy for the moderate among you to uphold truthfulness in their lives, yet beware the difficulty in sustaining such value as time goes by. Hard it is, as well, on those inadequately nurtured to adopt honesty. And it is similarly hard for those who are simply negative.
- If you decide to take the path of Truth and Honesty, then follow the steps of those who have preceded you and left their imprints in life. Learn not to oppose them for you might offend them.

- Finally, I tell you this! Practice heedfulness for, thus, you will be able to communicate correctly and be heard accordingly. When you speak, be brief and concise. A remarkable impression can be achieved with few simple and modest words."

The youth rushed their questions on him. Hence, he remained with them for a while to counsel and converse before bidding them goodbye.

On his way farther into the city, he halted at the Temple of Juno where young women gathered for their religious services. With cheerful cordiality, they greeted him.

"Are you coming to share with us some of your wisdom, Master?" A young woman asked him with hopeful eyes.

"Certainly, if you wish so," he grinned amiably.

"Of course we do!" the reply came unanimous.

They, at once, settled down on the steps of the Temple. Pythagoras remained standing yet his demeanor reflected his modest character.

"Dear sisters, I will be glad to give you four pieces of advice to apply as you venture through life. Heed me and learn, for only the Truth I tell you!!

- Above all, live by a grand sense of high moral values. Be modest and fair, so that the gods may hear your prayers.
- Do not worship the gods with sacrifices of blood and bodies. Instead, offer them something made by your own hands. Cakes would be a good example. And when you do that, do not exaggerate your offerings for that stance curtails your obligation. Know, instead, that the most righteous thing is the act itself.

- Love your husbands with all your hearts, the same way you love your parents. Neither oppose them, nor be submissive. Instead, perform sacred rites the same day of your union. It is lawful to do so for you are children of the earth.
- Now listen to this! Your gender is the most fitting among all the children of God for religious devotion. Take as example the Priestess-Medium of the Temple of Delphi. She always brings the unknown to light through oracles. Hence, I say, do not wear expensive garments as you do now. Instead, enter the Temple with extreme reverence and simple attire, void of any luxurious influence."

He spoke with kindness all along. At the end of his session, he announced, "Know that from now on, I shall refer to the unmarried and virgins among you as *Proserpine-Astarte.* The bride shall carry the name of *Nympha,* and the mother shall be named *Mater.* As for the grandmother, I shall identify her as *Maia.*"

That night, Pythagoras returned, to his small abode, elated. By contributing his wisdom to the youth of Crotona, he had granted them the opportunity to join the unique community he was about to start. In truth, he presently had succeeded in paving for them the good *way.*

* * *

His powerful charisma inspired and encouraged his listeners everywhere. The young Crotoniates were the first to have ever listened to him on Italian soil. His holy character impressed them in such a way that they decided, in spite of his refusal, to call him the *divine* rather than

Pythagoras. He maintained his preference in being referred to as the *Philosopher*.

Divinity, however, was not at all an inaccurate characteristic bestowed upon him. The divine powers he had effectively manifested, since his exploit with the fishermen, represented a good example for serious consideration.

In fact, an incident in the woods came to assert his divinity even more. A wild bear started to terrorize the inhabitants of the region of Daunia and beyond. The she-Bear caused havoc and destroyed properties. It attacked innocent people and inflicted pain and injuries. After every cruel deed, it prompted to retreat to the woods. The attacks continued on a daily basis until the Master took it upon himself to stop this.

Thus, he lurked on the outskirts of the city one of those days. The moment the huge bear stormed out of the woods to launch one of its brutal attacks, the Master dashed to stand, steadfastly, on its way.

The black bear hurled its large, heavy body at him. The growl it rendered prolonged, loud and deep. Saliva dripped from both sides of its jaw. Its paws, with the curved claws sticking out, knocked the air blindly trying to tear its obstacle apart. Pythagoras did not falter, nor did he move an inch. The beast halted a step away from him. It shook its massive skull angrily. Its jaw widened ferociously. Its bellow filled the air. Yet Pythagoras stood firm, unafraid. He looked at the animal squarely in the eyes, dominated it, subdued it, and held it in rein by his supremacy. The wild animal froze as if petrified.

"On your paws, now!" The Master commanded with a gesture of his right hand, his voice resounding low yet full of authority.

The animal abided at once. Pythagoras closed the distance between him and the beast while he muttered strange words in a velvety voice.

In total stillness, the wild bear surrendered to his vigorous caresses and gazed at him in blatant obedience. Without releasing it, Pythagoras extended a hand to the fruits of an oak tree nearby, and picked some to feed the animal. He then walked to the field, followed calmly by the bear. He grabbed some maize and acorns, and gently gave them to the animal to munch on.

For a while, he – the divine – rubbed the thick fur of the beast ever so tenderly. He then edged close to its ear. He commanded it never to hurt or even touch another human being again. Tamed for good and forever now, the wild bear rubbed its massive head on his side in a gesture of affection, or was it apology that it meant? Whatever it was, the subdued beast left meekly for the woods and towards the faraway mountains, never to be seen or heard of again!

The residents of the region spoke of what they had witnessed for years. His reputation as a divine man stormed through the cities of Italy and beyond.

Skepticism and doubt would sometimes challenge the Master in his divinity. Accordingly, he would make sure to prove their holders wrong every time. For those claiming his divine deeds on account of illusions, he would manifest his powers once again, and with strong faith and fervor.

When in Torentum one day, Pythagoras stopped to observe an ox in the field feeding on green beans.

"This is a forbidden plant!" he shouted, before he continued more calmly, "Brave herdsman, I advise you to tell your ox to eat other kinds of food."

The shepherd, stunned, burst out laughing for quite some time. With a sarcastic smirk, he retorted at last, "My fellow man, I am not sure what you expect! One thing I can tell you, I don't know how to speak in the language of oxen!" He snorted again, highly amused. "But, please! don't let my ignorance stop you. If you know yourself, then, you are welcome to tell it so!"

The Master shrugged off his shoulders and marched decisively to the ox. He knelt on one knee to address it. With his velvety voice, he explained why it should not feed from the beans of the field. The ox stood still, in attention, all the time that the Master took in communicating his reasons. To the shepherd's amazement, his ox nodded several times, turned to rub his head on Pythagoras' shoulders, and then toddled away. Bewildered and wordless, the shepherd gaped at him. Pythagoras smiled, bid him farewell, and continued on his way.

The tale of the ox spread through time. People came to know that ever since that episode, the animal never approached this plant again, or ate from it. It lived to an old age near the Temple of Hera and became regarded as sacred!

These feats, and others of similar or disparate nature, demonstrated that the powers of the Master comprised nothing of sorcery or magic tricks. They simply reflected the true manifestation of the *Divine Hokmah* that emanated directly from his mouth. He, in truth, held the power of the verb!

* * *

Pythagoras' followers increased enormously in the following months. The main reason behind this wondrous triumph surged from his input on the socio-political changes of Crotona and the adjacent regions. In addition to this, his spiritual insights, his teachings of wisdom, and his miracles drove thousands of people to his abode on the hill. These major incentives formed, in effect, the backbone of his mission.

One calm day in which Pythagoras worked inside his humble residence, vibrations of thrill drifted to him from his window. He tried to ignore them and reverted to his task at hand. He focused again on finalizing the basic procedures for the Order and the Doctrine. He believed that this plan would contribute a major impact on the process of improvement of mankind.

The vibrations intensified, along with the imminent sound of a crowd. The noise broke the chain of his thoughts. By need, he pushed his notes aside, stood up in annoyance, and approached his window. A multitude of people filled the center of the Institute, requesting his presence. He smiled with affection and stepped out on the porch of his house.

The crowd cheered in exultation at seeing him.

"Peace upon you, my friends!" he greeted them by lifting his right hand.

The mass responded with applauses. People called out his name, saluted him, and hailed him with words of praise. Pythagoras decided to address them with his wisdom, at once, in order to calm them down.

His voice rose strong above the noise. "Life, my friends," he proclaimed in introduction, and the crowd settled down. "Life resembles the Olympic Games. Its participants are of three different categories. First, the contestants who participate for the sake of the game; the second dwells among the audience and it represents those who attend for the sole purpose of engaging in commerce during the games. But the wisest fellows, I tell you, are form the third category! They are those who come simply to enjoy the show. They are the ones who find their happiness there."

"The ingress of men to this present life is like the succession of a throng within a society of different views and backgrounds. Some are influenced by the need of money and luxuries, which are the *first evils* that invade our homes and cities! On the other hand, there are those who abide by their love of power and dominion, and those who are controlled by their desire for glory. However, my friends, I tell you this! The purest among them all are those who contemplate the most magnificent and uplifting things in life. Those are the *Philosophers!*"

"Listen to me, and listen carefully! Nothing really happens in life by chance. Fortune cannot afford you what you strongly desire to possess, or endeavor to have. It is only by the *Divine Will* that things happen, in particular to good and pious men and women!"

His words appeared to make a strong impact in the minds and hearts of the people there assembled. He had just openly invited them to pursue Philosophy, and that was, in truth, what he had aimed to achieve all along. However, none seemed to heed a main component of his speech yet, as had been the case in many of his precedent ones. Up until now, no one appeared to understand that his term *'this present life'* referred to a doctrine of reincarnation!

"Human life," he resumed, "is divided into four stages: our Spring that sees us as children and youth for twenty years; our Summer that journeys us through adulthood for twenty years; our Autumn in which we enjoy our maturity for another twenty years; and finally, the Winter of our existence that encompasses our old age for twenty more years. Obviously, these periods are in union with the four seasons of our Mother Nature!"

On that note, the Master smiled to them with fondness, and without waiting for their questions and cheers, he waved farewell and went back inside. He intended for them to wonder on their own about the profound meaning of this factual statement. He deemed this analogy to portray the association and union, not only between humans and Nature, but with all the earthly creatures as well.

'It is but with the eyes of wisdom that we can discern their mysterious and unique resemblance,' he murmured as he reverted back to his work.

At sunset, one of those days, Pythagoras lived through a very strange occurrence. Accompanied by some of his disciples on one of his tours, he reached the River Kosas[36] (Casus) near Metapontium. They decided to stop for a rest. Pythagoras informed them that he intended to pay his respects to the spirit of the river and went to settle on the bridge.

While deep in contemplation, a strange whisper greeted him. He opened his eyes to look around then scrutinized the river for the source of the call.

"Fear not! I am your loving Father!" the voice intoned in the breeze.

Pythagoras realized then that the call reached him from the higher spheres of his divine inner realm.

"I place in your hands the foundation of the Kosmic Kingdom!" the voice commanded *sotto voce* yet it resonated strongly inside his being.

Back home, the day after, alone with his thoughts, he followed by heart the voice that had talked to him. He considered the feasibility of dividing the organization of his *Order* into two circles. The first would be the *Inner Circle* where only the *esoteric* knowledge would be explored. The mysteries of the known and the unknown would also be revealed to those qualified at the Initiation.

The second, the *Outer Circle*, would enroll all the other members who would live, or not, inside the city with the members of the Inner Circle. The Outer Circle would have access only to the *exoteric* rites of the cult of Apollo, the Supreme God, the One – the mystical Monad. The cult of the Muses would

---

[36] Some suggest that this incident happened over the river Nessos.

also be accessible to them. Along with that exoteric religious devotion, they would be led to seek a life of high social development.

Abiding to his vision, the Lover of Sophia undertook that day the establishment of the basic concepts of his *Doctrine*. He considered the first step to be the belief that man replicated the whole universe within himself; the second step, the belief in the immortality of the soul and, finally, the belief in reincarnation and the transmigration of the soul; in short, Metempsychosis.

As a matter of fact, Pythagoras envisioned the organization of the Order in a wisely process. He aspired to create both a religious-spiritual and a secular society of brothers and sisters. Moreover, when it came to the Doctrine, he integrated all the principles he acquired from the Canaano-Phoenicians, the Egyptians, the Chaldeans, the Zoroastrians, and the Hindu Gymnosophists.

Accordingly, the Pythagorean Society was born. It included a school of complete education that took into account mostly all the sciences of life. With careful studies of the theories, and the cautious performance of their practices, the novice should find the path to a *mathemagical* harmony of the spirit and mind with the universe.

That devise represented the arcane true Philosophy that he intended to reveal to both Circles within his Society. It would strongly evoke the rising of the human intellect towards the higher level of consciousness: God – the Universal Mind – to whom men and women would merge.

It would be, *ipso facto*, an inner actualization of the Truth. That Sublime Truth would absorb all people into its realm if, of course, they would aim for it of their own free will. A realm where the deepest impellers of faith would reside! It would be the true goal that every human being was created to achieve.

The Master was determined to make out of *Philosophy* the true religion of Sophia. And henceforth, his steady direction and close up guidance brought about the first prosperous phase of the exact model of the perfect city. Surely and steadily, he moved it towards the manifestation of the utopian way of life.

.7.

The City of a god

Towering above the metropolis of Crotona, the White City stood magnificent on top of the verdant hill. The majestic Cedars and the olive trees heightened the splendor with their evergreen leaves. The golden sunrays reflected on the immaculate ivory of the high walls. A tranquil serenity swathed the whole area with an eerie ambiance of peace that the birds praised with their melodious songs.

The outsiders stood always in awe in front of what they had surnamed the *Celestial City with Mighty Walls*. The great mystery that cloaked its very foundations kept impelling the youth of Crotona, as well as those of the adjacent cities, to seek admittance. In spite of the difficult rules of the Master, curiosity goaded many to venture inside its secrecy, with a passionate aspiration to discover the unknown. Yet, to enroll, young men and women should be introduced by their parents. Sometimes, it was one of the assigned Masters of the Pythagorean Society who assumed the introduction.

At the massive wooden gated entrance, one could admire the marble statue of Hermes-Enoch, the father of the spiritual laws. A cubical stone formed its stall where a skillful hand had carved the words: *No entry to the vulgar*.

Inside the city, an amalgam of scents emanated from a diversity of flowers that bloomed from patches scattered around in attractive geometrical forms. Every main edifice benefited from its own botanical courtyard; the Majestic Temple of the Muses, the humble residence of the Master, the two dormitories for men and women, and the gymnasium, which was under rapid construction, just to name a few. Several verdurous patios spread throughout the entire domain as if Eden had resurrected on Earth to reflect the unique harmonious rhythm that existed among the living elements of Nature.

The live-in disciples counted in the hundreds by then; some had remained with Pythagoras ever since Samos. Many of the youth of Crotona had soon joined in. Men and women alike had adhered to the Fraternity and abided by its rules. One could see, at that moment, young women in dainty tunics of different colors and shades walking down the hill in a row. They headed to the Temple of the grand goddess Ceres-Astarte on the shore. There, they would proffer the sacred rites to the young deity who personified the deepest mysteries of womanhood and Mother Nature.

Through the gates of the Temple of El-Apollo, the Sun God, men in white robes proceeded with devotion. Royally hoisted within the White City, the new shrine had witnessed, in the previous week, a grand opening ceremony led by the Master himself. Currently, the procession of the devotees entered the Temple to perform the rituals that would connect them with the Heavens above.

Then, to the right, the sports center...

The Pythagorean gymnasium differed, to a large extent, from those built in the other Italian cities. Even in its present incomplete structure, the athletic amphitheater promised to bypass any major gymnasium ever built in the region not only in size and beauty, but more importantly, by the new regulations of the Master. These rules, in fact, forbade all violent games and trivial palavers.

For the moment, active youngsters used the playing field to engage in mild sports. Some ran a court race, some competed in hurling heavy metal disks, and others darted their bronze arrows onto wooden boards. In the central square, some players performed a simulated fight in the form of Dorian dances. All the players abided strictly to the rules of the Master and avoided, at all costs, any brutal fight that could incite hatred and destroy friendships.

About the White City, people convened in various groups, here and there, to share their thoughts in a civilized manner that required freedom of speech and reciprocal respect. A sense of contentment reigned in their communication, for mutual esteem and tolerance led their hearts and minds. As instructed by the Master, such a method always allowed the revelation and recognition of the true-self.

As per the rules, new novices could enjoy a few days of unbound errands for personal acquaintance. Then, they would undertake a series of tests and trials under the strict surveillance of the Masters. Pythagoras attended these examinations, covertly, in order to observe and analyze the behavior and expressions of the new students. Having long studied the Human Physiognomy, he had mastered the art of determining the personality of the new novices from their features.

In reality, the Lover of Sophia proved to be a skillful observer *par excellence*. Minds and hearts yielded always to his stare and scrutiny. And since he cared for the City to encompass but the best potentials, he weighed every novice for the final admittance to his Society of Initiation. In addition to the cerebral potential and skills, a neophyte needed to excel in character and personality.

"The Truth I tell you! Not all wood is proper for sculpting a Hermes," Master Pythagoras often stated, and by wood he meant the novice seeking his Initiation.

As a matter of fact, crossing the cubical stone of Hermes-Enoch at the entrance did not ensure adherence to the Pythagorean Secret Society. A year of trials should be achieved while delving in the Master's several interesting topics on life issues. Based on the outcome, Master Pythagoras would ultimately decide on their admission. Failure would send them back home and back to their life as commoners.

* * *

As an alternative to the Egyptian cryptic tests of Memphis, Pythagoras adapted a test of endurance and cerebellum. The trial required from the novice to spend a night of complete isolation inside a cave at the foot of the hill of the White City. Memories of previous tales of monsters and phantoms, alleged to dwell near and inside the cave, made it harder on the beginners. In a state of mind that wrecked their nerves and tested their valor, they brazened out their hallucinations that could deceive their better judgment on the realities of the phenomenal world. Eventually, some had refused to submit to this initial psychological and physical test. Some had simply escaped in the middle of the night. Both categories had wasted, in consequence, their unique chance to continue the process of Initiation. Truth be told, many had failed the tests in overcoming the illusions of their minds.

Aristaeus, a young man from Crotona, undertook his assessment with eagerness. He looked forward, with bravery, to the aforesaid hard process of acceptance. However, when one of his Masters woke him up – in the middle of the night – without prior notice; he followed him, in disoriented confusion, into a special Spartan cell inside the White City.

"This is your test of acceptance, Aristaeus of Crotona," his sponsoring Master commanded in a dry voice that chilled the bones of the young novice. "You must decode one of the Pythagorean symbols. Once you find the answer, or simply give up, you will let me know by knocking on the door."

Aristaeus glanced around the dark, cold cell. He noticed a small candle, an old clay water jar, and a piece of bread placed on a bamboo mat on the floor. He shuddered and turned to his Master.

Gathering all his courage, he uttered, "What is it? I'm ready." He wished to sound more convincing. Under the circumstances, that was all he could come up with.

The Master nodded briefly. His eyes conveyed more challenge than approval. "Very well then. What is the meaning of the Square?"

Aristaeus lifted his eyebrows in puzzlement. His own question remained pending for the Master disappeared at once behind the door. The sound of the key turning inside the lock resounded in his ears akin a death knell.

What is the meaning of the Square?

He murmured once, and then twice, and for the long moments that elapsed. He finally sagged to the ground. He held his head with both hands while his mind labored for the answer. He drew the symbol with his index finger on the dusty floor to discern what hid behind it, or around it, or inside it. He tried it again and again. Nothing materialized in his mind. He started to panic. Time became his enemy. He bit on his now dusty nails. Sweat ran in rivulets from his forehead. He tried again. He refused to give in.

For the next several hours, he strove to decipher the meaning behind this simple shape. He completely tuned off all his senses to ignore the occasional weird sounds that swelled up from the dark areas of the cell. He even closed his eyes, at times, to avoid the hallucinations that distracted him.

A square... His mind repeated.

A square... a shape of a house... He tried to figure it out with its representation, yet no answer ensued.

He lost the sense of time. Thus, when his mind formulated the most probable answer, he realized that the exact hours of his isolation had escaped him.

A square is the shape of a house... which could be... the four sides of the world...

Of course! He leaped to his feet. "The square must be the symbol of the material world. It could not be otherwise!"

He charged to the door with renewed energy and knocked with vehemence. The sponsoring Master pierced him with curiosity when he came face to face with him.

At the smile of triumph that Aristaeus flashed at him, he uttered in doubt, "We'll see... we'll see. Go wash and meet me at the door of the Assembly Hall, inside the *homakoeion*"

"The Common Auditorium?" Aristaeus asked more to himself than anyone else. He knew that door very well for having seen it so many times; a door whose access had never been permitted to him, akin all novices.

Less than an hour later, both Aristaeus and his Master entered the Common Auditorium. Students, very much like Aristaeus, gathered in groups with their Masters, and a few recent members of the *Inner Circle*. Being a Pythagorean *listener*, thus an element of the *Outer Circle still*, Aristaeus joined his fellow members, who were deep in conversation, confidently.

The *Outer Circle* included some prominent personalities from Crotona as well as from the other independent cities of southern Italy – extending from Sybaris to Rhegium. Called the Pythagorists, these members usually enjoyed access to the lectures given by Pythagoras, yet without the rights to participate in the dialogues and discussions. They were surely not present there at the Common Auditorium, for no lectures were to be given by the High Master that day.

As a matter of fact, that day was very special to students, like Aristaeus, who were present and waiting to face their eventual fate. It was a day when they would be acknowledged with certain admiration into the Pythagorean Society or simply abandoned to their ordinary life outside the White City.

Aristaeus met some adepts of the second degree. From their exchange, he came to know that after their observance period of two to three years they had undertaken the Pythagorean *first degree*; a *Preparation* period of three to five years. Aristaeus heeded with admiration how their hitherto achievement had earned them the approval of Master Pythagoras. In accordance, they were now in the direct discipleship of the *second degree*, better known as the Pythagorean *Purification*.

Someone nudged Aristaeus who veered at once to face the mocking eyes of a member of the *Inner Circle*.

"So! Here he is, the new brilliant Philosopher!"

The sarcastic tone irritated him, yet he bit on his tongue not to reply.

"Come on, Aristaeus!" Another fellow joined in teasing him. "Tell us what you have discovered. Don't be shy. You did reach an answer, didn't you? So what is it?"

Beginners of his same rank chuckled in amusement. Others, however, smiled pensively, embarrassed themselves as if they had suffered the same bullying. The Masters, the *Sebastikoi*, stood in a discreet state of alert, apparently keen to his reaction.

Aristaeus felt a strong urge to retort with the same level of disrespect, if not more. He inhaled deeply. His hands in fists, he attempted to control himself. He knew the answer of the cerebellum test, and ached to hurl it on their sarcastic faces. Yet, he hesitated. He dreaded a mistake that could jeopardize his progress or trigger more pestering.

Somehow, he felt unable to articulate his deduction, suddenly doubting himself.

What if I am wrong? They will certainly mock me!

Irritated and humiliated, he struggled to dominate his frustration.

"Did the cat bite your tongue?" someone jested to general hilarity.

Aristaeus could feel the eyes of his Master observing his moves, his every gesture. He deemed his physical and moral conduct to be at stake. That realization infused him with more determination to stand firm against peer pressure. He recalled those rumors about novices reacting in dishonorable attitudes such as aggressiveness and tearful breakdowns.

The banters and harassment increased, tempting his self-control to a dangerous limit. His basic instincts urged him to retaliate with curses and insults! Many had done it before him. Many had surrendered to such heavy pressures on their egos. Many had ended retorting back with cynicism, and even curses on the school, the Master, and his disciples. Yet the rules forbade any kind of hostilities, for being the *second evil* inflicted on oneself and others.

Aristaeus resisted the temptation. He refused to yield. He gathered all his self-control. The moment he turned to step away, he sensed an overwhelming aura filling the Assembly Hall. He became vigilant to the imminence of another trial of illusions. He glanced around and discerned a sudden general stance of seriousness and awe. Total silence engulfed the hall in reverence.

Aristaeus followed the direction of all the eyes around him. He froze in anticipation. Behind the white curtains that separated them from the annexed hall, the silhouette of Master Pythagoras materialized.

The voice emerged calm and forthright to reach them like some supernatural mist would do; untouchable yet real. "The Truth I tell you. Those who have failed to deal with this test of morality, and assented to their *Ego* should leave at once, for they have betrayed the most elementary traits of friendship and respect towards the Masters. They will be immediately escorted out of the city, and considered dead to our Fraternity. The same rule applies to the members of the Inner Circle, for we consider them incompetent to continue further in their Initiation. The wealth they have entrusted to a curator upon joining the direct discipleship will be returned to them in double."

Aristaeus smiled inwardly, his self-confidence reinstated at once. He realized that, not only had he unlocked the puzzle of the Square, but he had also succeeded in standing firm against the harassment and sarcasm of the gathering. He, in fact, had thriven in controlling his reactions; something very few people could have done under such circumstances.

Encouraged, he stepped forward quickly and surprised himself by gushing out with fervor, "I think the Square means the physical world!" The resonance appeared strange to his ears. He blushed profusely.

A stunned silence responded to his enthusiasm. He had anticipated a comment or a reaction of some sort, but not this total stillness. He swallowed slowly. Cold sweat crawled down his back. His heart pounded fast; as fast as the wheel of time hovering in wait above the White City.

Then finally, "Who spoke?" the Master inquired, his tone strong, yet Aristaeus noted the clear hint of curiosity.

"My name is Aristaeus... Aristaeus of Crotona, Master!"

"Aristaeus... well son, listen," Pythagoras uttered with a pitch in his voice that hinted pleasure and affection. "You are not completely wrong. Let's say you are half-way right."

Relieved, Aristaeus made haste to affirm his zeal and goodwill, "Master! If you allow me! I can certainly proceed in interpreting the whole meaning of the Square, and other symbols as well. I will! Hardships and pains I shall overcome, and my very best I shall commit; all for the sake of discovering but glimpses of the ultimate truth!"

A faint sound behind the curtain ensued as if the Master cleared his throat to control his amusement. "I tell you this, Aristaeus. You possess the heart of a Lion and the will of an Eagle. You are therefore admitted into the Pythagorean Society. However, bear in mind that you must first undertake our observance period."

"Master... Thank you, Master!" Aristaeus answered, thrilled, and confident like never before. He noticed how the Master moved his head slightly for a quick look in his direction. Their eyes met in mutual respect, and then the neophyte gave his Master a gallant nod and a smile.

The beginners and students – of Aristaeus equal status – stood abashed, as Masters and members of the *Inner Circle* hastily gathered around Aristaeus. They shook his hands warmly, congratulated him for his achievement, and welcomed him as a probationary member in the Pythagorean Society.

* * *

At this particular moment in which the sun extended its morning light over Italian plains, Pythagoras ambled all by himself. He cherished these saunters that connected him to the peaceful and splendid Nature that characterized the Italian landscape, and almost every part of the Mediterranean world. These promenades often led him to the adjacent towns where opportunities to confer wisdom never lacked.

On that particular day, the Master performed something really unusual. While addressing the citizens of Metapontum, he appeared, simultaneously, in Tauromenium, known today as Sicily. The people witnessed his presence, in each of these cities, even though a great distance separated them, by land and by sea. Some ascertained having seen the *white man* walking on the water that linked both cities. Some alleged that he had overcome the distance, in so short a time, by means of a golden dart given to him by Abaris[37] – the old priest of the enigmatic Hyperborean tribe.

Whatever the means, such a mystical manifestation shocked the citizens of both cities, indeed. Eventually the news of such a phenomenon stormed through the country and beyond. The sages interpreted it as one of the god-like manifestations that made Pythagoras omnipresent.

Needless to say that time and events proved Pythagoras a true prophet. Among many of his amazing endeavors, he predicted earthquakes, and foresaw the death of friends he later buried, as seeds, in the bosom of Mother Earth.

* * *

Down in the crypt, inside the Temple of the Muses, a meeting of high interest was about to take place. Pythagoras and the *Sebastikoi* congregated with the nine sister-goddesses of harmony, arts, and sciences. The *Sebastikoi*, known to be the leaders and Masters of the Inner Circle, assembled eagerly around their Great Master. The occult

---

[37] According to historical records, the priest Abaris, the Hyperborean, joined the Pythagorean community at later stage. Hyperboreans were a mysterious people that had probably originated from the mountains of the northern region, the birthplace of Apollo. They are said to have built the first temple of Apollo at Delos. Some say that they are the ancestors of the Celts.

lesson that followed was aimed at examining the esoteric properties of Numbers.

Previously Initiated by Pythagoras into the hidden knowledge of Sophia, the *Sebastikoi* devoted nearly all their time to *theoria*. They indulged, as such, in pure speculations. They spent their time in meditation of the Divine Truth based on the Pythagorean Philosophy that relied on mathematical theories and their direct application to life.

The Master started. "Before we take on the secret of the two most important Numbers, I should tell you a matter of high importance. Today in the afternoon, one of our brothers died in a tragic accident after falling off his horse and hitting his head on a sharp rock by the side of the road, outside the White City. Now, since you are assuming the role of religious functionaries of the Order, you should carry the body, first thing in the morning, to the Temple of Apollo. In the middle of the terrace, where we raised an altar for the outside religious ceremonies, the body should be placed. Certainly, you should not burn the body of our brother into ashes. It should, instead, be wrapped up with a white piece of cloth for the body to revert back to its first nature. And hence, fellow brothers, you must only burn fire all around and near the cadaver to exorcise the bad spirits! Verily I say unto you; this ritual is undeniably one of the most mysterious of all religious ceremonies, for fire comprises, in fact, the power of the One."

A moment of reflection passed before Pythagoras resumed his teachings to his closest disciples.

"The two most important numbers, my friends, are *One* (1) and *Ten* (10). I will explain the reason in a while and elaborate on the hidden properties of all the numbers from *one* to *ten*. For now, know that the Numbers are the measure of all things. Each number has its own personality, whether it is masculine or feminine, complete or incomplete.

"*One*, the number (1) is the *Monad*, the Universal Mind that diffuses through everything," he proceeded to elucidate the symbolic meaning of the numbers. "*Ten*, the number (10) is the very best number because, not only does it contain the first four numbers: one (1), two (2), three (3) and four (4), it is also the sum of all of them: one plus two plus three plus four equals ten. $(1)+(2)+(3)+(4) = (10)$. Ten is the ensemble of the ultimate Truth!"

"Listen and heed! The act of Creation occurred by the invisible power of the *One*. It is a solitary, all-embracing whole in which everything is truly interconnected."

He paused for the brief moment it took for him to glance at them.

"The *Ten,* or the whole, is the superlative manifestation of this interrelated reality. Adding to that, *Harmony* is the mysterious binding agent whereby every existing atom, in this vast Kosmos, is related to the other."

He waited for them to reflect on the knowledge he had just imparted. He meant for them to absorb the deep meaning behind his statement before he continued.

"Listen to this and listen carefully. I'm using the word *Kosmos* for the first time to indicate a *well ordered and harmonious universe*. The Kosmos is, in fact, an immeasurable musical instrument in perfect tune with itself. Its vibrating numbers produce melodious tones that resound almost everywhere. Hence, both the Universe of gods and Man, Heaven and Earth, the Macrocosm and the Microcosm, are all linked together eternally. They do reflect the same harmonious proportions we examine in mathematics. Yes! But this is only achieved through the Divine Numbers, which are the primal reality."

"Now, to really invoke the powers of the Kosmos like an Initiate should, there is no need to perform prayers and rituals. Instead, put thyself in *synchrony* with them. And so, if you use the same numerical proportions as those of Heaven, then and only then, dear brothers and sisters, would you be definitely able to vibrate in the same frequency of Heaven. Your spirit would call forth the Heavenly Spirit. It would descend upon you like a white dove from the sky."

It would descend upon you like a white dove from the sky...

The sentence reverberated for a long moment in the secret chamber, and deep inside their inner realms. The Philosopher wanted to ensure that they would always, and only, seek and long for Heaven.

He waited because his next revelation would surely incite, even more, their desires to synchronize themselves with the Numbers that existed behind the powers of the Kosmos.

"This approach, without a doubt, allows me to hear the *Music of the Spheres,* and therefore live in Harmony with the universe!" He asserted with great confidence. He read clearly in their eyes a new fiery aspiration.

"The Kosmic music of the Muses should be imitated here on Earth, starting with our own White City! Only then shall we move on to the other neighboring cities. If this is done successfully, I assure you that we will achieve a state of *Homonoia*; a true and strong union of minds and hearts among all people on Earth!"

They were all in wonder for a while, dreaming and imagining that incredible, yet difficult to accomplish, union of all the people of Mother Earth.

"To finish, for now, our lesson of the day," he brought them back, not to disturb their imagination but rather to strengthen their dream of a better world. "I tell you this, my friends, be like your Master, act like him. Do not be afraid to approach the gods... Together, let us build a Kosmic Kingdom... here on Earth!" the Philosopher ended his dialogue.

With this passionate invitation, he had just imparted his *Sebastikoi* with the keys to the heavenly Kingdom, and moved them into a higher level of intellectuality. Its *modus operandi* exposed, they should know by now how to live in its replication, which was the Kosmic Earthly Kingdom. His explanation of the strong connection between Heaven and Earth revealed to them a Kosmic Unity. He had managed to artfully sketch the exact trail that joined the *above* with the *below*.

He had widely opened the door of self-realization to his Inner Circle. And he had, unquestionably, made all of this appear to be in alignment with his own philosophy.

The state of *homonoia* that he had envisioned, and aimed to create on Earth, could seem an impossible task to achieve. However, the construction of the Kosmic Earthly Kingdom, via mathematics and numbers, would enact nothing more than the reproduction of the Kosmic Heavenly Kingdom with the God Al-Apollo as its Eternal Ruler. How to realize it? That remained, indeed, the biggest question of all.

However difficult the task ahead, his powerful *will and faith* never lessened, or halted, in front of the immensity of such a mission. As a matter of fact, the inspiration and the direction of the Divine Hokmah in him worked as his greatest inner allies. They guided him through the right path to ultimately succeed in establishing his White City to be the *City of a god*.

* * *

Two years and a half into the observance period, Aristaeus of Crotona adhered officially to the Pythagorean Secret Society. He earned the right to wear the brass necklace engraved with the distinctive *five-pointed star* of the Fraternity. With the *Preparation* period ahead, he readied for that phase, which required three to five years from him.

Consequently, the time duration of the *first degree,* known as the Pythagorean *Preparation,* would firstly vary according to the level of Intellect and the mental evolution of the neophyte. Secondly, it would differ according to unknown variables, uncontainable circumstances, which might play against him along the way, such as infirmity, a death in the family, emotional breakdown, and other things of the sort.

Throughout the first Initiation level, the novices would not be allowed to see the Master who always conducted his lectures from behind the curtain in the *Common Auditorium.* The same procedures applied in his cave, set for his lectures, at the right border of the White City. Known as the *akousmatikoi,* they profiled the Pythagorean Outer Circle as being the *Listeners,* or the *Auditors.* Their participation was strictly restrained to only attending the conferences.

Believed by his followers to be the *Son of Hokmah,* Pythagoras possessed a true spiritual and religious essence that a student with an exoteric inhalation could not absorb clearly, nor fathom easily. For that particular reason, he chose at will to sit behind the curtain and conceal his physical appearance, so to speak, from his *akousmatikoi.*

Differently from the general public living in the White City and to which Pythagoras clearly appeared when addressing them, he deliberately chose to hide himself from the *akousmatikoi* during his lectures because he mostly communicated with them in parables. His *akousmatas,* those magnificent symbolical terms and enigmatic allegories, contained double meanings; one exoteric and the other esoteric. The *akousmatikoi* always struggled to comprehend their significance. Only the Masters, the very few *Sebastikoi,* and the most excelling members of the Inner Circle, understood, perfectly well, the esoteric meaning behind the symbolism of Pythagoras' parables.

From this perspective, when the Master mentioned the *Chant of the Mermaids*, he in fact meant the Harmony of the Spheres. When he spoke of the *Islands of the Blessed*, he betokened the Sun and the Moon. When he conveyed the image of the *Dogs of Persephone*, he certainly implied the Planets. And when he discussed the *Lyre of the Muses,* he expected the Initiates to fathom his reference to one of the Constellations!

Therefore, his audience focused completely on his words in order to comprehend the meaning. The *akousmatikoi*, in turn, were mostly ignorant of the hidden meaning. They, nonetheless, respected at all times the silence required during the lectures. They abstained, no matter what, to contest or discuss the teachings. They acquired a comprehensive knowledge, void of any detailed explanation, demonstration, or even reason – the latter being the most powerful of all human mental abilities. Thus, they meditated upon the parables on their own, or conferred among themselves in groups of two or three members. When it happened that some members of the Pythagorean Outer Circle disagreed over a certain theory of the Master, the debate never developed into a dispute. It quickly ended when any one of them issued the statement *Autos epha-ipsi dixit,* which meant "He (the Master) said it". As a result of that conformity, they all strove in maintaining and preserving the testimony and words of the Master.

In addition to the *akousmatas*, his lectures to the *akousmatikoi* contained clear elementary instructions relating to ordinary everyday life. These were subjects he communicated with the general public. In fact, at that time, Pythagoras preferred to abstain teaching them the mysteries of life or what dwelt beyond its physical manifestations. He contented himself to insinuate, and sometimes openly declare, their important connection to the universal laws and fundamental truths upon which the Listeners should base their queries. His words triggered their primordial faculties of intuition and inspiration. With every new revelation, a flicker of light seeped into their psyches for future self-accomplishments.

* * *

Early in the morning, when the sun appeared in the East, Pythagoras waited for his disciples in his cave, his head bent in serene meditation. The many apertures of the upper rock that formed the roof filtered in a few warming sunrays. His head now bathed with them. His disciples would be along, any moment now, for their lessons of the early day.

The birth of every new dawn on the Pythagorean City represented a new prospect of resurrection for the human spirits that longed to hear the Master; the Son of El-Apollo. And every Rising Sun, being nothing less than the rising of the god Apollo, re-creating life in the wide visible Kosmos. Despite being portrayed as the One, the *Not Many*, Apollo formed all Numbers in the unseen Kosmos.

In the garden around the Great Temple of Apollo, the young neophytes used the bedecked basins to submit to their washing ritual. They then proceeded, in steadfast reverence, inside the Temple. Whether they belonged to the Inner or Outer Circle, they all undertook the morning exercise of memory recollection as part of their essential training. They were required to recall the events of the previous day in their exact order.

In truth, the preservation of memory constituted a prime method for the fortification of knowledge acquired over the years. The sciences, experiences, and wisdom bestowed by the Master formed real treasures that required protection and memorization for as long as possible. They certainly recognized that without good memory, everything ended in vain.

Therefore, deep silence shepherded their prayers and meditation during that inner trip back. On their way out, they gathered in small groups to meander through the alley under the royal gate of the Temple. They discussed some of the imperative social issues related to the teachings of the Master. Others sat on stone benches and chanted hymns to the God. Moments later, they all strolled through the well-structured avenues of the White City. At the intersection of two streets, they met with a group of students coming from the square of the gymnasium.

All together, they headed now towards the Sacred Garden around the cave, known also as the habitat of the Initiate. For having earned the right to see the Philosopher, only the Members of the Inner Circle outstripped the restriction of the shielding veil of truth, and joined him inside. Members of the Outer Circle congregated outside in patent anticipation of the morning lecture.

Minutes later, the poised voice of the Master drifted to greet them with warmth. From behind the curtain set inside the cave, his silhouette basked in the sunlight of the Divine Inspiration of the sacred teachings. The Lyre in his hand, he posed like a real musician.

When he started his speech, his words traveled as swiftly as the speed of Light. He appeared in a transcendental state, like a Son of the Sun – the son of Al-Apollo, whom he confidently called *Father*. His firm and yet melodious voice resonated loudly to reach the neophytes in the Sacred Garden outside. The magical tunes of his dearest instrument, the Lyre, accompanied his words in tender melodies.

Pythagoras believed that his music produced a powerful yet soothing effect on both the physical and psychological levels. For that particular reason, he often combined his everyday teachings with the miraculous effects of his music on his audience.

And as usual, his words began full of wisdom and right to the point. "Verily I say unto you: Women and men are all equal in this Society. Both genders should assume their roles with much tact and efficiency while conforming to our tradition. We should all behave as one family; one for all and all for one! The Truth I tell you. In spite of the many differences between both genders, some women have the ability to become Philosophers, and may undoubtedly join the Inner Circle."

"Heed me. I reveal myself only to the members of the Inner Circle for they have succeeded in completing their *Preparation* period and moved up to the Second Degree that is the *Purification.* To them only, I communicate the wisdom kept and concealed in my heart for so long. I call them the *mathematikoi.* These Initiates, men and women, trek slowly and silently beyond the veil and into the secrets before they ultimately start their spiral ascension towards the Divine."

He granted to the meditation that followed enough time for his neophytes to ponder on this revelation. The soft tunes of his lyre prevailed under the game of his fingers.

"Wrong are those who claimed that wisdom could be found by men and for men only!" His voice spoke out what his spirit believed. "Listen to me, and listen well, for I only reveal you with the Truth. Sophia belongs also to women! Alongside the accomplishment of their domestic duties, and their most innate roles as creators of life and mothers, women have all the rights in the world, and all the capabilities, to seek and preserve wisdom. Indeed! For women are known to be wonderful custodians," he affirmed with the steadfast tone of conviction.

"Dear brothers and sisters, I end my oration today with an advice that you should consider as essential and carry as holy at all times in the depth of your hearts. Love your parents and honor them for they have always loved you dearly. Look upon your father as you would look upon God; the Creator of the Kosmos. There is nothing more revered than the value of a father. Look upon your mother as you would look upon the generous Nature, the Mother of humanity, and of the fauna and flora. A Mother nourishes her children with deep joy and remarkable care. Mother, what a beautiful phenomena!

"In Truth, the love you hold for your country, as you must, stems from your primal childhood feelings of love towards your mother ever since she was your guardian.

"And, to speak with finality, behold the following important truth. Our parents were not given to us by mere coincidence! Not at all! Only the ignorant deems it a coincidence. In reality, such things do not exist, for everything occurs for a clear reason of the Divine Plan; an *Essential Will*. Things truly happen, the way they happen, by necessity, and due to a superior order of the Number. Behold that truth, dear brothers and sisters, and behold it well."

The Master ended his discourse and disappeared, further into the depth of the grotto... into the depth of his thoughts. He knew that such knowledge remained undeniably difficult for the *akousmatikoi* to grasp. Even the few *mathematikoi,* those closer to him, would not understand, but only slightly, the full meaning of his final statement. In fact, that knowledge would remain vague in their minds until they attained the great mysteries, akin to the *Sebastikoi*; those few leading members of the Inner Circle who had achieved the mysterious path towards the truth.

* * *

Later, sometime around midday, the Pythagorean novices offered prayers to their minor deities: the gods and the good spirits. They then sat quietly for their lunch, composed of bread, honey, and olives. Sometimes vegetables, milk cakes, and fruits were added. The non-vegetarians among them enjoyed a meal made up of meat or fish.

Based on their motto *a healthy mind in a healthy body*, the afternoon saw them exercising in the gymnasium. Some ran for miles, others built up their muscles by throwing disks and hurling arrows. Some of them engaged in wrestling, which they practiced in the form of Dorian dances. Others jumped with weights in their hands. And, while they considered these sporting activities a must – to train their bodies the way they educated their minds – they reveled in the physical and moral benefits of the games.

The routine of the day continued, afterwards, with the Pythagorean Listeners devoting themselves to poetry and history, be it individually, or in small groups of two or three. The importance of poetry was ascribed to its mythological context, which contained highly interesting theological and philosophical figurative forms.

As the sun edged down on the horizon, they allocated some time for essential contemplations. Some meditated with hindsight on the early morning lessons of the Master. Others converged in small groups that walked in the garden around the Temple of Apollo while sharing their inputs on their recent studies.

The moment in which the sun disappeared behind the sea, they headed for their bath before assembling for their common prayer. During the open-air ritual, young men and women burned incense on the outside altar of the Temple of Apollo. With magnificent hymns, they eulogized El-Apollo, the One and the Father. With Cedar, Laurel, and Oak branches in their hands, raised up in veneration, they honored their gods. Ceres-Astarte, Mother Nature to all living beings, received her share of incantations, followed by exaltations to Diana, the protector of the Dead.

Reputed for their strong faith, the Pythagorean brothers and sisters of both Circles always honored their divinities in the White City. They strongly believed in consulting their gods, the source of all good, for guidance and enlightenment. Hence, they carved their images in fine splendor on brass of spherical forms. Brass held a particular importance in that work of art, for they deemed this metal to be the most appropriate, beside the spherical shape, to operate as a divine receptor.

When the night fell smoothly on that heavenly City and the stars appeared softly in the large celestial realm, they gathered for their dinner in the Assembly Hall. Since they had abstained from consuming any strong drink during the day, they could now allow themselves some wine. Halfway through their meal, the youngest among them joyfully recited some poetry. However, an older brother might critique it at will.

Their dinner ended an hour and a half later with the due honor to their Master. They all stood up, raised their goblets, and cheered to him. They then chanted delightful hymns to their divinities, to their parents who fostered them, and to the Fraternity.

In peaceful spirits, the *akousmatikoi* headed to their homes to join their family members. The *Sebastikoi* and the *mathematikoi*, in turn, retreated to their secluded dormitories in the *homakoeion*. All dressed in untainted white, they stretched down in their beds of white sheets and covers. Before they slumbered their night away, they performed the rite of memory recollection. Hence, all behaviors, actions, and words of the day withstood a profound assessment, an honest self-examination of their conscience. Only then did they allow for the calmness of the night to engulf them in the peace that presided over their sleep.

269

* * *

Apollo rose again in the early morning to find his so-called son already waiting in the cave. His head bent, Pythagoras surrendered in devotion for the Light of Apollo to bathe him and for His Divine inspiration and wisdom to anoint him. Basked in serenity, he soon received his *mathematikoi* inside the cave while his *akousmatikoi* assembled outside in the sacred garden.

With a poised smile, he grabbed his lyre. He stared at the *mathematikoi* settling around him in a semi-circle. He then moved closer to the curtain to address his neophytes and those outside as well.

"Brothers and sisters! May the Sun Apollo shine upon your day as in your mind today, and grant you the needed enlightenment. Happy am I, indeed, to be able to give you some crucial advice. Heed it and adopt it in your life, for by it you shall find the Golden Way[38] towards the Divine Virtue.

"I am delighted that you are honoring the Supreme God El-Apollo, the Immortal gods and the Divine Law that spoke about them, in order. It gratifies me, as well, to see you venerating the honorable heroes, and the spirits of the dead, and revering your parents and relatives, and finally, the oath.

"The Truth I tell you! No one will find, either in words or in ways of life, anything more perfect than *Philia*, friendship. Philia is a universal law of mutual attraction and interdependence. Philia is a

---

[38] The Golden Verses were written later by one of the Pythagorean masters, sometime around the fourth century BCE. His name remains unknown to us. Yet they, undoubtedly, reflect to a big extent, the spirit of Pythagoras, his teachings, and of course, the essence of the Pythagorean lifestyle. The Golden Verses are presented in seventy one lines. The reader can get to know a big part in this book. The teachings of Pythagoras, here stated, are from different sources, including the Golden Verses.

270

Kosmic force that attracts all the elements of nature into harmonious relationships.

"Thus, select your friends and life associates according to what affinities you share with them. Among all the people you may encounter in life, whether here or outside the White City, elect them from among the ones who excel in virtue. You must realize that a friend is another self that you should honor like you honor a god. Friendship is equality, and among friends everything should be common. Do not get into fights with them. Do not reach the destructive level of hatred towards them, especially for insignificant, silly mistakes. Yield to kind words and helpful deeds as far as you can, for ability is near to necessity.

"Pay attention to the following advice; I ask you today to cast your pride away, for it is better to live a life of modesty than of egotism. When you are happy, do not exaggerate your expressions of laughter. And when you are annoyed, hinder your anger from your faces.

"I tell you, do not spend in excess like those careless of what is good, nor be parsimonious. Opt for the middle path, as moderation is always best. So chose the average way instead.

"Think wisely before acting, to avoid foolishness. It is the worthless man who gets in the habit of speaking and acting without tact and consideration. Only perform such acts in a way that you will not regret them later.

"I advise you to practice a lifestyle of purity, never of debauchery! Avoid all deeds that might cause envy. See that you always perform and undertake what holds no harm to you. Discard any attempt to embark on matters that you ignore, but learn what is necessary. In Truth, this is the way to ensure a more pleasant life for yourselves.

"A major advice, my brothers and sisters, is for you to recognize that death comes to everyone. Know that wealth will sometimes be acquired,

271

sometimes lost. Whatever your destiny and whatever your grief, as mortals by divine probability, bear them without complaint. Yet, it is only right to improve your existence as much as you can. Remember this; fate does not confer so many sufferings on good people.

"A golden rule for you to know, my friends, is that many words befall men, wicked and noble alike. Do not be astonished or constrained by them. If a lie is told, endure it with gentleness. Whatever I tell you, carry it out to fruition, yet let no one persuade you by word or deed, to do or say, what is not best for you. Be liberal and candid.

"I strongly recommend for you to adopt simple garments that are always clean and chaste. Do not adorn your bodies with gold or the like, especially when you enter the Temple to perform religious rites. Purity, I tell you in truth, is a sign of equanimity and justice in reasoning."

The *mathematikoi* and the *akousmatikoi* appeared riveted. Nothing could disrupt their attention, neither the heat of the morning with its twitters of birds, nor the colorful butterflies over the bushes. Their concentration revered the Philosopher of all time. And the Philosopher spoke, indeed, words of pure, authentic gold.

"As for what you consume, my brothers and sisters, I warn you against eating meat and fish. This kind of food reverts you back to your natural instincts. Do not eat beans, either! My observations and experience assert the interference of this plant with the process of lucid thinking. It distorts the prophetic visions during our meditations and dreams. Instead, drink as much water as you can, and wine but in small quantities, for they are both beneficial to the body. And so, you should not be neglectful of your physical health! Exercise your body. Consume your food and beverage with moderation to avoid regretting the detriment of any excess.

272

"I also advise you, brothers and sisters, to conform yourselves to the practice of restraint over your appetite, sleepiness, sexuality, and angry behaviors. Always abstain from doing shameful deeds, be it to or with others, and be it in public or in private. Instead, respect yourselves above all so you can respect others. Therefore, exercise Justice, not only in words, but also in deeds!

"Another golden rule I offer you, my friends! Do not kill, and never harm any human being who might endanger you, your family, or your beloved. It is more just, or rather holy, to be injured than to end the life of a person. I tell you but the Truth; our final judgment is mysteriously related to our actions here in this life.

"Heed my advice, my friends, and heed it well. It is of great importance to love life and to have compassion for all living forms. Do not kill harmless animals but treat them with kindness. Do not kill at all, for whatever the reason. When feeling threatened, defend yourselves for this is always justified. Do not cut trees, for they are beautiful and significant. The Cedar tree in particular, my friends, is to be highly respected and preserved, for it is the symbol of the Initiate!" The Master paused for a moment behind his curtain, yet his lyre prevailed with its soothing tunes.

The neophytes outside kept their eyes on his silhouette, their minds pondering on his golden advice and their hearts on that barely visible god-like figure who might judge them according to their deeds! Yet, the voice that spoke carried no judgment or admonishment whatsoever, just love and care in the tones and contents of the message.

"On Holy days, do not cut your hair or forget your religious services. Beware of offering your services for the sole purpose of increasing your profits! Stay religiously conscious and honest when enacting spiritual ceremonies. Pray to the gods for success, and get yourself to work!

"My final advice today, my friends, is to undergo a clear examination of your conscience every night. Always ask yourselves what wrong have you done during the day. Hold yourselves responsible for your shameful error, if any. Meditate on the duties you have failed that day, and rejoice in the good deeds you have achieved!"

The Master finished his speech. Silence prevailed inside the cave and outside in the Sacred Garden.

Truth be told, Pythagoras never deemed himself a divine judge, but mainly a Master to be duly respected, and his teachings to be adequately absorbed and applied. Most importantly, he considered himself a friend, who taught with much love and care all the necessary qualities that should help his followers live a good, a perfect life. He cared to embody the role of an older brother in his Fraternity. He throve for his charming friendship to liberate them from present and potential troubles and worries. Undoubtedly, he believed in standing as the ideal role model of the Philosopher. Therefore, his devoted and generous approach towards his people meant to instill their minds with an essential moral virtue that could ameliorate their socio-cultural behavior.

As a matter of fact, he lived virtuously by those same precepts and, therefore, what he preached and tutored always instigated the admiration of his followers. Their respect for him increased with each passing day. In consequence, they never doubted him and never hesitated to abide and live by his rules.

Always in a white linen tunic, he epitomized the god of their White City. He abstained from any intake of wine during the day. He adopted a strict vegetarian diet that consisted only of bread, honey and vegetables. He loved all his disciples dearly and equally, yet restrained religiously from any sexual desires, and abstained to love any woman in

274

particular. He never laughed foolishly nor behaved cynically. He neither mocked nor punished any of them. In conclusion, he loved them with pure and divine feelings.

* * *

She was beautiful indeed. Her ebony mane cascaded on her fine shoulders and down her back to the waist. The green eyes, on her tanned face, brightened with anticipation. Alone on the green grass of the Sacred Garden, outside the cave, the young woman stood bathed in radiance by the sunrays. The neophytes glanced discreetly at her as they left the site of their morning lecture and headed to their duties of the day. Some lingered. They waited for the few confessions allowed after the discourse. By turns, they entered the cave and sat on the floor of the outer side of the veil to confess their personal issues to the Master, he, the Son of Light. When her turn came, the woman, in reverence and modesty, swathed her head with an elegant blue veil, then went in.

From behind the curtain, Pythagoras bent his head in attention to the confession of the woman.

"I want to tell you a secret, oh, Master," she murmured shyly and her soft voice rang a bell in his memory.

"Go ahead my child," he encouraged her with affection and focused at once on his duty at hand.

"I'm attracted to a certain man, Master, and I..., I think I'm in love with him. When I look at him, love overwhelms me. His words pierce my inner realm just as the first sunrays penetrate the soil of the Earth. And inside me, everything shivers, Master!" She admitted with fervor, and then paused for a while, probably thinking what to say next.

An extraordinary quietness echoed strongly inside the walls of the cave.

"Carry on my child. I'm listening," he goaded her to proceed.

"Sometimes, I'm so besieged by his voice that his profound words reach me unfathomably. This whole situation perplexes me greatly. I don't know what to do or how to think correctly. He has the power, and certainly the vision, but he keeps it to himself. What shall I do, Master?" she sounded desperate and it touched his heart.

There was a strange kind of tranquility for a few seconds.

"Why the despair my child? Is your love for him forbidden? Is he married, or has he rejected your feelings?"

"Oh no! None of these, Reverent Master. He... well, how should I put it... He just doesn't know it. I'm not sure he has even noticed me at all!"

Somehow, he felt for her. "Then, why don't you tell him what you feel? You ought to have the courage, my child. Courage is a value we uphold."

"Courage? Oh Master, I have none!" She sounded distressed, her voice tearful. "Honestly? I'm afraid he might reject me! He...," she hesitated as if weighing how to reveal the identity of the man who stole her heart.

Pythagoras then recognized the woman from one of her previous confessions.

"Theano," the softness of his voice meant to comfort her in her pain. "Why should he reject your love for him? Tell me, who is he?"

A long silence ensued in which the Master waited with patience. He knew of her previous pleas as well, for she earlier struggled through her queries for faith.

"Theano," he intimated with a firm kindness, urging her to speak out.

"Master, he... he is...,"

"Yes, Theano?"

Impelled by his tone of commandment, she rushed on her words, "He is the intimate friend and lover of Sophia, the Philosopher who prepares me to understand the secrets of life. He teaches me who I really am!"

"Is he one of the Masters?" he prompted to ask before he realized that she might have meant... *him!*

"You mean...?"

He saw her bowing her head from behind the curtain.

A mask revealed. Time stood still.

Pythagoras, the Grand Initiate of great spiritual life – he who always thrived on the occult powers of nature – sagged back in astonishment. He had renounced *women* since the very beginning. He never thought of loving in that sense, and especially not one of his disciples! He had directed all his energy and feelings, always and uniquely, to his White City and his followers whom he loved equally, based on the quality of *Philia*.

Theano's revelation came unscathed from any seduction, but rather, a statement of untainted love. He suddenly became aware of her pleasant scent, which grabbed his senses. Completely beset, he wondered in the silence of his thoughts, w*hat is happening to me?*

The Master had long since learned to control his senses, squelch his emotions, and conquer all kinds of seductive illusions. However, this spell differed from anything he had ever experienced before. It swelled up, real, inescapable, and undeniable! Her strong spiritual glow, and her vivid mental vibrations penetrated his inner realm and ensnared him completely.

Without further hesitation, he lifted the curtain. There she was, the lovely Theano, the daughter of Brontinus of Crotona – an Orphic who had become a Pythagorean. In truth, the Philosopher had never suspected that she might nourish any such emotion for him. She had, indeed, succeeded in hiding it all along!

In her mid twenties and of medium height, Theano, with her beauty and youth, could have been married by then, but her fate apparently had decided otherwise.

From her father, Pythagoras knew that since childhood, she had always displayed a strong affinity for the spiritual world. The mysteries behind life had attracted her interest back then, and goaded her, still today, to grab all the opportunities and attempt to unlock their secrets.

He studied her soul through that special spark in her green eyes. Since becoming a Pythagorean sister, this was the first time they had come as close to seeing each other face to face or talk without the obstacle of the curtain. He knew, of course, the depth of her intellect for he had frequently attended, in secret, the many tests and trials of her probationary period. Akin all novices, Theano had undergone his clandestine scrutiny. She had completed the experimental period with an outstanding success and, at this stage; she adhered to the Pythagorean *Preparation* phase – the *first degree*. Her strong personality, her acute spirit of inquisition, and her spiritual intelligence made her emerge as an exceptional student. Her uniqueness had stood out from the start, not only among women but also among the brothers of the Pythagorean Society.

Looking at her now, the Master deemed her, somehow, a gift of fate. Without taking his eyes from hers, he stood up slowly. He grabbed her hands in his with affection to lift her to her feet. The softness of her skin touched him to the core of his heart. Their eyes hooked. The intensity of the moment reflected in the love her soul conveyed to him.

Time stood still.

It stood for some time...

Then, he saw it: their future together, a perpetual union that their fate claimed loudly in the quietness of the cave.

The moment her hands left his and she turned to leave, his heart shivered. An emotion, new to him, fastened his attention on her, walking the lane back to the Temple. She glimpsed at him over her shoulder. Her smile appeared to compete with the sunrays basking in her silhouette. He snatched himself from the magic of the moment to revert back to his cave and his thoughts. His mind fought his heart. The struggle between his intuition and rationality escorted him all day. Confusion unsettled him all night long. After all these years of restricted Initiation, the Master found it hard to accept that his heart had yielded to the love of a woman!

Is it possible? But how? What was that powerful emotion that took my breath away and entrapped me to that young beauty? Is it love or simply affection?

Affection! What kind of affection could trigger such physical desires that render me helpless and powerless?

Affection... love... physical desires...

What is the difference then between these emotions?!

And so it happened that the long night took him by surprise.

.8.

Initiation
The Theology of Numbers

Beyond question, the paranormal character of Pythagoras produced a major intellectual impact, not only on the minds of his followers but there, where his reputation and messages reached all through the Mediterranean cities and towns. Residents and visitors wondered, questioned, and speculated. And yet, whatever the stance, skeptical or trustful, all received the seeds of his wisdom.

Bound to his Philosophy and method for a better life through his magical potency, his followers abided religiously to his wise teachings, and to the vast knowledge he introduced. His adepts felt the rise of their individual energy that made the realization of their primary goal possible: the harmony with the Kosmos!

Harmony, as Pythagoras taught, was the universal law adroitly orchestrated by the Universal Mind; the *One*, the Great Monad. There, resided the essence of the great mysteries, and the invisible order of numbers manifested, in shapes and sizes, within the mundane world.

Inside the *City of a god*, some remained *Listeners* by decision of their Masters, or by their own personal choice. These Pythagorean Auditors represented the majority of that society. They were the *akousmatikoi*; the *Outer Circle* who lived with their families – in their own private homes – inside the City, and sometimes outside. They only attended the lectures of the Master during the day, in the outer Sacred Garden of the cave. They acquired the teachings of the Philosopher through the method of the *akousmata*; an allegoric form of

280

speech. Contrary to the *Inner Circle* Disciples, they were allowed to keep their belongings, or assets, in spite of the fact that Pythagoras deemed the material possessions to be harmful to *theoria*; the meditation of the Divine Truth. Moreover, the *akousmatikoi* could choose to adopt a vegetarian lifestyle if desired, although that rule did not necessarily apply to them.

Similarly, when deemed competent, some followers engaged the *Inner Circle* by free will, or by decision of the Masters. Few young *Listeners* grew to be *mathematikoi* in time and through hard work. The third group within the Pythagorean Society was the *Sebastikoi*. They stood as the religious functionaries of the Order; the leading members and the Masters of the Inner Circle. They resided with the *mathematikoi*, lived like monks in the *homakoeion,* and slept in an annexed common dormitory. Wholly detached from any material wealth, they shared their goods with generosity, and abstained from eating meat and fish.

And again, akin to their Masters, the *mathematikoi* devoted their time to *theoria*. Hence, they dealt with pure thoughts and engrossed in the contemplation of the Divine Truth. They embodied the avid inspectors of the esoteric properties of Numbers. Accordingly, they took into serious consideration the spirit and essence of their Master's Philosophy, which encompassed mathematical theories, and their practical applications to life.

They would meet in secret sessions under the chamber of the Temple of the Muses. Pythagoras would stand in the center of their semi-circle to address them. He frequently conferred them with the imperative rules of their allegiance to the Fraternity, be it at the beginning of their clandestine lessons, or at the end.

"Brothers and sisters of our esteemed Order," he would say daily, "I ask you to endorse strict

281

loyalty towards each other, as well as to your Masters and me! Practice confidentiality and adopt communalism, for, in truth, they are of critical importance to our Secret Society!"

In point of fact, he insisted in reminding them of their major significance to their Society. Needless to say, they never argued or hesitated to abide by his rules with foremost devotion.

* * *

One day, the year in course was 513 BCE, one of his uncle's students brought an urgent letter. The moment it reached his hand, he shivered with unexpected emotion at its negative vibrations. *Bad news!* His intuition muttered. He hesitated, his eyes riveted on the scroll of papyrus. All too slowly, he untied it, unrolled it, and read.

Uncle Pherecydes is dying! His heart moaned in pain.

The message heralded his uncle's last days. Bed stricken with a fatal illness, he requested the presence of his nephew. The messenger urged him to travel as soon as possible. His hands trembled on the papyrus. The vision of his beloved uncle, flailing in his bed, smudged the words into an eerie appearance. Tears blurred his vision. His heart cried. He sagged on his chair.

Pherecydes, his primary source of great knowledge and wisdom, was dying! Pherecydes and his teachings; the science of Cosmogony, the immortality of the psyche, and his concept of reincarnation... A Sage in the real sense of the word who had led him in his primordial steps towards Sophia then guided his interest to the Egyptian profound Initiation...

It had been so long since their last get-together. Memories – long forgotten – surged with force in his mind, memories of his father, his beloved mother, and his teacher, Thales.

Are they all gone, without me being by their sides for the final farewell? His heart grieved at the thought. He suddenly feared to loose his uncle, his teacher, without seeing him again.

Leaping to his feet, he grabbed strength from the pain itself and walked out of his dwellings at once, his decision made. He did not dawdle in his preparations to leave Crotona the same day. Time could impede the very last chance to spend some valuable time with his agonizing uncle. He prompted to gather his *Sebastikoi* in order to brief them on his resolution. Acknowledging the capability of his officials, he entrusted them with the Society. The same night, he set sail for Greece with two of his closest Disciples: Archippus and Glorippus.

The ship sailed through the Mediterranean Sea towards the Grecian archipelago of the Aegean Sea. Half way through the journey, a fierce storm disturbed the peaceful dawn, angered the sea, and rocked the ship all too violently. Women bawled in fear. Children cried in terror. The sailors shouted as they scurried to contain the damages. Nature riposted with increasing fury at their desperate attempts to manage the precarious situation.

Caught amidst the chaos, Pythagoras fought his way to the captain's compartment and scuttled up the narrow stairs to the roof. Archippus and Glorippus ran after him in panic, dreading to lose him to the storm. Unconcerned by the rain drenching him, he stood on the platform with his legs spread apart firmly for an equilibrium that was hard to achieve. Yet, determined, he defied the wind that throve but to flatter his purple robe. He raised his right hand towards the sky and pointed the left towards the sea. With a fierce voice that thundered over the current tumult, he commanded, "As below, so above!"

Time ceased for a moment...

His disciples halted in their race abruptly behind him. Aware of being on the verge of a new outstanding exploit of their Master, they held their breath. In a gesture that bound the Earth and Heaven together, he conjured with authority, "Elim shalam likum... Melki yam... Melki rouh... Shalam!"

The strange ancient mystical words knocked the tempest down with an extraordinary power. The furious nature capitulated. The waters of the sea quieted down. The rain abated. The ship stabilized. The wind waned away. Bewildered, his disciples froze in absolute veneration.

Sailors and passengers gawked around them in total disbelief and confusion. They followed the direction of the pointed fingers of the few who had witnessed the magical feat of the Master. Stunned, they gazed up at this majestic figure on the platform. His serene authority radiated on them, transforming their awe into adoration for that man with godly powers who had just saved their lives.

With his typical modest tranquility, Pythagoras made his way down, and through the crowd that stepped back in respect at his passage. For him, such a heroic act was nothing more than the result of utilizing his *mathemagical* powers to pacify the sea, appease the wind, and stabilize their sailing conditions. In spite of his unpretentious attitude, no one dared approach him, not then nor during the remainder of the journey. They would scrutinize him discreetly from afar, keeping to what they considered unanimously to be their human rank. A few more courageous passangers queried about him with the two disciples. Eventually, the talk of the ship, for the last ten days and nights before they reached land, circled around Pythagoras the Mathemagician, the Master of Sophia – the son of Phoenicia with amazing authority.

Reaching Syros, the small isle facing Miletus in the Aegean Sea, Pythagoras smiled tenderly as he recalled his primary education on that Phoenician colony. Pherecydes had lived there almost all his life[39]...

And now, the crucial phase called *Death* awaited him.

What is death but a passage to another dimension of a more sublime existence?

Pherecydes had always believed the veracity of that notion. How would he now face that terrifying moment? That was still to be seen.

With his two disciples in tow, Pythagoras took the lane leading to his uncle's house. The exotic plants of the island bloomed on their path. He remembered, with a blend of ache and affection, the beautiful moments in which he had meandered around with his uncle. He reached the terrace of the residence where he had spent years studying under the guidance of Pherecydes. He halted in order to touch the wooden bench and connect with his memories: those magical instants with his Lyre, mostly at nights. A faint sound of steps and murmurs made him turn around. Pale and downhearted, a dozen students stood around in small groups. Ache pinched his heart. He sympathized with their anxious wait for the departure of their teacher, whom they already mourned. He introduced himself briefly, and communicated to them his own sorrow. He then went to sit on the bench to bunch up his strength, and control the flow of his sadness. His faithful companions, Archippus and Glorippus, remained with the students to grant them comfort.

A moment later, one of the neophytes moved towards him. His head slightly bent, his voice low, he offered to escort him inside the house. Pythagoras nodded a silent consent and followed him. More students, their faces withdrawn and their

---

[39] Some have suggested that the meeting between Pherecydes and Pythagoras happened on the isle of Delos, near Syros, but there is no such historical proof.

eyes tearful, lingered in the hall. At this point, he lost all effort to smile. The vibrations of grief in the air overwhelmed him. Wordless, he proceeded at once into his uncle's bedroom, followed by his escort.

Bed stricken Pherecydes, his eyes to the ceiling, waited with stoicism to pass to the other side of Life. His face carried the grayish tint of death, and the contortion of pain. Pythagoras halted at the sorrowful sight; 'a scene he had envisioned upon receipt of the letter, yet too painful a reality for him to absorb. As if sensing his presence, Pherecydes turned his head slowly. Their eyes met. An intense current of emotions and memories fused between them for long moments of joy and sorrow. The teacher smiled widely. His eyes brightened.

"Pythagoras..." he whispered, in a tone loaded with love and relief, and his wrinkly hand extended towards him.

Pythagoras rushed to grab it in the warmth of his own grasp then leaned to kiss the feverish forehead of the dying man. Pherecydes motioned for the student to leave them alone, which he did quietly. Without waiting for an invitation, Pythagoras sat on the bed rim, as close as possible to face him.

"Uncle..." he murmured, in a tearful tone, then added in respect, "Master..."

Although he had surpassed his Master in the knowledge of Sophia, he still deemed him his grand mentor to whom he owed his utmost esteem. *Respecting our Masters* was one of his favorite principles that he constantly reinforced in his White City; a stance he expected from all his disciples to take to heart.

"How are you, Pythagoras?" Pherecydes asked in a low tone.

"I'm fine, uncle."

"I've heard about your Society... and the great mysteries around it...." A series of coughs interrupted him. He murmured an apology and continued, not without trouble, "I hope... you are not facing... difficulties in... maintaining the organization."

"Not to worry, uncle. Everything is going well. I have things under control."

"Tell me how." His interest was patent in the eyes he focused on his nephew.

"Simple, uncle, I've divided the Fraternity into two circles, an inner and an outer. Accordingly, I'm keeping it all in order under the close scrutiny of the *Sebastikoi*: the religious functionaries of the Order."

Pythagoras briefed him on the structure. He restrained to impart but the bare minimum as the old master looked suddenly withdrawn in his agony. He seemed to struggle with his breath, and with the pain that distorted his features.

"Pythagoras, my beloved neophyte... my dear nephew.... I asked for you... for two main reasons," he mumbled as if the words affected his feeble capability to breathe. "The Society... first, of course.... I'm extremely happy for this success. But son... beware of envious people."

"I am, don't worry. Be still now. Don't speak too much!" He fretted, concerned that his uncle would collapse under the effort of speaking, for the coughs interrupted him with an anguishing frequency.

"No, son... Time is running... Heed me... before it is too late," he pleaded with a broken voice that meant to be a command. "Your mother, son... before she died... she asked a favor of me. I was in Phoenicia... at the time. I saw her... always so beautiful and graceful... my dear sister...." He stopped. Tears streamed on his craggy face and disappeared through his thick white beard.

"Yes, uncle?" With a kind yet firm tone, Pythagoras urged him back to the present, and out

287

of the painful memories that seemed to torture him at the moment.

His uncle turned his weepy eyes to him and murmured, "She worried about you, son. She wanted you to... to think about yourself for a change... to have a wife, a family. It was her wish... her most loving and deepest desire... I promised her to convey to you her message... I am sorry I couldn't before. But... here you are now, aren't you, son? And that is not too much to ask anyway."

Pythagoras smiled softly to the eyes probing him for an answer, yet he abstained to comment, for his mind dwelt in the idea. Such a wish from a loving mother would come true one day with Theano.

It was planned by the One; he thought, realizing that he and Theano would be joined forever. In truth, he started to believe, now more than ever, in the inevitability of that union.

"Pythagoras!" The trembling voice requested an answer.

"Uncle, dear. I believe we have enough time to talk about that during my stay. My main concern and purpose is to serve you now. I intend to remain at your side for as long as it takes."

Pherecydes nodded with a faint grin that betrayed his great relief. A tear shone in the corner of his eye. In spite of his belief in the immortality of the psyche, he whispered, "Time... yes of course... but we don't know how much more is left."

Pythagoras went silent.

So did the room for a long while.

The days elapsed much too quickly on, this, their last reunion, and yet too slowly for the man suffering the daily agony. Pythagoras nursed his uncle with devotion and love. He would not leave his side, sleeping in the chair facing him. His priority focused on transforming his uncle's last days into as much of an enjoyable and peaceful time as the circumstances would allow. He would make him laugh at his jokes, and distract him with tales of his many trips. He would feed him, wash him, and change his tunic. When the coughs became stronger than bearable, he would hold him by the shoulders with tender care. Thus, when Pherecydes stared at him with gratefulness a moment before his sense of the physical world wilted and collapsed, the old master departed with a happy smile on his serene face.

On that memorable day in the history of the Island of Syros, Pythagoras buried his uncle near a Phoenician temple on the island. The funeral ceremony hosted all those disciples who had received the deep impact of Pherecydes' faith.
His epitaph read:

> *"All adorned with modesty and virtue,*
> *All wisdom was summarized in him,*
> *Even after his death,*
> *His spirit lives a delightful life."*

And so it did. Pythagoras had no doubt that Pherecydes had touched immortality with his psyche!
In respect and honor to the memory and value of the deceased, Pythagoras remained for a month with the students Pherecydes had left behind. He dedicated that time to reinforce the important teachings they had acquired through the years. He urged them to keep the memory and wisdom of their master well alive in their hearts.
Only then, reassured of the accomplishment of his mission, did he pack his meager belongings. He left for shore with both of his faithful disciples. There, they took the first Phoenician ship in destination to Italy.

* * *

Pythagoras resumed his life and responsibilities as soon as he reached the White City. Satisfied with the successful trials of some of the Outer Circle, he approved their admittance into the Inner Circle in order for them to pursue more profound truth. Keen to have them as his direct disciples, he soon summoned them to the ritual ceremony. He intended to sanctify them, for them to become his Pythagorean *mathematikoi*. Inside the crypt of the sanctuary of the Muses, he prepared himself to receive them, standing at his sides, his skillful *Sebastikoi* adepts and a few *mathematikoi*.

The nine Muses, regarded as the goddesses of harmony, sciences, and arts, stood in wait. Divided into three categories for the three elements, the Muses consisted of the three superior goddesses. The first category presided over the sciences of Cosmogony, covering both Astronomy and Astrology. They mastered the art of divination, and managed both the concept of life and of death. They also handled the spirits of the *au-delà* and their reincarnations. The second trio, the middle Muses, presided over the sciences of Man, which covered magic, psychology, and medicine. The last group of three regulated all living forms in the mundane world as well as the four elements that shaped life: *fire, wind, water* and *earth*.

The new Disciples, numbered in ten, finally entered the crypt with utmost reverence. Although hoods covered their heads, their faces seemed to radiate with expectation, for they were about to penetrate, at last, the secret domain of the Master. Their eyes reflected their awe and wonder at the scene in front of them.

In turn, Pythagoras received them with the respect and honor they had earned from him. He gazed for a moment at Aristaeus of Crotona then his heart warmed when he met Theano's eyes.

With a serene smile, he shared their joy, for he would soon reveal to them the Great Mysteries of

Life. They had come, in fact, to undergo a higher level of the Pythagorean system; *Purification*, known also as the *second degree*. From there onward, they would receive the esoteric knowledge from mouth to ear, so to speak, for the simple reason that the essence of the Occult Doctrine resided purely in the enigmatic science of numbers. It is followed by the concept of the universal evolution of the manifested realities that would undoubtedly lead them to the understanding of the final abode; there where the human psyches reside. Hence, they would certainly become like gods since they would achieve a sublime unification with the Universal Mind. *De facto*, the process embodied pure Occultism – the real *magic*.

In principle, all former Initiates of the Ancient World had come to know the basic forms of the science of numbers, the esoteric sacred meanings of the twenty-two alphabetical letters, and the hidden essence of geometrical figures. Secretly implemented by the High Priests, this secret science existed in the Phoenician sacred tradition and in the Egyptian system. It also transpired in the Babylonian method, the Zoroastrian mode, and the Hindu Initiation. These secrets had remained hidden from the vulgar, the common populace, for it contained the keys to the occult world. They would only emerge during their ceremonies of Initiation.

Pythagoras had adopted their structures and developed them into an effective and more profound system. In short, he had created a new way known as the Pythagorean method inculcated to his disciples at that second degree. At any rate, the principles of foundation behind the *Theology* of Pythagoras were deep-rooted in the science of sacred mathematics, the world of numbers. Eruditely formulated, and meticulously purified, his theology became equal to the sacred verb of the Phoenician-Egyptian tradition of the Great White Fraternity.

At that very moment, inside the crypt, the nine goddesses moved to surround the majestic statue of Hestia-Isis; the perfect goddess veiled with mystery. Her left hand held a torch that emitted a translucent light. Her right one was pointed towards the Heavens. Isis represented the guardian of the divine essence, which existed everywhere. She symbolized Sophia: the Divine Hokmah.

Pythagoras stood steadfast at her feet, as if he was her son Horus. The long purple robe, which he wore over his white tunic and purple belt, reflected his divine image. The religious functionaries of the Order, the *Sebastikoi,* flanked him from the right and his few *mathematikoi* from the left. In front of him, the soon-to-be mathematikoi waited in reverence.

He gazed at each one, in turn, to examine their souls then issued with authority, "Fellow young brothers and sisters, I command you to honor the coming words with a tranquil soul. By adhering to the Inner Circle, you will undertake a purification of your body. Only then will you be able to control the tricky and exigent desires of the physical world. To be more precise, I imply the strong sexual energy that you must completely eliminate from your life, for the time being."

The disciples did not seem to have any problem with that. No reaction emanated from them whatsoever. Relieved, Pythagoras moved on to the revelations he intended to impart as a start.

"Today, you will learn the four important rules concerning the knowledge of the occult sciences. Listen and listen well to the Truth of the primary elements of Sophia that I am about to reveal to you!"

"First, know that Mathematics reside at the deepest level of reality. That is why I have named you *mathematikoi,*" he added with a smile. "Mathematics is a theoretical science that helps you seek the mysterious world of numbers in order to meditate upon the Divine Truth. Mathematics shall guide your thinking process, and make your analysis sequentially clear. It is, indeed, the second best form of mind purification, certainly after Philosophy. It will elevate you towards the realm of reality, where you should reside in order to build the world."

The disciples shared murmurs of excitement and grinned with enthusiasm. The idea of mastering reality and building a new world infused them with a new energy patent in the sparkles of their eyes.

"The second principle, my friends, concerns the benefit of Philosophy to the psyche. In truth, it is the highest form of purification. Brothers and sisters, you are the future Philosophers. Know thyselves!"

The new mathematikoi gasped in elation and a few fervent whispers ensued. With a hand gesture, the Master claimed stillness in order to carry on.

"The third principle reveals to you certain symbols that shall engage you directly through your journey into the Inner Circle. These symbols carry mystical meanings that shall arouse the unconscious in you, and make it conscious of itself; and that, in order to awaken the state of your intuitive knowledge."

"The fourth principle, my friends, implies the Divine Powers that were implemented, *de facto*, within your individual psyche at the beginning of your life. Not only from the moment you were born, but from the very instant of your conception! The Truth I tell you! These powers shall levitate you through Initiation to unite you with the Central Fire of the Universe; the Divine Spirit that is the Great Monad."

Their most serious spiritual expedition into reality's realm had just started. They would come to float beyond time and space to penetrate, then merge, with the *hieros logos* of the Master; that sacred discourse that would expose to them the Ultimate Truth of Numbers.

"The Number is not an abstract quantity. It is indeed a real and active virtue of the Supreme One; He who is the Source of Universal Harmony!" The Mathematician asserted in their direction. "The Number is also a factual and dynamic asset of the harmonious structure of the Psyche. It is the wisest! Numbers are the Divine Powers that are in action within the Macrocosm and the Microcosm. They are the movers of the Kosmos and the rulers of all forms and ideas. They are gods!"

"I tell you, now and always, do not speak of God without putting some light on, for God is the True Light. Accept Him with a free spirit!"

He paused for the ritual of Light that would allow them to reflect on the important concept of light and God. Hence, the *Sebastikoi* handed over a torch to every new *mathematikoi*. In turn, the disciples proceeded to the purified fire smoldering in the center. They enkindled their torches and walked back to their places. There, they placed them into receptacles, built for that purpose, in the ground right in front of them and uncovered their heads. Their faces shone with a new light.

"Now listen all!" Pythagoras drew their attention back to him. "The *One* (1) is not just a number but the creator of all numbers. It is the primordial harmony, the unbecoming, the unborn, the unmade, and the unformed. It is the Central Fire that diffuses in everything, and circulates through the circumference of existence."

"By its High spiritual nature, it is not at all Hermaphrodite – male and female – as some have assumed! It is in fact the **Monad**, or the *monas*. It is the Intelligent Spirit that moves by itself; without being divided or manifested, being unique, eternal, and unchangeable. The *One* is the Universal Mind, or *nous*, which initially pervaded the Kosmos and summoned it out of chaos, by sounds and harmony, before guiding it into an order of Divine Origin."

"The *One* epitomizes God, or Good, the Source of life, and the hidden Essence of everything that moves and changes through a harmonious measure of Intelligence. The *One* profiles the **Unity Point** that contains Infinity. It is the Absolute Creator whom I have called *Father*. His sign is Light and Fire; the Life Force and essence of the whole. I have dedicated the *One* to the Sun, to El-Apollo!"

"The Truth I tell you! The ultimate goal of Initiation, brothers and sisters, is to come closer to *Him*... to the Father," the Philosopher, thus ended his explanation on the nature of the first principle. He glanced at them sitting wordless in awe in front of him.

Parmiseus of Metapontium uttered in a husky voice, "You have generously invited us to become like you, Master...." He hesitated for a second that reflected his need to clarify a matter.

With a gentle nod, Pythagoras encouraged him to proceed.

"With all respect, Master, I concede to the veracity of such a feat, since it is you who states it. I do not argue that," Parmiseus advanced, with a frown of puzzlement, his tone deferential. "However, I wonder: how can we possibly come nearer to the *One*, to the Father?"

Pythagoras questioned in reply, "Has anyone seen the Master of Time and Space?"

A moment of silence echoed inside the crypt.

"No... and a thousand times no, of course! It is only by merging with *Him* that you could feel His essence. He is the Invisible Spirit; the Source of Intelligence that exists in the heart of the Macrocosm, and of the Microcosm that you are. Know that the personal spirit incarnated in each one of you, is like water, agitated by the deeds of the mundane world. You are required to sooth it down through the serenity achieved by meditation. Thus, you must purify it to make it clean and clear. Then and only then will you achieve the Great Unity, by simply harmonizing with *Him*."

"Thence, God the Father will resuscitate in the depth of your conscious mind. Subsequently, you will participate with celestial grace in His great powers, and enter perfection to dominate matter by the sole command of your Intellect and will. Accordingly, and with faith in your heart, you will be active like *Him*."

With that wonderful revelation, and in the total secrecy of their Assembly, the *Mathemagician* finished his session on the first number, the *One*. In accordance, he conveyed his new disciples into a serious state of reflection.

* * *

Some of the *mathematikoi,* who had previously entered the higher level of esoteric knowledge, excelled in exercising their minds through further contemplation of shapes and numbers. They penetrated the essence of the manifested reality. On the other hand, the newest *mathematikoi* spent their time meditating on the nature of the number *One* and its profound meaning.

Later, both Circles convened in the Assembly Hall as one family of brethren for their habitual common meal.

In the afternoon, the Inner Circle worked, in progressive measure, on the purification of their minds through the study of esoteric mathematics, revealed by the Master.

"Exercise in measure," the Master repeated often, and they fully abided by his words.

When the stars appeared in bright dots in the deep blue sky of the night, the *mathematikoi* lay down to sleep in the common dormitory next to the *homakoeion*. The mystical sound of the lyre drifted to their ears and glided all over the place.

296

Sometimes, in order to relax and unwind all fatigue, conflicts, stresses, and anxieties of the day, Pythagoreans of the Inner Circle would chant spiritual songs, or express themselves in poetic verses. Songs and poetry, along with the sense of joy infused by the soft melody of the Lyre, would induce them into profound serenity.

The powerful effect of the music, which Pythagoras performed for them at night, gushed out in significant, mystical rhythms that penetrated with finesse into their deepest realms. It gently purified their minds, reinforced their intuitions, and awakened their psychic faculties, ultimately triggering pleasant and prophetic dreams.

In the concealed dimension above their dormant physical bodies, their astral forms floated in a free, subtle manner. They vibrated as fast as the speed of light. Feathery, weightless, the astral light traveled beyond time and space to cross the threshold of the deepest level of existence. It soared like the Phoenix over that very fine thread that linked the Microcosm with the Macrocosm.

"Sleep, dreams, and trances are the three most important keys to the world beyond; there, where the knowledge of the psyche and the art of divination are acquired," Pythagoras would often declare.

They could feel him whispering softly in their ears.

His words would linger in their thoughts. With *plaisance* in their hearts, they would recite certain verses before surrendering to the silent night...

> *"Allow not sleep to close your eyes*
> *Before three times reflecting on*
> *Your actions of the day*
> *What deeds done well, what not,*
> *And what left undone?"*

* * *

297

A spiritual melody of the Lyre roused up the *mathematikoi* from their sleep. The words of the Master imparted, "Music is that very power, which links Man with the Kosmos of the gods."

Awakened by then, they intoned after him:

> *"As soon as I wake up,*
> *In order I lay*
> *The actions to be done*
> *The coming day"*

"Listen, brothers and sisters, your goal – that once was mine – is to heed the music of the gods, who are numbers. You can perceive it with your psyche but only when harmony – which is the most beautiful of all things – purifies it, and only when the power of music releases it."

Perfectly fathomed, the words shepherded the *mathematikoi* through their morning preparation. At any rate, not only did Pythagoras enhance his enigmatic parables with music when addressing his people but he used it also, and mainly, for therapeutic healing.

A keen observer of the human mind, he strongly believed in the capability of musical rhythms and melodies to work as antidotes for psychic troubles. In fact, his musicology had revealed to him the therapeutic effect of certain tunes on the afflictions of the soul; those related to emotions and passions; like depression, lust, envy, pride, and rage too. Moreover, the experimentation of his own compositions on his ailing subjects had attested to their *mathemagical* healing powers on a variety of spiritual and physical disorders. They had proved to enhance humor and develop sensory conditions, resulting in significant psychological equilibrium.

* * *

The statue of Hestia-Isis, encircled by the nine Muses, loomed over the Master as he stood to confer his teachings. The Lover of Sophia resumed the Theology of Numbers from his *hieros logos.*

"When the *One,* or the Monad, decided to manifest itself, it became *Two.* That is the Dyad of indivisible essence, but of divisible substance. The *One* acted on the **Dyad** to produce the numbers. Therefore, the Dyad is not a number by itself, but rather, a two-pointed division, a confusion of unity, a **line.** It contains, on one side, the male-active principle which is Energy, and on the other side, the female-passive principle which is Matter."

"Consequently, the Dyad represents the conflicting union of the will of the *Eternal Male* with the faith of the *Eternal Female.* These two essential divinities created the visible phenomenal world. They embody Adonis-Baal and Astarte for the Phoenicians; Osiris and Isis for the Egyptians; Bel and Ishtar for the Babylonians; Heaven and Hell for the Persians; and Shiva and Shakti for the Hindus. The Dyad is dedicated to the Moon, or Juno, which is the second luminary."

After this insightful explanation, Pythagoras paused to examine the reaction of his disciples. Their minds seemed at work. He gave them time to absorb his introduction of the number 2.

When enlightenment showed by degrees on their features, he nodded in approval and then proceeded, "So, the Dyad generated the physical world known as the **Tryad**. The Tryad exists everywhere, being the first physical number. It is the psyche that I compare to a **triangle.** It, in fact, gives life to the Kosmos from its three atoms of Fire, Air, and Water."

"As you have already learned, the Microcosm, or Man, is composed of three dimensions; the Body that means Strength, the Spirit that means Beauty, and the Mind representing Wisdom. Similarly, the Macrocosm, or the Universe, is composed of three

299

spheres of existence: the Natural world, the Human world, and the Divine world."

"I have dedicated the Tryad, the number Three (3), to Jupiter. It is a perfect number indeed, for it is the symbol of Truth manifested in the mind, Virtue in the spirit, and Purification in the body. The Phoenician tradition identifies this Trinity with Anat, Adonis and El, while the Egyptians associate it with Isis, Horus and Osiris. The Hindus, in turn, correlate it to Sarasvathi, Vishnu and Brahma."

"The Tryad constitutes the key elements of life in the Kosmos. And this is a fact! Along with Creation, there is Evolution that passes by all the levels of life forms; from the mineral to the vegetable, to the animal, and finally, to the human."

"However, here is a twist. The third element of the Tryad represents the mundane world of suffering. But why is it so? You may ask why, of course! Could anyone advance a suggestion?"

The question threw the disciples into confusion. Pythagoras did not expect them to know. He, himself, had strove through many years of quest and Initiation to attain that kind of knowledge. He nodded pensively at the thought, and gave them a cheering smile.

"I will tell you why, brothers and sisters. Your goal now is absolutely akin to mine when I first embarked on my spiritual journey. It is to revert back to your original state – to the primordial unity with the Monad – and that, by ending the material and instinctive evil elements within yourselves. When we, humans, entered the Tryad, we subsequently lost the vision of the Sublime Reality that is the *One*. As a result, we have remained stuck between the divine world that seeks to absorb us upwards in its perfection, and the natural animal-human world that pulls us downwards into the depths of the ground."

"Verily I say unto you! Man resulted from the smart evolution of the animal. Divinity surged from

300

the smart evolution of man. Thus, in order to attain that sublime state of holiness, you must break out from all the evil deeds of the dyad, or dualism. You can achieve it by uniting your three dimensions with your psyche, which is nothing more than your *Individual Monad*. When you accomplish that state of concordance, your Individual Monad will finally come to unity with the Great Monad."

With this new revelation, the Master concluded another important session of his esoteric teachings.

The minds of the *mathematikoi* set to work, once again, on their individual contemplation of the Sacred Discourse of the Master. Weariness took over and they decided for a long respite in the garden of the temple to ease their mental strain and refresh their vigor.

Their thoughts blended with the fresh air as they absorbed the peaceful mood of nature around them. They wondered, inwardly, if they would be able to accomplish that harmony with the Monad, and regain their alleged lost vision. When, hours later, they headed to the cave, one common question escorted them inside. Would they ultimately evolve into a god-like state of perfection and power?

Determined and highly motivated, they convened, for weeks, in the secrecy of the cave for magical rituals. They utilized, accordingly, the power of the Tryad for their own sanctification and purification, which they performed with profound dedication.

* * *

Every Initiate of the ancient world had, at some time in his or her life, experienced a different method of Initiation. Yet all these great systems, and most importantly the ones of the Phoenicians and the Egyptians, encompassed relatively similar meanings, and identical understanding of the True Sophia.

301

These mystics had discovered, through Initiation, the basic and most essential elements of all the sciences in general. They had definitely grasped the *law*, which governs the existence of the various living forms, and their way of evolution. These sages had gravitated around, and inside, the Inner Circles; and rotated away from the profane world to come to recognize that the essence of all religions was the One Superior Reality: the Divine Hokmah!

A full moon reigned in the sky above. Its silver rays teased the game of the waves below, fighting against the shadows of the night. They bathed the couple that ambled on the beach. Their feet left their prints on the sand, side by side, yet not touching. The White City, on the hill above, loomed with majesty over the shore and witnessed, in silence, the peaceful walk and private conversation of the twosome. The Master and his beautiful disciple discussed life and the role of its Mysteries in their being together.

"I strongly believe that our encounter has not been the deed of coincidence, my dear," the voice of Pythagoras floated melodiously with its statement through Theano, the ocean, and the air. "Believe me, it is rather, how shall I put it," he paused for a while before continuing. "It is a static probability of the Divine Will; a necessity in the world order of the Number...."

Whatever personal matters they shared remained secret to their surroundings, for his voice became a declaration murmured to her ears, and Nature witnessed her smile of utter happiness.

Their promenade conveyed them to the Temple of Ceres-Astarte where the young *mathematikoi* gathered for the session of the nightfall. Poised and composed, Theano joined them while the Master took his stand to start his lecture. A stillness of anticipation prevailed, broken only by the sound of the waves pounding their rhythmical tempo on the high walls that held the terrace of the temple. He bent his head for a minute of reflection, in which he gathered his thoughts to focus on the lesson he was about to contribute. He then looked at them with a warm grin of greeting.

"Good evening, my friends."

"Good evening, Master," all the ten disciples replied almost in one voice.

"Tonight, I shall unveil the number Four, the Tetrad or Tetraktys. It symbolizes the Kosmic Creator embodied by the Logos; the hidden archetype of the universe. The number *Four* completes the process of Creation because it begins with the *One* – being the point of Fire – then moves to the *Two* that epitomizes the line of Water. At this point, the process shifts to the *Three* – being the surface of Air – to finally reach the *Four* that portrays the solidity of Earth."

"The Tetraktys is, in reality, the true **Sacred Decade**, for the basic principles do exist in the first four numbers 1, 2, 3, and 4; the sum of which is equal to 10, which stands as the best number. Thus, I have arranged them for you in a way that forms a triangle with the *One* at the top, then the *Two*, the *Three*, and finally the *Four* at the bottom."

"Here it is!" He unrolled a large papyrus to disclose the sketch of the triangle.

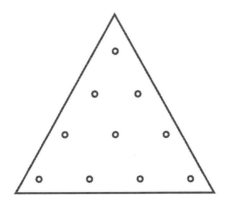

"The number (4) is the most important key in Nature. In fact, it is the Key-Keeper. Many important natural phenomena come in groups of four. The most significant one describes the four levels of existence, which are: Being, Living, Feeling and Realizing. Another major group of four forms Nature itself, and it comes in the four elements of Fire, Air, Water, and Earth."

"Four is the **Perfect Square** of equality and regularity. It is the symbol of Moral Justice. It stands between the subject and the object in a horizontal direction. The vertical line describes the Divine Laws in a conscious and energetic method. Hence, all powers and vibrations of the physical and spiritual planes are engraved within the Perfect Square. And the name of Him, *Alim*, or *Abba* – the Logos – is equal to the sacred number *Four*. I therefore have dedicated it to the Sun!" The Grand Hierophant of Sophia proclaimed with finality.

Silence prevailed in their current state of awe. He anticipated a reaction from them. None came for as long as their eyes reflected their personal rumination on these vital teachings. With the confident patience of a true Master, he waited quietly for their eyes to lighten up in comprehension.

When they all did, one after another, he indicated his satisfaction with a smile. He invited them then to stand up and proclaim the most requisite and solemn oath of all times. And so, under the faint phosphorescent light of the celestial stars, and the infinite kingdom of the Most High, the *mathematikoi* swore in a unanimous voice:

"I swear by him who has transmitted to our minds

the Sacred Four, the Tetraktys, High and Pure,

> *the Root and Source of ever flowing Nature,*
>> *The Model of the gods."*

Their affidavit resounded all over the terrace of the Temple. It reached high above the hill, and inside the White City. It resonated with the waves of the Mediterranean Sea and the Ether of Space. To them, this sworn declaration constituted the supreme affirmation, for it determined, without a doubt, their religion and faith.

The soft breeze of the Divine Spirit entered their realms.

Calm was the night.

* * *

From behind the hill, early the next day, the sun soared up in radiance and warmth. The place of the meeting had changed for the new lesson. Inside the crypt of the Temple of Apollo this time, the *mathematikoi* gathered in a half circle. In front of them, the Master smiled to the Sun, and then at them.

"Good morning, my friends. Today, we proceed with my Theology of Numbers," he announced at once. "The number Five (5), the **Pentad**, is in truth the most important and powerful number of them all. It stands in the middle of the number *Ten*. It is central in its position, a circular number that comprises five circumscribed circles. The *Five*, in fact, characterizes the return of everything. And by that I mean the return of the Psyche into itself, there where purification and knowledge abide to the *Cycle of the Pentagon*; A Great Cycle that rotates in harmony, and commands the movements of the Kosmos[40]."

---

[40]   The Pentagon, or the State Department in the United States of America, is undoubtedly based on the Pythagorean idea of the Cycle of the Pentagon. Of course, the US State Department is ideologically built not with the idea of commanding the movements of the Kosmos, but rather, those of Earth. From here, came the idea of

"The *Five* is the symbol of the five atomic shapes that exist hidden in Nature. They consist of the Pyramid, the Cube, the Octahedron, the Icosahedron, and the Dodecahedron. These geometrical shapes represent, in a systematic and respective order, the five elements of Fire, Earth, Air, Water, and Ether. However, nothing is really pure of the existential matters, since Earth partakes in Fire, Fire in Air, Air in Water, and Water in Ether."

"As we know, there exist, aside from the sun and the moon, five other spheres that float with affinity in the small visible space. Accordingly, five major zones divide our Sphere: the Earth. We have the north cold zone, the south cold zone, the summer zone, the winter zone, and finally, the equator zone."

"The number *Five* is a merger. I have named it *marriage* for it contains a male-odd number, the Three, which is limited and determined, and a female-even number, the Two, which is unlimited and undetermined. The sum of these two numbers, 2 and 3, equals 5."

"Now, here comes an important point," Pythagoras took a step forward. He then looked at his ten disciples standing in a half-circular formation in front of him with great honor. "Heed me," he uttered. "The esoteric and spiritual symbol of the number 5 is the *five-pointed star*. It is the **Pentagram** of our Great Society. It is, *de facto*, the sign on your chests denoting your official adherence to the *first degree*. In our secret language, it means *death to reveal;* a term that connotes the death and resurrection in our system of Initiation. Each line of our star intersects with another line in the proportions of macro to micro. *Five*, my friends, is dedicated to Hermes-Enoch, to Mercury!"

---

building an American Empire.

"It symbolizes, mainly, the *Kosmic Man* that is the Microcosm of the Macrocosm; the thinking and conscious man. Therefore, drawn on a Pentagon, *Five* epitomizes, in my perception of matters, harmony and health. In accordance, I have selected it to be the secret sign of our Fraternity!"

In a unanimous reaction, the disciples hailed their Master with enthusiasm. Hymns resounded in honor of the Fraternity to which they proudly belonged. Pythagoras let it be, happy with the general mood that lifted their spirits in glee.

Amidst their cheering, he marched to the entrance of the Temple and they followed him. He raised his hand to command their silence to which they abided at once. The mid-day carried to them the caress of the breeze and the sound of the waves. A solitary eagle glided high in the sky with its long broad wings spread out. It claimed, by such display, the magnificence of its flight. By his will and *mathemagical* supremacy, the Master summoned to him the predator. His hand in a fist, he extended his arm firmly. At once, the Eagle revolved on its circumnavigation, and vocalized a faint screech in response. To his disciples' bewilderment, it scudded down in a plunge, directly towards them.

At the darting of the powerful raptor, they swiftly stepped back in an instinct of survival. They exclaimed in rapture as the Golden Eagle slowed down to land smoothly, like a messenger of God, on the arm of their equable Master. Pythagoras caressed it gently. He then whispered some mystical words close to its small head that bent to heed the message of the Master. When he looked into its golden eyes with a smile of complicity, the Eagle responded with a repeated screech. The Master then raised his arm and commanded it to freedom. The subdued predator fluttered his wings widely, lifted in the air, and took off to its realm, high above in the sky.

In the days that followed, the *mathematikoi* performed several religious and magical ceremonies inside the Pythagorean sanctuaries. They employed the power of the Number *Five,* drawn inside a circle, to beckon the good daemons. In a similar manner, they would often exorcise the bad ones; those non-human disembodied souls from around them to impede their many disturbing interventions in their lives.

* * *

Vibrations of excitement swelled up inside the crypt of the Temple of Apollo where the members of the inner Circle convened. On his stand, in front of them, the Master readied to reveal the next teachings of his *hieros logos.*

"Good morning to all of you, dear brothers and sisters," he greeted them.

The usual kindness in his voice blended with a tone of authority that only great Masters like him knew how to employ with effective tact.

"Today, we move up to the **Hexad**, the number *Six* (6). It is the primary perfect circular number. It is the regular figure for marriage. Why? You must wonder," he tempted with a smile, then, lifting a sketch to their attention, he explained, "Look at these figures. *Six* is the Union between the male and the female. The male has for sign a downward triangle in the following shape (▼). The female is represented by an opposite triangle in this upward shape (▲). Together, they form the six-pointed star[41]."

---

[41]   In almost all Ancient Religions, the male was represented as the God-Energy descending from Heaven (▼) and impregnating the female, Earth (▲). One of the most famous examples to such an archaic belief could be seen with Giaia, Earth, and Zeus, the Most High God of Ancient Greece. In Greek Mythology, Zeus has been often regarded for his divine insemination of Giaia. And so, Zeus made life beat in her bosom.

"In concordance, the triple spirit descending from Heaven (▼) interweaves with the triple receiving matter of Earth (▲). The *Six* is sacred to the goddess Astarte, known also as Aphrodite. It is Venus which, as we know, is the morning and the evening star. For that reason, the holy day of Venus is Friday; the sixth day of the week."

"Now, *Six* is also an important number for it represents the six levels of natural life. The first level encompasses the *seed* and starts from the bottom. The second level takes in the *plant life*. The third comprises the *animal life* and the fourth the *human life*. The fifth is the *angelic life,* which profiles the mediators between men and gods. And finally, the last and sublime echelon at the top of this hierarchy is the *godhood life*."

"Listen and listen well! Six cubed (6×6×6) is equal to two hundred sixteen (216). In truth, it represents a very mystical number, for it is a generator principle of the spirit! It repeats itself by its spherical structure that produces an eternal recurrence of approximately the same events in both the spiritual and physical worlds. Matter is not at all infinite in the Kosmos! Know thyself! So, in fact, every two hundred sixteen years, the spirit of man travels around the Circle of Necessity in order to incarnate a new and different body. The Truth I tell you! That Cycle of Reincarnation commands the state of being of every mortal!"

This outstanding conclusion ended his discourse. Without further comment, he reached for his Lyre, and settled on his chair to play a sacred tune while his disciples were absorbed in due reflection. His voice soon drifted soothingly as he chanted the Homeric verses VII, 5-60 from the Iliad to illustrate the reality of Reincarnation.

The song related the death of Euphorbus, one of the previous Avatars – or lives – of Pythagoras himself! A brave warrior, Euphorbus had fought and perished in the Trojan War.

The Master intoned beautifully:

*"He fell, thunderously, and his armor
clattered upon him
and his hair, lovely as the Graces, was
splattered with blood, those braided locks
caught waspwise in gold and silver.
As some slip of an olive tree, strong-
growing, that a man raised in a lonely place,
and drenched it with generous water, so that
it blossoms into beauty, and the blasts of
winds from all quarters tremble it, and it
bursts into pale blossoming.
But then a wind suddenly in a great
tempest descending upon it wrenches it out of
its sand and lays it at length on the ground;
such was Euphorbus of the strong ash spear,
the son of Panthoos, whom Menalaus
Atreides killed, and was stripping his armor."*

When Pythagoras ended chanting the death
of his own prior existence, Myllias of Crotona, one of
the exceptional *mathematikoi* in the group, argued
in doubts at the reality of reincarnation.

Pythagoras looked at him sternly and
declared patiently, "Verily I say unto you, brother
Myllias, that in your previous life, you were a King,
and not just an ordinary King, but the legendary
Phrygian King Midas."

Myllias gawked at him for a moment of
wordless astonishment then managed to exclaim in
a faint voice, "A King! A legendary King... me?"

"Yes!" Pythagoras did not soften the look he
pierced Myllias with. "And honestly speaking, I
strongly urge you to take that long trip to Asia one
day soon, and perform the expiatory rituals at your
previous tomb!"

Wordless, indeed, Myllias remained all day.
He tried to deal with the shock of such an
astounding revelation. He wondered painfully what

great sins he had committed in his former life that required from him a due expiation!

That same day, the disciples came to know that their Master considered of essential that his disciples understood the great law of reincarnation. At their queries, he revealed four of his Avatars. As he declared, he had lived as *Aithalides*, the son of Hermes; then *Euphorbus*, the Trojan hero. He had incarnated, as well, as *Hermotimus*[42], and finally as *Pyrrhus*, a fisherman from Delos."

Fascinated and excited, the disciples asked him if he could see into their spirits and tell them of their former lives. To the delight of some, and the consternation of others, he did. In fact, considering the time appropriate to teach them the secret process of *Anamnesis*, he caused many to recollect the memory of their previous incarnations! _

* * *

Walking together on the beautiful sandy shore at eventide became a pleasant habit for Pythagoras and Theano. They both enjoyed these private moments in which they shared their past, present, and potential future. They delighted in knowing about each other on a more personal level. When Pythagoras deepened his conversation with her on the nature of the number *Six*, he certainly meant to prepare the ground for the realization of his aspiration, and ultimately, the last wish of his late mother. The prospect of marriage between them materialized, in fact, in her mind the way he saw it; the perfect alliance of the manifested natural life. As she rejoiced in the thought, their conversation

---

[42] It could possibly be Hermotimus of Clazomenae, a Greek philosopher who first proposed, before Anaxagoras, as per Aristotle, the concept of the mind being primary in the cause of change. He declared that physical entities are constant, while the mind instigates the variation.

dragged, until dusk caught them, still together, on the shore.

When the first pink tinted the horizon, he uttered, "Time for the lesson, dear," he reminded her with a tender smile. "The others might be waiting for me at the Temple."

She smiled back at him, and the adoration in her green eyes touched him deeply. He hastened his steps towards the Temple of Ceres-Astarte, and she matched his eagerness with an energy that pleased him. On the terrace of the temple, she joined the other nine disciples with a simple look of respect towards him, and he appreciated her tactful attitude. Taking his stand in front of them, he focused at once on his teachings.

"Good evening to all of you, brothers and sisters. Today, before the sun completely disappears in the horizon, you will have learned the value and meaning of the numbers *Seven* (7) and *Eight* (8)."

"Seven is the perfect number of life and its ideal vehicle. In truth, it combines the three higher elements of the spirit with the three lower elements of the body. The fourth level, or shall I say, the middle one, is the mind. As such, it shows the great relationship that exists between Man and the Divine Monad. It represents the active mind, the godhead."

"The **Heptad**, *Seven*, is associated with the seven heavenly bodies that form the Music of the Spheres. These heavenly entities are also related to the seven days of the week. This association is best described as follows: Moon for Monday, Mars for Tuesday, Mercury for Wednesday, Jupiter for Thursday, Venus for Friday, Saturn for Saturday, and finally, the Sun for Sunday!"

"Listen now and listen well, for the Truth I tell you! The manifested universe is also a constituent of seven, and so is the microcosm, or man, who is organized into the seven levels of evolution. These levels start at the bottom with the *physical body*. The *sidereal body* ensues at the second level and the *desire body* at the third. The fourth level, being the Mind, is the stage of equilibrium, as I mentioned before. The fifth corresponds to the *human spirit* and the sixth to the *vivid spirit*. The seventh level betokens the *divine spirit*."

"You should know by heart that the symbol of seven is the **Seven-Pillared Temple**. It means the Initiate. It is Sophia, and for that reason, I have dedicated this number to Jupiter."

Pythagoras waited for the questions that usually came up after his lecture, when none ensued after a few minutes; he decided to move on to the next number.

"Fine! Since there are no questions, which means all is well understood, let's move on to the number *Eight* (8)!" He proposed with a grin of approval. "Know, my friends, that *Eight*, in fact, is the **Octad;** the first actual cube. Its relationship with the Kosmic harmony allows a perfect balance that regulates everything in the universe. Hence, know that two cubed is eight, and 2+2+2+2 equals 8. It is also the source of all the musical ratios, and it is greatly associated with the Music of the Spheres. For that reason, I have called it the Embracer of Harmonies, or *Harmonia*, after the name given to the wife of Kadmus who was one of the Kabirim of Phoenicia."

"*Eight*, my friends, is also related to the principles of safety and steadfastness. It is the symbol of lasting friendship and of Love too! Because those emotional relationships have a healing effect, *Eight* can symbolize medicine and health, as well. Thus, I have assigned this number to Eshmun, the Phoenician god of medicine and dedicated it to the Air element."

"In conclusion, my final concept on this number is that *Eight* represents the balance that adjusts the combination of the three subjective aspects, and the five objective facets of the human consciousness."

His discourse for the night ended with this statement and, as usual, he took his Lyre to play some music while his disciples were immersed in their meditation.

* * *

Inside the crypt of the Temple of the Muses, the next morning, the *Mathemagician* continued where he had stopped the night before.

"The number *Nine* (9), the **Ennead**, is the Number of Justice *par excellence*. Its square root is three, 3×3 equals 9, and 3+3+3 equals 9. It is called Horizon, or Oceanus, because it represents the crossing line between many important sequences. For example, it is the passage between the Number *Ten,* and the other numbers that led to it. With the *Nine*, which represents the spiritual number of our Mother Earth, the perfect nine months of gestation are completed for birth."

"*Nine* is also the number of the Muses, the nine sister-goddesses of harmony, arts, and sciences. On the other hand, it relates particularly to Terpsichore – the Muse of movement and dance. *Nine* embodies a powerful sacred number, for it is composed of the nine aspects of the Divine Energy, best described as follows:

> Heavenly three: Father, Mother, and Son.
> Humanly three: Mind, Matter, and Spirit.
> Elementally three: Fire, Water, and Air.

"To you, my friends, I should certainly reveal that I tried three times – nine days each, in twenty seven phases – until I successfully completed the process of self-purification. Subsequently, I've attained a high spiritual perfection," he avowed as a statement to the power of this number.

314

He then granted to himself some time for recollection, and to his disciples, moments of reflection.

Quietness waned when he opened up for questions. The debate that ensued dragged on for an hour. Due to the weariness that showed on some of his disciples' faces, he dismissed them with his insistence that they take a long break in the garden. He set a time at night to resume his teachings. Some showed reluctance but abided in consideration to the others who welcomed the rest.

When they came back at night, refreshed and smiling, Pythagoras was ready for them.

"Let's discuss the number *Ten* (10), the **Dechada**, which is the greatest number of all!" he started as soon as they resumed their places around him in a semi-circle. "*Ten*, my friends, is the perfect Number *par excellence*, for when we reach it, we simply revert back to the *One*! And thus, the process of Creation will repeat itself *ad infinitum*. In that regard, *Ten* is related to human fate, and I have dedicated it to the World and the Sun!"

"The Truth I tell you! It is not a coincidence that you are the 10 chosen disciples to enter the Inner Circle at this round. It is also not a coincidence that the power of the Number *Ten* is so faultless, for it is the vessel that holds all things through a single form and power. It shapes the *Cycle of Necessity*, planned, as such, by the Divine Will. It also represents all the Divine Principles that evolve and rejoin in a new *Unitas*. *Ten* is the ensemble of the Absolute Truth. It is Heaven!"

"Listen to this once again – the numbers: One plus Two plus Three plus Four equals Ten. These numbers, joined together in this way, compose the **Sacred Decade** of the gods. These are the gods that hold the Kosmos together, as well as all the manifested laws of Mother Nature."

Pythagoras paused for a minute. His power radiated upon his disciples. Their stances reflected impeccable attention and enthusiasm.

"Let me conclude the *Theology of Numbers* by imparting that Numbers are not a creation of the human mind, but rather, a mystical existence of its own. They reside outside the intellect of man, or of any living form. As you have undoubtedly realized by now, there exists a certain hidden mystery in the Numbers. In fact, it is not by coincidence that the *One* created the Numbers, but by Divine Reason and Logic."

He then halted to stare at them, one by one.

"Numbers, my friends, absorb – to a great extent – from their origin: the Great Monad, the reality of all things. Hence, if you want to discern the properties of Numbers, you must meditate upon their meanings. You will definitely commune with them. They are gods!"

"Know that it is not-at-all easy to understand that concept. But if you achieve it, believe me, dear brothers and sisters, you will then become yourselves. You will utterly become what you are in reality: gods!" He concluded, with finality and smiled encouragingly.

An imposing stillness prevailed over space and time.

Silent was the night...

.9.

Initiation
Cosmology and Theology of the Psyche

In mid-winter of the year 512 BCE, a tyrant, by the name of Telys, raided the political territory of Sybaris; a city adjoined to the northern borders of Crotona. From the very start, he masterminded, covertly, a dangerous scheme that triggered the countdown of a powerful revolution against the government. The state of affairs promptly degraded. The negative impact on the city worsened quickly. The Oligarchic rulers fled to the democratic safety of Crotona. Naturally, the authorities granted them political refuge, and sheltered them in the safe haven of a Temple that ensured their total protection.

With this vacancy in the government, Telys took fast control of Sybaris. He imposed his oppressive autocracy, and levied drastic legislative changes. Consequently, discomfiture prevailed among the Sybarites, who ended yielding to the new ruler – few by fascination and most by fear.

The Crotoniates turned their eyes and hearts towards Sybaris. The political deterioration of its adjacent neighbor unsettled them. At that time, some of the Pythagorean brothers resided in Sybaris, as part of a mission that consisted of studying the mentality of the local youth. The anguish for their safety proliferated among the Crotoniates and the Fraternity.

Their angst proved justified. With such a tyranny in force, brutality eventuated. The new political body committed a major crime, whose dreadful consequences affected the Pythagorean

317

Fraternity. Kidnapped and incarcerated, for no particular reason, the missionaries suffered the viciousness of despotism. Some even met a brutal death.

In an adamant attempt to subdue Crotona as well, Telys hastened to dispatch two messengers, from his government, to its authorities. The irony of diplomacy, at this stage, was that it required Crotona's own ambassador to Sybaris to accompany them. And so it happened that Crotona received his clear-cut message, commanding submission, and their ambassador reported the dire crimes committed against the Pythagorean missionaries.

As one would reasonably expect, the authorities ranted and raved in indignation and grief. Their anger whirled to outrage when they read Telys' dispatch to them. The tyrant ordered the immediate delivery of all political refugees, fault of which he would execute more Pythagoreans.

The threat threw the authorities into horror and uncertainty. People of peace and compassion, themselves, they could not fathom, for even a minute, the idea of forfeiting the refugees to a sure, atrocious death, or even worst! On the other hand, to risk the casualty of more Pythagoreans shook them deep to the bones. While in their debate, a delegation took off to announce the bad news to Master Pythagoras.

Despite his profound grief and resentment, he reacted with wisdom and control, requesting time to ponder on his decision. The fate of his disciples was at stake! Thus, he retreated to his cave, and to his lonely meditation. His resolution taken, hours later, he summoned two of his disciples, and went to meet with the authorities. The moment he stepped inside the House of Senate, his imperturbable attitude assuaged the fear of the authorities there present, and abated their anxiety. His verdict, however, disturbed them, "No negotiation with villains," he declared firmly.

In spite of their perplexity, they abided in total trust.

Crotona would not yield to the demands of such a criminal, no matter what!

In accordance, their rejection to any attempt of negotiation ensued resolute. Astonished by the reaction of the peaceful city, the Tyrant confronted a steadfast resistance from Crotona. Upon realizing his defeat, he veered his frustration and rage against his own messengers. He sentenced the Crotoniate ambassador to death. Still unsatisfied – his sense of cruelty insatiable – he ordered the sanguine massacre of all the Pythagorean captives.

Such an atrocious act obviously broke all connection between the two cities. The Sybarite Oligarchic political refugees remained out of sight, and well protected inside the Temple of Apollo. Nevertheless, a state of alert settled in, to oppress the residents of both cities in their daily lives. The sense of security and peace waned, as terror of a possible war haunted their days and nights.

* * *

Upon Pythagoras' decision and his instructions, life resumed inside the White City, as did his lectures. He intended to provide his disciples with a state of mind that would lift their spirits from the world of visible forms, and into the hidden essence of all things. His Theology of Numbers was, indeed, a great mystical science. It constituted their admission into a more Sublime Reality that would enhance their perception of the Intelligent Fire: the Divine Monad, the creator of these forms, and the mover that kept changing them.

That particular day, the disciples settled down on their usual places inside the catacomb of the Temple of the Muses. Pythagoras watched them pensively with fatherly affection. He decided that the time had come for him to Initiate them secretly into the Pythagorean *Perfection.* This *third degree*

319

comprised a dual path: the Science of Cosmology and the Science of Psychology. Both esoteric sciences deal profoundly on the Mysteries of Life.

"It is not by the air which I breathe, nor by the water which I drink, that I should ever blame myself for revealing the Mysteries to you, dear brothers and sisters. Honor them with wisdom," he cautioned them in a firm, yet kind voice that opened his way to their hearts.

"Listen now - *Fire* exists in the center of the Universe. The Sun is nothing more than its reflection. This *Fire*, I tell you, is the conscious Universal Mind – the Great Monad!"

"The planets have developed from the *Sun* to revolve around it, and form what I call a *small universe*[43]. The invisible Anti-Earth, which is the Spiritual Urantia, started its rotational movement first. The Earth, the Moon, and the Sun followed it, in that order. The Sun operates as the central provider of life; it is the generator of fire and energy in a more relative proportion. Venus tagged along then Mercury, Mars, Jupiter, Saturn, and lastly the Zodiac.

"That *Small Universe* is enveloped by an exterior fire. Beyond it stretches the infinite void. And from that void, the *small universe* breathes in and out the infinite air."

"There exist, indeed, an endless number of small universes that are governed by the same order of the Number, like ours, of course. However, each one of them assumes a specific role within the immeasurable Kosmos. I use the word *Kosmos*, once again, to remind you that it indicates *a well-ordered and harmonious universe.*"

"After its creation, the Kosmos has surely continued its existence, upon a Divine Plan.

---

[43]   Pythagoras named the Sun and its rotating planets 'small universe', which is what we call today 'Solar System'.

Eventually, some of these planets should present a great probability of maintaining some form of physical life, somehow similar to ours on Earth – the Sphere of Generation. It is certainly my ratiocination that intelligence, and spirits, as well as life of some kind, inhabit part of the entire ensemble of these small universes."

"Behold, my friends, the important role that Earth – the sphere of the visible – assumes in its small universe. It is on its surface that occur all the operations of the incarnation and disincarnation of the spirits. On the other rotating spheres, say around the Sun, and perhaps on the moon, there exist spirits who are relatively higher than those who took physical bodies on Earth. However, much **higher** spirits, almost as spiritually pure as *Fire* or *Light*, live on the Sun, which is a solid reflection of the Intelligent Fire: God – the Great Monad. Think about it! The day is young and long, and the sun is still shining. Take your time to reflect on the Kosmos, its universes, and its spirits!"

With that unexpected note, the Master finished his first session of the third degree. He left his disciples to ponder upon these Mysteries by themselves.

Later, at nightfall, the *mathematikoi*, both young men and women, took a walk along the sandy shore on the outskirts of the White City. The sky was clear... Majestic! It exhibited the celestial bodies, as in a beautiful display of *objets d'art*, strangely suspended in the spacious void above. Akin to a sacred kingdom with unreadable signs, the sky enthralled the humans, down on Earth.

The *Mathemagician,* with his white tunic and purple robe on his wide shoulders, walked a few steps ahead of them. With calm confidence, he led his Inner Circle of 10 disciples to the Temple of Ceres-Astarte for the lesson of the night.

"Look at the sky," he intimated when they reached the terrace of the Temple. "Observe the

321

space with the sharp eyes of an eagle, and take your time. If you manage an intelligent scrutiny, you will perceive the movement of all the elements of space. Yes, right! Everything in the Kosmos moves. Can't you see it?" he inquired, while his eyes pierced the sky, as they did.

Moments later, a voice issued, somehow hesitant, "I think I saw something. I guess so. Yes... I can see that now!" Aristaeus of Crotona confirmed with excitement.

"Wow!" Theano exclaimed in awe. "I have never noticed it before in my life. This is so beautiful!"

Pythagoras glimpsed at her with a tender look then reverted back to the stars. "Yes it is, indeed," he murmured, for he never ceased to admire the beauty of Creation. "Nothing stands still," he commented musingly, and went into silence in order to give the other disciples enough time to discover that discipline on their own. As brothers and sisters would do, they shared their thoughts, helped each other to see what they had discerned, and exchanged their enthusiasm like young explorers would do in the face of a new discovery.

Pythagoras raised his voice above their talkfest to deliver, "As I told you previously, Earth is a Sphere. Today, learn that it has, in effect, a double movement. You have studied that it revolves around the Sun, the *Sphere of the visible fire*. Tonight, know that it rotates around its axis at the same time."

"All the spheres of our small universe move in a circular path around the Sun, in a west-to-east direction, and at a constant speed. Remember that five other spheres glide in harmony with our Earth, sun, and moon."

"What is really interesting is the fact that every sphere that consorts with the Earth around the Sun makes a specific sound, according to the speed of its rotational movement. The sound pitches higher and higher, the farther away any particular sphere stirs from Earth. The musical tones are calculated based on the distance. On that account, the distance from Earth to Moon is one tone (1). From Moon to Mercury, it is one-half tone (½), and from Mercury to Venus, it is one tone (1). The length from Venus to the Sun stretches one and a-half tones (1½), and from the Sun to Mars, one tone (1). Mars extends at one-half tone (½) from Jupiter, which stretches at a distance of half a tone (½) from Saturn. The distance between Saturn and the Zodiac measures one tone (1). Hence, from these seven varying tones, a coalition of sound takes form. It develops into a perfect septenary melody of Nature. It is Harmony – the Music of the Spheres – the music that we cannot discern because we hear it all the time."

Theano gasped in amazement, widened her eyes at him then looked up to the sky. Pythagoras, somehow, felt touched by her feminine reaction. His heart smiled, but his appearance remained composed. In a cool voice, he resumed his explanation, where he had left off when interrupted by her.

"Listen, my friends! If you really aspire to perceive the Music of the Spheres, you should start by listening to the beats of your own hearts, and then to the sound of the rotating Earth. That is actually feasible through meditation and the creation of a perfect void in your inner realm. Why? You would ask. And my answer is: because it will allow you to *tune* yourselves, and your heart beats, onto the same musical numbers of the heavenly bodies."

"Now, look at the Moon. The part we see, at this very moment, increases or diminishes according to its angle, which faces the Earth, and its other half, which is directed towards the Sun. When the Earth, or any other sphere, stands

323

between the moon and the Sun, an eclipse occurs. Think about it! Take your time. The night is young and long," he recommended with finality.

At the time, the Moon illuminated the part of the Earth where they stood on the terrace. The tide kept crashing, with some intensity, on the high walls below. The sound of the waves reverberated high. It crossed the long distance of the Mediterranean Sea to finally reach a safe haven, out of the dark void. The resonance ricocheted smoothly on the shore, there, at the foot of the hill of the Majestic White City.

Then, silence echoed peacefully in the body-temple of every *mathematikoi*.

Would they hear the beating of their hearts?

Would they listen to the cry of their Mother Earth?

Would they heed the Music of the Spheres?

* * *

As if with a sigh, the Moon – the nocturnal Queen of the sky – disappeared completely from its watchtower. Night turned to day. Time came for the Sun – the King of the sky – to rise high above, and give light to the world, and sight to the living.

At the center of the White City, a delightful melody drifted from a modest house. The tempo accelerated to be heard everywhere. Inside his small residence, the *Mathemagician* relaxed while he played a mystical melody. The delicious moment shattered unexpectedly. A woman stormed inside his dwellings, yelling in pain. Through her lamentations, he understood that her uncontrollable ache resulted from the affliction of a disease.

She, a housewife from the Outer Circle, in her mid-age, pleaded for his help. Calm and composed, he invited her to sit at his side, and while performing his music, he addressed her with a soothing voice.

324

"Dear lady, you assume that you are sick, but you are not. Other people may have told you so, but I tell you, fear not. Your pain results mainly from some disorder in your system."

"I don't... understand," her broken voice interrupted him tearfully. "What are you saying, Master? I am really... terribly ill... What do you mean by... a disorder... in my system?" The woman blurted amidst her sobbing, totally confused.

"Dear Lady, your system is made of vibrations, like the notes I'm playing now. At this very moment, the mystical vibrations of my Lyre communicate intelligently with yours to set them in order. It's a truly magical process."

She was stunned, speechless.

A few minutes later, she walked out of the house, relieved from her pain, and cured from her illness. Realigned, so to speak, she became *in tune* with herself, and thus, healed and healthy again.

This episode was one of many in which Pythagoras performed his healing powers. Sometimes, he would visit the sick members of his Society to heal them, as he would openly state.

Down, inside the crypt of the Temple of the Muses, that morning, the Master lectured his disciples on Cosmology.

"The Kosmos, I tell you, is not continuous and linear like a river. It is instead circular and cyclical like an egg. The same applies for Nature, as we have previously observed. Thus, the Kosmos and Nature are alike. Everything in existence repeats itself. This recurrence of events in the Kosmos occurs because of the spherical form of the stars and planets that revolve in circles around the Sun."

"Know also that the sphere is perfect, and so is the circle. They are perfect because all the points that exist on their surfaces, or circumferences, are at the same distance from their centers. Our Earth is then perfect, so are the Heavenly Bodies!"

"Listen, I assure you, fellow brothers and sisters, that it is only by pure thought that you can logically deduce the laws of Nature and those of the Kosmos. Mathematics will reveal to you a pure Kosmos, accessible to your Intellect in which numbers and shapes are perfectly connected with the natural order of existence."

He scrutinized his 10 chosen disciples who appeared motionless as if their minds dwelt in a different orbit, somewhere amidst the stars, the planets, and the sun.

Moments elapsed...

"Now!" Pythagoras snapped, interrupting the chain of their thoughts to haul them back to Earth; the sphere where they belonged. "Let's consider a right triangle. The sum of the squares, of the shorter sides, is equal to the square of the longer side. Hence, a2 + b2 equal c2. Let me show you how by a simple demonstration."

He drew its sketch on the wall while explaining again to demonstrate his theory through mathematics. "Here it goes!" He pointed to the completed triangle.

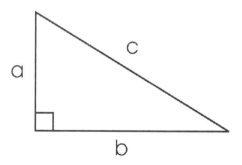

"There are infinite numbers of regular polygons as in the infinitude of the Kosmos," he continued his tutorial. "I would, however, focus here on two of the five solids mentioned earlier. The Cube, for example, contains six sides. It represents Earth. Now, when we unfold its sides, we obtain a cross of seven squares; the Symbol of the Initiate!" He asserted while he showed them in a drawing on the wall how the Cube was transformed into a Cross.

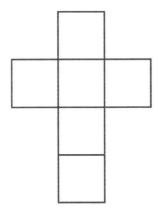

"I told you previously that the Earth is the Sphere of Generation. It is so because souls come down to it continuously through birth, and always ascend out of it at death. Hence, they follow a circular movement in an order of necessity. And thus, to become an Initiate, one must rise up and above this circle, and I, esoterically, mean above the cycle of life and death."

"There, above the Cube that symbolizes Earth, which has not yet unfolded, I place the Dodecahedron that represents the Heavens. This important solid contains twelve pentagons as sides. In a mystical mode, I associate it with the Ether of Kosmos which is, in truth, the quintessence of the Heavenly Bodies. It is the fifth element, and the purest form of the Kosmos."

"Listen and listen well! The Ether is a very flexible essence that moves through all visible matters. Through it, the Divine Mind exercises its sovereignty upon the world. It is, indeed, the Great Medium between the Invisible and the Visible, between the Spirit and the Matter. Verily, I tell you

327

now, and this is a very crucial issue, no one outside the Inner Circle should ever know the Great Mystery of the Dodecahedron and the secrets within it!" He came to a halt and observed...

These Pythagoreans understood well that the deepest Mysteries of Nature and Life, revealed and taught by the Master, should be highly respected at all times. They should be admired wholeheartedly, yet kept well concealed from the ignorant in order to protect them, and save them from the profanation of the outside world.

Hence, the Master commanded them to pledge total secrecy, which they did in a solemn and unanimous voice. He then proclaimed their silence on the sacred doctrines to be symbolized by a particular clandestine sign that displayed an Ox over a Tongue.

Ox over the tongue!

Only when reassured that the Mysteries would be well kept, did he resume his extremely informative lecture. "In the Kosmos, there exists a series of opposites developed from the eternal conflict between the finite and infinite principles. There are, actually, ten opposing principles of being, at the very heart of existence. However, since *Ten* is a perfect number, as discussed earlier, these ten opposites fit, accordingly, within the Kosmic existential harmony. For that reason, I assert that *Harmonia* is Balance! It displays the unification of the compounds and the multiples, and the agreement of the opposites. Just like music!"

"*De facto*, music, my friends, bears a dual value. It is, in reality, one of the greatest, if not – I confidently stress – the greatest expression of Harmony! The truth I tell you, my dear *mathematikoi*, Harmony is nothing less than a clever, manifested impulse of the Divine Law that brings order to chaos and agreement to conflict," he explained then added, "Here! I will draw for you a comprehensive table that describes best these ten opposing principles."

Having said that, he grabbed a papyrus, and sketched, bringing the table to their attention. Exhibited in such a way, the opposing effects of the principles appeared clear to them. The explanatory table read:

Achieved	Not Achieved
Limited	Unlimited
Odd	Even
One	Plurality
Right	Left
Male	Female
At rest	In motion
Straight	Crooked
Light	Darkness
Good	Evil
Square	Oblong

Master Pythagoras explained further, "Once combined, these pairs of opposites, called duals, produce a material third that is obviously their synthesis. Everything in Nature is dual. Nothing is complete without its opposite. Only together could they form a perfect balance, a stability, and a natural physical union. However, they can never generate a supernatural, a spiritual, or even a mental union with the Great Monad!"

With this revelation, he concluded his tutoring of the day. He grabbed his Lyre and played a brisk melody. From their places, his disciples studied the table and shared their thoughts in quiet voices. They then made their own individual drawing of the table on a piece of papyrus to keep. They also drew from the wall the right triangle and the Cube that transformed into a Cross.

At the time, around two hundred *mathematikoi* had been enrolled in a succession of 10 disciples each period, under his direct apprenticeship of the sacred *Hieros Logos*. On the other hand, the *akousmatikoi,* who learned in parables and allegories, numbered a thousand members.

Led by his wisdom, these two groups, along with the *Sebastikoi* before them, formed the perfect society – the Pythagorean Society. Whether they gathered in the Assembly Hall, on the terraces of the Temples, down by the crypts, or in the Sacred Garden of his cave, they would eagerly congregate to heed his profound doctrine.

To their attentive gazes, he disserted about Life, and all its related matters. His vast knowledge educated them on most life Mysteries and Divine meanings.

Days and nights together constituted a perfect balance of earthly luminosity – earthly, for their time duration differed from Eternity. His teachings abided by the same order of division, in the sense that he conferred them in two timely and opposite parts: some in the mornings and some at nights. As a result, he complied with a balance of earthly opposites at all times.

And yet, Eternity prevailed in waiting...

* * *

The night carried the beauty of the spring, along with the breeze that caressed the faces of the students and their Master on the sandy beach. Seated in the middle, a young musician played the Lyre, the way Pythagoras had taught him for so long. The melody drifted, enchanting the mood, the way the aroma of the nearby fields wafted, blending with the smell of the sea. The stars grinned at them in millions of tiny lights. The aura of the Master appeared to match the regnant one of the Moon. However, like all great Masters, he fared, in that confident modesty of his, unconcerned by his radiant strength. His aim totally converged on the youth and his guidance to their enlightenment. His lecture that night broached a particular question raised by Opsimus of Rhegium, one of his *mathematikoi.*

"Why, Master? Why bother seeking the secrets of the stars and the planets, say the Kosmos, if it is to have death continually lurking ahead?"

The Master nodded with a smile, for he understood the quandary of his young student.

"Verily I say unto you, brother Opsimus, the physical world of the Kosmos that displays all the stars and planets in such a wonderful manner for us to admire, is not at all a real matter! It is but a passing form of things and shapes that are in eternal transformation. In fact, what your eyes perceive is just a phantom existence of the hidden Truth; *Maia,* the Universal Soul which disperses matter in the infinite space, and then changes it into Kosmic Fluid, or what I call: the Ether."

His words echoed in the night.

Stunned by this new revelation, Opsimus gawked at him then at the sky above then back to him.

With a kind smile, void of any hint of admonishment, the Master enjoined, "Have you forgotten your oath, brother?"

Ashamed, Opsimus lowered his eyes. He muttered under his breath the most solemn oath of all times:

> *"I swear by him who has transmitted to our minds the Sacred Four, the Tetraktys, High and Pure, the Root and Source of ever flowing Nature, The Model of the gods."*

The student at his side tapped him on the shoulder in a friendly gesture of sympathy and smiled at him.

"The truth I tell you," the Master prompted in a firm inflection of warning. "Fear not death for it is an illusion, an ever changing state of existence!"

A general nod of consent ensued in unanimous response.

"Master, if I may," Alcmaeon of Crotona requested to speak. "I would appreciate your opinion on a very strange incident that happened to me, almost a year ago."

"Go ahead, Alcmaeon, ask!" Pythagoras goaded him with an encouraging grin.

"In fact, Master, I meant to consult with you, about it, for a while now," he revealed then halted in hesitation. "But, the opportunity never arose, really," he said, as in apology, to which those friends at his sides nudged him teasingly.

Someone gushed out from behind him with exasperation, "Say it, Alcmaeon. Say it!"

Alcmaeon shrugged his shoulders as if to tell them to leave him alone. He waved his hand in a gesture of annoyance to which a general chuckle sprung out. The smile of the Master widened in amusement.

"Yes, Alcmaeon, say it, I'm listening," he invited him gently.

"Yes, Master. See, one night, I don't quite remember which night, I sat alone on a rock in the fields, like I do sometimes, under the moonlight. Out of nowhere really, a man came by and took a seat at my side without a word. His profile appeared familiar to me. He remained silent for a long while, until... well, until he turned to look at me, and...," he halted, uneasy.

"Yes, Alcmaeon?" The Master pressed on in a tone of encouragement.

"He looked exactly like my late father!" He spurted out and prompted a glance of dread at his fellow *mathematikoi*. No mockery ensued as he had expected. Instead, the general stance became serious and attentive.

Encouraged, he pursued, "We spoke for some time before he disappeared. I don't quite remember the topics of our conversation. I frankly don't remember even how he disappeared. He vanished... just like that! What could that possibly mean?"

"My dear Alcmaeon," Pythagoras addressed him with affection. "It only means one thing. You have, indeed, communed with your father. That's the reality."

Several students gasped at the answer, and some, very few nodded pensively as if such a weird experience was not new to them. Silence prevailed among them, leaving the ground to the sounds of nature, and to their inner thoughts to reflect on that statement. Even the Lyre player stopped the game of his fingers on the cords of his instrument.

The Master let it be. A sense of peace engulfed him as it always did when he revealed a truth. For a moment, his eyes met the adoration in those of Theano; bright green that bespoke of her hidden love for him. It was a swift instant, but enough to warm his heart for her.

He cleared his throat and broke the silence to give voice to his wisdom, "The truth I tell you, brothers and sisters, the Kosmos is but an imperfect reflection of the realm of the gods. It falls short of the Divine Archetypes – the Numbers – that perfect reality that conveys to us a glimpse of the Truth through Mathematics. The Absolute reality, therefore, is not material but rather spiritual, and it emanates from the ideas within the Numbers. Hence, these ideas, you should understand, are sacred and higher than all forms and shapes."

"Every small universe, or Kosmos, contains a partial element of the Universal Soul. Small, incomplete, yet essential, such an element evolved in the central Sun of a Kosmos. Driven by an impulsive power, and a special measure of the Divine Mind, its evolution took millions of years." He paused for a thought, but before he could continue, he was interrupted by a new question.

"Excuse my sudden intrusion, Master, for my query cannot wait any longer. What about the Higher Spirits living in the stars and planets?" Archippus inquired. "You mentioned them before, and I have been wondering about them ever since."

"Right, Archippus. This is an important question. Heed me! Higher Spirits are actually divided into two categories." The Master affirmed with a smile. "First, there are those known as the living Spirits, which are beings – like us – living on stars and planets, exhibiting only a spiritual form; they don't have bodies. Secondly, there are those known as the Forming Spirits, also called the Divine Forces. No doubt these spirits betided from a superior order, God – the Father – who is the Great Monad. These invisible and immortal spirits, or gods, played an important role in the Kosmos."

Bewildered, and yet eager for more, Archippus did not wait another minute, but dashed to ask, "Oh! And how did that happen?"

"Well, brother, you will be interested to know that the Secret Doctrine of the Ancients teaches that, long ago, these gods directed the formation of this world, the Earth. They formed it through the five elements which, as we know, are: Earth, the solid state; Water, the liquid state; Air, the gaseous state; Fire, the energetic state, and lastly; the Ether, which is the subtle, and sub-atomic state of matter."

"The Truth I tell you! All planets befell from the Sun, and submit to the managing forces of attraction and rotation. Each planet represents an expression of the Universal Mind, and thus, it contains a kind of pre-psychic energy, which somehow differs in shape, but not in essence, from any other planet orbiting around the Sun. It assumes, as well, a particular role to play, and a special function to achieve, in the evolution of that Kosmos."

"What about the evolution of humans, Master?" Hipposthenes of Crotona asked from his spot on the last row of the group.

"Here it is, brother," the Master replied, patiently. "Our Sphere, the Earth, went through many phases of evolution with its Animal-Human life. Although the laws of evolution are one-and-the-same for almost all beings that dwell in space, I will explain, for you, the most important issue that relates directly to us, humans, as you inquired. Bear in mind that this particular Animal-Human evolution occurred not only by the *Law of Nature*, but also by an eternal *Law of Divine Generation*. You should also comprehend the fact that Time is the Spirit of the World!"

"And so, when the new species of Mankind surfaced on Earth, some Initiates identified it as a race of spirits, of superior monads. In fact, at some point in the history of the Earth, a long time ago, this new genus of Mankind had incarnated in the progenies of the previous ancient Animal species. And thus, this superior race boosted the Animal species one step higher in evolution, by transforming it into its Divine-Human spiritual image. It is truly a hierarchical process of intelligent evolution from Animal to Mankind and later, from Mankind towards the Divine-God."

Baffled by his last statement, the ten *mathematikoi* became very still. No comment arose, not even among them. Their incomprehension did not go unnoticed by the *Mathemagician*. With his notorious determination, he refused to end such an important session of his Sacred Discourse without being fully understood. He turned to the Lyre player and requested, in a murmur, a different rhythm of music. At once, a different tempo streamed to activate the brainwork of the *mathematikoi*.

335

Pythagoras believed that certain styles of songs positively affected the states of mind at special hours in each season. At that moment, for instance, he knew – all too well – the heavy load that burdened his students' minds.

With the new melody, some voices rose timidly to follow the cadence. Others joined more assertively. Incited, their hands clapping, all the *mathematikoi* started to intone in one harmonious voice. A song of unity emerged to produce a powerful sense of euphoria. Long blissful moments carried them through the remainder of the night at the beach on that cool lovely night of spring.

An hour later, their lofty mood escorted them all the way to their last bedtime ritual before absolute quietness took over the night...

... And yet, in the depth of their unconscious and conscious minds, the intelligent evolution lurked in waiting.

* * *

The sun broke through the morning mist that surrounded the White City. A procession of believers, all dressed in white, the color of the Pythagorean Society, walked the narrow path around the hill. With great reverence, they headed towards the Temple of Ceres-Astarte. Like a river of pearls, they connected to one another, validating the same feelings of existence.

Reaching the Temple, they crossed the threshold of the entrance from the right gate, for their Society deemed the *right* to be lofty, good, and divine. Theano, along with the Pythagorean women, practiced inside the temple one of their most sacred rituals of all times. With a great sense of devotion, they offered, at the altar, delicious homemade cakes, and beautiful bouquets of flowers that they had picked from the fields, on their way to the goddess.

Their gifts proffered in due form, they stepped out from the *left* gateway, considered low, evil, and dissolved. They lingered outside, on the terrace, enjoying the peaceful breeze. They conversed about life, and about both the good and the bad that dwelt through existence.

Soon, Theano – that beautiful Italian girl with a symmetrical body, and long black hair that gleamed under the sunrays, had lost interest in the female debate. The Sun and the sea seemed to concord in a game of beauty where the rays from above hit the undulations of the water below, producing amazing glitters. The sea impelled her forward to the banister and away from the group of her friends.

Her face, gorgeously tanned by the Mediterranean sun, created a contrast with her bright green eyes that seemed to be looking somewhere far beyond – she was looking at the sea. Pensive, she remained engrossed in her thoughts on the essence of life. A *mathematikoi* for some years now, she lifted her mind to a higher and deeper level of consciousness. She reflected on her previous spiritual journey through the realm of Numbers, the gods. She tried indeed, to hear the Music of the Spheres, to taste from the fruit of the tree of life, to know the good from the bad, and to touch the divine light through the knowledge she was receiving.

The image of Pythagoras took shape in a sparkling vision. She closed her eyes for a moment to inhale the total blossom of her love.

"Theano! What are you doing over there? Come back here!"

She ignored her friend's call. Her thoughts deepened in the recognition that her union with her beloved Pythagoras in matrimony must be decided very soon; its happenstance a sweet reality.

"Theano?" The voice edged closer, her friends joined her at the banister.

"Hey! I might be wrong, dear, but you do look very much in love!" Tymicha – the wife of Myllias of

Crotona – who was one of her friends, teased her and the others chuckled in glee.

Theano yielded her personal feelings, no longer strong enough to hide them. After all, her friends had shared most of her daily life for years. She smiled at them with a faint nod then declared with grace, "Love is a soul, sick with longing."

Her clear voice echoed in the very heart of existence.

Her friends giggled in response. She shared their laughter in her honesty and purity of heart.

"Who is he, your love, Theano?"

"Ah! That... I cannot tell you now!" She dashed out. She whirled on herself, her eyes closed in ecstasy. She stopped, saw their disappointed faces, tilted her head sideways and uttered an apology, "I'm sorry, but I can't." She felt the heat on her face.

"Oh... come on Theano! Of course you can, tell us!" Cheilonis, her closest friend exclaimed, hurt by what she thought to be a lack of trust from Theano. "You cannot possibly hide the love of your life from us!"

"We love you, you know that Theano, don't you?" Melissa – another young woman – contended, pulling her by the sleeve. "You know that we will be very happy for you! Come on dear, say his name!"

Kratesikleia, the eldest among them, grabbed her by the waist to whisper close to her ear, "Theano dear, we have been friends for such a long time. Don't act this way as if you don't trust us. Share his name with us!"

Theano looked into the blue eyes that expressed motherly care, yet she could not make herself reveal the secret.

"Come on, come on! Don't be shy!" Vavelyca – the youngest of all – exclaimed, seizing both her hands and whirling with her on the terrace, laughing and repeating, "Say it, Say it!"

Theano burst out laughing wholeheartedly then screamed, "Okay, okay, but stop! I'll tell you who he is, but stop it, you are making me dizzy!"

The young girl abided. In a flash, Theano found herself surrounded by a tight circle of avid eyes and bright smiles of anticipation. She took a deep breath, fixed back her long hair, and disclosed with a delightful beam, "My love, my friends, my eternal love is none other than the Master himself!"

"The Master!"

"What?!"

"Oh... Theano!"

The shock was unanimous. The smiles vanished at once. Their eyes widened. Some gasped in astonishment with their hands to their mouths. Some frowned and shook their heads in disapproval. Their awful looks of compassion revealed, their assumption, that such a love was hopeless, and it mortified her. For them, the Master was simply a god.

Her joy was deflated by their reaction. She turned on her heels and walked away without another word.

Just around that same moment, the image of Theano took shape on the documents Pythagoras held in his hands. He halted his work on the new lessons planned for his *akousmatikoi*. From an aperture in the rock of the cave, the sunrays bathed him with an unexpected sense of her presence. In his mind, she stood staring at him with that particular look in her green eyes, which communicated the desire of her love. He, who had long lived outside the Circle of Necessity, akin to a true Initiate, felt awesomely weakened by his strong emotional feelings towards her.

Although a divine man, a Son of God who had heeded the Harmony of the Spheres, eaten from the tree of knowledge, and touched immortality, he seriously considered marrying Theano. He strongly believed that the divine order of Numbers had planned their encounter, and it stood now behind his possible physical union with her. It came to his mind then that the reason might lay in the fact that both he and Theano represented the *fallen models*, so to speak, of the One.

Marriage must be decided... and must be decided soon! He concluded with determination.

* * *

As seen by the esoteric teachings, two opposite and contradictory movements govern the world. They are parallel and strongly interconnected. This dual mechanism consists of both the material evolution and the spiritual evolution. It works on all levels of life.

The Fire-Energy begets the manifestation of God - the Great Monad - in the matter, and feeds it. This is to be considered the material evolution of the Kosmos and the Life that spawns out. On the other hand, the spiritual evolution is a whole process of conscious development of the Individual Monads, and their continuous trials to escape the Cycle of Death and Rebirth, or the Circle of Necessity. And when this happens, they re-join the Great Monad, the Central Fire that has formed them in the first place.

* * *

At last, the *mathematikoi* accomplished the entire program on Theology of the Kosmos, also known as Cosmology. Subsequently, Pythagoras determined to instigate their instruction on his sacred science of Psychology, called Theology of the Psyche or Soul.

Be it by curiosity or by high interest, the basic questions that human beings have debated through the ages constituted the main focus of the new program.

Who am I?
What am I?
What am I doing here?
Whither do I go?

For them to unlock the great Mysteries of all time, they would have to seek, and ultimately find the answers to these questions. Dwelling in this eternal dilemma, the Psyche always struggles to avoid falling into the duality of Darkness and Light, or more precisely, of evil and good.

Underneath the Temple of Ceres-Astarte, down in the crypt of Proserpine, the *Philosopher* assembled his 10 closest disciples. That day, he invited them to penetrate the narrow portal of the Psyche that would directly lead them to the discovery of the invisible world.

Thrilled with anticipation, they felt completely ready to undertake that fascinating adventure. They had purified their bodies through a period of sexual abstention and strict diet. They had trained their physical appearance to become symmetric models of Nature. They had fortified their minds by the intellectual assimilation of the knowledge of Sophia, Music, and the Esoteric Mathematics of the Sacred Numbers.

They were indeed ready!

"Know thyself, and you shall fathom the secrets of the Universe and the gods," with authority, the *Mathemagician* summoned them to enter into a direct relationship with the Psyche, with their Souls. "Fellow brothers and sisters, behold the *Sanctum Sanctorum*, the Holy of Holies that beats high and deep inside your realms!"

In a unanimous voice, the *mathematikoi* hailed an enthusiastic avowal of obedience and commitment. They strongly believed the Truth to be the Ultimate Arcane behind their existence, and all existence as well. They comprehended its dwelling, deep inside each one of them, to perfection. They understood that the external fell short of the Divine Light that shone beautifully, and ever brilliantly, within.

"The Truth I tell you! Every human Psyche is a partial element of the Great Soul of the World, and

I mean the Great Monad. The human Psyche, *de facto*, lives throughout all the kingdoms of Nature. It started as a mere blind force at the Solid level. It behaved as a self-reliant, active force at the Plant level. It then vibrated through the receptive and instinctive impulses of the Animal level, and it lastly reached the Human level, which stands as the highest form in natural life. There, the Psyche tends towards the conscious Individual Monad. I tell you this! The psyche resides at all the levels of life forms where the *anima* and the spiritual energy evolve. Their evolution is gradual, and it transpires relatively through a series of incarnations."

"So, the farther the living beings ascend in levels, the more the dormant faculties of their Individual Monads develop. That occurs by originating from total blindness, and ending with intelligence. Hence, the pre-psychic force is forever related to the elements of Water and Earth, in both the Solid and the Plant levels. However, after death, the psyche of the Animal life sojourns in the condensed element of Air, for it is strongly attracted by the gravity of Earthly life. It then returns to Earth to embody life repetitively. The human Psyche, however, is solely related to the Fire element. It returns, after death, to the Central Fire or Eternal Light, to be judged. If found guilty, it will take a physical shape here on Earth, once again, in order to redeem itself from the errors made in the previous life. If found innocent, it will then unify with the eternal light, and that occurs only after completing the cycle of reincarnation."

He paused for a moment. His right hand on his forehead, his eyes closed, and his mind in deep reflection...

"If you allow me a question, Master," a young mathematikoi, by the name of Dinocrates of Tarentum, advanced in puzzlement. "How then could you explain the evolution of the Animal psyche into the Human Psyche?"

342

"Easy! Envision this while I explain," Pythagoras invited him to figure it out while he set forth to prove his theory. "Evolution, which constitutes the transformation process from Animal to Human, could never have occurred without the prior existence of some properly formed Kosmic Human Psyches. These must have descended to Earth from other spheres of existence, and built a preliminary spiritual essence in the Animal psyche to infuse them with divinity at a later stage."

"How, Master?" Hipposthenes of Crotona wondered out loud. His pleading tone drew some faint smiles around him. "I don't quite understand! Do you really mean that we came from the outside space?"

In a swift motion, Pythagoras' inquisitive eyes browsed all the students, and noted their blank looks of incomprehension. For the second time now, they had failed to grasp this important concept of his. Previously, at the shore, their blankness had made him request a change of tempo from the Lyre player in order for their minds to develop the seed of his notion. He had meant to avoid overloading them with his teachings at the time. However, today he was adamant for their understanding.

"Let me put it in a more comprehensible way," he proffered with the intention of imparting more details to aid them in their comprehension. "Our Human Psyche did not originate from Earth. The Kosmic Psyches, which shaped our Humanity, had existed long ago, on other spheres of very slight material density, almost insignificant ones. In the beginning, of course, these Psyches were invisible, pure spirits with great spiritual, divine, and mental faculties. With time, they changed, because their incarnations and re-incarnations occurred lightly and easily. They, in fact, developed into semi-corporeal bodies as they moved down from one sphere to another in this great Kosmos."

343

"As the spheres consolidated on their way down to Earth, they slowly condensed into physical forms. As such, they gradually lost these faculties, called energies. On Earth, the last material level of heavenly descent, they materialized into Human beings. A great deal of their aforementioned energies waned. This is the *Fall of the Ancient Man* from the Kosmic Garden of Eden – from Heaven down to Earth."

"This *Fallen Man* was physically modeled as such due to his interconnection with the fleshly substance of the Animal form, and its related elements. On the other hand, the *Ancient Man*'s Psyche achieved the impregnation of its residual spiritual and mental essence into the Animal psyche, and that in order to endow it with the left-overs of its divinity."

"Therefore, on Earth, the Human Being remains in a constant state of tension because the material world diverts him from his ultimate goal. His goal was and always will be the redevelopment of his *Intelligence*, through a chain of reincarnations that would reinstate his lost *Spirituality and Divinity*. And from that moment on, his reincarnations on Earth are not merely a fall into matter anymore, but rather an elliptical ascension towards the higher spheres. Why? Because Earth, as I said, has fashioned his final physical level! Hence, his ultimate mission is to become what he was, and is in reality, a Son of God. You should not be amazed at this knowledge for, in truth, we are the sons and daughters of the Earth, but also of a Celestial Race. Know thyself!"

With these words, the *Mathemagician* finished one of the most important parts of his secret Initiation. With a great satisfaction, he discerned the comprehension in his students' eyes and smiles. In fact, their looks conveyed a divine light.

He smiled widely.

* * *

Life in that *City of a god* consisted of a daily conduct of Equality, Justice, and Freedom. A strong belief in friendship, as well as a great sense of Love and Peace, engulfed the ever-increasing Pythagorean Fraternity.

Night surged with an incredible calmness. The stars filled the sky with scenic lights that paved the way for the Moon, the Queen of the sky, to reign over the streets, the houses, and the temples of the White City. The *mathematikoi* convened with enthusiasm for another esoteric lesson at the terrace of the Temple of the Muses, there, where the Master once summoned the Golden Eagle. Pythagoras resumed the promulgation of his wisdom. He presented them with the *Divine Psyche.* He discussed its inevitable ascension, back to the Heavens above, where it truly belongs.

"The Psyche, or Soul, is invisible and immortal. It is a self-moving unit, or Number, divided into three elements. The first, being the *nous* or mind, is the seat of Intelligence. The *phren* comes secondly. It epitomizes the feeling, the instinct, and the *raison d'être*, or the vital principle. The third element is the *thumos*, passion, representation, and performance."

"*Phren*, the vital principle, resides in the brain and heart of both Humans and Animals. The *thumos* dwells only in the heart of both species, formed of the same natural elements, and sharing the same natural life. However, only the *nous* – the mind – characterizes the essential self of Man alone, and is eternal with God."

"Listen, my friends, and listen well! The Psyche represents the Astral Essence of the physical and mortal body that holds, within itself, an Eternal Spirit. It is through its power of action that this Spirit has formed the human spiritual body that is the Psyche. Thus, the Psyche, serving on the sensitive level, is the instrument that moves and

345

animates the physical. Without it, the body remains an inert force."

"I have named the Psyche: the *Subtle Chariot*. It's the secret chariot that, upon the physical death, lifts up the Spirit from Earth to the Kingdom of Heaven – the Divine Excellence. When this transpires, the *thumos* – passion – returns to Earth. And the *Phren* – the vital principle – is eliminated. The disembodied Psyche will…"

"Excuse me, Master. I am sorry to interrupt you," Glorippus cut him off with a frown of perplexity.

"Yes brother?"

"What happens to the mind at this stage?"

"At this stage, the *nous* joins the Universal Mind, God the Great Monad."

"I see…"

"Master, you were saying something about the disembodied Psyche?" Hippon, one of his young mathematikoi hurriedly asked. "What happens to it?"

Pythagoras nodded. "Right brother, I shall continue. Figure this out. Perplexed and confused by its new state of disembodiment, the Psyche cannot fathom whether it is dead or alive. It enters then in a state of ecstasy that prevails in the Ether as long as it revolves in harmonious movements with the Kosmic Music. When heard, the Music of the Spheres releases the Psyche from all links with the Earth left behind. At this stage of new existence, the Human Psyche starts to distinguish its divine nature, and contemplates the gods for a while before meeting with them. Then and only then, great feelings of peace and love infuse and embrace it in a state of illumination."

"My friends! Never forget the other non-human disembodied souls that pervade the air above us, subsist around us, and intervene in our lives. These angelic and demonic daemons fashion our dreams, impart us with health and illness, and appear when you beckon them through divinations, oracles, and rites of purification."

He stepped forward and asked around, "How many times have you performed the sacred magical ritual of the Pentad inside our sanctuaries? How many times have you used the power of the number *Five,* drawn inside a circle, to exorcise the bad daemons?"

By this note of alert, he invited their questions. He waited patiently for as long as it took them to deal with their individual speculations.

At last, the *mathematikoi* – Leocritus of Carthage – broke the silence, "Master, how would the Human Psyche be judged in this case?"
The question was relevant. His interest shone in his eyes, and in the fast pitch of his voice.

"That's a very good query, Leocritus. When the Psyche comes to meet the gods face to face in the Ether, its deeds are weighed at once on the scale of Life. If found worthy, and equitable in the goodness done, and in the *peace and love* lived, then to be reborn in flesh would be unnecessary since the Psyche would have earned the right to join the gods. Hermes, the Gatekeeper, guides these purest souls to the realm of gods, and away from Earth."

"On the other hand, a corrupt and guilty Psyche is condemned to return to Earth by the load of its own wrongness. Imprisoned by Hermes inside a new body on the Sphere of Generation, it assumes its punishment of self-purification through the cycle of death and rebirth. It remains entrapped inside that *wheel* until it accomplishes a total purification from every wrong and evil committed along the cycle."

"In order to attain the desired freedom, the Psyche must control the illusions of matter, and live the virtues of a good life. At that stage, it would have developed its intelligence again, gained back all its spiritual faculties, and realized the beginning

347

and the end within itself. Once reverted to its pure and sacred reality, the Psyche ascends to enter into the Divine State of the Universal Soul – Maia, and merge with its Light. It ultimately becomes one with the Great Monad; the Divine Intelligence."

At that revelation, most of his Disciples expressed their elation; most, but not the *mathematikoi* Leon of Metapontium, who stood up to prompt, "Master, a question please! When the Psyche unifies with the One, does it lose its individuality?"

Impressed by the pertinence of the inquiry, the Master regarded him with respect. He then observed his audience and said, "Brothers and sisters, Leon has advanced a very intelligent question here! Pay attention and listen carefully. The highest state in the evolution of man is not the act of merging into the unconsciousness of the Universal Mind, but rather the act of sharing the *Supreme Consciousness* in creative action!" He proclaimed to the hearing of all, and to the echo of their heartbeats.

Waves of awe followed. Grins of delight drew on the faces of those who had fully grasped the meaning behind such a strong statement.

"Yes, my friends!" Pythagoras lifted his eyebrows in amusement, smiled in response, and nodded with satisfaction. "And the greater news is that when the Psyche is unified with the One, it becomes a pure Spirit, which is a controlling power. It does not lose its personality at all! In rejoining God, it accomplishes, in fact, its own individuality. It attains the highest status of Man, which I call the Kosmic Man level. This Kosmic Man is a half-god. Therefore, the Intelligent Light of the Great Monad, I tell you with faith, feeds this half-god eternally!"

He halted as the murmurs of wonder surged from the Assembly of his *mathematikoi*. He could feel their positive and passionate vibrations reaching him. They exchanged their feedback with each other, and he let it be for a while. Theano stared at him with sparkles of delight and, for a moment, the beauty of her soul fully transpired in the green ocean of her eyes. His heart swelled with emotion, yet he remained composed. He readied himself to convey the last revelation of his *hieros logos* for he was about to complete the *third degree* Initiation of *Perfection.*

"Therefore, brothers and sisters," he started in a strong tone to compel their soundless attention. "Knowing is willing, loving is creating, and being is shining the truth and beauty of becoming a god."

With that, the *Mathemagician* unearthed the final Truth. His eyes shone bright, and his body seemed transfigured.

Silence reigned, so did the stillness that captured his Disciples. The Truth overwhelmed their capacity to utter a single sound. Their eyes reflected a sober worship towards their Master, who had just asserted their potentiality to become half-gods. But, more importantly for Pythagoras, their souls shone with the depth of their comprehension. Their spirits relished in the eagerness of their next phase; the ultimate expedition that would make them like God!

Man's end is to become like God - a god!

In fact, they had finally realized that this was the fate of every atom in the Kosmos, and of every small universe in space.

Silence prevailed. The Heavenly sky and all its bright stars witnessed their wonder, and beheld among them the imminent rising of new gods.

Quiet was the night.

Truth be told, Pythagoras was the first man on the Grecian Land to say "I tell you the Truth". The Truth, which he had just proclaimed, formed a bond between Heaven and Earth, and between gods and men, to combine all of them together, in a Society of friendship, justice, and wisdom. This Pythagorean Society accomplished the first Human experience of joining the Exoteric to the Esoteric, the Semi-Sacred to the Sacred.

As it came to be, the Pythagoreans walked the middle path of life. Akin to their Master before them, they stood out in the Center of their existence with their particularities, and expanded towards the Circle, the Universal. Within a bond of true friendship, they practiced the first monastic life ever witnessed in the history of humanity. They lived as meditative thinkers, philosophers, scientists, and secularizers. While others had failed before them, they succeeded in uniting both justice and wisdom in their collective conduct of daily life.

In view of that, the White City of Pythagoras embodied an earthly order, successfully manifested from the Heavenly Kosmic City; an efficient and harmonious city!

* * *

One Sunday afternoon in the month of August, a beautifully memorable day befell on every mind and heart in the White City. The Sun radiated in splendor over the gracious procession of young women in white. From the Temple of Ceres-Astarte on the shore, they advanced through the narrow passage around the hill, and all the way into the White City.

On both sides of the street that led to the terrace of the Temple of Al-Apollo, people of all ages hailed at them, and cheered with excitement and joy.

At the head of the procession, Theano appeared more gorgeous than ever; her eyes sunny, her smile bright, and her cheeks tinted with the pink hue of shyness and warmth. Her wedding tunic carried the *five-pointed star* on her chest. Her bouquet of white roses, and her simple bridal wreath of white sweet alyssum, gave her the appearance of an angel. From the crowds, petals of roses drizzled on her. Her joy increased as her heart swelled with emotion.

Approaching the Temple, Pythagorean dancers surrounded her with the sacred Dorian dance that welcomed her into the Circle of Marriage; one of the many within the Great Circle of Necessity. Theano, her steps light, followed the melodious tempo of the Lyre with graceful movements until she reached Pythagoras, waiting for her at the steps of the terrace.

Time came to a standstill.

She admired her future husband, magnificent in a royal purple robe over his white linen tunic. She deemed his white beard seemly to the beauty of his age. Never had a man carried his late fifties with such nobleness. Or so she thought.

Pythagoras met her with the eyes of his soul before smiling widely at her. All too slowly, her eyes in his, she ascended one step up while he hastened three steps down to her. He took her hands in his. His gaze warmed her face with delight.

"Shall we?" he murmured in a husky tone that touched her deeply.

"Yes my love, for ever," her heart replied out loud.

Hand in hand, they traversed the terrace, crowded with happy people. Fellow members waved at them with great enjoyment. Their guests from Crotona saluted their passage with affection. Guests from other adjacent cities nodded in respectful attention. Theano felt overwhelmed with happiness.

The couple halted for a second at the gate of the Temple of Light. The velvety melody that drifted to them was but the prelude of the hallowed atmosphere that received them inside. The altar radiated under the sunrays that diffused in from the openings of the walls. Theano gasped in admiration. In tacit response, Pythagoras squeezed her hand tenderly. At that moment, the melodic music of the lyre faded smoothly to give way to the sacred hymn that eight Pythagoreans of the Inner Circle intoned to El-Apollo. At once, the noise from the terrace gave way to a unanimous deferential quietness. Pythagoras and Theano continued their way to the altar. There, they stood in veneration, their hands joined together.

The *Mathemagician* uttered the sacred words, the ineffable name, to summon the Spirit of the *One* to descend upon them. Out of nowhere, as if by magic, fume of incense wafted and blended with the sunrays to encircle them. They breathed in the powerful aroma with delight. Without unlinking their hands, they turned to face each other. Their eyes dwelled together in the vision of the manifestation of the Eternal Truth in their union.

By marrying Theano, Pythagoras finally touched the peak of achievement in the manifested life. He in fact had completed the fusion of two opposite, yet complementary, human beings. Their love justified their union, just as they believed. They were in truth *fallen models* of the *One*, just as Pythagoras had previously perceived in his contemplations. Deep down within himself, he admitted his surrender to *the Woman*, whom he had always rejected.

He, the *Philosopher* with a vow of chastity; he who had consecrated all his Love to Sophia – the great wisdom – in the invisible abode of the *One*; he, Pythagoras, had ultimately fallen for the love of Theano, one of his Disciples, a woman dwelling on Earth, the Sphere of Generation!

Outside the walls of the Temple, that evening, on the wide open terrace and all around, the Pythagorean Society, and their guests, celebrated the phenomenal union. Pythagoras, and his lovely bride Theano, participated in the celebration of their marriage with unveiled happiness.

Music, dance, and a bit of wine, until dawn...

.10.

The Martyr of Sophia

Two years after the massacre of the Pythagorean missionaries, the tension between Crotona and Sybaris skulked in the shadows of iniquity. The Sybarite political refugees subsisted under the protection of the local authorities in the safety of the Temple of Apollo. The menace of an imminent war remained a major cause of disturbance for both populations. Their peace of mind and sense of security remained scarce. Forcefully, the state of vigilance prevailed in spite of the absence of any real sign of hostilities, other than what their speculations concocted.

Until one day, Telys, the Tyrant, surprised Crotona with a formal dispatch in which he demanded the immediate abdication of its political protection on the Sybarite fugitives. He threatened the authorities with ghastly repercussions if they would not consent at once. "Let it be certain in your minds that, the House of Senate, the Pythagorean Society, and the city of Crotona will bear the consequences if you refuse to abide to my demand at once."

Bound by their previous agreement with Pythagoras, whom they trusted without limit, the authorities stood up to the tyrant... In spite of the significant threat of his powerful army, they resisted the political pressures with faith and determination. They refuted his intimidation, and rejected his demand.

Along with their written rebuttal, their reply contained the same strong statement that Pythagoras had ensued two years back. "We do not negotiate with criminals."

353

In the same toughened tone, they reminded him that Sybaris owed its freedom to Pythagoras, like many other Italian cities. They condemned him for massacring the peaceful Pythagorean missionaries; a cruelty that remained hard to forget and forgive. They ended their missive with "The great independence and democracy of Sybaris, offered by Pythagoras, was a gift from the Heavens and the god Apollo. This blessing bechanced the city well before you captured it and turned it into an autocracy and a haven for miscreants."

The news reached Crotona quickly. Rumors have it that after reading their reply, Telys went mad... very mad!

The days that elapsed did not pacify the revived antagonism, quite the opposite. Telys ranted and raved in his own kingdom of tyranny until he finally declared war on Crotona. The Crotoniates, in turn, never took the necessary precaution in fortifying their defense, or reorganizing their small military force. Despite the two-year tension in which they had tarried, their alert had remained minimal until that moment. Crotona had failed to work on enhancing its military capabilities that subsisted scarcely and deficiently. At that crucial time in its history, Crotona started realizing, in mounting horror, that its defensive army would not stand a chance in front of Telys' powerful one!

Thoroughly aware of their dangerous deficiency, Pythagoras engaged in intense speculations. He probed his means to save Crotona, and ultimately his Fraternity. In disquietude, he debated his own philosophy of nonviolence. War contradicted all that he stood for, and all that his principles stood on! He had often proclaimed, "War is the leader and legislator of massacres."

The sole idea of hostilities quaked his being in abhorrence. Yet, as an Initiate of the *first order*, he heeded the voice of duty, a voice he could not ignore, urging him to take action. He concluded that the defense of the self, and of the beloved ones, would justify his response to the imperative call.

His decision made, he summoned one of his members, Milo, an ex-warrior who had endorsed the Pythagorean way of life. Considering the high level of crisis, Milo appeared unsurprised by the request of his Master. His mission, in fact, transpired as a natural *causatum* of the looming danger. To reorganize and train the army became his fervid focal point. The peaceful man he had become in the Fraternity beckoned, at last, the meaningful purpose of his past. At this very moment, the fate of Crotona, and eventually of the White City, its members, and families, rested in his hands! That was indeed a huge responsibility he pledged to undertake to the last detail.

He, therefore, embarked on the sacred mission entrusted to him for his warfare expertise. With a fierce determination to carry it through to fruition, he strove for days and nights in training the army, and all those who volunteered to join in. In his Pythagorean spirit, one main aim dwelt all along; to save the innocent population from a bloody onslaught that was about to unleash on them at any time. In a few weeks, he throve in the organization of an army of hundreds of soldiers; all geared up to defend their beautiful city, their beloved homes, their peaceful wives, and their innocent children.

While the specter of death edged closer, and accelerated the beats of every Crotoniate heart, Milo explained calmly its inevitability. He reassured them that death was, simply and mainly, a means of access to a more sublime reality. There, in the middle of the city square, he stood on the podium, a blatant reflection of a powerful and fearless warrior. His feet apart and his shoulders straight, his eyes infused his army with bravery, as did his confident words. His voice, dominant and firm, addressed the men he had molded into perfect soldiers during the recent arduous weeks.

"Soldiers and people of Crotona, listen to me! Those who die for a higher cause, like this one, shall be honored. They shall be remembered as heroes, saviors, and men of valor! I ask you, what could be more praiseworthy on this earth than saving human lives? Can you deem, in truth, any deed to be more principled than such an exploit?"

There was no answer. The plaza vibrated with anticipation. Eyes reflected a unanimous fierce pledge of resistance against the attackers to rescue, at all cost, what was most precious to them.

Time was running...

...and running too fast until obscurity broke through, darker than ever. The stars hid their lights behind peculiar clouds that swirled above Crotona like an ominous presage. On that early winter night of the year 510 BCE, blasts walloped in repetitive strikes that propelled the citizens out of their beds. Mothers scuttled to their kids in wails, and men to their weapons in angst. The ferocious attack shook the borders of Crotona. The ground quaked. Massive dust clouds were formed by the hooves of hundred of horses slashing the wind in their course. Women cuddled their children tighter to them. Younger men charged out to help the soldiers.

Crotona resisted with courage.

The assault persisted for days and nights yet the strong Sybarite army failed to score any advance into the territory of Crotona. Their front-line soldiers broke down in a matter of days. Milo did not hesitate. He retaliated with an offensive blitz on the city of Sybaris. His masterly tactic aimed at paralyzing any possible, and further, onslaught from the backup positions, as well as from the defensive lines of the enemy. His martial strategy took the Sybarite Generals by surprise. They assumed that their front-line troops would have already conquered Crotona. The fury in which Milo retaliated confused their alignments.

The battle raged in the heart of Sybaris for weeks, until Milo and his fearless army overpowered the Sybarite military completely. A wrecked city surrendered in total defeat. The sound of the battle waned to the stillness of wretchedness. The streets and alleys pervaded with the smell of destruction and death. Soon the sinister sobs of the women gushed out as they mourned their bereaved. Children cried. The wounded moaned.

The Crotoniate soldiers could not show but sympathy to the sufferers. They acknowledged them in fairness for being the victims of the greediness and cruelty of their ruler. Telys attempted to flee with some of his close associates. Caught at the outskirts of the city, he came to experience the humiliation of defeat and the bitter taste of captivity.

That day, the astonishing victory of the Crotoniates that crashed down on the powerful, and once unbeatable, army led by Telys, with naught but a hundred fierce men, was written in the pages of history. As a result of that unmatched success, Sybaris became an integral, and official, part of the State of Crotona.

* * *

Spring came with a renewed vigor that year. Flowers bloomed all over the fields in multicolor splendor. A brisk fragrance suffused the air of Crotona to the delight of the citizens and residents who enjoyed the restored order in deep gratitude. War had ended, never to return again, just as they had hoped and prayed for.

In the White City, inside the cave of the Initiate, the group of 10 *mathematikoi* huddled with patent enthusiasm as they waited for their Master. They had finally attained the final level of their

Initiation, and gained in consequence the rightful access to the *Fourth Degree,* known as *Baptism.*

The grotto enfolded them in a sense of security akin to what must have been felt by those cavemen who had resided, in similar caves, at the dawn of humanity. Yet, unlike their ancestors, who had feared the unknown while evolving from the animal-human species into the humanoid complete form, these young Pythagoreans faced their evolution with strong confidence. Today, fate would make history.

After having confronted the mystical obscurity with their power of will and their years of education, the *mathematikoi* readied to join, at last, the Divinity that glowed inside their minds.

The moment their Master stepped in, with his usual serene confidence, his vibrations of glory imposed silence on them. Theano smiled; her eyes in adoration. The hearts of the other disciples pounded faster. The crucial time had arrived. They all stood set for their Baptism.

With that assertive, yet soft, tonality that characterized his voice, the Great Master summoned the first *mathematikoi* in this group, Aristaeus of Crotona, in private, to be baptized.

"Stand in the darkness of the cave, there, so I can *see* you clearly," he uttered the strange words with authority. "Stand with your feet closely together so as to form with your body a vertical line. Now, stretch your arms to the sides to beget a horizontal line," he guided him into the required body position. "Behold my friend that you are now the representation of the Number *Four.* You are the cross in which you have been crucified. This crucifixion is of your lower-self, and by that I mean, the four elements that have formed you in the scheme of existence. You are now dead!"

Time stood immobile for a few moments.

"I now command you! Walk out of the darkness and into the light!" At that, he pointed to a spot lit by the sunrays seeping from an aperture in the rocky roof. "Now, stand there with your legs and arms spread out to your sides. Stand still!"

The radiant beams of Al-Apollo shone upon the head of the *mathematikoi,* and bathed him in glorious light.

"At present, you have grown to be the revelation of the Number *Five,* a Pentad, which resonates in the whole universe through the power of the Dodecahedron, the Heavens. You have become the *Keeper of Justice,* just like the salt preserves from decay the food it touches. The truth I tell you, the new element of Ether has permeated you in order to resurrect you to your higher-self. Therefore, I hereby baptize you in the name of the Central Fire, the Great Monad!"

"My brother, at present you hold the Truth. Comply with its light that glimmers in the depth of your being. Hold on to it as your daily guide in life. Practice it to its full extent. Be wise and prudent in the use of the powers you have so deservedly gained. Remain at all times conscious of your deeds and endeavors. Preserve forever your good will. Abstain, at all costs, from using these powers in moments of anger or hatred, for those negative emotions perturb your better judgment, and evil would persist in haunting you. Heed my warning brother, for such misuse would cause those powers to rebound on you many times and destroy you!"

"Maintain a perfect equilibrium in your life, within the harmony of the truth that shines in your intellect, the virtue that vibrates in your spirit, and the purity that dwells in your body. You must never forget, not even for a moment, the Macrocosm that beats inside your inner realm - the Microcosm that you are. Also, heed its beats in the heart of life itself. Only then, at that stage of permanent attainment, will you come to realize the presence of God, and sense Him in a transparent way; Him, the Universal Mind, who lives in the whole of existence."

In turn, the other 9 *mathematikoi* there present undertook the private rite of *Baptism,* one after the other. An atmosphere of peace and serenity invaded the cave. From far above, a subtle music reached their inner ears. A new aura of wisdom and enlightenment wrapped each one. The place appeared radiant as never before.

Master Pythagoras smiled with a great sense of exaltation. His customary modesty failed to overcome the irresistible pride he felt for them; having achieved that stage, after so many years of study and Initiation.

"My dear mathematikoi," his voice surged husky with deep affection. "You have made it so far, and I am, indeed, very happy. Yet, my teachings do not end here. Behold, now and forever, the three most important Laws that rule us. The Truth I tell you! Evolution is the law of life. Number is the law of the Universe. Unity is the law of God!" He imparted in such a solemn tenor that the walls of the cave seemed to vibrate.

"Verily I say unto you my last words, engrave them in your hearts! The Eternal Truth resides higher than any matter conceived, or yet to be conceived, seen or unseen. Lofty, it reigns far above the act of marriage betwcen a man and a woman, or any union of the opposites. Eternal Truth is the Great Monad, the *One* to whom you cannot unite, unless you eliminate the devious work of dualism. Such exploit depends strongly on the power of your minds; your own Individual Monads."

Pythagoras needed, *ipso facto,* to ascertain that his sacred teachings would prevail unscathed by his recent compliance to the work of dualism through his *earthly union* with Theano. Dualism, in his sensible perception, remained the work of evil. It was an obstruction to holiness and to the *heavenly union with the One...* although he had truthfully achieved oneness with the One, earlier in his life.

And so, in the concealment of their Initiation, the Disciples of his Inner Circle received the final teaching of his *hieros logos*. With the *Baptism* and his last recommendations, the *Mathemagician* ended their edification on the Mysteries of the Universe, and the secrets of the gods. Truth be told, Pythagoras, had entrusted the keys of his White City to these few *mathematikoi* whom he now beckoned Masters like himself. Their new sacred mission was to teach, and Initiate future disciples into the esoteric knowledge of the *Philosopher*.

Hence, proclaimed masters by the Great Master himself, they joined him behind the curtains to attend to the *akousmatikoi*, when gathered in the evergreen Sacred Garden. Eagerness vibrated in the air as hearts and minds waited for the knowledgeable thoughts of the day. Yet, that particular day differed from all the other ones. The strong emotion of farewell oppressed their hearts.

"Brothers and sisters, allow me to express my sincere gratitude for the strong commitment you have proven to our Fraternity," Pythagoras spoke from behind the curtain. "My dear *akousmatikoi*, I shall leave you, in a while, in the righteous hands of your fellow brothers and sisters, the new Masters. From here on, they will take charge of the remaining portion of your Initiation. As for now, I shall impart you with the last three recommendations of importance that you must never forget."

He went into a silent minute of contemplation in which he gazed pensively at each one of the new masters around him. He then reverted back to, what turned out to be, his last speech ever given in the White City.

"Listen and listen well, my friends! First, hold on to the philosophy that no one must take away from you. Verily I say unto you! Your inner-selves enclose what is similar to the Universal Mind. Therefore, make of your bodies temples of God!

361

Finally, if one day you decide to honor God, and pay Him homage, then you must know Him, and imitate Him."

He breathed deeply and then uttered, "Stay in peace!"

With that heartfelt wish and blessing, the Great Initiate finished his brief discourse, fulfilling, by it, his final *akousmata*.

* * *

Pythagoras, in his early sixties by then, weary of the hard long path he had chosen to tread, sighed in great relief at his decision to relinquish his responsibility as head of the Society. His heart ached for a family life in which he would devote all his time and energy to his wife Theano, and to his future children.

Pythagoras might have ended his mission, yet his humble house in the White City remained his abode. And there, life pounded with another strong rhythm, as his family grew and developed. From his seat at the window, he felt overwhelmed with a peaceful joy. Damo[44], his first daughter, cried for her meal in the arms of her mother; his beautiful and beloved Theano.

He observed them with that compassionate heart of a god, or simply of a fine, married man. Delight invaded him upon the realization that he and Theano had *de facto* succeeded in creating a life. Hence, they had participated, with God, in the great work of creation.

Soundless, he stood up to approach her. His arms wrapped around her waist to enfold her backside to his chest. His mouth to her ear, he whispered softly, "What could be more honorable than the miraculous accomplishment of creating a life?"

---

[44] Some historians say his daughter was called Myia, but the general knowledge is that she was named Damo.

Theano leaned on him, "Nothing, dear, in truth, nothing could ever be more divine," she murmured, with affection, and granted him a radiant smile and a look of pure love. Their baby girl went silent, all of a sudden. They both turned their immediate attention to her. As if she had understood their statement with joy, she beamed at them._

That peaceful happiness would, however, wane at nights when his beloved Sofia harassed him about the illusion of such a dream.

A fantasy! He would heed her protest. *This is but a fantasy of your unconscious mind. This is but a deception meant to reassure you that this union is simply an imitation of the work of God!*

One of these perturbed nights, Sophia whispered to him in his dreams. She awoke him to assert her rightful position in his mind. She explained to him that his marriage, and ultimately the procreation of their daughter, could not be the labor of the *One*. She insisted that it was mainly, and truly, the reproduction of the work of the Dyad; the essential divinities that had created the physical world.

At that, Pythagoras concluded, not without a great sense of relief that the previous harassments had not actually transpired from Sophia, but from the evil exertion of the number *Two*! And that night, although still perturbed by the recent assumptions of his failure as a holy man in the act of duality: marriage; he slept in peace with himself.

* * *

Months sped through the year. The Pythagorean Society, led by the new Masters, lived well and in peace. The White City kept to its bright and enigmatic existence, each and every day. The smooth *modus operandi* accounted to the fact that the keys of its unremitting success subsisted in the good hands of the best Philosophers.

363

The Society lived on the goods the members shared in a genuinely fraternal way-of-life. They also relied on the generosity of the people of Crotona who never ceased to provide them with aids and provisions. In truth, their gratitude for their victory against Telys prevailed deep and solid, for Crotona had developed into a powerful and rich state ever since its victory!

Unquestionably, the new Masters, the Philosophers, preserved Pythagoras' accomplishments as sacred. They carried on their new positions based on his method and philosophy. They strove so religiously to imitate their Master that the Kosmic music of Heaven, the Music of the Spheres, appeared to duplicate itself in the White City.

Upon their own achievement, they pondered amongst themselves on the prospect of having that Kosmic replication manifested in other adjacent cities and beyond. In their minds, they conceived the idea that such a potential success would give rise to the creation of a *homonoia*, a union of minds and hearts, all through Magna Graecia. For them, the great Master Pythagoras embodied the perfect prototype of the Kosmic man. He, the *Philosopher,* personified the supreme status of man. *Ipso facto*, all Philosophers represented the finest guides of Society.

Yet, their project of expansion remained impossible since Pythagoras had solemnly bound them to the secrecy of his Initiation. Consequently, the Inner Circle could never divulge any of the Inner Secrets to the outer world, regardless of the pressure, or reasons. The ox of utter secrecy had sealed their tongues for evermore.

As a matter of fact, this form of arrangement had constituted one of the most sacred rules enforced on every Initiate of the Ancient world. Confidentiality prevailed, for all such Societies of

Initiation, as the best policy of protection, against all blasphemous violation.

Never surrender the Heart of Mystery to the vulgar, for it would break down and shatter in ways in which the beasts of illusion could consume. Every time the *Mathemagician* had issued that warning, they had always replied with their oath of steadfast silence, and avowed their loyalty to the secret doctrine entrusted to them. They would also pledge commitment to his name, their Master, the extraordinary man who had imparted them with the Sacred Four; the *Tetraktys*, High and Pure, the root and source of ever flowing Nature, and the Model of the gods.

And secretive they prevailed, despite the difficulties that eventually ensued while assuming their mission. Sooner or later, mistakes would crop up while someone strove to teach without delving into the essence of Truth. Hippasos of Metapontium, one of those recent masters, faced such an issue when instructing a group of Listeners on moralities. While some of the Masters handled the teachings of the natural sciences, and others the social problems within the Society, Hippasos tackled the topic of moralities.

At the time, the Pythagorean Outer Circle of the *akousmatikoi* counted over one thousand and five hundred members, whereas the Inner Circle, the *mathematikoi*, along with the Philosophers, added up to four hundred. That escalation in the numbers of adepts in both Circles resulted from the fascinating, and peaceful, *way of life* Pythagoras had envisioned and applied through an efficiently organized system.

Unlike the supreme Philosopher Pythagoras, the new masters did not need the shield of a curtain to teach. They simply convened with their Listeners in different places every time; a hall, a garden, or other tranquil spots around the White City.

That particular day, Hippasos discussed corruption with his group in the nearby field.

"...thus a corrupt man is better off dead than alive," he inferred, looking at their attentive gazes.

"Master, would such a man rise to Heaven, or descend to Hell, upon his death?" The pertinent question took Hippasos aback.

Still for a moment, he pondered on how to reply to this Listener without exposing the taut secrecy of the Mysteries. For an explanation was required from him, a Master assigned to teach! In the seconds that trailed, he sought for the right answer to one of the most important questions ever to be asked by curious Humans. He could have explained, right there and then, the secret doctrine of metempsychosis if, and only if, their minds were ready to fathom the depth of such knowledge.

"He goes to... hell, I suppose," he ended, sharply, to attenuate his spasmodic reply.

"But, Master, what is Hell?" another *akousmatikoi* riposted.

"Well... Hell is a place of pain where all the wicked people dwell in continuous suffering, as punishment for the evil deeds they committed in life."

"Where is Hell, then?"

He thought for a while.

"Listen, Earth is, in a way, like Hell. Plenty of suffering and injustice exist here on Earth where people live as a punishment for the bad deeds they have committed at some point in time," Hippasos released with a bit of relief. He had finally said it, hinting at it, yet without revealing the plain truth, or so he had assumed! "Can you grasp this, brothers and sisters? Is the idea clear to you?" He queried, doubting that they would be able to understand, or perceive, beyond the appearance of life and death.

A more relevant question cropped up, unsettling him. "What is Heaven, then, Master?"

That's it! Hippasos thought in annoyance. He considered ending the discussion at once on the excuse of an urgent matter, simply because his pledge for secrecy forbade him from revealing the truth about the esoteric Heaven.

He hesitated.

That would be so unlike the ethics of his Master Pythagoras, to leave matters unanswered, or unattended. He pondered on how his Master would have handled this situation. He then decided to simply impart them with a general and inexplicit idea. He smiled inwardly and went for what he deemed to be the best answer under such circumstances.

"Heaven is a place of Love and Peace," he stated with confidence. "Heaven is a place up high, there where you would rise based on your good deeds in life."

"It must only be populated by good people then!" An akousmatikoi advanced in wonder. "We'll surely like it, right?" he said genuinely to his friends then asked eagerly, "Where is this beautiful place? Can you show it to us?"

Silence filled the place. The Listeners waited for his answer while he fought against his strong wish to reveal the truth.

"Heaven is the very Ether of existence," he decided to declare, assuming that a general innuendo would satisfy their curiosity for the moment.

"What do you mean, Master?"

"How does that happen, Master?

"So what is Heaven, in fact?"

Truth be told, Hippasos had assumed that such profound questions would never surge on him, since he had reached the fate of the corrupt man in his lesson. He was being charged and his mind was only trained to deal with the subject of morality, not spirituality. However, the questions poured out, pressuring him further. The eyes probed him with doubts about his ability and erudition, or so he felt. It was already tough for him to fight his internal conflict. He sweated profusely. He heard it then, the murmurs he had much dreaded, the words whispered among them,

"He doesn't know...."

"He is not a good master...."

"Listen to me, everyone!" He countered with authority then rushed out on his explanation, "Heaven is the fifth element that floats everywhere beyond the four element of Nature. It is not atomic, but rather spiritual. It is the Dodecahedron!"

The stillness of confusion captured them.

He could detect their perplexity in their blank eyes, and in the faces that gaped at him. Some of them frowned then, obviously trying to ponder on his words, which must have sounded quite strange. He could sense the momentary emptiness of their minds.

Hippasos realized, belatedly, what he had done. Irate, he walked away the moment a student opened his mouth to ask further explanations. His feet stomped the lane towards the Temple, with the same angry rhythm that his spirit bore. He had just revealed the hidden properties of the purest and most sacred secret of all times, the secret of the Dodecahedron! And he would have to face the consequences soon. Anguish grabbed him by the throat.

The ox of sheer secrecy had fallen off his tongue.

That infamous day befell on him sooner than he had expected.

Early at dawn, the *Sebastikoi*, the religious functionaries of the Pythagorean Order, summoned him without delay to the Temple of Apollo to stand trial. Hippasos, his heart in torment and his body heavy with numbness, abided at once. The moment he crossed the threshold of the gate, he swallowed with difficulty and halted. He knew the formalities, and delaying the confrontation would not help him in any way. His fellow philosophers, the new Masters of the Inner Circle, formed two parallel, straight lines, from the entrance and all the way to the altar. Eleven of them in each side, they stood like judges in wait.

Great Master Pythagoras is not here! He is nowhere to be seen, yet, he would certainly appear... and soon enough! Hippasos mumbled under his breath.

Hippasos grabbed his courage in both hands, and moved forward under the severe scrutiny of his fellow brothers and sisters from both sides. In shame, he plodded with leaden steps to the center of the Temple where he stopped and remained motionless.

In his disgrace, time seemed endless until Pythagoras walked in from the right side: the high, the good, and the divine direction. His glorious aura escorted him behind the altar. His white linen tunic and purple robe stated his position as supreme judge. In seconds, the trial would start with the masters of Philosophy assuming the role of jurors and witnesses at the same time.

"Hippasos," Master Pythagoras spoke, his voice calm, too calm for Hippasos not to heed the hidden tone of disappointment and anger. "It was a real honor for me to become a Master at one time in my life; the same applies to you and your brothers and sisters. Verily I say unto you! You were assigned with the most honorable mission of all times; teaching the listeners."

"Yes, Master! And that's exactly what I was doing!" Hippasos prompted to answer in self-defense.

"Right, Hippasos. None of us ever doubted it. It is certainly fine and commendable to teach morality to the Listeners, yet to reveal the secrets is utterly unacceptable!" Pythagoras snapped. "You took an Oath of total secrecy, Hippasos! Have you forgotten?"

Hippasos trembled at the admonishment, and bowed his head in shameful silence. *An ox over the tongue!* He muttered beneath his breath.

"You broke the most important rule of our Society by divulging the most Sacred Secret of our teachings!" The supreme judge spat. "Are you aware of your crime, Hippasos?"

The disgrace felt heavier than ever. "Yes, Master," Hippasos mumbled and closed his eyes. "I am deeply sorry, Master! I really am... I mean, to have betrayed your trust... and the trust of all the Assembly here gathered."

"You have, haven't you? You should be sorry, indeed!" Pythagoras admonished. He scrutinized him pensively then looked at the Assembly and asked, "What shall we do about this betrayal, brothers and sisters?"

The question echoed in the Temple, sinister like a creepy menace that chilled the blood in the veins of Hippasos. He veered to the Philosophers with imploring eyes. But there was no kindness in the looks that pinned him to the floor.

His heartbeats throbbed faster and louder. Cold numbed his hands. His neck and back dampened with the cold sweat of dread.

"Expulsion!" A voice prompted and was soon followed by others. They all sentenced him, unanimously, out of their sacred circle.

Hippasos bowed his head, and his shoulders sagged in defeat. He understood that nothing could be done to have them change their minds, or even mellow their hearts. He himself deemed his transgression unacceptable. He should have stood stronger, and more faithful, against the pressure. Now that the final decision had ensued in unison, his spirit broke down under a terrible sense of loss.

370

Pythagoras took a very profound breath. He sighed deeply as if the decision was hard on him too. He then issued with authority, "In the name of the Great Monad, personified by El-Apollo, the God Most High, and in honor to our Heavenly White City, I, the Lover of Sophia, the son of Hermes-Enoch, expel you, Hippasos of Metapontium, from the Pythagorean Society forever and ever!"

The verdict fell harsh on Hippasos, and shattered him. An acute sensation of burning hurt the eyes he lifted at his Great Master. Abiding to the formalities, Pythagoras turned his head away, so did all the twenty-two Masters of Philosophy as the accused walked back towards the entrance. He dragged his heavy feet out of the Temple, and all the way out of the White City.

Fraught and beset, he meandered in the wilderness, his pain acute and his crying loud. In a while, the Fraternity would declare him officially dead to them, and that hurt his soul severely. His heart bled at the notion of it.

That same day, the Fraternity did in fact declare their brother, Hippasos, dead to all. They erected a cenotaph in his name, in the Square of their White City, to be seen by all. The memorandum read in clear letters of green color:

> *"Here lies, Hippasos of Metapontium,*
> *A Pythagorean brother for seven years,*
> *A Master for almost two years,*
> *He broke the rules of our Society,*
> *Divulged its most sacred secrets,*
> *And then... died."*

* * *

A couple of years later, another beautiful soul infiltrated the womb of Theano, to Pythagoras' delight. Months after that, a baby boy came into the light of life, where he was to journey under the name of Telauges. Be it a coincidence, or an act of divine intervention, the new baby boy bore a great deal of resemblance to his father, while Damo, their first-born daughter, displayed an astonishing similarity to her mother.

"Just, it is so. A perfect equilibrium in our work of creation, or better said, procreation, for we were given children in our images!" Pythagoras shared with great interest.

Theano smiled widely at him then gazed at her two children lounging in front of them. She chuckled with delight and nodded in consent. Happiness prevailed in the haven of the Great Master.

* * *

Peace and happiness carried the Pythagorean Society through the years. The Dodecahedron assumed a perfect position on the Cube, or in other words, Heaven was positioned on Earth. It crowned the White City with the golden color of the gods. Its unique lifestyle kept compelling more and more people to join. Within the Outer Circle, there existed the Pythagorists; a group composed of prominent persons from Crotona and other Italian, independent cities from the South. From Sybaris to Rhegium, these individuals had joined the Fraternity to acquire wisdom and enlightenment from the Great Master. In fact, its excellent reputation took the Mediterranean region by storm. Among the prominent citizens of Crotona who expressed high interest in adhering, was Kylon, a rich man.

In the year 502 BCE, the Magical and breathtaking White City overwhelmed Kylon, the moment he stepped in. Two members of the Fraternity received him with kind reservation and led him to the Gymnasium. There, the games quickly caught his attention. Later, he abided to their invitation to participate in the discussions held by a group of Pythagorean students. His interest increased, and months later, he commenced his initial tests under the close scrutiny of the Masters. His oratorical skills and strong leadership favored his achievements on all the trials. The masters, however, still speculated on the kind of leader he could be. At that stage, it was still early for them to decide, for there was something about him that they found a bit disturbing.

When the hour of truth came for him to face his monsters, he walked fearless to the deserted cave at the foot of the hill for the next decisive trial. The tales of beasts, phantoms, and ghosts, alleged to exist there, held no credibility in his mind. He knew the area all too well for having sneaked around it sometimes during the day. To face it at night stirred but his sense of challenge. Thus, thrilled with anticipation, he settled in for the nightly trial.

Just a single night, he thought cynically. *Easy!*

He grinned broadly and slouched on the cold floor. He bent his knees so he could rest his elbows on them, and started to mumble a happy song, while his eyes examined the area around him. After a while, boredom took over. He leaned his head back on the rocky wall, and closed his eyes to sleep. An instant later, he snapped them open at a sound that echoed deep inside the cave. He leapt to his feet and started checking the dark spots. Finding nothing, he shrugged his shoulders, went back to his spot, and attempted to sleep once more.

Less than an hour later, he prompted his eyes open widely at the warm breeze that basked briskly on his face and arms. A cold sweat dampened his tunic and his back. He frowned. He swallowed with difficulty. Something new to him, something called fear, grabbed him by the throat. He rejected that feeling, and decided to inspect the cave again. Yet, this time, his heart pounded faster than usual. Somehow, he seemed to hear faint sounds but could not see any living creature around!

The sensation of warm blasts of air on his shoulders reiterated several times during the night, impeding his rest. It triggered his doubts on the existence of supernatural creatures, somewhere in that darkness. Suspicion, as well as the threat of the unknown and the unseen, shook his courage and unsettled him. The eerie obscurity escorted his ruminations all night long on the possibility of such a weird existence. Against all creepy sounds and sensations, he held tight onto his pragmatic mind, and stout determination to overcome the trial.

And he did, yet not without internal scars! The experience of facing the illusions of his mind had resulted tougher than he had expected. Stepping out at daylight, a nuisance dwelled in his thoughts. He needed a good, long, and restorative rest to be able to undertake the next test that would give him rightful access to the Fraternity. He knew that the next test related to a moral examination of his ethics and values. This achievement would be required of him in order to proceed into the Initiation of the *first degree*, called the *Preparation* period.

However, the subsequent trial did not come as expected. A sponsoring Master surprised him by leading him, without prior notice, to a Spartan cell inside the White City.

"This is your next test, Kylon. You are to stay in here and decode a Pythagorean symbol," he informed him dryly. "Find out what is the meaning of the Triangle. When you get it, or if you simply give up, knock on the door and you shall be released. Otherwise, I will come for you when the time is done."

Left to this, Kylon sagged on the floor. He looked around the gloomy cell with annoyance. He frowned at the sole piece of bread placed on a bamboo mat, and at the clay jar of water next to it. *Dinner!* He sneered before delving deeply on the solution to the question. Hours elapsed on his attempts to decipher the secret meaning behind that strange geometrical form. With his index, he drew it several times on the dusty floor to discern what hid behind it, or around it, or inside it. Nothing! He started to panic. Time became his enemy. He bit on his, now dirty, nails, swiped at the sweat running down in rivulets from his forehead and tried again. Yet nothing would come to his mind. And he refused to give in.

The door creaked and opened to reveal the same Master who had led him in.

"Your time is over, Kylon. Come with me." With that lackluster order, he turned his back and disappeared without waiting for a reply.

Kylon leapt to his feet and dashed behind him all the way to the *homakoeion*, the Common Auditorium. There, without a word, the Master opened the heavy door of the Assembly Hall and let him in.

Kylon noticed, at once, the presence of several neophytes like him, and a few recent adherents of the Inner Circle and their Masters. They all appeared to be expecting him to reveal the secret he had reached in his meditation inside that Spartan cell.

"Have you reached an answer?" his Master then asked, all too softly. "What is the meaning of the Triangle? In case you forgot, that was the question."

Kylon stood still like a statue. Known as an accomplished speaker, his tongue, this time, was hooked to the query of the geometrical shape. He couldn't talk. The answer didn't come, and the question lingered in the air for some time.

"Well... say something!"

"Can you?"

"We cannot wait all day long for your answer."

"He can't speak... the cat got his tongue."

375

"Is this the philosopher we came to listen to?"

"A statue with no soul will certainly not talk."

These cynical questions and comments poured in on him at once from every direction. The beginners, like him, laughed and sneered. The Masters, on the other hand, stood there, observing his probable reactions.

Their abstention to interfere irritated him. Although he knew that this was a test of morality, or the sort, he could not stem the fiery anger that ignited in his being. Whatever the importance of the test, or his determination to win, he deemed his dignity and pride to be above all this humiliation. His arrogance was notorious. And, at this very moment, the banters and mockeries incited his most base temperament into reaction!

Damn it! He thought, and *Damn it,* he snapped out loud. He lost control of his temper and unleashed his anger, cursing the School, the Society, the Masters, and Pythagoras.

Cursing and insulting are to be considered the 'second evil' inflicted on one's self and others, Pythagoras had often warned.

His sponsoring Master grabbed him by the forearm and pulled him firmly back. In a calm voice full of authority, he admonished and rebuked him for yielding to the negative impulses of his ego. His Master then informed him that he had just lost all privileges to remain in the White City. Kylon stormed out in a fury. Two brothers followed him to the gate as the procedures required.

Kylon understood, too late then, that all his money and fame would never influence the decisions of the Masters in allowing him to become a Pythagorean brother... and not even a Pythagorist! The last words of his Master harassed him all the way down the hill.

Kylon! You lack the three most important qualities that could have changed the outcome. We

376

require respect, the value of friendship, and the desire to seek knowledge and wisdom. You came seeking prestige instead, because of our reputation. There is no place for you here, Kylon. You are dismissed!

Kylon delivered a diatribe against the perspicacity of that Master. He knew that the Fraternity would soon raise a monument commemorating his expulsion. His disgrace, as he deemed it, would last for posterity, and he could not tolerate it! The moment he reached his home, revenge had taken shape in his wicked mind, and lasted for the remainder of the day. During the sleepless night that trailed endlessly, he analyzed the possibilities, devising a plot that would annihilate Pythagoras and his Society.

My name will last for Posterity, yes! But not in disgrace!

* * *

A few months later, the year now 501 BCE, Kylon founded a socio-political club to which he enrolled a great number of Aristocrats from Crotona. Through it, he gained the friendship of most of the city's wealthy and prominent citizens, among which, a certain, Ninon became his fervent right-hand.

Soon enough, all the financial power invested in that club transformed it into a dominion of hatred and anger. Like mad dogs, these perverted minds howled furiously, and lurked for the right moment to strike on the *Silent Pythagoreans*. They soon arranged for an oratory platform in the city square, and issued a mass invitation to their speech. On that day, they introduced Kylon to the public.

Minor members and several fans scattered among the audience to cheer and applaud loudly, which, as expected, goaded the surrounding citizens to tag along. Kylon felt great; his ego gratified and his sense of leadership incited as never before. He elated in anticipation. His speech ready in his mind, he lifted his two fists up to launch his first attack on the Pythagoreans. His aim? To incite a riot against the White City and its Master Pythagoras!

"Blasphemy!" he roared.

Astounded, the audience held their breath at once.

"Citizens of Crotona, how could we accept to follow a man claiming god-ship? I ask you, who is he really, that man who calls himself a Master, a Lover of Sophia? Blasphemy, I tell you! How dare he claim to be the Son of God Apollo? How could you possibly tolerate such sacrilege, and keep yielding to him as if you truly believe in his profanity?"

Gasps of dismay gushed out louder and louder from the crowd that stirred in revolt. Eyes widened in shock at such a strong verbal attack on their beloved Pythagoras. Kylon had expected that first reaction. He did not give them time to unleash their repulsion on him.

In a stronger pitch heavy with menaces, he proclaimed high and loud, "Beware, people of Crotona! Behold the fury of God Apollo for it will crash on the city, destroy every home, and annihilate every child of yours!"

A wave of tremors hurled the audience in total silence until a male voice shouted in disapproval, "We have witnessed his miracles!"

Many people around him acquiesced at the top of their voices. Kylon interfered at once to impede the failure of his iniquitous scheme.

"Miracles! What miracles? If he has truly performed any, I can assure you that the power of Apollo, the Great Light, has nothing to do with it!"

Murmurs of denial cropped up. Many shook their heads in rebuttal. Kylon understood that he should strike harder, and immediately, before he lost ground.

"My friends! I have been there myself, and can attest in all sincerity. Pythagoras and his Inner Circle always gather inside a dark crypt, like devils inside the earth. Away from the light, in the very gloom of the night, they often convene by the sea, like creatures of darkness."

He sensed some significant sudden fear from the audience. Encouraged, he pressed on, "Yes, my friends! Those alleged miracles could not have been performed but by the power of darkness!" He proclaimed in condemnation.

The members of his club, there present, ranted in fury against Pythagoras and his Inner Circle. Yet, most of the crowd remained openly annoyed by these deceitful accusations. Kylon overheard the word 'envious' snapped in his direction.

"Your claims are wrong!" A woman yelled. "The Master cannot be blaspheming since he has erected a Temple for Apollo in the White City!" She argued with vehemence, her features distorted in annoyance.

Kylon knew her to be one of those fervent Pythagorean partisans. He stepped forward, and ogled down at her to intimidate her, and subdue her into silence.

She looked at him squarely in the eyes in defiance, and stated out loud, "Master Pythagoras worships God Apollo with vehemence! He venerates Him as a Father. Many of us can attest to that fact! He lives as the Son of Light, so how can he possibly be the son of darkness? You immoral liar!"

To Kylon's great displeasure, shouts and cheers of approval responded to her.

"Woman, be quiet!" he snapped at her, attempting to regain control of the situation.

She retorted, adamantly, "No, you listen! Are you really... really talking about the Pythagoreans?" then looking around her, she pointed an accusing finger on him and yelled, "This man is insane!"

379

A general laughter shook the audience.

She turned on him then and snapped, "You don't really mean the Pythagoreans, right? Because if so, you just have to look at them to know, like we all do, that they are not what you claim! They live in perfect harmony with nature, and in perfect friendship with each other. They are a genuine and perfect Fraternity of love and peace! Have you seen the white purity of their clothes? This is what, and who, they are! Pure and clean!"

Stillness besieged Kylon at the patent reality of her argument. He quickly rummaged his mind for something valuable to retort with.

"Fellow citizens, this woman might be right about the appearance, but that is only the outer shell of what they really are! Heed the one who has witnessed the truth of their deception! I, as well, deemed Pythagoras pure and clean, and genuine. That's why I joined his fraternity some months ago. He was my ideal! I even left everything behind, all my wealth, my easy life, my family, and my home, in order to be one of them. Yes, fellow citizens, I did! I even succeeded at all their tests, and they welcomed me in their Assembly Hall!" He lied shamelessly. It stimulated him to observe the sudden meditative interest such a statement got him. He rubbed his jaw and continued, "then, I came to watch their deceitful claim...," his voice broke as if honestly disappointed. "Oh, how shocked I was when I realized that this Assembly Hall was naught but a den of demons. Everything was just the iniquitous façade of a clever trick! A hoax fabricated, not only against the God Apollo, but also against all the good, trustful people of Crotona!"

Kylon paused to give time to his proclamation to sink deeply into their minds.

"The truth I tell you, my fellow citizens, all the works of Pythagoras, and his alleged Masters, are never performed openly, but only inside the underground crypt. Why my friends? Why! Ask yourselves why?! Haven't you ever wondered?"

No one answered. He noticed the frowns, in secret delight. Almost everybody there appeared engrossed in their thoughts.

He pressured further, reiterating the same notion but worded differently. "Do you really think that this is a Fraternity of love and peace that live in perfect harmony with nature? Know this: that their white clothes are meant to reflect a good, angelic image with the wicked purpose of hiding their true dark selves. That is in fact a perfect disguise! Ask me, I have been there. I saw the plain truth!"

A hot debate eventuated. His followers applauded. Some others expressed their admiration of his leadership. Others, however, protested fiercely, revealing their faith in Pythagoras, and their affection to the Pythagoreans.

"This is absurd ... total nonsense!" Someone countered him in strident revulsion.

Many echoed his reaction with the same intensity.

"You are completely wrong, Kylon!"

"You are changing the facts to mislead us!"

A woman darted forward and screamed in the chaos, "Kylon! May the God Apollo punish your wickedness severely! We are not blind as you presume!" At that, she climbed on the platform and addressed the gathering with a strong voice of authority. "My friends! Let me remind you, and refresh your memory. Pythagoras consecrated his marriage with Theano in the Temple of Apollo! What does that mean to all of you here?"

Most people in the crowd approved high and loud. Their cold eyes now on Kylon demanded from him a factual reply that might overthrow the strong statement put forth by the woman, or so he thought.

Unable to deny it, he went speechless. He had failed to alter the facts. *For now*! He fumed inwardly.

The bold woman thundered down the steps, off the stage, cursing Kylon and his club. In a frenzy, she forced her way through the crowd. Some followed her at once, others looked intently at him in wait for a rejoinder. His stillness lingered, and the plaza emptied gradually; too fast for his taste. Only his members stayed to pierce him with sharp glances of disappointment. Humiliated, once again, because of the Pythagorean Fraternity, he lost his temper. He reaped further abhorrence against Pythagoras. He seethed and raged hysterically, right there on the stage of his defeat. His insults erupted stridently. Yet, only his members witnessed this abject discharge.

Such a disastrous failure, though, did not undermine his determination to destroy the Pythagoreans, on the contrary. The Aristocratic Lobby soon summoned its most powerful members for an urgent, and top-secret meeting, in their headquarters. There, in their underground Lobby Hall, at the heart of the city of Crotona, they plotted clandestinely against the Fraternity.

The primary purpose of the summit was to analyze the reason for their recent fiasco. They concluded, almost unanimously, that to taint the religious image of Pythagoras, in a public place, would result catastrophic. Someone suggested exploiting the strong weapon their own wealth posed, instead. Eyes brightened and smirks evolved at the notion. Soon a demented frenzy ensnared them as they developed a scheme to best fit their aim.

In the days that followed, they invested big amounts of money in buying, discreetly, the loyalty of many poor, and not so poor, Crotoniates. When money would not work, they would offer jobs, or promises of better careers. The Lobby would write their names on a waiting list. They used the phony pledges as a successful tool to gain their allegiance. The result exceeded even their wildest expectations, and their methodic plan!

Due to the masses of people that enrolled, based on interest, the Lobby opened several branches around the city for Kylon to hold his secret meetings with the new adherents. He met them all, group by group. He worked on manipulating their minds. He convinced them that Pythagoras focused mainly on distracting the young generation away from the gods of Greece by converting them to his way of life.

"Pythagoras is a true Charlatan, a real Demon in disguise. He will steal everything you own, and all that you live for," he often stated, and they accepted the lie as true.

The number of new members increased by the day. Public debates continued. However, to his displeasure, very few would join the newly adhered poor souls in applauding his public speeches. He strove for a grand crowd and for the interest of the major entities that did not come. Yet, he would not give up easily. He summoned the most influential and prominent members to the biggest clandestine summit ever organized by the Lobby. They assessed the previous debates, and emended their decisions in order to proceed further.

"There are always some new citizens who believe my words every time I address the public," Kylon affirmed with arrogance. "Our emergent list attests to that fact. Isn't that right, gentlemen?"

They grinned with heinous satisfaction, and nodded in agreement.

"However, I have decided not to assail, or even mention again, in public, the alleged holy image of Pythagoras. I shall instead speak of something else, something even more credible than that, something that will leave a great impact on the mind of Crotona. And I promise you, gentlemen, that, at our next meeting here, we will be counting the new adherents by the hundreds!"

They all cheered to that. With a renewed eagerness, they poured their immoral astuteness into their plan. They studied and elaborated the new plot that Kylon and his dangerous assistant, Ninon, had churned out. They decided then on a date for another public debate to which they would invite more and more people.

"This will be it, gentlemen," Ninon exclaimed with stout confidence. "I can feel our victory already!"

A general applause responded, followed closely by fists pounding rhythmically on the conference table, and feet on the floor. The cadency accelerated into an archaic clamor for war. The walls vibrated. Excitement heightened in intensity.

Kylon could have sworn he saw the demons in the red sparkles of their immobile eyes. He raised both hands to command their silence.

"Aside from the impact of my influential and credible oratory," his voice blasted with self-importance, "the large number of fellows, whose loyalty we have purchased, will be a great asset for us in the crowd. Their loud cheering and continuous applauses on my next speech will certainly affect the others!"

He certainly had it all planned out in his impious mind. Whether he would succeed in winning over the whole crowd, or not, in his next public appearance, he would still raise major doubts on Pythagoras' views and on his Society. Damages would be deep and permanent, he swore inwardly.

* * *

Less than a month later, Kylon and his Lobby watched, with great satisfaction, as the plaza filled with people of all ages and classes. Soon, the place could not encompass all the attendees, be it adepts or just curious people. Women stood at their windows, youngsters climbed on the roofs, men jammed the area, and some even sat at the edge of the platform to avoid getting stampeded. Kylon considered with excitement the hard work of his Lobby in the past weeks. Actually, they had done a better job than expected. The sight infused more arrogance in his heart. Never had he seen such a huge crowd, and they came to listen to him!

Ninon leaned to whisper in his ear, "I believe you will never get another chance like this, Kylon. It is now or never...."

"Are you implying, Ninon, that we go for plan B?" He taunted, without turning his eyes off the growing crowd.

"Absolutely!" Ninon exclaimed in a murmur.

"So, be it! You will handle the Lobby then."

"Don't worry. I have them under control."

They exchanged a quick look of complicity. Ninon nodded discreetly and, with unconcealed pride, Kylon marched firmly to his spot on the stage to deliver what he reckoned to be his last and hopefully fatal attack on the Pythagorean Fraternity.

He smiled widely at the crowd. *There is no place for error this time*, he thought to himself.

"Citizens of Crotona, thank you all for coming. As some of you already know, I am here to talk about Pythagoras and his Society. For the newcomers, I must say that I still believe that the man, Pythagoras, is way more dangerous than you could ever imagine. Yes, my friends! He is in fact a tyrant with an occult power. Why? You might wonder! Well, my fellow citizens, let me call your attention to the obvious fact that he deems himself of a divine race, while he considers you but a herd of sheep to be led and commanded!"

He ignored the gasps of astonishment, and the incredulous looks of his own Lobby. With this unexpected introduction, he had broken his pledge to them to change his previous tactic, thus sparing the holy image of Pythagoras. True, he had promised them something totally different, more plausible, and more effective. Yet, he and his right-hand man, Ninon, knew best how to crash the enemy, Pythagoras!

"How is that?" a female voice from the audience asked in doubts.

"Well, you people don't have a say in the politics of Crotona, right? You do know that the authorities set the rules, but what you don't know is that they consult with Pythagoras on when, and how, or if, the rules should be implemented. What does that mean to you? It simply means that Pythagoras is in fact the one who rules our city! It means that he has crowned himself the God-King of Crotona!"

His powerful proclamation impelled the shouts and yells of his members, as well as of the mass of his followers among the crowd. Curses spurted against Pythagoras and his White City. Faces twisted in hatred against the alleged god. As for the Lobby, they reacted with mischievous smirks. They seemed to consider the way in which he had worded his speech to be very interesting and cunning.

"Hold on there, people of Crotona!" A strong male voice shouted with such authority that it subdued the roar of the people.

Kylon glared at the direction of the warning that had interrupted the emergent rage he wanted so much. From among the multitude, the caller, a notorious politician, darted towards him. In a flash, he climbed the few steps, reached Kylon, stood face to face with him, and stared, fiercely into his eyes. Kylon held his breath and froze in astonishment.

The politician veered to the audience. "My fellow citizens!" his voice thundered. "You can't possibly believe what this man claims! Pythagoras is a blessing to our city! Pythagoras has envisioned our matters rightfully and fairly. Remember the war!

Remember Telys, the tyrant! We would have all turned into ashes if Pythagoras had not interfered. How could you forget the key role he played in making us win the war? It was his great wisdom and his effectual support that overthrew the fierce and unbeatable army of Sybaris! Thanks to him and only him, Sybaris has become part of the State of Crotona. Isn't that a huge victory he has granted us, and our posterity, with his acumen and integrity? How could you forget it? Shame on you! Yes, shame on you! Ungrateful citizens! We owe the saint man our safety and security. We owe him our new wealth and work opportunities. We owe him the peace that this Kylon and his club are trying to shatter and disgrace!"

Stillness fell on the plaza at the accuracy of the facts. Many nodded in agreement, his rational historical input accepted as true. Even Kylon agreed inwardly, yet he could not afford another public disaster, especially not this time! He pondered quickly on how to turn the tables on the authorities as well.

He sneered in the secret recesses of his mind. "Yeah, right!" he spat out in a bitter tone. "We won the war. But tell me, fellow politician, how has the government rewarded the people for risking their lives in the battles? Tell the citizens here what you have really done to compensate the families for the loss of their martyrs" he shouted with a rage that echoed like a thunderbolt.

The politician blushed then went pallid.

"No reply? Of course, you can't answer this," Kylon snickered then veered to address the crowd with a thunderous voice, "because I tell you, citizens of Crotona, nothing has been given to you in exchange. Nothing!"

Mesmerized by his counterwords, the audience gaped at him, as if paralyzed by his wrath. Having grabbed back all their attention, he decided to strike fast and hard, for he knew he had successfully touched a painful nerve in them.

"The lands, my friends!" he yelled to their consideration. "All the new lands and properties, acquired from that war, have been divided between the political body and the Pythagoreans! Know that they worship each other as gods, and regard all of us here as brutes!"

"That is not true!" Someone retorted from the back of the crowd, probably a friend of the Pythagoreans. "Liar! Imposter! That's not true at all!"

Before he could add another word, a lobbyist knocked him down with a blow to the back of his head. Rendered silent and unconscious, he was immediately dragged out of the plaza, and thrown in an alley.

Kylon smirked with wicked pleasure. Adamant in his hate, he delivered to his audience, "You pathetic citizens! How could you have let them fool you for so long? Tell me, please, how can you still trust them, even now? Come now, open your eyes! Look at the facts! This has been naught but an immense conspiracy against you, innocent citizens; pure exploitation, fabricated by Pythagoras and his followers in alliance with the political body!"

Fury stormed through the mass akin to an unruly tsunami. Like vampires thirsty for human blood, members of the Lobby and the growing group of Kylon's followers gathered there, in the plaza, unleashed their rage first, to be followed then by the crowd; the greater part of it.

"Death to Pythagoras!"

"Death to his Society!"

"Kill the fraud!"

"Annihilate the Fraternity!"

Ugly condemnations roared and barked in all directions. The crowd went wild, their anger feral, and the plaza boisterous.

Chaos and ruckus reigned.

All those friends and followers of the Pythagoreans scurried away, running for their lives.

Kylon bellowed, "Wake up from the spell cast upon you by that dark sorcerer! Walk by me now, and you will never regret it! You shall never feel betrayed, never again! Your social and political rights will be granted to you in full. Walk by me, citizens of Crotona, and every coin that you lost will be returned to you! Trust me! Walk by me... Walk by me!" he kept repeating in a metrical litany.

Excited, the multitude pounded the floor with their feet and shouted, "Kylon! Kylon! Kylon!"

It took him some time to command their rowdiness into some semblance of quiet order. He fathomed in ecstasy the dangerous state into which he had driven them, yet, he still strove to fuel them even more.

"Listen to me! Let us judge them without a hearing! Yes! The same way in which they have condemned us! Together, let us persecute the swindler who has corrupted our youth; that impostor who has robbed them of their souls, and away from the gods of Greece!" his voice blasted, his body launched forward with his fist up. "We must strike... and strike powerfully!"

"Death to Pythagoras!

"Burn the White City!

"Kill the impostor!

They roared over and over again until foam spit out from their mouths like mad dogs, ready to attack, and tear at human flesh. Like automatons, they lurked in wait of orders.

Kylon and his Lobby relished in the luscious taste of their remarkable triumph. They shared, with a grin, the rotten evilness of their hearts.

And so it cropped up. The Lobby vowed to launch a strong attack on the White City upon devising a well-organized plan that could annihilate the Pythagoreans to the very last one. They had sworn to do that.

That night, alone in his bedroom, Kylon stood in front of his polished bronze mirror, dreaming of glory and fame. His eyes shone with the red color of wrath. His reflection embodied the very personification of evil; a man thirsty for blood and destruction. Somehow, that image of himself fascinated and excited him. He laughed out loud. And, for a while, the sound reverberated in the silence of the creepy darkness.

* * *

Those who had witnessed the uproar, and feared for their relatives and friends, scuttled to the White City. In panic, they asked to see Master Pythagoras. Their hysterical requests urged the Masters to rush them in, at once.

In growing angst, he heeded their frantic reports. He had barely had time to urge them back to their safe dwellings, when the Maters darted in with some more feverish visitors: his few, close politician friends. They reported the same tale without contradictions. Pythagoras took the threat on his people very seriously.

His eyes probed the anxious politicians in front of him. "When?" His tone betrayed his internal torment.

"We don't know! They did not divulge it!" The man who spoke kept twisting the cord of his belt in edginess.

Pythagoras turned to the older official who rushed to say, "We were tipped, on our way here. Kylon and his rabble are now in the pre-final stage of preparation." His nervous tic twisted his right eye again and again. His hands quivered on his cane.

The younger politician halted his fretful pacing at last to press on him, "Master Pythagoras! It is just a matter of time!"

Pythagoras walked to his window. He gazed at Crotona for a long while, then observed the horizon for any sign that might belie his presage.

"What about the Senate?" he finally asked in a murmur. There was no reply, he turned to probe the politicians with a commanding voice. "With whom are they siding? Do I have their loyalty? It is crucial for me to know immediately. Will they help us defend our White City?"

The important question met with total silence. Their eyes reflected their deep sorrow and anguish. They shook their heads in shameful negation.

"We cannot speak on behalf of the Senate, nor in favor of all our fellow politicians, but we, the eleven of us, are here to stay with you until the end, if you want us to," the older politician offered with emotion.

Pythagoras nodded.

Time stood still while he struggled, in the secret of his heart, to cope with the deep pain of abandonment and betrayal. The precarious outcome of such a crisis tortured him. He had always refused to acknowledge the vision of the imminent destruction his spirit had revealed to him.

Beware the envious souls...

Pherecydes had often cautioned him against their dangerous deeds. He had even warned him about it in his deathbed. Had his uncle foreseen, as well, the brutal end of the White City, or was it his nephew that he meant? Whatever his message, time proved him more than just a wise man.

He was a prophet with foresight!

Pythagoras deduced, with respect, then reverted to the problematic condition that had entrapped him. Dismissing the eleven politicians to safety, he summoned all the members of the White Society for an urgent Assembly. At the time, the Outer Circle counted two thousands members, and the Inner Circle, six hundred. In a state of apprehension, they assembled on the wide terrace of the Temple of Al-Apollo.

Pythagoras emerged in all his glory, his long white linen tunic draped with his purple robe over his shoulder. His *mathematikoi* stood at his sides and his *akousmatikoi* just behind them. He stared at his devout people for a long painful minute before he uttered.

"Dear brothers and sisters, thank you for coming on such short notice. As most of you probably know by now, this is a matter of extreme emergency. Heed and behold my words. The time has come indeed, and the waiting has ended."

The sorrow of his heart reflected in his voice, and rendered his bizarre statement incomprehensible to them. He could read their fretfulness and confusion in their eyes. He sighed deeply and decided to enlighten them with the blunt truth with no further delay.

"My friends, evil is about to heave its vengeance and odium upon our White City. Unfortunately, nothing can be done to impede the imminent fury. Nothing...," his voice broke in profound sadness.

Gasps ensued, eyes widened in shock then fear and murmurs wafted like a brisk wave that prompted to turn into cries and wails.

"Please!" Pythagoras urged them. "Do not panic! Let us remain composed to plan for our safety! I urge utmost discipline and self-control. Let us face our predicament with wisdom and clarity."

He continued talking to them in a soothing, even tone that meant to assuage their fears and impose some sense of order. When he felt them ready to heed him, he raised his voice to announce, "Everybody is free to leave the White City, and seek shelter somewhere else," he declared. "No one, I repeat, no one should assume, in any way, that he, or she, should stay any longer. I just ask you to uproot and spread around the neighboring cities. I also urge the *akousmatikoi* among you to depart at once for the sake of their families," he pressed on them in spite of the raucous refusal of many.

He raised his hand to command their silent attention. "Listen to me! There is something you should know! As you spread around, you might fail to identify a fellow member of our Fraternity. We can't allow such an outcome, not when we have shared so many years together. You should keep in contact with each other. I will reveal to you now our secret handshake so you will be able to distinguish each other outside the White City. Use it when greeting each other from now on. Remember, you are all brothers and sisters of our Great Fraternity, and whatever the separation, you owe support to each other!"

At that, he murmured a brief order to his Masters at his sides. They stepped forward from among the Outer Circle. From one to another, they communicated the secret sign of the Fraternity. In turn, the members were prompted to practice among themselves. The Inner Circle already knew it and had been using it for a while now.

"What are you going to do, Master?" a woman previously cured by Pythagoras asked him with tears in her eyes.

"Fair lady, your care surely touches me," he replied with sincerity. "The Truth I tell you! I shall never abandon you, or this great White City. I will not turn my back on all the love and peace that have infused its sky all these years! No, and a thousand times no! This is what I have lived for, and this is what I shall die for," the *Mathemagician* claimed his allegiance with a voice full of emotion, and a tone strong with certainty.

"Master!" A *mathematikoi* exclaimed in fearful protest.

"My decision is irrevocable, brother!" Pythagoras asserted firmly.

"Then, if this is your decision, we shall stay with you until the end!" A young *mathematikoi* affirmed his allegiance and loyalty.

"We shall die with you!" An *akousmatikoi* acclaimed high and loud.

Many echoed then waited for his orders.

In truth, the silence that ensued pierced a hole in the sky above, and reverberated deep down in the land below.

"No... and a thousand times no!" Pythagoras shouted at last. "You, all of you, must leave for good. You must not die now, but live instead in safety, away from here. The essence of friendship, morality, and loyalty is deeply rooted within you. Your mission now requires that you relegate it to the generations after you. This is my last recommendation to you! Heed it as sacred and apply it as such," he ordered. "My beloved friends beware the growing ominous danger. Leave in peace, and do it immediately!"

Suddenly tired, the Master sought by himself the Temple of the One for meditation and solace.

* * *

Early one autumn afternoon, almost a month later, Pythagoras, alone with his thoughts, meandered through the Sacred Garden of his cave. The leaves of his Cedar trees and Oak trees had turned from the orange color of maturity to the blackish yellow one of death. At that moment, they made their final way to the ground, stating their smooth decline, one after the other. The wind blew swiftly, and scattered them through the beautiful garden and beyond it. Pythagoras observed that significant motion of life before he resumed his walk at an even slower pace. His feet felt heavier, and his shoulders laden. Slothful and listless, as if almost defeated, he realized that the end of his present life had finally come._

He already grieved the departure of most of his people. He knew that at this very moment, the remaining families of his Outer Circle were about to leave. In spite of his disapproval, a few of them had chosen to stay, like the *mathematikoi*. That decision of theirs worried him deeply. Yet, he could not force them to run for their lives and into safety. Even at this stage, he still conformed to the free-will and democracy ideal he had applied and implemented in his own city. He had hoped that with the days following the warning, they would come to change their minds. Yet, they kept going on with their daily-lives, almost normally, regardless of the state of maximum alert.

Pythagoras turned to the sea. In a flash of memories, he recalled his very first trip with his father, then the several others that had journeyed him towards his destiny. He smiled faintly. At this moment in which the sun glowed with wonderful titian hues before setting for the night, he recalled the tale of the Phoenician man seeking the end of the world, there where the sun touched the sea, like it did now. Yet today something was different. Pythagoras perceived it in the way the Mediterranean Sea swallowed the sun into its very depth.

It was the year 500 BCE.

A sudden gloom befell the White City. He gazed for a while at the black clouds and felt their sinister foretelling. In a brisk motion, they extended above him like the shadows of death. His eyes searched for a glimpse of light from the moon. Yet, the clouds swallowed the astral body in its darkness. Night fell in from all sides akin the augur of an unavoidable demise.

Pythagoras knew then.

His eyes, burning with an internal ache, browsed his surroundings before they closed for a moment. Somehow, he discerned the faraway pounding of a marching army. *A thousand probably*, his mind estimated. His spirit flew, beholding the horrible sight of the dark mass of heinous creatures storming towards his White City.

Torches and long spears in their hands, they hummed like some nightly beasts craving for their prey. Pythagoras snapped his eyes opened. Cold sweat dampened his back.

He ran as never before to order an immediate evacuation. As previously trained, all the families scuttled frantically through the two narrow passages, the right and the left, known only to the members of the Society.

In fretfulness, he screamed to Theano to follow him quickly. He grabbed his two small children in both his arms. He scuttled through the secret passages. He halted when Aristaeus of Crotona ran to meet him half way.

"You know what to do!" He prompted in his ear and handed over his precious children to his most faithful Initiate.

"Fear not, Master. They will be safe with me," Aristaeus assured him with firmness then his voice broke, "Master..."

"No, brother!" Pythagoras commanded him with resolution, impeding an emotion that could weaken his wife, already in tears. "Remember, I am about to pass to another life. We all do. My time has come. That is all."

He veered to Theano and engulfed her in his arms in his first public display of husbandry affection. He would have kept embracing her forever had the sounds of the marching death not loomed closer by the minute. He murmured words of love and caution to her ear then informed her what he had agreed on with his loyal Initiate, "Aristaeus is now in charge of you and the children, Theano. He will make sure to find you a safe shelter in a neighboring city. Trust him, dear. He has pledged his life to protect you and the children as his own family."

Before releasing her, he delivered his last spoken will to her ears. Yet, Theano would not let go of him. She clung on to him, crying her heart out. He swallowed hard. He missed her already.

"The children, Theano... you should save our children," he urged her with the only reason he knew that would make her abide.

Aristaeus understood then what to do. He shoved her daughter into her arms, kept her son with him, grabbed her by the elbow with his free hand, and darted with them towards the secret exit. Pinned to the floor, his vision blurred, his heart dying, Pythagoras witnessed how his beloved family disappeared through the passage.

A strong blast urged him back to the imminent catastrophe. He realized that the enemy had reached the main gate. The terrible sound as the statue of Hermes-Enoch smashed down on the ground by the entrance, reached him achingly. The bolted gate trembled under the violent assaults. The fierce attempts of the Pythagoreans to hold it did not appease the Master. He knew that it was merely a matter of time before their resistance waned and the gate crashed opened. He quickly summoned some of his top Initiates. They ran to the Temple of the Muses, and scuttled down inside the crypt. There, in safety and secrecy, Pythagoras entrusted the *Secret Word* to his elite, whom he had honored with the noble name of the *Trees of the Garden*.

"I'm sending you around the world to continue cultivating the seed of Sophia. You must never forget to nourish it with drops of water, sparks of light, pulses of life and beats of love. Go now, brothers and sisters... Go!"

Complying to his last recommendation, they pledged their most binding and solemn oath of all times:

"I swear by him who has transmitted to our minds The Sacred Four, the

Tetraktys, High and Pure, The Root
and Source of ever flowing Nature, The
Model of the gods."

In tears, they bid their Master farewell then charged out of the City, and towards their holy mission.

Pythagoras walked out to face his destiny in courage.

Tears, he had none, other than those mixed with the blood of his shattered heart as he contemplated the hungry fire flames licking, then swallowing the main gate. His people retreated, avoiding the blaze that burned everything to ashes. He witnessed in pain the ferocious hatred of his foes storming into the city. He beheld their indescribable rage, savagely exterminating every living person along their way.

His soul endured the excruciating blows his Silent Pythagoreans received in sacrifice to Sophia, as the creatures of darkness struck them blows to the head, pummeled their bodies, and slashed their throats. The clean white robes marring into crimson red as dozens of bodies collapsed to the ground; white doves bleeding away the purity of their lifestyle to a violent and unjust death.

The criminals set the place on fire. The wails of children and women, who had stayed behind, could not impel them to stop the cruelty of their crimes. In pain and revolt, innocence sobbed from the very depth of its essence. Motherhood moaned away its last breath, as the barbaric extermination forged its way through it. Cries ricocheted all around. They echoed among the collapsing walls, on the streets, and between the alleys. As the heat of the attack decreased, lamentations and weeping emerged from the few terrified women left alive, holding to their bosoms the cadavers of their loved ones.

The odious bellows of victory gave Kylon a sense of cowardly reassurance and safety. Only then did he decide to cross the threshold of what had stood, just moments ago, as the stoutest and most forbidden gates to him. Elated, he rode his horse through them then halted abruptly at the hellish sight all around him, which filled him with fascination.

The criminals he had created that past year had succeeded in turning the White City of *love and peace* into a bloody bath of death and destruction!

Motionless, he contemplated the outcome of his wicked scheme. A great sense of victory filled his being all the way to the depths of his depraved soul. With it, came the scent of fresh blood, torn flesh, and blazing ashes; mixing together the reverberations of triumphant cheers from his army with the moans of the wounded, and the dolorous wails of women and children. What struck him then, with a more acute sensation, was the terror and anguish that suddenly grabbed at his capability to breathe. Akin to the portent of drums, heralding his own damnation, his heart hammered painfully in his chest, blurred his vision, and waned his hearing. Breathless, he watched as his rabble set fire to the Temple of El-Apollo first and the Temple of the Muses next. His own horse whined and startled in revolt. It became difficult to control. Its head snapped left and right. It pulled back. It whined again, louder, and shook feverishly trying to dismount its rider. Kylon grabbed the bridle tight, veered the animal towards the exit, and darted out of the nightmare he himself had generated .

Meanwhile, inside the underground chamber of the Temple of the Muses, Pythagoras and some of his *mathematikoi* prayed to their God El-Apollo and to the three superior goddesses of the Muses; those who presided over the sciences of Cosmogony, who mastered the art of divination, and managed both concepts of life and death. They also handled the spirits of the *au-delà* and their reincarnations. The prayers were in preparation for their final passage into another existence.

A thunderous blast shook the foundation of the Temple where they stood. An earsplitting sound reverberated back to them.

"The Temple!" someone yelled in dread.

Pythagoras dashed forward. His group rushed behind him. They scuttled up the spiral stairs. They penetrated the hall of the Temple. Horror brought them to a brutal standstill. The fires of hell reigned in fury.

A huge piece of wood crashed on fire at their feet. They jumped backward, awakened from their shock. Quickly, they snatched their cloaks from their shoulders, and tried in frenzied despair to subdue the flames around them. In no time, their tunics had caught on fire, so had their hair and beards. The smell of burnt flesh soared. Cries of agony spawned. The flames engulfed them.

Pythagoras sobbed faintly as he whispered in the smoky air that he breathed in for the last time:

> *"I'm the one,*
> *standing on the throne of Sophia,*
> *a son of man.*
> *I leave the Earth*
> *and return to myself*
> *before I fly to the Great One."*

He then collapsed. The flames consumed him in a flash. His Psyche, *his Subtle Chariot*, lifted his spirit up in resurrection. It soared high above, free, towards the Father of Life and into the Heart of the Central Fire... into the Great Light[45]!

---

[45] Some historians claim that Pythagoras fled the White City to Metapontium where he found refuge. Returning after the attack had ended he later died at the Temple of the Muses after fasting for forty days. We, however, do not deem this historical claim to be logical and acceptable. A strong character and sublime visionary

Down on Earth, the aftermath of greed and envy prevailed throughout the White City. A carcass of black stones, and smoldered wood, miserably subsisted to claim the last vestiges of an empire built from love in purity, and consumed by fire in odium. The thick black smoke forged ahead, and spread thicker and thicker to pollute the air, and diffuse a venomous stench all over the region, and far beyond it. The flora bent in sorrow then perished. The greenery yielded to its extermination, not without shrieks. The Cedars lifted their burning arms in prayers of sacrifice. The birds fled far away to grieve in silence the annihilation of their heaven on earth.

And high above in the sky, a white eagle soared and glided for a long while, witnessing, in protest, the extermination of the *City of a god...*

---

such as Pythagoras could have never fled the White City, and everything he had lived for. His magnificent contribution to humankind proved the courageous man he was in facing trials and danger. Based on his ideology and principles, Pythagoras considered death as a passage to a better life. He could not therefore fear death, since he considered the 'Psyche' to be immortal. Moreover, the alleged forty days fasting period is just a symbolic idea.

Appendix

Many years after the massacre, the Pythagoreans continued to spread all around Magna Graecia. They resided mostly in the major cities of Tarentum, Metapontium, Rhegium, and Sicily. Their persecution persisted wherever they went, being a minority. In order to recognize each other, they adopted secret handshakes, signs, and passwords.

At a later stage, some Pythagorean families returned to their native city of Crotona. There, the authorities allowed them to settle down under the strict condition that they would not practice politics at all. Reunited once again, even if in small numbers, they convened in secret at the same diminished hill where the White City once stood in all its majesty.

Aristaeus of Crotona, who had best endorsed and understood the Pythagorean teachings in their entirety, led the Society. Theano[46], on the other hand, assumed the guidance of the Pythagorean women. Her daughter Damo took charge of the young girls. Taught and guided by both her mother and Aristaeus, Damo grew to treasure the secret writings of her father, the Great Master. She later married Meno the Crotoniate, and earned the first place as a philosopher at the altar of life. As for Telauges, the son of Pythagoras, he evolved into one of the best Masters of his time. He was the one who initiated Empedokles into the Pythagorean Doctrine.[47]

---

[46] Works on *Cosmology, Construction of the Universe, Theory of Numbers, Theorem of the Golden Mean*, and *On Virtue* are often accredited to her.

[47] Some historians and modern thinkers believe that Theano was not the wife of Pythagoras but rather the name given to his much beloved school. In accordance, these historians assume that his children were but his favorite disciples. However, at the lack of credible proof, such an assumption is to be discarded as untrue.

Without a doubt, the Pythagorean Society expanded to a significant extent after the terrible death of the *Philosopher*. Unfortunately though, the Society later split into many diverse, and yet important factions. Such divisions encompassed the scientific, spiritual-religious, and political fields.

Around 460 BCE, the Society endured another fierce suppression that burned all its meetinghouses into ashes. That happened while some fifty to sixty Pythagoreans held a top-secret meeting in the House of Milo of Crotona, in that city. Assassins attacked them unexpectedly and killed many of them. Those who survived the ferocious attack fled to Thebes in Greece, and to other places throughout the Mediterranean World.

These brutal acts and persecutions failed to destroy the will and faith of the Pythagoreans. The Order subsisted for many years and functioned significantly well in fact. Among the distinguished Pythagoreans, emerged the notorious names of Archytas and Philolaos, both natives of the city of Tarentum. However, sometime around the third century BCE, the Pythagorean Society ceased to exist again, and for a long while.

At the beginning of the Roman Empire, around the first century CE, the Pythagoreans resurrected once more, like the invincible Phoenix, and succeeded in regaining their power. Yet, with time, they strove to maintain their position and status within the Empire. When the Emperor Constantine decreed Christianity as the official, and only, religion of the Roman Empire in the fourth century CE, the Pythagoreans became an unwelcome minority.

Nevertheless, through the consecutive ages, ever since the Pythagorean Order started, it succeeded in influencing a large mass of people. Among them, many became famous philosophers like Plato and his Academy, Apollonius of Tyana, Plotinus and his small circle, Nicomachus of

Gerasa, Moderatus, Numenius of Apamea, Kronius, Thrasyllus, Porphyry of Sur (Tyre), Iamblichus of Chalcis (Anjar), Ammonius Saccas and his group, and many others.

Truth be told, Pythagoras has marked humanity to a significant extent. His adepts and followers left their spiritual and social impact on several other sects, and religious societies, that flourished around the Mediterranean Sea.

The Essenes (from Asayas, *healers*) appeared sometime around the fourth and third centuries BCE at Mt. Carmel, and through a major part of Galilee, if not all of it. Entirely different from the Qumran Community of the Dead Sea, the Asayas assumed a lifestyle similar to the *way of life* of the Pythagoreans. They shared their goods, prayed at sunrise, practiced silence, wore white linen tunics, and treasured the Mysteries well.

Jesus Christ was their ultimate revelation.

The Therapeuts, those healers who lived like hermits in secluded groups through the deserts of Egypt, presented, as well, the same Pythagorean influence.

Strangely though, the religious community of the Druses, that lives to-date in Mount Lebanon, and in some parts of the Middle East, endorses a particular occult doctrine in which Pythagoras stands as one of their Seven Sages!

Likewise, comes hitherto one of the most enigmatic and problematic secret societies of all times; the brotherhood of the Freemasons. Similar to the other sects, influenced by the Pythagorean doctrine, they have adopted many of its ways and concepts. To date, Pythagoras embodies their *Peter Gowar* who is greatly honored within their higher degrees.

At any rate, the Pythagorean teachings continued to infuse the Mediterranean World for hundreds of years after Jesus Christ, and until the early Middle Ages. Sometime around the sixth century CE, the Society and its concepts endured another strict prohibition, until around the mid European Renaissance when the Pythagoreans resurfaced, once more. Later on, it reemerged as a completely esoteric system.

If truth is to be told, humanity owes Pythagoras a great deal of Knowledge, and in many different fields. He stands as the organizer of spiritual laws, as a pioneer in mathematics, both in its exoteric system with the Theorem of Pythagoras, and the esoteric one with his Theology of Numbers. In Astronomy through his Heliocentric System; in Music for his Invention of the Monochord; in the Organization of the Perfect City with its innovative Social structure, and finally, in Philosophy!

Pythagoras strongly believed that Philosophy could undeniably shed some light on our most pressing life queries, and certainly shape us to become *Lovers of Wisdom*, as he had once been. He is, indeed, one of those very rare prophets who made us realize that our sole purpose in life, and our very last end, is to become like God.

In all truth, the Doctrine and Philosophy of the *Mathemagician* are well and alive to this very day and... they shall never die!

There are men and gods,
and beings like Pythagoras.
(The Pythagoreans)

Bibliography

English

- Iamblichus, *Life of Pythagoras*, translated from the Greek by Thomas Taylor, Printed in Great Britain by the Haycock Press Ltd, London, 1965.

- Gorman Peter, *Pythagoras a Life*, First published in 1979 by Routledge & Kegan Paul Ltd, Printed in Great Britain by Lowe & Brydone Printers Ltd.

- Strohmeier John & Westbrook Peter, *Divine Harmony - The life and teachings of Pythagoras*, Berkeley Hills Books, California, 1999, 2003.

- Russell Bertrand, *A History of Western Philosophy*, A touchstone book, published by Simon & Shuster, Inc. 1972. Printed by Murray Printing Co, Forge Village, Mass, NY, USA.

- Hastings James (Edited by), *Encyclopedia of Religion and Ethics*, Printed in Great Britain by Morrison and Gibb Limited, T&T. Clark, Edinburgh, London, 1930, Volume X.

- Herodotus, *The Histories*, Printed in the United States of America, Published by Barnes & Noble Books, 2005, New York, USA.

- Davies Paul, *The Mind of God*, First published in Great Britain by Simon & Schuster LTD, 1992.

- Blavatsky H.P, *Isis Unveiled*, Printed in the United States of America by Versa Press, First Quest Edition, 1993, Volume I & II.

- Blavatsky H.P, *The Secret Doctrine*, Printed in the United States of America by Versa Press, First Quest Edition, 1993, Volume I, II, & III.

French

- Laerce Diogene, *Vie, Doctrines et Sentences des Philosophes Illustres*, Tome 2, Traduction, notice et notes par Robert Genaille, GARNIER FRERES, Flammarion, Paris, 1965.

- Schure Edouard, *Les Grands Initiés*, Rama-Krishna-Hermès-Moise-Orphée-*Pythagore*-Platon-Jésus, Librarie Académique Perrin, 1960 et 1997, pour la présente édition.

- Mattei Jean-François, *Pythagore et les Pythagoriciens*, Editions Que sais-je? Presses Universitaires de France, Paris, 1993,1996.

- Saint-Michel Leonard, *Pythagore Les Vers d'Or*, Éditions ADYAR, Paris, 1995.

- Gobry Ivan, *Pythagore ou la naissance de la philosophie*, Editions Seghers, Paris, 1973.

- Ghyka Matila C., *Le Nombre D'or*, Editions Gallimard, Paris, 1976. _

Made in the USA
San Bernardino, CA
11 July 2016